THE COMPLETE AIR ADVENTURES
OF GALES & McGILL, VOLUME 2

Frederick Nebel

FREDERICK NEBEL

THE COMPLETE AIR ADVENTURES OF
GALES & McGILL
VOLUME 2

BY
FREDERICK NEBEL

ALTUS PRESS

BOSTON • 2017

© 2017 Altus Press • First Edition—2017

EDITED AND DESIGNED BY
Matthew Moring

SERIES EDITOR
Rob Preston

PUBLISHING HISTORY
"Crate Crashers" originally appeared in the February, 1930 issue of *Air Stories*.
"High-Flying Highbinders" originally appeared in the March, 1930 issue of *Air Stories*.
"Siren of the Wind" originally appeared in the April, 1930 issue of *Air Stories*.
"Winged Salvage" originally appeared in the May, 1930 issue of *Air Stories*.
"South of Saigon" originally appeared in the June, 1930 issue of *Air Stories*.
"Bloodhounds of the Sky" originally appeared in the December, 1930 and January–March, 1931 issues of *Wings*.
"Sky Scrappers" originally appeared in the May, 1931 issue of *Air Stories*.
"The Skyline Two" originally appeared in the August, 1931 issue of *Air Stories*.

THANKS TO
Joseph Laturnau, John Locke, Joel Lyczak, David Saunders and Sheila Vanderbeek

TABLE OF CONTENTS

CRATE CRASHERS

Gales and McGill—birdmen of fortune—back on the sky frontier! Trouble rides their wings. Hongkong and Canton turn a cold shoulder. Then a crimson-streaked map plots their flaming course.

HONGKONG WOKE up one day to find Gales and McGill among those present. Now this was considerably more significant than it sounds—if you don't know Gales and McGill.

It was said on that coast, anywhere from Shanghai to Canton and on down to the Straits Settlement, that whenever these two birdmen of fortune showed up, trouble would be certain to follow as a matter of course. If they did not start trouble, it was alleged, they attracted it. It just goes to show what a reputation can do.

There is no gainsaying the fact that they were soldiers of fortune. It would be futile to deny that they played a spectacular role in the late Chinese civil war, that they got mixed up in a tong war in Singapore; that they took a whirl in a native uprising down in the Dutch end of Borneo.

No one will deny, either, that they saved a British outpost beyond the Yangtze, and at another time rescued an American newspaper woman on the farther reaches of the Pearl.

Yet they were considered a burr in the sock of any city that had the misfortune to number them among its visitors.

Popular opinion surged up against them in Hongkong as soon as they flopped their ramshackle crate down on a mangy piece of terrain back of the city and almost piled up in a ground loop. This was not poor judgment, but poor landing conditions.

The monoplane itself was of unknown vintage, but the OX5 was fairly new.

A wise-cracking newspaperman, seeing two synchronized Vickers poked along the cowl, asked if there was a war going on.

McGill, that sawed-off, hammered-down, red-headed Mick, said, "Buddy, there's always a war where we are."

The newspaperman pointed to the large *G-M* painted in black letters on the red fuselage.

"General Motors might get sore at that."

"That don't stand for General Motors, brother."

"What then—General Murders?"

"Ain't you the bright boy! That stands for a kind of hard-boiled partnership. Me and that good-looking guy over there, Bill Gales. Get it—Gales-McGill, not incorporated, and unlimited. We fly anywhere, any time, do anything except shoot a man in the back. No charge accounts and no cut rates."

"Are you sure you've never shot a man in the back?"

"Listen, son. One more blow-out like that and you'll do a nose-dive and never get over it."

IT DID not take them long to find out that Hongkong resented their coming and wished to expedite their departure. The newspaper gave them unfavorable publicity, and several official notes urged them to move on to other parts.

As a matter of fact, the boys were hard up financially and were on the lookout for anything that might enable them to build up a comfortable bank-account. Their presence there was mentioned in cables to other cities and was also a topic for conversation in the swanky bars and hotel lounges.

It began to get on McGill's nerves. He was a wild-cat to begin with, and when he began to show signs of licking anybody who looked disapprovingly at him, Gales told him to calm down. Gales was the younger and cooler of the two—a lean, clean-clipped man, with keen blue eyes and a fine straight mouth above a neat, square chin.

The upshot of it was that McGill stayed in their hotel room, remarking that he could resist anything but temptation, and he was sorely tempted to haul off and knock the supercilious hotel clerk for a tail spin.

And it was while he was sulking in the hotel room, a couple of days later, that the door smacked open and Gales strode in with a smile twitching at his lips and a twinkle in his eyes. He scaled a piece of paper across the table and said:

"Read that, partner!"

It was a cablegram:

> Understand you are in Hongkong stop can offer something big if you come immediately to number ten Sing Fu Street Canton stop please answer.
>
> JOHN SMITH.

McGill rolled his cigarette from one side of his mouth to the other, squinted against the rising smoke, and then squinted at Gales.

"Sounds good."

"What I thought!"

"Well, cable him."

"I did."

McGill grinned and stretched his arms. "Boy, looks like we're going to eat some sky!"

"It sure does, Mike. See what popularity does? We ought to thank the guys in this town. If they hadn't put up such a howl and let the whole world know we were here, this chum in Canton would never have heard."

McGill took a puff. "What d' you think it means, Bill?"

"A job."

"Yeah, I know. But what kind?"

"We'll have to find out. The new Far East Commercial Airways has a field in the northern part of Canton and we'll land there if they like it or not. Ten to one this job is something big, else this chum would never have cabled. Let's pack up and breeze."

"Yeah." McGill pinched out his butt. "Say, Bill."

"Uhuh?"

"First, suppose you go out for a walk, just a little one, and on the way out tell that hotel clerk I'd like to see him in my room."

"Why?"

"I want to plaster him."

Gales chuckled. "Forget it, Mike. We've got work to do. We want to make Canton before dark, and we can't afford to let a pin-headed snob like that cramp our style."

"Just one, Bill—just one nice clean sock in the—"

"Mike, old tomato, keep your pants on and pack that bag. Contact in half an hour!"

McGill shrugged. "Well, suit yourself, big boy."

CHAPTER II

JOB FOR AN EAGLE

WHEN THEY reached the *G-M*, they put lightweight coveralls over their neat white suits. A knot of curious natives had been standing around, and others came up and joined them.

Gales went around warning them to keep back, then hopped into the rear cockpit of the dual-control crate, closed the radiator shutters and pulled out the choke, with the throttle slightly advanced.

"Ready, Mike!" he called.

McGill went around to the front and heaved several times on the prop, to get a fresh charge of gas in all cylinders. Then he yelled, "Contact!"

Gales turned on the ignition and replied, "Contact!"

McGill heaved on the prop and the motor roared to life. Gales shoved back the choke and let the motor warm up while McGill prowled around looking at the flying wires and inspecting the empennage.

When the motometer showed a temperature of 160 degrees, Gales opened the shutters. He pulled back the stick to keep the tail down and proceeded to rev up. The motor howled, and Gales' eyes flicked the instrument board. Oil pressure 50 pounds; 1450 r.p.m.s on the tachometer.

McGill was looking up at him, hands on hips, butt drooping from one corner of his mouth. Gales nodded and eased up on the throttle. McGill pulled away the chocks and stowed them in the after part of the fuselage. Then he vaulted nimbly into the front cockpit and pulled down his goggles.

They had to taxi down to the far end of the field to get into the wind. The ground was rough and the scarred old bus creaked and grumbled. Gales swung it around at the end of the field, settled down, and opened the throttle. The *G-M* lurched forward, rocked, gathered speed, steadied, and slammed down the field.

Controls in neutral, air speed at forty, she cleared the ground and soared low over a group of buildings. Clear of the buildings, Gales pulled back slightly on the stick and reached for a thousand feet of altitude.

Wheeling over Hongkong, he attained two thousand, then leveled off and headed for Kowloon.

The OX5 was knocking off 85 miles an hour when they crossed over Kowloon and passed up the broad mouth of the Canton River. The sun was a white burning eye in a cloudless sky, but the air trail was not very smooth.

Repeated down-drafts smacked the *G-M* like a sledge-hammer, and her wires creaked like old bones. Vertical air currents struck her from above and below, and time and time again the partners were jerked up from their seats, and safety-belts strained. Bright skies do not always mean a smooth air trail, whereas gray, sunless weather often indicates a trail smooth as velvet.

McGill called for the controls and Gales gave them over. The Irishman took the crate up to seven thousand feet, then power dived to three thousand, leveled off and went into a crazy barrel roll. He came out of it grinning, and Gales shook his fist.

"We're up to make time, you sawed-off half-pint!"

McGill could not hear, but he laughed and fish-tailed wildly. Gales waggled the controls, wanted them back. McGill put his hands over his head, and Gales took control. Looking around, McGill grinned.

TWO HOURS later they circled over Canton, which lies at the junction of the Pe-kiang and Canton rivers. A square-walled city, cut up by canals.

Down in the southwest corner they could see the neat foreign concession. North of it were four old forts. Many temples shone amid the hodgepodge of Chinese dwellings, and on the river were thousands of houseboats.

Well away was the tarmac of the Far East Commercial Airways. Just outside a huge metal hangar, they saw two huge passenger planes. Gales eyed the wind-sock.

He throttled down to idling speed, and the *G-M* slipped into a long glide. Gales banked her gently over the hangar and slid smoothly toward the field, nose down. Ten feet above the field, he pulled back on the stick. The wheels struck, the plane bounced gently and lumbered along.

Gales roared the motor and then chugged along toward the hangar.

A delegation was there to meet them, and the absence of brass bands, flags and cheers was noticeable. But the two tramps of the air had become hardened to this sort of thing, and both grinned as they jumped out.

The Field Superintendent said. "I believe you are Gales and McGill."

"Right the first time!" said McGill. "Glad to know you, brother. Just thought we'd drop in for a spot of tea and see how the old air business is getting on. You're looking fine these days!"

The Superintendent was very dignified. "You realize, of course, that this is a private field. While we cannot prevent citizen planes from landing, I assure you we do not encourage it, especially men of your notoriety."

Gales said, "I'm sorry, naturally, that necessity forced us to land here. We shan't be long, however."

"You had better not be," sliced out the Superintendent.

McGill was on the point of delivering some tart back-talk, but Gales sensed this and silenced him with a dagger look. They passed through the airport station, got into a taxi and drove off.

"Ain't we popular!" chuckled McGill.

"Very," nodded Gales. "Another thing, if you don't cut out cracking wise whenever a guy gets high-hat, I'll take a crack at you myself."

"I didn't say a thing."

"You were going to."

"Well, I didn't."

"Well, let's drop it."

Into the turbulent, teeming heart of Canton, through squalid, ragtag streets cluttered with hawking Chinese. The partners sat back like lords of the earth. The taxi slewed from left to right, wheeled around corners, bored through the shifting throngs.

Presently it drew up before a mean, dirty-faced house in a dim, narrow street. Number 10 Sing Fu Street. Perplexed, the two birdmen alighted.

"What a dump!" muttered McGill.

Gales paid the fare and then looked at the door. "Sure is, Mike. Well, let's try it."

HE KNOCKED. The door opened and an old Chinese looked out through square, steel-rimmed spectacles. Gales showed him the cablegram.

"Enter," bowed the Chinese.

They went into a dark hallway, feeling their way behind the Chinese. They were led into a room, comfortably furnished in the Oriental manner and redolent of incense.

"Will you be seated, gentlemen?"

They sat down, looked about warily. The old Chinaman said:

"If you will be good enough to wait here, all will be well. I shall not be long."

Bowing, he backed out of the room. The door closed.

"Well!" breathed out McGill.

"I don't know what we've got into, Mike, but we're going to see it through."

"I'll say we are. The old boy looks like he's got a couple of brains knocking around in his head. But I'm darned if I can see any jack hanging around in this dump."

"Calm yourself, old-timer. I've got a hunch there's something big in the wind."

"Yeah. Butt?"

"Thanks."

They lit up.

When the door next opened, a tall, slim man entered and stood just inside the threshold while the door clicked softly shut behind him. He was well-groomed and carried himself with fine dignity.

A stick hung on his arm, and a Panama hat was in his hand. Gray hair powdered his temples.

"Gentlemen." His hand was extended.

The two partners shook. Then the man crossed the room, laid his hat and stick on a chair and sat down. He waved his hand casually.

"Won't you sit down?"

They sat down.

"Of course, my name is not John Smith," he went on, and smiled mildly. "But it is necessary that I be known to you as John Smith. Very necessary. I want to assure you that what I have in mind is very honorable, though it may not seem so. Also, before we go into details, I must have your word that whatever may pass between us will go no further."

"Of course," nodded Gales, showing interest.

"Sure," clipped McGill.

Smith inserted a cigarette into an ivory holder. "You cannot realize what depends on the success of this venture in which I have called you.

"You cannot realize what depends on failure.

"I called you here because it was common gossip that you were in Hongkong. I know your record, and I do not think it a particularly unsavory one. I believe you are men of honor, otherwise I should not have cabled you."

HE STRUCK a match and calmly lit his cigarette. Then:

"There is a certain vitally important document which we believe to be in possession of a certain man. A great deal depends on our securing this document. When I say a great deal I mean it in terms other than monetary.

"To work with me, you must first believe that I am an honorable man and that I have no thought of self. My position prevents divulging my name, and I named this rendezvous because otherwise we should have been spied upon.

"There is danger—to you, I mean. There is great danger. Hence I am willing to pay extremely well for your services.

"The man who is my enemy, and who is the enemy of many others, goes by the name of Volskoff. He is scheduled to fly to Shanghai tomorrow morning in the *China Queen* of the Far Eastern Commercial Airways.

"We suspect that he is carrying this document, and we want it, to prove many things of which now we have merely a suspicion. It will be found, no doubt, in a small leather dispatch case which he carries.

"The method of procuring it, without killing him and without harming anyone else, is up to you."

McGill shrugged. "Bill here is the brains of this outfit, Mister. It's up to him to lay plans, then I follow 'em."

Gales had keened his eyes. "It may be possible, Mr. Smith. The risk—"

"Is great, I realize. If that document is placed in the proper hands, the reward is ten thousand dollars."

"Whew!" whistled McGill.

"A thousand advance," added Smith. "The document may be delivered here, or to Number 26 Sun Gow Street, Shanghai.

"There is a man there who, if you say, 'We are from Canton,' will reply, 'How is Mr. Smith?'

"To that man you may give the document. He is short, rotund, with a white mustache. The little finger of his left hand is missing. He may be called Major White, though that is not his real name."

Gales stood up. "I think I have an idea."

"I knew it!" chuckled McGill.

Mr. Smith took a roll of bills from his pocket.

CHAPTER III

SKY-HIGH PERIL

CHINA IS a land of intrigue. Fortunes have been made and lost there. Men have become emperors over night, and over night they have become corpses too.

The winds of chance and of destiny are variable, and a king today may be an outcast tomorrow. Men have worshiped in temples, and later those temples have been ransacked and laid to ruin. Beneath the yellow calm of an Oriental face may lie berserk passions, and death—that is, somebody else's—is not taken seriously.

White men from the far corners of the Western World have gone out there to range the snag-toothed coasts or penetrate the God-forsaken hinterland. White men have tried to establish empires of their own in the far embattled hills.

Gold—or the things that stand for gold—have drawn the good, the bad and the indifferent. And many a man has felt the thrust of a knife in his back down where the city streets are dark, and found oblivion eternal in the blacker depths of the river.

In the waiting room of the Far East Commercial Airways there was a certain amount of activity. Baggage was being weighed on the big scales, and each passenger was also weighed with his baggage, and the total was carefully set down by the clerk.

The man who had first arrived and taken up a position beside the desk, was tall and noticeably reserved. He wore a wide-brimmed hat of Bangkok straw, a drooping mustache and smoked glasses and he leaned upon a stick. He had reserved passage under the name of Henry Brownstone. In reality he was Bill Gales, and the mustache and smoked glasses were affected.

He had listened closely when each new arrival appeared at the desk, and when the clerk said, "Have you much luggage, Mr. Volskoff?" Gales took careful stock of his man.

Volskoff was of medium height and build, rather well-dressed, and of an age somewhere between thirty-five and forty. He carried himself with an air of importance. He was swart, clean-shaven, and had very dark eyes. He looked powerful and able to take care of himself.

The Field Superintendent came in, checked up on the luggage, and ran an appraising eye over the passengers. He did not recognize Gales. The baggage was trundled out to the field on trucks, and then the gate was opened to admit the passengers.

Gales tagged along behind. The big all-metal plane was good to look at. She was bi-winged and powered with three Armstrong Siddeley engines of 385-425 h.p. each. These were calculated to drive her at about one hundred miles an hour, and when fully loaded she weighed almost eight tons.

The baggage was being loaded into the after part of the big fuselage. The passenger entrance was abaft the wings, at the after end of the row of windows, and passengers reached this by means of a movable stepladder of three steps.

Inside, there were two rows of single seats with an aisle in the middle. Forward was the fireproof bulkhead that separated the cabin from the pilot's cockpit, and on this bulkhead were a clock, an air-speed meter and an altimeter.

Gales saw Volskoff take a rear seat and appreciated his judgment. Gales took one a little farther forward, on the opposite aisle, flush with the trailing edge of the lower wing.

THE MOTORS were running over slowly, and the white-jacketed Chinese steward was seeing to it that everybody was comfortable. There were fifteen passengers, and most of them must have been first trippers, for they looked more than a little apprehensive.

In the roof of the cabin, at equal intervals, were three squares of doped fabric, attached to each of which was a rip-cord. These were emergency exits in case the plane landed in water or took fire in a land crash, and were torn open by merely yanking the rip-cord. Aft was the pantry and wash-room, and beside each seat was a menu suggesting drinks and sandwiches that might be had en route.

The door was closed and barred. The pilot was revving the engines. The copilot looked back into the cabin through the slot in the bulkhead, then closed it. The chocks were hauled away.

The engines roared. The big plane vibrated. Some of the passengers looked at one another and grinned weakly. There was a slight jerk, and the *China Queen* was moving. The engines roared louder and the plane moved faster, streaking down the field.

The take-off was scarcely perceptible. Eight tons rose into the air and drove steadily over the edge of the field. Up—up, ponderously, doggedly, efficiently.

To Gales it was commonplace, humdrum, but to many of the passengers it was a new adventure. There was hardly any motion, and the bank and turn at two thousand feet was deftly maneuvered. Up two thousand more, and then level flight—the giant silver bird soaring majestically over the river and heading northeastward into the arms of morning.

Gales looked around and saw Volskoff reading a paper. Who was this man, and what or whom did he represent? That was a cruel, bitter mouth he had, and dark eyes that could become savage under stress. Who was Mr. Smith, that tall, quiet-spoken gentleman with the gentle smile and the straight gray eyes?

A document. A document of great importance. Gales noticed the small leather dispatch case on Volskoff's lap and wondered why that document was of such great importance. Then he looked out of the window, down upon the wilderness over which they were now cruising at ninety miles an hour.

Two hours from the drome they sighted the sea, and the plane banked over it and then thundered up the coast. Stops would be made en route at Amoy, Foochow, Hangchow, and thence to Shanghai.

Gales slipped his hand into his pocket and felt the smooth steel of his automatic. He had no intention of reaching Amoy. He grinned behind his mustache.

He was on the port side, looking toward the land.

His gaze kept shifting upward, and presently he saw a speck in the blue above. His eyes keened.

The speck grew in size rapidly, plummeting from the sky. It was a bi-plane.

It swept down past the *China Queen,* and Gales saw the large *G-M* on the fuselage. Then the bi-plane leveled off, zoomed and hovered five hundred feet above the rear of the *China Queen,* maintaining that relative distance.

Gales shot a glance at Volskoff. The man was twisted around in his seat, his cheek pressed to the window. After a moment he turned front, picked up his newspaper, rumpled it, and pretended to read. But his eyes kept shifting to the window.

Gales rose and made his way aft to the washroom. He came out a moment later and returned down the aisle. One hand was in his pocket.

He stopped beside Volskoff and with his other hand grabbed the dispatch case. Volskoff's mouth opened, but his outcry was smothered by the roar of the engines.

Gales' gun was in his hand.

ONLY TWO of the passengers saw what was going on, and they were petrified. The others, having heard nothing, were serenely watching the scenery. The steward was in the pantry. Volskoff was red with rage.

Gales opened his coat and clipped the dispatch case on to his belt.

Still covering Volskoff, he reached up and yanked the rip-cord of the nearest emergency exit. A blast of wind thundered by and all in the cabin looked around, startled.

Gales leaped up, clawing his way to the top of the fuselage. Volskoff dived for his legs, but he was a split-second too slow.

Gales, fighting the wind now, clung to a vertical strut. He saw Volskoff's head appear in the opening and threatened him back with his gun. He clawed his way to the next strut forward, took a look upward and saw the *G-M* heading downward.

Muscles tense, he reached the next strut and found himself beneath the forward edge of the upper wing. The wind bludgeoned him, but he managed to fight his way to the top of the upper wing, and clung there while the *G-M* flattened out above.

He could see the *China Queen's* pilot, up in the nose of the plane, looking back and shouting. It was dangerous business, and the pilot dared do nothing but maintain an even keel.

The *G-M* drew closer, and Gales could see McGill's goggled face peering down at him. The red-head was grinning! Everything depended on how expertly he managed that old rattlebox.

And McGill was an expert when he had to be. He edged closer, and Gales crouched, both hands now gripping the edge of the big plane's wing, head twisted and eyes glued on the approaching bi-plane.

He removed one hand from the wing. The wind almost turned him around. He reached up. The bi-plane's landing gear was just over his head. He straightened and the wind carried him off even as his hands gripped the *G-M's* axle.

The *G-M's* nose went up and she cleared away. Gales hung suspended in mid-air until they were well clear. Then he muscled up and over the axle, while the wind ripped at him and whistled past his ears.

Bit by bit, fighting desperately for every inch, he reached the lower wing, fought up to it, hugged it to regain his breath, then caught the rim of the front cockpit and piled in. Automatically he buckled on the safety belt.

When he looked around, he saw the grinning, freckled face of McGill, and McGill waved. Gales grinned, too, and then looked down at the *China Queen*, which was keeping to its course.

Well, he had the dispatch case. But this was really only the beginning. Radios and cables would be buzzing with the news of a skyway robbery. A net would be spread.

And Volskoff—no, this was not the end of Volskoff. Because China was the background—land of intrigue, high adventure, quick, untimely death. And law? Law only in theory!

CHAPTER IV

FOUR DIE

NUMBER 26 Sun Gow Street, Shanghai....

Gales stepped from the riksha, paid the coolie and told him to be gone. He watched the riksha disappear around a bend in the serpentine alley. He was alone, a lean young man in neat whites, a white blur in the shadow-ridden street.

He looked at the dark face of the narrow door. There was no light. There was no light in all that mean, forgotten street. It seemed as if life had packed up and quietly walked away. Down the wind came the faint murmur of other streets. Came a dank odor of decay, too, of things left to rot.

Gales knocked at the door. The echoes rushed back at him and clicked down the alley. In one hand was the dispatch case, in the other his gun, hidden in his pocket.

The door opened like a ghost door, and a cave of darkness yawned.

A low, soft voice asked, "Gentleman wish to see whom?"

"Major White."

"Gentleman will enter?"

Gales hesitated, wishing for some light. There was a scratch, and then a match flamed in a thin yellow hand. A young, wedge-shaped face appeared in the glow.

"Will enter?"

Gales stepped into the doorway, and the young Chinaman closed the door softly, then led the way silently down the corridor and up a flight of narrow, creaking stairs. The match went out, and Gales stopped, feeling his gun, which he was tempted to draw.

But a second match scraped against the wall, and the Chinaman continued.

At the top Gales saw a sliver of light projected from a door open on a crack. Toward this the Chinaman continued, and pushing it open, stood aside to let Gales pass in. The room was large, furnished with a desk and littered with books. The door closed.

The Chinaman stood there, his head slightly on one shoulder, a quizzical half-smile on his lips.

"You must pardon the disorder, sir. I am a student."

"I've come to see Major White," said Gales simply.

"Yes. I shall summon him, if you will make yourself at home. There is some tea, if you wish it. I shall be not very long."

Gales nodded and sat down. The young Chinaman put on a hat and went out.

Mystery. What the devil had he got himself into? Much the same process here as in Canton. You came to a dark back-alley, entered a silent house, and were told to wait. This was a system.

Was he, then, a cog in some gigantic under-cover system? Not a cog—a tool. He resented this, but then thought of Mr. Smith, who certainly bore the hallmark of a gentleman.

So he waited, smoking cigarettes. He and McGill had landed their plane on a beach south of Amoy, and Gales had come north with the dispatch case by railway. It would have been suicide to fly the *G-M* to Shanghai, or to any large city on the coast.

After an hour of restless waiting he heard footsteps outside the door. He stood up. The door opened and a short, chunky white man stepped in, followed by the young Chinaman.

Gales said, "I am from Canton."

The man smiled. "How is Mr. Smith?"

GALES RELAXED. "You are Major White, I take it."

"Yes, yes. I had a code message that you were due to arrive. The city has been agog over the robbery staged on the *China Queen* and the spectacular getaway of a man with a mustache wearing smoked glasses."

Gales grinned. "I favored a disguise."

Major White chuckled good-naturedly and stroked his close-clipped mustache. He had red cheeks and twinkling little blue eyes, and he kept flipping the watch-chain that spanned his vest.

"Then you have been successful?"

"Here is the dispatch case," said Gales, "if that is what you mean by successful."

"Quite. Ah, I see it is locked!" He turned to the young Chinaman. "Lee, have you a knife?"

"Indeed, sir."

Lee took a knife from a drawer in the desk, handed it to Major White, and the latter slit the case open. Reaching in, he drew out a packet of papers wrapped in oilskin.

"I believe there is nine thousand dollars coming to you," he said. "Good work."

"I shall put that amount into your hands before another hour. H'm. Let's see."

He broke the seal that held down the oilskin flap.

He was drawing out the flat sheaf of papers when the door burst open and three swart men charged in with drawn revolvers. One of the revolvers exploded.

From its muzzle burst red searing flame, and Lee, the young Chinaman, opened his mouth and his eyes wide. He tried to speak, but his teeth closed in a terrible grimace, his hands flew to his chest, pain wracked his face. He fell headlong.

Gales, with the agility of a cat, bounded sidewise as his own gun leaped from his pocket. Major White clutched at his pocket. Gales fired point-blank at a man who was swinging a gun toward him, and that man staggered as straight lead smashed through him. The other two roared.

Major White had his gun out, but another gun burst into flame and the Major wilted, firing as he went down, and that shot of his bored through the heart of the man who had shot him.

The other, seeing the papers drop from the Major's hand, dived for them. But Gales dived, too, and the other snarled as they came together. Neither got the papers, but both turned on each other, and the swart man's gun belched.

The shot fanned Gales' forehead and slammed through the ceiling. Gales struck with the barrel of his gun—struck at a swart, dodging head—hit it and sent the man reeling sidewise.

Blood streaked his cheek, and Gales plowed into him to sidetrack another shot; caught the gun-hand and wrenched it savagely.

The man cursed and heaved, kicked with brutal intent and caught Gales in the stomach. Gales, gritting his teeth, struck again with his gun, and the blow, landing square on the man's head, dropped him senseless to the floor.

GALES STOOD spread-legged, awed by the cyclonic suddenness with which death had swooped upon the room. He stared at the dead Chinaman. He stared at Major White, who stared upward as only the dead stare. They must have been trailed to the rendezvous.

He bent down and picked up the packet of papers. He shoved them back into the oilskin envelope. There was nothing he could do here. Those shots must have been heard. Others would come here—even the police, perhaps.

He grabbed his hat and plunged through the open door. He raced down the creaking staircase blindly, stumbled as he came unexpectedly to the bottom. Jumping up, he groped on toward the hall-door, found it and yanked it open.

As he leaped into the street he was confronted by a knot of curious, babbling Chinese. He struck right and left, taking no chances. They yelled loudly and tried to hold him, struck at him and kicked at him. He went through them like a whirlwind, and dashed on down the crooked alley.

He ran until he reached a crowded street, and then he walked rapidly, elbowing his way through the crowd. He kept on walking, with no idea of where he was going. He stopped at last on the Bund, sought the shelter of cool shadows and stood mopping his face.

He felt his pocket. The document, that in a few minutes' time had cost four men their lives, was still there. He knew no address other than the one in Sun Gow Street. After what had happened, it would no longer be a rendezvous. And the document—a passport to death—was open and in his possession.

He muttered, "Now I have a right to see what it's all about. By George, I'm going to see—and that other nine thousand be hanged!"

That being that, he strode briskly along the Bund to his hotel.

CHAPTER V

THE RIDDLE

MIKE McGILL sat by a fire of driftwood on the lonely beach, smoking a cigarette and watching the surf cream white over a saw-toothed reef. The stars were on parade, and the moon hung high, and the spell of the night enveloped the sea and the jungle.

But McGill was lonesome. The beauty of the night made him feel that way. He had lived on nothing but fish for almost a week, and he dared not take the *G-M* up for a spin because all their fuel would be needed when—and if—Bill Gales came back.

He missed Bill. There was nobody to argue with him. He felt down at the mouth, and wondered why he hadn't married that Swedish masseur back in Providence, R.I., four years ago—considering that she'd asked him. Of course, she had stipulated—*no more flying*. That was the reason.

"I wish Bill would come back," he said to the sea. "I don't like this spot. There ain't a soul here. Not even a Chink. I couldn't talk with a Chink but I could pick a fight with him. Little excitement—"

He stopped, startled by the sound of his own voice. He grinned to himself, sheepishly. A guy sure had the willies when he talked out loud to himself. Well, try whistling.

There was a sound back in the bush. McGill looked around, his hand on his gun. The firelight danced about him, glinted on his red hair. Sounded like horse's hoofs.

A voice through the silence, "Hi, Mike!"

McGill jumped up. "Hi, Bill!"

Gales rode out of the darkness, accompanied by a gaunt Chinese astride a mule.

"Bill, you big bum you!"

They shook vigorously, Gales chuckling. "Back, Mike, all safe and sound."

"Who's the guy on the jack?"

"Just hired him at Amoy yesterday." Gales turned to the Chinaman, paid him for the hire of his horse and his service as a guide, and then unloaded four five-gallon drums of petrol from the horse he had been riding.

"Good thoughtful old Bill!" said McGill.

Gales then dismissed the Chinaman, and the latter forked his mule and led the horse away with him into the night. Gales lit a cigarette and sat down by the fire. His eyes were narrowed thoughtfully.

"Let's hear the dirt," said McGill.

Gales related what had taken place in Sun Gow Street, and McGill cursed because he had missed the fun.

"Fun my eye," said Gales. "You and I, Michael McGill, seem to have got ourselves into something more than we bargained for."

He drew the oilskin envelope from his pocket. "This is something of vital importance. Come closer and look it over."

THEY CROUCHED by the fire, and Gales spread out a map of China. "Look at this, Mike. Notice the lines drawn in red ink, and the various X's.

"Notice the red circles around Canton, Hongkong, Hankow, Hangchow, Wuhu, Amoy, Foochow, Ningpo and Shanghai; and beside each circle a number. Canton: 25,000. Wuhu: 15,000. And so on.

"Now notice that all these red lines diverge from one spot, in Hunan Province. See?"

"Yeah. But what does it mean?"

"I'm blamed if I know. Here's something else," he said, opening a sheet of yellow paper. "Look. Here's a list of thirty planes. Five two-motored bombers; three tri-motored transports; six scouts; sixteen combat planes, ten of which are two-seaters.

"And look—beside each plane or group of planes is marked the maximum speed and cruising range. Mike, this is somebody's report!"

"Yeah. Whose?"

"I don't know. Maybe Volskoff's. Or maybe he was just carrying it for somebody else. Now this looks, mighty gigantic to me. On the face of it—I mean all this flying equipment—it seems absurd. There is no foreign power in all China, to my knowledge, that possesses such an array of crack fighting equipment. I can't understand it."

"Well, cripes, if you can't, Bill, I'm sure I can't!"

"It's so big, Mike, that I'm all keyed up, and there's only one thing to do: see this Mr. Smith in Canton and make him let us in on the mystery. There's a good chance for adventure here that's worth far more than the remaining nine thousand dollars, and I'm blamed if I'm content to be just a tool in a thing as big as this."

"You took the words right out of my mouth, big boy. Let's eat some sky in the morning. Of course, we can't land in Canton, but we can land somewhere near there."

"Right!" Gales shoved the papers back into the oilskin envelope. "Old tomato, there's something big, mighty big, in the wind, and I've got a hunch that wind's an ill one! And I've got a hunch we're going to pancake on somebodys' merry-go-round."

"And how, brother—and how!"

CHAPTER VI

STRANGE WINGS

THE FIRST flush of the sun found the *G-M* bowling along at four thousand feet. Below, mists hung in broken layers over the wild coast and the sea was a vague gray blur. The air trail was smooth, and the OX5 was kicking off ninety miles an hour.

McGill, in the front cockpit, was at the controls, and he had promised to cut out all aerial wisecracks. Gales was scanning the morning with binoculars. He had slept well and the feel of the vibrant plane was tonic to his birdman's heart.

This nondescript old crate had carried them thousands of miles, in fair weather and foul. It was like a faithful old dog— not a prize, high-priced dog, but a good, reliable old mongrel. It wasn't much on looks, and it was a great deal noisier than any plane had any right to be.

It was a tough old bird, dented and patched, pocked with old bullet marks, but always ready to meet the worst in a slam-bang, bull-dog manner. It had, in short, personality—at least to the two men who owned it.

The sun came up in a wild blaze of scarlet, spilling its color over the lean long reaches of the sea, tinting the gauzy wisps of cloud that rode high beneath the roof of the world, and flashing on the wings of the vagabond plane.

Gales swept the brightening sky with his glasses, looked past McGill's head through the shimmering disc of the prop. A small dot held his attention—a small dot dead ahead and far away.

He leaned forward, peering intently. A plane—no doubt one of those passenger planes bound north. It would not do to be seen and recognized. That plane would be carrying a wireless outfit and would send out the news that the *G-M* had been discovered.

He lowered his glasses and wiggled the stick. McGill looked around, then raised his hands, the signal that he was off the controls. Gales took them over and at the same time motioned for his partner to look ahead.

McGill took his own glasses and screwed them to his eyes. After a moment he leaned back and nodded. Gales indicated that he was about to change his course, and McGill made a gesture signifying that he understood.

Gales kicked right rudder bar, shoved right on the stick, and the left wing tilted upward as the *G-M* turned in toward the coast. They crossed the line of surf and held their new course for five miles, then swung south again at five thousand feet. This course would be at least seven miles west of the route used by the passenger plane, and at that distance recognition would be impossible.

But events did not follow what Gales had supposed would be the natural course. The oncoming plane had changed its course and was now heading inland toward the *G-M*. McGill looked around and shook his head disapprovingly. Gales banked and headed farther inland, and then, pulling back on his stick, hit the air trail for eight thousand feet. It was significant that the other plane also chose to make altitude.

Gales throttled down and shouted to his partner, "Mike, she's probably an official plane out to get us. We can't fight her. We'll have to lose her."

"Suppose she fires on us?"

"We don't fight till we're cornered!"

GALES HAD no wish to enter combat with government planes. They had never done this in all their wild career. Their duels in the air had been with outcast planes.

But this new plane was certainly making for them. Gales went into a steep bank and turn, leveled off and then zoomed mightily. The old crate throbbed in every fibre but chewed the air like the bulldog it was.

At fourteen thousand feet Gales straightened out and looked overside.

The bright yellow monoplane, whirlwind motored, was climbing rapidly. A two-seater, with a machine gun swiveled from the rear cockpit. A sleek bird, finely steamlined, with military wings built for speed and maneuverability and a minimum of lift. A fast, first-class fighting plane.

Up she came in a businesslike manner, then swung off and shot beneath the *G-M's* tail. McGill, looking down, saw the machine gun spit quick puffs of smoke. A stream of lead slammed through the after part of the *G-M's* fuselage.

McGill swore a sizzling blue streak and smacked his hand down on the synchronized Vickers. Gales yelled for him to leave it alone. McGill swore mightily.

Gales ran for it. He power-dived with the throttle wide open, and the wind screamed past like a maniac, shrilled keenly in the wires, hooted along the fuselage. He leveled off at two thousand feet, flung a look back and upward, saw the monoplane loafing about. He gunned the motor hard and went howling over the coast, out over the sea, then upward and away, burning the wind.

The yellow plane took up the pursuit. It overhauled the *G-M* ten miles at sea, and its gun cut loose, and Gales saw one of his center struts chipped in a dozen places. Another burst hammered the head-rest fairing, and stray shots twanged through the landing wires.

McGill was red with wrath. He glared at the yellow plane and shook his fist. Then he stared, and a moment later was yelling at his partner:

"No—markings—Bill! No—government—plane!"

Gales looked. McGill was right. There was not a single marking on either wing or fuselage. The plane was an unknown.

McGill looked to his gun, and his lip curled. At the same time Gales stood the crate on one wing and cannoned through the air in a wild circle. The yellow plane dived from aloft.

The *G-M* straightened out on the other's tail and for the first time McGill's gun talked a language it knew.

The first burst raked the monoplane's empennage, and she keeled off, then zoomed like a frightened bird. Gales followed, but to no avail, because that monoplane had him licked for speed.

He throttled down and loafed in a wide circle. A thousand feet above loafed the monoplane, marking time.

Then it suddenly dived, a yellow streak in the sunlight, straight for the *G-M*. Gales kept to his circle, and as the other shot by he went into a barrel-roll, and the monoplane's fire missed wide.

Gales dived after it, tailed it down toward the sea, and McGill's gun blazed furiously.

THE MONOPLANE fishtailed, then banked sharply and went screaming away for safety. Gales banked still sharper to break its wide turn, and McGill's gun crackled and put a stream of bullets into the left flank of the yellow plane.

Staggered, the plane took a skidding right turn and then stood on its tail as it bit the air for altitude. It was a fast plane stacked against a slower one with a wizard for a pilot.

But none the less the yellow bird was dangerous. As if angered by the insult of being driven off by the vagabond *G-M*, the monoplane swooped with a vengeance, and a clatter of lead raged in the metal behind Gales' head.

Savagely he stood the *G-M* on its nose and dived for the sea, as the monoplane screamed past his tail. Recklessly he leveled off a few hundred feet from the waves. Then full throttle and stick slightly back, and a bedlam of wind and howling wires as he fought for altitude.

Down came the monoplane on a wave of fresh courage. And Gales, mad to the core, stuck the nose of his plane straight toward it and ripped every last ounce of energy from the roaring 0X5.

And the hot gun of McGill blazed upward at the descending monoplane, and lead tore through its belly, riddled its wing. It had planned to drive the *G-M* back down to the sea, but its pilot and gunner had not reckoned on the wild courage that manned the battered bi-plane.

The yellow plane shot by low overhead, and as it did a sheet of flame enveloped it, torn aft by the blast of the wind. Gales grimaced and bit his lip. It was terrible, but those fellows had forced the fight. He banked and turned his plane around, then leveled off and throttled down.

Below was the doomed monoplane, spinning and flopping downward in a world of flame and oily smoke. The sea received it, or what was left of it, and a puff of steam billowed, then faded into thin air, and jets of burning oil smoked on the water and then died.

Gales dropped the *G-M* in a number of easy spirals and drifted over the spot. Nothing remained but bits of charred and broken wings, and even as he watched they slipped from sight. Gunning his motor, he climbed to six thousand feet, then throttled down.

McGill looked around and said. "Well, that's that!"

"A strange plane, Mike," shouted Gales. "More outside the law than we are, because she carried not a single marking. I'll bet Volskoff was behind it."

"Yeah. But what's behind Volskoff?"

Gales shrugged. He did not know. But he felt that he and Mike were becoming enmeshed in a vast net of grim and somehow terrible mystery.

He drove the *G–M* southward with steel determination. He felt certain that somewhere in brooding, yellow China lay a deadly serpent.

CHAPTER VII

THE LOST RENDEZVOUS

LATE NEXT afternoon Gales was walking along Respondentia Walk, overlooking the Canton River. Respondentia Walk is the smart promenade of the Foreign Settlement. But Gales was on his way to yellower, dirtier China; and once beyond the walk, he hailed a riksha and climbed in.

The document was in his pocket. Determination was in his heart. He and McGill had thrashed things out and were resolved to find out what sort of net they had been drawn into.

Toward this end they were willing to forfeit nine thousand dollars. If the wiseacres of Hongkong had heard this, they never would have believed it. But the wiseacres of Hongkong were not adventurers, so they could not understand.

The riksha wound its way down a teeming Canton street, where itinerant merchants sing-songed their wares; where pot-bellied Chinamen sat in doorways smoking long pipes, and a scrawny beggar played on a wheezy flute, and half-naked children sat in the gutter. Here the blazing sun streamed down on dust and dirt and fruit and fish and the ragtag squalor of a careless street. Tinkling glass and the wheezy flute and the brazen clang of a gong and the strident discord of a thousand voices.

Gales, birdman of fortune, weaved through this tapestry of life, and seeing it—and smelling it—longed for the clean sweet thrill of an air trail.

At last, Sing Fu Street.

But a perplexed frown bent his brows as he neared Number 10. For what had been a house was now a mass of ruins.

Alighting, he stood beside the riksha. Ragged walls and a mass of crumpled stone. There was no doubt in his mind that Number 10 had been bombed.

In the short space of a minute he became aware of the appalling fact that he was in possession of a document that could not be delivered to the man who would understand it. Smith's rendezvous must have been discovered by his enemies.

Gales felt at a loose and dangling end. The information which he held in his pocket was valuable and vital to somebody. Because of it four men had died in Shanghai and a mysterious yellow monoplane had been sent out by some unknown power to destroy the *G-M*.

There was no way of locating Smith. To begin with, that was not his true name, and he had given no address other than this one, which now was no longer an address but an epitaph.

Gales was certainly in a dilemma. Disgruntled, he turned to board the riksha, and in so doing his gaze chanced to wander up the dark front of the building opposite.

Framed in an open window on the second floor was a face. A familiar face.

The swart, deadly face of Volskoff!

It took restraint on Gales' part to sit down nonchalantly in the riksha, wondering if Volskoff recognized him without the disguise he had used during the skyway robbery. He told the coolie to get going, and as the riksha moved off a slug banged through the top of Gales' topee.

Instantly he leaped, certain that he had been recognized. That shot had been fired from a silenced revolver, and a second shot rang on the pavement an inch behind his heels.

HE FLATTENED against a house-wall on the same side of the street, out of range, while the coolie, forgetting his fare, went galloping off with his riksha. Gales hurried away along the house fronts. Looking back, he saw Volskoff and three other men burst out of a door, point toward him and then take up pursuit.

Gales took to his heels. He'd be cursed if Volskoff would get the papers back again, and he knew that if he stopped and tried to shoot it out, he would certainly be killed. He loved life, and he had no keen desire to throw it away in a Canton back-alley. Besides, he could not forget that the papers which he carried bore tremendous value.

He banked around the next corner and pounded swiftly along. He saw Volskoff and the others dogging his footsteps.

Turning another corner, he raced along and was soon in a crowded street. He swung into a narrow passageway that led to another crowded street, and he hurried through the shifting throngs, from street to street, a clean-clipped young white man who drew the quizzical glances of the mob. For white men do not hurry in Canton.

Finally he jumped into a riksha and told the coolie to stretch his legs in the direction of Respondentia Walk.

And when he reached the Walk he alighted and strode briskly away. He went down a wharf and dickered with the owner of a power sampan. They came to terms and Gales boarded it and sat down beneath the mat awning. The sampan chugged off and headed up the Pe-kiang River.

Ten miles beyond he left the sampan and struck out through low bushes. And a mile inland he came to a small field. At one end of the field stood the *G-M*, and perched on the coaming of the front cockpit was McGill.

"Hi, Bill! Back so soon?"

"Yes, old tomato. And no luck. That dump in Sing Fu Street has been blown up, and now we're stuck with a riddle that can only be answered by Smith—and Lord knows where he is. I saw Volskoff. In fact, he took a shot at me."

"The pup!"

"What I thought, too."

"D'you get him?"

Gales sat down and lit a cigarette. "Didn't try."

"Why, Bill!"

"You would say that, you Mick. There are times when I choose to run, and that was one of them. Remember, you wild-cat, that I'm carrying somebody's gold-mine in my pocket."

"Well, yeah, that's right, too. Now what?"

Gales sighed. "I wish I knew." Then he drew the papers from his pocket and studied them again.

McGill leaned over his shoulder. "Wonder what them numbers mean?"

"Might mean anything. Not the population, I'm sure. Not even the white population. Maybe—say, maybe they stand for a certain number of persons in each city and town."

"What persons?"

"Dunno. Maybe— Now I wonder if they stand for the number of persons who can be relied upon— Oh, dammit, I'm getting a war on the mind again. Blamed if I know, Mike. These X's, though—maybe they stand for outposts.

"Say, there's an X not far from here—about two hundred miles west. See it? Right in the wilderness. If there's something there, we can't miss it."

"What you got up your sleeve?"

Gales showed a new and intense interest. "Old tomato, we'll have to solve this riddle ourselves. To begin with, we look for this place marked X. What say you?"

"Big boy, do your stuff!"

Five minutes later the OX5 was roaring up over the Pe-kiang River.

CHAPTER VIII

X STANDS FOR—

THEY DROVE west over a raw wilderness, beneath a brazen sky. The air trail was rocky, and the *G-M* bounced over bumps and staggered beneath the walloping down-drafts. The wings swayed and jerked, and the tail slewed.

They crossed a river that looked like a narrow thread of silver woven into a tawny background. Low hills and broad plateaus and flat, steaming swamplands passed beneath them. The sun was wheeling westward, too, and the wings of the vagabond plane gleamed like sheets of red metal.

McGill was at the controls, and Gales had a worn chart before him. He saw another river flash beneath them and placed it on his chart. An hour later they crossed still another one, and all of these flowed south to join the upper Canton.

When they crossed the Kwei, Gales put away his chart and looked at the map he had taken from Volskoff. Not far beyond the Kwei—perhaps fifty miles—there was an X. He wiggled the controls and McGill gave them over.

Nothing was beneath them now—nothing but a yawning, savage wilderness. McGill took his binoculars and kept looking downward and Gales proceeded by dead reckoning. When they had covered sixty miles from the Kwei River, he banked and circled downward. No town—no hint of life—met their searching eyes. They continued to fly low and in wide circles, going back fifteen miles, then going ahead again.

Suddenly McGill looked back and pointed downward. Gales peered over the edge of the coaming. He saw nothing. He shook his head.

McGill yelled, "Cleared land!"

Gales looked again. Yes, there was a field down there that, on second glance, seemed strange in the midst of that wilderness.

He shoved forward on his stick and dived, flattened out at two hundred feet and went howling over what looked like an excellent place to land.

But he saw nothing else. Booming over the tree-tops at the farther end he rose steeply, circled above and then throttled down. The *G-M* whistled downward, banked gently over the trees and slanted down again toward the field.

Gales made a three-point landing on one of the smoothest bits of terrain he had ever struck in all China. The *G-M* rolled to a stop, and Gales shut off the ignition.

McGill muscled up and forked the coaming. He shoved up his goggles and looked at Gales.

"Well, Bill, what do you think?"

"I think that this land has been cleared and made into a first-class tarmac. Let's stretch our legs."

They leaped to the ground, lit cigarettes and roamed their eyes over the forest wall that surrounded the' field. Suddenly Gales pointed.

"What's that, Mike?"

"Let's look."

SIDE BY side the partners crossed the field and entered the timber. They came upon a large square structure made of logs and chinked with mud. No windows, but a door securely held shut by a huge lock. They looked at each other.

McGill grinned. "Big boy, your hunch led to something."

"The hunch says we should break in here, Mike."

McGill drew his gun, stepped to one side, and fired at the lock. Lead whanged against steel.

"Again, Mike!"

Bang!

The lock fell to the ground.

Gales pushed open the door, and a familiar odor assailed their nostrils.

"Petrol," said McGill. "I'll get the flashlight."

He ran over to the plane and came back grinning. He shot the beam of light in through the door as they entered.

Drum upon drum of gasoline was stored almost to the door, to say nothing of motor oil.

McGill muttered, "Hot dog, Bill!"

"Red hot!" said Gales.

They backed out, tingling with excitement.

"Now we know what these here X's mean," exclaimed McGill.

"Yes, sir! And there are plenty of X's on this map. Landing fields and re-fueling stations. For what, Mike? For the thirty planes named on this list!"

Out came the map.

"But why, Bill?"

Gales said, "God knows! And these red lines—I'll bet my hat that they indicate air routes, and the best air routes to all the cities around which you see red circles. And you will notice, old tomato, that all these lines—all these routes—start from one point, about four hundred miles north of this spot!"

"Go on, Bill."

"We certainly are going on! We're going to help ourselves to oil and petrol here—and then we are going on to the place from which all these red lines start!"

McGill cracked fist into palm. "Bill, we're on the trail of something dirty, so help me!"

"We certainly are, Mike! We'll stay here until morning. And we'd better find a place where we can roll the bus into the woods out of sight."

THIS THEY did, with a deal of labor, and then carried drums of petrol from the storehouse and loaded their tanks. They stowed six extra drums in the fuselage, fifteen gallons of oil.

By this time dusk was descending, and they sat down beneath the wings and munched biscuits and tinned beef. Night followed the dusk, and the stars came out over the wilderness. They were about to roll into their blankets when Gales stood up and listened.

"Hear that, Mike?"

"Yeah. She's a big baby."

They went out onto the field and peered upward. They heard the drone of motors, but saw nothing. But presently lights appeared in the south, and the drone increased in volume. Against the network of the stars they saw a large shape moving northward. They saw lighted cabin windows.

"Tri-motored," said Gales.

"Yeah. And she's doing about a hundred."

The big ship crossed directly above them, then passed. The lights grew dimmer, the sound of the motors faded. Then lights and sound died in the darkness. The two partners remained in silence for a long moment.

"Can you beat it!" muttered McGill.

"I'm boiling with curiosity, Mike! By George, what's a crack transport plane doing in this wilderness? It doesn't seem real. It's ominous, old boy."

"I don't know where you winged that ten-dollar word, brother—but in my language, it's just plain lousy. Let's catch some sleep. I crave an early take-off."

CHAPTER IX

THE EAGLES FALL

THE PARTNERS took off with the sun, circled for altitude above the field, and then headed the *G–M* due north. Hills, wild and tangled, rolled before them, and as they were approaching Kweilin these hills assumed the dignity of tawny mountains. The town of Kweilin was a mere blur from nine thousand feet, and as they roared northward and the mountains began to billow in greater numbers, they tacked on more altitude to get away from the air bumps.

The next town of Chuanchow gave them an opportunity to check up on their course, and then all signs of life were left behind and the wilderness yawned again beneath them and as far ahead as they could see. The OX5 was knocking off her customary r.p.m.s, and all the instruments on the dash were registering normally. A crash would mean certain death, for no plane could land in that tangle of rugged mountains.

But the partners had faith in the OX5, and there was plenty of fuel and oil. One of them was always scanning the sky with binoculars, for if a plane had crossed during the night, it was logical to suppose that one might turn up at any time during the day.

The wind was from the north, and blowing strong, and though the speed of the engine was ninety miles an hour, Gales reasoned that actual speed over ground was not more than seventy. The prop was screwing into the air with a vengeance, and the wind was a bedlam of screams, hoots and claps like thunder. Cloud scud streamed beneath them and above them, and sometimes they bored through it, and it smoked about their heads.

At a little past noon Gales began to look around for some town that would correspond with the mark on the map—the mark from which all those red lines diverged. He throttled down long enough to tell McGill that by his reckoning they ought to be somewhere near their goal.

McGill nodded, and then Gales knocked off altitude and dropped way down to look the country over. He hedge-hopped over the floor of a tangled valley, and on either side of him reared buttressed mountain walls. He saw not the slightest hint of habitation.

He pulled back sharply on the stick and rose to avoid a beetling mountain that loomed ahead. He banked and then circled, swooped down into other valleys, zoomed over other mountains.

It seemed incredible that any life could exist in this half-forgotten hinterland. Yet there must be a strategic point somewhere, he reasoned, else why did all red lines meet there?

Continuing north, he found a towering mountain ahead, and rose gradually to clear its embattled crown. Updrafts and downdrafts were numerous and bad, and the old crate lurched and hobbled like a man three sheets in the wind.

The top of the mountain drew nearer.

THE NOSE of the plane rose at a steeper angle, and the *G-M* cleared the top with three hundred feet to spare. Below stretched a valley, surrounded by mountains—a valley perhaps three miles long and a mile wide, hemmed in by sheer walls.

McGill was pointing and shouting, "Look, Bill—look!"

Gales saw. He saw roofs that glinted beneath the vertical rays of the torrid sun—many buildings—a vast field.

He throttled down and loafed along. Was this their objective? It struck an odd note in the midst of that teeming wilderness. It had all the appearance of a mirage.

The *G-M* drifted down the wind. McGill had taken over the controls, and Gales was peering keenly through his glasses.

Orderly rows of sheds at one end of the field. Behind them, other buildings—one group in a large hollow square, another group set apart in a compact cluster. A water fall tumbling down the mountain, and smoke rising from chimneys. This was not on the official maps—Rand-McNally did not show it.

Gales felt a premonition of danger. McGill was floating the plane nearer the field, at four thousand feet, and losing altitude casually. Presently Gales could see little dots moving about on the ground—dots that were men.

Suddenly the men began to disappear. The *G-M* cruised downward, and with every passing moment Gales wanted to tell McGill to pick up and run, but curiosity was tugging at him, even as it was tugging at McGill.

The sheds—of course, the sheds were used to house planes. That cluster of buildings must be dwellings. The other buildings that formed a hollow square—what were they? From them rose columns of smoke.

McGill banked at a thousand feet and advanced the throttle. Gales called for the controls and McGill gave them over. Gales gunned the motor, and the exhaust howled as he swept off and upward.

From the edge of the timber burst three puffs of smoke. The *G-M* jerked violently, and Gales saw fabric trailing from the edge of his left aileron.

He banked sharply. Three more bursts came from the edge of the timber, and lead—heavy lead—whanged through the fuselage.

The OX5 roared. From another point on the rim of the timber two more puffs of smoke shot into view, and lead carried away a streamline strut between the upper and lower wings and snarled through one of the metal ribs.

Puffs of smoke came from new parts of the forest, and Gales knew that they were trapped. There was only one thing to do—run for it. Throttle wide, he cannoned the *G-M* away from the field.

But three bursts exploded directly beneath him, and at the same time there was a horrible crash of metal and wood, and splinters flew past the birdmen's heads. The motor still roared, but the plane began to drop!

Gales' heart jumped a beat. The base of the propeller had been shot away, and the prop itself was spinning to earth.

Down went the *G-M* in a long glide. There was nothing to do but land, and the field sprawled before them. Gales shut off the ignition. He thought of the papers in his pocket. He cursed. But not for long. The business of saving his plane from a crack-up was all-important.

Men were running out on to the field from all quarters. They had seen the plight of the *G-M* and were waiting to receive it.

Gales watched the field rise up. He handled the controls gingerly. The wheels struck with a bang. The *G-M* bounced six feet in the air, wavered, then hit the earth again and rocked along drunkenly to a stop.

A moment later it was surrounded by an angry mob; men in breeches and boots, some of them wearing flying helmets with the flaps up. There was one who wore a swanky uniform and carried a big automatic pistol.

"Out—you two! And careful how you move!" he roared.

THE PARTNERS left their cockpits and leaped to the ground. Gales stood straight and keen-eyed, his mouth a grim slash. McGill had his fists doubled and his lips were curling.

"So," said the man in the swanky uniform, "our hidden anti-aircraft guns brought you down."

"Obviously," clipped Gales.

"And what about it?" snapped McGill, ripe for trouble.

"'Shut up, Mike," cautioned Gales.

"I'll not shut up!" barked McGill.

The officer folded his arms and rocked on his feet. "How nicely you came down! I must say that at least you men are expert flyers. But you must admit that our gunners are expert too."

"Expert?" laughed McGill. "Ha! What a joke that is! You fired all over the sky and then by luck connected. I've done better than that after an all-night drunk."

The crowd parted as another man came striding through it.

"Well!" Volskoff came to a stop and jammed his hands against his hips. "So!"

A wicked smile drew at his lips and his dark eyes gleamed.

"Who's this piker, Bill?" asked McGill.

"Volskoff."

Volskoff stepped forward and slapped Gales' face. "A pretty disguise you wore in the *China Queen!*"

Gales' fists doubled. "You keep your hands off me, stranger!"

Volskoff laughed. "You do not like it, eh? Well, I do not like being robbed. Where are those papers you took from me?"

"Where do you suppose?"

Volskoff turned to the men. "Search him!"

Six men leaped upon Gales and almost ripped the clothes from him.

"You big bums!" howled McGill, and sailed in like a wildcat.

A roar went up, and a dozen men piled on McGill, struck him and hammered him to the ground. Meanwhile the papers were taken from Gales, and when the crowd stepped back, McGill rose, wiping his face and cursing colorfully.

"Ah!" exclaimed Volskoff. "These are the papers! So you did not find it so easy to dispose of them, eh? You were blocked in Shanghai, and when you returned to the rendezvous in Canton you found it demolished. Well, well, this is one great joke."

McGill snapped. "Go ahead, wise guy—laugh your block off!"

Volskoff laughed loud and long. "So we have in our hands the famous Gales and McGill! It is very much like that old adage about the curiosity that killed the cat. Indeed, indeed!" Volskoff seemed immensely pleased with himself.

The partners were marched across the field, past the sheds, and through open doors they saw planes of various sizes. They were taken on toward the cluster of buildings, and into the largest. Then into a large, grimly furnished room.

BEHIND A desk sat a mountainous figure of a man with a spiked gray beard and gray hair clipped close to a bulging head. He wore a gray uniform coat, decked with medals. He had big, heavy eyes, and a tight, brutal mouth that contracted strangely with loose, fleshy jowls.

He leaned back, took a puff on a long, sweet-smelling cigarette, and eyed the two captives darkly.

"Very good, Colonel Volskoff," he rumbled.

"Our gunners brought them down nicely, General," replied Volskoff. "The little one here, the Irisher, is rather difficult."

"And I'm going to get difficulter, brother," threatened McGill.

Gales kicked his shins by way of urging silence.

The mountain rumbled. "I am General Petrovosk."

"I am Lieutenant Michael Flaherty McGill!"

The mountain erupted and a ponderous hand smote the desk. "Have done with this levity!"

McGill turned to Gales. "What the hell is levity, Bill?"

Gales' lips whispered, "You idiot!"

The mountain subsided and took a puff on the cigarette. "You do not seem to comprehend the seriousness of your position. Perhaps it does not occur to you that you have dropped into the jaws of death!"

Gales was quick to say, "You have the papers. Why must we die?"

Petrovosk attempted a satanic grin. "Do you suppose that we would permit you to leave here after you have discovered the vital heart of the New Empire?"

"New Empire?"

"Yes, the New Empire. A New Empire is about to be born in China. At the proper moment word will flash to all the great cities. The chosen in each city will stand by. The rest will be obliterated.

"England—America—France—will be thrown out of China. The present government will collapse. A great mandarin will be the new emperor, and I, General Petrovosk, will assume dictatorship."

"That's impossible," scoffed Gales.

Petrovosk scowled. "Impossible? No. For years we have planned carefully. We will take our enemies by storm—and from the air. We have the greatest fleet of fighting planes in all China. You saw our sheds. The fastest planes procurable. And all of them were built here. The materials were brought overland to build the first three transports, and then the transports brought in the materials to build the others.

"You see these electric lights. We generate our own power by means of the waterfall. We have manufactured our own bombs. And through the country there are landing fields, hidden away, and reserve fuel. And you say impossible? No.

"We have worked long and hard. We have agents in all the cities, and in Shanghai is the wealthy mandarin who will become emperor. We will strike before the powers can amass. Canton, Hongkong, Shanghai will fall beneath our air attacks—and other important cities.

"Ha-ha! And I shall be dictator!"

SILENCE FELL upon the room. Then Petrovosk chuckled. "Of course, I tell you this, because dead men relate no tales—and very shortly you will be among the dead."

Gales said, "So you intend to start a civil war?"

"Exactly."

"And though this mandarin will be emperor, you will be dictator. You will run the show—and amass the wealth."

Petrovosk bent his brows. "I do not like your tone."

"I predict for you," said Gales, "a miserable failure."

"Silence!" thundered Petrovosk. Then, "Colonel Volskoff, imprison these men while I meditate upon a choice manner of death for them."

"Indeed, General."

The partners were marched out of the room, out of the house, and across a courtyard. They were thrown into a bare, damp room, and the heavy door banged shut. In the gloom, they stood and regarded each other. McGill grinned.

"Tough, pard."

"Kind of, Mike."

They had been close to death many times before, but never as close as they were now. Gales pulled out a packet of cigarettes.

"Have one?"

"Yeah."

Gales struck a match, held it for McGill, then lighted his own.

"And they got the papers back, too," he muttered.

McGill gushed smoke through his nostrils. "Yeah. But I've got a duplicate."

"You—what!"

"Sure. When you were sleeping last night I got to thinking about things. I borrowed your original, made a little fire for light, and did some copying. It's back of my undershirt here."

"Mike McGill, you rate a lot of brains lately!"

"Yeah. But look at the ditch we're in."

They sat down and puffed glumly on their cigarettes. The dark angel of death was hovering near.

CHAPTER X

McGILL CUTS LOOSE

EVENING BROUGHT rain—rain and thunder and sheet-lightning. The rain thrushed against the single window of the prison room, and the lightning flared intermittently, showing the partners sitting against the wall, side by side.

After a while the door opened and Volskoff swaggered in. With him was a smaller man who carried a lantern and wore a monocle. Both were smirking, and it seemed that both had been drinking.

Volskoff, carrying a swagger stick, smacked his thigh and laughed. "Ah, the rats in the corner! Ho! Ho!"

McGill leaned close to Gales and muttered, "Bill, I'm going to sock that palooka before he's much older."

"Pipe down," cautioned Gales.

The man with the monocle teetered around the room and then banged the lantern down on a bare table. He hiccoughed and sat down on a stool.

" 'S truth, Colonel, a pair of rats! Ah—h'm—'s truth!"

Volskoff stood with legs spread, hands jammed akimbo. The lantern light played on his swart, cruel face. His eyes were glittering coals behind narrowed lids.

"Major Plitz, the humor of the situation paralyzes me. There they are—two insignificant fellows who call themselves soldiers of fortune. Imagine!"

"'S droll," hiccuped Major Plitz.

"Quite droll. They have caused us no end of annoyance, and Destiny was kind enough to play them into our gentle hands."

"Mos' gentle, Colonel," nodded Major Plitz.

Volskoff took three brisk steps toward the partners and rasped, "Scum, stand up!"

McGill said, "Lay off that baloney, brother!"

Whack! Volskoff's swagger stick cracked across McGill's head.

Gales snapped to his feet, a lean shaft of vibrating anger.

"Damn you, Volskoff!"

"You—shut up!" barked Volskoff. "At attention, both of you!"

McGill stood beside his partner, red with rage, his fists knotted.

Volskoff relaxed and cackled dryly. "So-o! There is still fire in the potential corpses."

"You're drunk," said Gales tartly. "Get out of here and leave us alone!"

Major Plitz staggered to his feet, weaved about and remarked, "Such monumental insolence!"

McGill snapped, "You shut up, small change, or I'll haul off and spend you all over the place."

"Enough from you, Irisher!" sliced in Volskoff. "It pleases us to dally with you two a while. You thought you were very clever when you robbed me of that document. You thought you were very clever when you shot down one of our planes.

"Well, you will pay, both of you. Tomorrow morning you will be tied to trees and machine guns will tear both of you to ribbons. Major Plitz and I will man the guns. Is that not pleasant?"

Major Plitz wobbled up, removed his monocle, polished it, then replaced it over his eye. "Mos' pleasant, eh? Hic—from the legs up, Colonel. First we shall break their legs—then upward, quite systematically. But we shall avoid the heart so that we may reach the brain. 'S droll!"

McGill exploded, "You lousy little squirt!"

PLITZ CHUCKLED, then reeled forward and struck McGill square in the face. It was too much for the red-headed Mick. He sailed into Major Plitz and sent him hurtling against the wall.

Volskoff jumped for McGill, and Gales, mad to the core, swung an overhand right that connected with Volskoff's ear and turned him completely around. With a bellow of rage, Volskoff streaked for his gun.

Gales cannoned for him and planted a pile-driving shot to the point of his jaw. At the same time he grabbed for Volskoff's half-drawn gun, and in the tangle the gun spun away and slid into a corner.

As for McGill—hell hath no fury like a red-headed Irishman struck. It is almost safe to say that Major Plitz was not certain whether it was McGill or a bolt of lightning that hit him. As he staggered away from the wall, McGill cut loose with an uppercut that sliced the air in twain and stopped with a terrific shock against Major Plitz's jaw.

The major did a tail spin. He not only did a tail spin, but added to that a barrel roll. The landing was far from being a three-point one. The major cracked up on a hard field of stone and promptly conked out.

Gales, under ordinary circumstances a man who favored tact to brawn, was now a savage rapier of vengeance. He gave Volskoff no quarter. He fought clean, clean as a slim, fast blade. Volskoff never knew what exactly happened, that is certain. It seemed incredible that a man could hit so fast and with such deadly accuracy. Gales finished him, did a neat, workmanlike job; polished things off with a nicely timed left hook that sent Volskoff skidding into a corner from which he did not rise.

The two partners looked at each other.

"Now what, Bill?"

Gales' lips were tight. "Our only chance, Mike! Swipe Plitz's uniform. I'll take Volskoff's. Quick, old tomato!"

They went to work rapidly. Five minutes later they were attired in gray uniforms. Over these they swung the rubber capes, and pulled the rubber hoods up over their uniform caps.

"Let's go, Mike!"

They went out into the storm. Thunder rumbled. Lightning blazed and crackled. They strode across the courtyard, past the house wherein they had first met General Petrovosk. Through the wet murk they could see many lighted windows, but no one was afield.

Gales led the way. They had done what it was reasonable to suppose no one had expected them to do. They had fought their way out of a tight corner. Volskoff had simply under-rated their hard-boiled nerve.

Two men appeared out of the murk, slushing through the wet mud. They mumbled and saluted as they went by, heads down against the wind and the rain. Gales and McGill strode on. They had never heard such terrific thunder. The world shook and trembled, and sheet lightning blazed.

On they went, along the edge of the field, past rows of sheds that contained fighting planes. At the end of the row they stopped. Next to the last shed stood the old *G-M,* shorn of its propeller.

"Poor old man!" sighed McGill.

They stood for a moment while the rain thrashed against their rubber capes. No one was in sight. They had to lean toward each other to make themselves heard above the bedlam of the storm.

"We take a plane, Mike," said Gales. "God knows if we can take her up in this weather, but it's our only chance. We've got to get back to civilization and warn somebody of this hellish scheme to pitch China into another war."

THEY TURNED to the nearest shed and slid back the door. The intermittent flashes of lightning showed them a sleek white two-seater, with a machine gun jutting above the rear cockpit.

"She's a two-twenty Whirlwind, Bill, and some crate!"

"Get in front, Mike. I'll yank the prop."

McGill hopped into the front cockpit, advanced the throttle a bit and pulled out the choke. Gales turned the blade several times to distribute the oil. Then he yelled, "Contact!"

"Contact!" yelled McGill.

Gales heaved on the blade and the motor burst into a roar even as a clap of thunder shook the universe. Gales stood out front, gripping the pistol he had taken from Volskoff. He hoped that no one had heard the burst of the motor, but he was ready to shoot it out with anyone who might show up. Grim, watchful, he stood in the rain while McGill warmed up the motor.

No one showed up, and after a few minutes McGill jumped out, and between them they rolled the plane out of the shed. Then they jumped in—McGill in front, Gales in back.

Gales took the controls and began taxiing the plane farther down the field, away from the buildings. At the very end he swung the monoplane around, ran his eyes over the dash, and then gunned the motor hard.

A flash of lightning showed him a lot of men running from the buildings. The throttle bit in hard, the motor howled, and the plane lurched through the darkness. It gathered speed, slashed through the rain. The running men were nearer now, waving their hands. The partners crouched low in their cockpits. The wheels lifted. Rifles and revolvers began to crackle and lead whined past their heads and snarled in the metal fuselage.

The plane thundered up over the buildings, was swallowed by the night; rose mightily into new flashes of lightning. At a thousand feet Gales kicked left rudder bar and shoved the stick to the left. The plane banked and then climbed again, and at three thousand feet Gales looked at the lighted compass. He set a course southeast, and a few minutes later the air speed meter was showing a hundred and fifteen miles an hour.

Their getaway had been spectacular. In this chaos of darkness no plane would be able to find them. For the present they were safe, and Gales, knowing what mountainous country lay beneath and ahead of them, attained an altitude of ten thousand feet.

And he reasoned, too, that their getaway would precipitate the attack of the New Empire upon the far-flung provinces of China. They had the secret now, and they would take it out with them. It was imperious that he and McGill get to Canton and rouse the unsuspecting powers. The Whirlwind roared mightily into the snarling teeth of the storm.

Thunder vibrated along its ribs. Lightning flared, and crooked forks of it speared the clouds, and rain hammered like leaden pellets against the windshields.

None but a pair of reckless sky-eaters would have taken a crate up under such conditions. And none but Gales and McGill were better fitted to weather that devastating storm and carry the ominous news to Canton.

CHAPTER XI

THE RUMBLE OF WAR

A **BRUISED** sun rose out of the east. Long, soggy cloud streamers still spread themselves across the sky, but the sun, rising ponderously, drove them away, and crimson color smeared the morning.

The monoplane wheeled high over Canton. Its nose dipped, and it streaked down over the Canton River. McGill, at the controls, picked out the flying field of the Far East Commercial

Airways, and throttled down. The wind keened through the flying wires, and the wings pillowed gently on the air. The wheels met the field with hardly a jar, and McGill taxied along toward the hangars.

Gales jumped out as the plane stopped, and was met by the Field Superintendent.

"By Jove!" exclaimed the Field Superintendent.

"Now don't get hot, friend," said Gales crisply. "We're here to see the authorities, and we don't intend to be held up."

The Superintendent yanked out his gun. "Now as you are, both of you. You staged a robbery in the air, and now, by Godfrey, you come here with a plane which you've obviously stolen! This is too much! I shall turn you over to the law!"

"You pig-headed son of a jumping jackass!" yelled McGill.

"Now look here," said Gales. "You're wasting time. At any moment Canton may be shelled by the planes of a hidden power. We're bringing news to forestall that—or to attempt forestalling it. For the love of God, put up that gun and listen to reason!"

By this time half a dozen other men had come out on the run, and all carried guns. They closed in on the partners. Gales talked himself blue in the face, but to no avail. They were rushed across the field, into the station, into an automobile. The automobile roared away toward the heart of the city.

They were dragged into a large, important-looking building. They were kept waiting in an anteroom, while the Superintendent went on in to interview some man higher up. A minute later he popped out.

"Come in, you two!" he snapped.

Gales and McGill strode doggedly into a large, sumptuous office.

Behind a polished mahogany desk sat Mr. John Smith.

SMITH SAID to the Superintendent, "You will kindly leave me alone with these men."

"Yes, sir. They're bad characters, sir. Staged a robbery in the *China Queen,* and now they're here with a crack new plane, obviously stolen."

"I will see you later, Mr. Harris," said Mr. Smith quietly. The Superintendent swept out, and the door closed behind him. Smith smiled. "Well, gentlemen. Sit down. Have a cigar." Gales did not sit down, neither did he take a cigar. "I didn't know you were a governmental head," he challenged.

"That was my intention—that you shouldn't know. Now what is the fellow Harris all worked up over?"

"You ought to know."

"Yes, yes—the plane robbery. The rendezvous at Number 10 Sing Fu Street was blown up. I also learned that the rendezvous in Shanghai was found. Major White was killed. You got away."

"Yes," said Gales, "and came here and found Number 10 in ruins. I had the papers but I didn't know where to go with them. So Mike and I, after trying to make out what the map meant, started out to solve the riddle."

Mr. Smith leaned forward, eyes keening. "Yes?"

"And we've found out! Back in the mountains there's an enemy about to strike!"

Smith stiffened. "I say!"

"Perhaps the best fighting fleet in all China! They've been planning this for years—a General Petrovosk—"

"Ah, Petrovosk!"

"And this chap Volskoff."

"Quick, man!" said Smith. "What else?"

Gales turned to McGill. "Mike, those papers."

McGill produced his copies, saying, "We made a copy of the originals, Mister."

"But where are the originals?"

Gales told him—explained how they had been shot down, described the place in the wilderness, told of their escape in the storm.

Smith spread the papers. His eyes widened. His jaw set hard.

"As I thought!" he exclaimed. "My suspicions were well-founded. Volskoff was taking those military reports to the rich mandarin in Shanghai. That mandarin obviously is financing this new rebellion. We had some secret agents working, but we could not find any concealed military strength. You understand, since we were working merely on suspicion, we could not come out in the open. This map—and this report of fighting units—confirm our suspicions. But... I must say... this map is perplexing."

Gales said, "The lines diverging from that one spot to all the cities indicate, I believe, air routes. The X's indicate emergency landing fields and petrol stations.

"What the big numbers mean, I can only guess."

"So can I," said Smith. "They indicate the number of people upon which this new power can depend. And I daresay that even now this hidden place of which you speak is in code communication with all their agents. This—this is stupendous!"

"It certainly is," said Gales. "Those planes are new and fast. We came down in one that got up a hundred and twenty-five an hour against a bad wind."

Smith sat back, his cheeks drawn in, "Gentlemen, the safety of China, and of all the white people in China, is in dire peril. What do you intend to do?"

"Do!" exploded Gales.

"Huh!" grunted McGill.

AND GALES said, "We intend to carry on. Why the devil do you suppose we came to Canton in a stolen plane?"

Smith put out his hand. "Gentlemen, shake! There is nine thousand due you, and I shall see—"

"Let that be put over," said Gales. "This is no time to talk about money. Action—and fast! For all we know, those fellows may be on the wing."

The door opened and a man came in and said, "Sir, there seems to be trouble brewing in the city. Riots have broken out, and houses are being stoned."

"Mr. Moore," said Smith briskly, "get in touch immediately with the Chinese Military Commandant and urge him to call out a regiment. Urge him to patrol the streets and guard all public buildings.

"Summon the military attachés of the various foreign governments.

"Send wireless messages in code to the embassies at Hongkong and all important cities, warning them of impending civil war, and asking them to secure all available aircraft and stand by."

Mr. Moore was aghast. "You mean, sir—!"

"I mean that we are under a cloud of impending war. Quickly, Mr. Moore!"

Mr. Moore went out, and Smith stood up and paced the room. "Let's see. A French and an English cruiser off the Bund. Two American cruisers and three English at Hongkong. Three regiments of Chinese regulars in Canton. Two Chinese planes and four British here. I say, men, as veteran fighters of the air, what would you suggest as the first move?"

Gales said promptly, "Blow up all the reserve petrol stations as indicated by X's on the map."

"Fine thought! Now look here. In an hour's time the Chinese military heads, along with the representative military heads of all foreign nations, will meet. I am going to suggest that you be put in charge of the first combat unit we can scrape together."

"I'm sure we'll like it," said Gales.

Smith suddenly turned and looked through the window. He pointed. "Look! A riot! At the entrance to the Foreign Concession! There comes a column of Chinese regulars—!"

The door burst open. Mr. Moore was waving a telegram.

"Hongkong reports a bomb explosion in the Foreign Office! American Marines have landed to quell riots! I say, sir, this is ghastly! I—I—"

"Calm, Mr. Moore—calm does it," said Smith gently.

Shouts and the rattle of gunfire rose from the streets. The Chinese regulars were driving the rioters back from the Foreign Settlement.

McGill suddenly clipped, "Say, I'm going down and join that fight!"

"No!" said Smith. "You are meant for bigger things than riots. Remember—the main death will come from the air!"

Mr. Moore wavered, "My wife, my babies—"

"Take it easy, chum," put in Gales. "Those planes haven't arrived yet."

His lean, muscled face seemed to hint that they would have a hard time arriving.

Gunfire was still rattling....

CHAPTER XII

FIGHTING WINGS

THE MILITARY powers that he met, talked, and came to prompt decisions.

Gales was appointed flight commander of the first combat unit. A check-up showed that four British bi-planes, two of them single-seaters, and two Chinese planes, were available.

The Far East Commercial Airways suspended passenger service and offered three tri-motored planes for the protection of the city. These would not leave Canton, but would take off as soon as the enemy was sighted.

Machine guns were rushed out to the field, to be installed in the cabins.

Hongkong had mobilized four planes, and Shanghai ten, two of which were citizen sports that had to be armed. There were three Chinese planes at Nanking, and one at Amoy.

The trouble was that no one could foresee where the enemy would strike first. Wires were kept open, and the cities were in constant touch with one another. Government buildings were being heavily guarded, and the ground defense units of each city were waiting with anti-aircraft guns. A later report said that four planes had flown down from Peking to join the ten at Shanghai.

Gales decided on action, planning to blow up the emergency fueling stations of the New Empire and head in the general direction of the hidden airdrome over the route marked on the enemy's map. Out at the flying field, he looked over the six planes that would join his own. McGill had grabbed a brush and a can of black paint, and on the fuselage of the stolen monoplane he hastily scrawled:

G-M-2

Gales called his co-pilots together and gave them brief instructions. Simms and Harkness, Kent and Derwent, had the two-seaters. Marlin in one single-seater and Jarvis in the other. The Chinese planes were bi-winged, gunner in the rear cockpit. Ah Wong and Lu Yen were in the first, Chi Sung and Tai Fu in the second.

When Gales finished talking and joined McGill, the latter had just put the finishing touches to his paint job.

"The wind'll have to dry it, Bill," he grinned. "How's things?"

"Put the paint pot away and get ready to take off, old tomato."

McGill hopped to it, and the other planes were already warming up. Gales took the front cockpit of the *G-M-2*, and McGill came running up to work on the prop.

The *G-M-2* was the first to take off, amid the rousing cheers of thousands gathered at the field. The sleek white monoplane streaked down the field, roared free of the ground and dug its prop into the wind. One by one the others followed, circling above and finally forming a flying wedge, with Gales and McGill in the lead.

GALES LOOKED back, saw that everything was in order, and then gunned his motor hard. The others picked up speed too, and the combat unit left Canton behind and drove resolutely northwestward. McGill had his binoculars out and was eternally scanning the heavens.

When they reached the first emergency field, Gales signaled for the other planes to go aloft and stand by. Then he shoved forward on the stick, power-dived, leveled off at five hundred feet and throttle down, poked lower to find the fuel house.

McGill picked it out in the timber, and then Gales rose again, banked and turned and hefted a bomb, one of ten he had been given at Canton. Peering downward, he let the bomb drop. A moment later a great tower of flame cascaded upward.

McGill grinned. Gales waved and zoomed mightily. When he leveled off at eight thousand feet, the others fell behind him, and the flight continued in unbroken order. Two hours later he found another field, and laid waste to the fuel house. Flight was resumed, and McGill kept his endless vigil with the binoculars.

They were high over a rugged wilderness, and it was late afternoon. Gales had another X in mind where they could land for the night and refuel. It was two hundred miles beyond, and within three hours' flight of the military headquarters of General Petrovosk.

McGill thumped him on the head, and Gales looked around. McGill pointed ahead, his mouth working rapidly. Gales peered intently and saw some dots against the blue beyond.

McGill had risen in his cockpit and was motioning to the planes behind. Then he sat down again, tightened his safety-belt, and trained his glasses on the dots ahead. His lips moved as he counted the dots. Then he poked Gales, and held up ten fingers.

"Ten?" yelled Gales.

McGill nodded.

Gales yanked back on his stick and zoomed mightily. The other planes followed, and at twelve thousand feet, high above that ragged, saw-toothed wilderness, the *G–M-2* roared toward the enemy, his six planes hard behind him. Ten against seven.

McGill said, "Just about our size!"

CHAPTER XIII

COMBAT!

A LEAN-FLANKED blue monoplane, boasting twin synchronized machine guns, started the show. Stabs of flame winked like red eyes. Lead hit like a riveting hammer on Marlin's single-seater.

Young was Marlin, not long out of an English Public School. His white teeth bared and his hands throbbed on his own clattering guns.

Jarvis, in the other single-seater, looked over. Granite-jawed, veteran Jarvis. He banked swiftly. His lip curled as he hammered lead into the blue monoplane. An enemy two-seater, crimson-winged, bent toward him. Its gun spat. Jarvis saw his windshield ripped away, and glass splinters thrashed across his face. Little threads of blood appeared on his cheek. He cocked up an eye, cursed, and power-dived—leveled off and screwed upward.

Gales and McGill were after a big green two-seater which they had driven away from Kent and Derwent. The two-seater was on the run, and Gales had his throttle wide open.

The two-seater made a fast, screaming turn, standing on one wing. Gales kicked left rudder bar and shoved his stick to the left. McGill's gun rattled and he laid a line of bullets along the green plane's fuselage.

The enemy gunner retaliated with a vicious burst that ripped up the metal partition between front and rear cockpits. McGill roared and cut loose again.

Flame billowed. Gales pulled up and swung off. The green plane hurtled earthward, winged with fire, trailing a smudge of heavy smoke.

The *G-M-2* had no time to breathe. The partners were set upon by two fast single-seaters, and a burst from below riddled the leading edge of the left airfoil.

Gales gunned the motor hard, and went plowing into the thick of a fight that was raging between his own two single-seaters and a pair of enemy two-seaters. Cross-fire snarled in his fuselage.

He ripped around a curve at the nearest enemy plane, and a concentrated hail of lead from McGill's gun made a sieve of its vertical fin. Another burst swung forward and laid open its fuselage.

The plane ducked wildly. It crashed head on with Marlin's single-seater. Petrol tanks exploded and both planes were enveloped in a world of lurid flame. Locked, shattered, they tumbled earthward.

Jarvis, the veteran, grimaced, shook his fist at the world in general, cursed fiercely. Then his jaw set, and his fast little plane streaked toward an enemy single-seater that was diving for one of the Chinese planes.

His guns talked in a bitter tongue, snapping lead through the shimmering propeller. He saw the enemy pilot throw up his hands, twist, slump downward. That plane sailed off serene as a bird, rose gently, then stalled, flopped over and went into a tail spin.

AT THE same time one of the Chinese planes got an enemy two-seater in a bad way, and a relentless stream of lead finally reached the two-seater's gas tank, and she billowed with flame and plunged downward. A moment later the other Chinese plane, set upon by two single-seaters, was riddled, broken—its men killed—and the plane pitched down hopelessly.

From above came Gales and McGill, and the two planes ran for it. Gales took after one and chased it in a wild power-dive. Down—down, with wires and wings straining, full throttle on, and the wind howling past like a thousand demons.

And death came to the single-seater—but not from McGill's gun. The brutal force of the wind ripped away her wings. A broken, tattered thing, she plunged on downward like a plummet and was smashed to smithereens against a mountain side. Gales leveled off sharply, gunned his motor and hedge-hopped over the top of the mountain.

Aloft, the fight was as furious as ever. Five enemy planes had been downed. Marlin and one of the Chinese planes had been downed. The forces were even now—five to five.

There was that man Jarvis, quick on the stick and the gun, fearless and reckless. The plane beneath his hand was like a magic wand. He swung it thus and so, whirled it over and over, went into tail spins to avoid enemy fire, but came out of the spins like the expert he was.

He chased a two-seater through a cloud bank, came out of the gray murk almost on the other's tail, dived almost into its rear cockpit, while his guns pounded. The pilot was shattered.

The plane jerked out of control, and the gunner waved his hands. He tried to leap out. The plane lurched and he was caught in the flying wires. Down went the plane, twisting and tumbling.

Five to four. Now Gales and his men had the advantage, and they made good use of it. It was war, and there was no quarter given. The four enemy planes, perhaps losing some of their original dash, tried to bunch together, like wolves, for general protection.

Jarvis, in his single-seater, and Kent and Derwent, in their two-seater, cut off a straggler and dragged him out of the group. The others tried to turn after them, but Gales and McGill, followed by Simms and Harkness, cut them off. And the remaining Chinese plane drove the leading enemy from the pack and chased it in a wide circle. Thus the group was broken up.

Jarvis and Kent and Derwent cornered the enemy two-seater at eleven thousand feet. Jarvis was a fierce and accurate blade. A screaming climb carried him above the enemy. A crazy loop took him well forward of it and back on his trail, heading for the other's prop. A blast from his gun drove the enemy aside in a skidding turn.

At the crucial moment it side-slipped, and was full in the eye of Kent's gun. That gun spoke death. The enemy crumpled. Both men twitched and heaved, and the plane, staggering, stuck its nose downward and was lost. Far below, flame spurted from a mountain.

THE REMAINING three planes lost heart. They tried to get away. But they were blocked by men who were determined to fight to a finish.

Simms and Harkness got another two-seater, found its petrol tank with a terrific burst of lead. That plane became a diving torch.

Another plane exploded under terrific fire driven by McGill, and flame streamers roared from its cockpit.

The last plane dived. It streaked earthward, with Gales and McGill and that old veteran Jarvis after it.

Blind with fear, the pilot lost judgment. He tried to clear a mountain top, but his left wing cracked against a tree. The plane slewed wildly, cut a swath through tall timber, crashed finally against a tree that would not yield. Flames shot up, blotting out a mass of twisted metal.

Gales and McGill zoomed. Jarvis paced them on the way up. He waved a hand, and his head flung back with a gesture of victory.

CHAPTER XIV

THE EAGLES SWOOP

A CAMPFIRE glowed in thick timber. Nine men sat around it, smoking. Twenty yards away was the edge of the timber, and beyond that a field. At the edge of the timber were lined up five fighting planes.

Gales was saying, "At break of dawn we'll help ourselves to petrol from the store-house and go on toward the seat of this New Empire. I don't know what we'll meet there, but our aim is to destroy it.

"Thus far we've mopped up one of their crack fighting units. That gang, I believe, was bound for Canton. Which means that for the time being Canton is safe. I want to say, now, that all you men were first-rate in that scrap, showing good judgment and excellent fighting ability."

Said Captain Jarvis, "Young Marlin was a fine lad, Gales. And so young to die. 'Tis a blooming pity it wasn't me they got. When Marlin went down I saw red all around me. And the two Chinamen, too—young, brave lads, and gentlemen to the core."

He sighed, and there followed a long moment of grave, dead silence.

Then Lu Yen said, "They died for China, for humanity. A noble, heroic death."

The fire crackled. McGill kicked on some more wood. One by one the men curled up on the ground and went to sleep.

At the crack of dawn they were up, refueling their planes. Gales explained the lay-out of their destination and gave brief, pointed instructions.

Then he and McGill climbed into the *G-M-2* and took it up. The others followed, and when they were all up, Gales dived, leveled off above the woods, and heaved a bomb that blew up the remaining store of petrol.

At ten thousand feet Gales led the way northward, high above the rugged, savage wilderness. No sun was out. The sky was a dull gray leaden dome, and mist banners streamed beneath them. The wind was from the west, and Gales had to figure on a considerable amount of drift.

All the planes were pocked with bullet holes, but the motors were running in good order, the guns had been reloaded and each plane carried plenty of reserve ammunition, and a number of small but effective bombs. Jarvis, reckless man, was smoking a cigarette, biting the air with keen, windy eyes.

Gales turned the controls over to McGill, took out binoculars and began scanning the sky. The country looked familiar, and he was certain they were on the direct route to the headquarters of General Petrovosk. There was always the risk that another squadron might be aloft, and Gales deemed a constant vigil vitally necessary.

Often he looked around, to find his other planes constantly in tow. What was taking place elsewhere in China, he could not hope to know. He and his men had at least eliminated one crack combat unit and—he was sure of this—saved Canton from a night air raid.

Presently he picked out the mountain behind which, he reasoned, was their destination. It lay far distant, a dim blur, but the general contour of it was familiar.

He signaled McGill to gather in some altitude, and a moment later the *G-M-2* was rising powerfully.

THE OTHER planes followed, and at twenty thousand feet Gales took over the controls and leveled off. He looked around to make sure his planes were behind him. The men had their orders, and some of them waved. McGill looked to his gun, spat overside, and stood by.

Gales shoved his stick slightly forward, advanced the throttle. Flame streaked from the exhaust, and the *G-M-2* started to scream through the wisps of cloud. Up to full throttle.

Motor roaring and wings tearing through gray fog, the *G-M-2* cannoned downward. One-forty—one-fifty miles an hour. A white streak in the changing gray murk, a bolt from the sky. The wind tore, hammered, howled, shrieked. Wires keened stridently.

Gales crouched over his stick, head shot forward, jaw set, eyes straining through goggles. The top of the mountain rushed at him. Beyond were the buildings, faint dots—and the field. The mountain lunged up and then rushed beneath.

The *G-M-2* screamed toward the field, and four hard-flying planes screamed behind. Four planes were on the field—two transports and two bombers. Men looked up, waved their arms, ran for shelter.

The *G-M-2* cleared the timber at one end of the field and howled in level flight at two-hundred feet of altitude. McGill leaned out and heaved a bomb.

It struck beside one of the bombers, exploded, and metal and fabric sailed into the air.

Behind came Captain Jarvis, a dead butt stuck in one corner of his mouth. Up and down went his arm.

Boom. Up went a tri-motored transport and down came the scattered pieces.

There were Kent and Derwent—Kent at the controls and Derwent hefting a bomb. Down went the bomb. It struck the other bomber and the plane sprayed its parts all over the field.

Gales drew back on the stick and barely cleared the buildings. As he shot over, McGill heaved another bomb, and one of the buildings fell apart like broken chalk. Jarvis, coming next, threw another bomb, and another building blew up, and stones and dust fell back with a roar.

Gales banked sharply and headed back to blow up the hangars. As he pounded over the timber, puffs of smoke rose, and the tip of his right wing was torn away.

He kicked the right rudder bar, and McGill let a bomb drop. Great trees were uprooted and fell sprawling into the field. Two hangars collapsed.

The planes tore 'round and 'round the field. Anti-aircraft rifles were hard at work, and the air hummed with singing lead.

The Chinese plane met doom on a sharp turn. It blazed like an exploded shell, and a fragment of its shattered engine ricocheted off Jarvis's fuselage.

Gales spotted the gun that had done the work, and as he dived he looked at McGill and jerked a thumb downward.

THE *G-M-2* flew almost level with the tree-tops, and McGill's gun cut loose and sprayed lead and death at the men manning the gun. Another gun put a line of lead through the *G-M-2's* tail, but Gales zoomed mightily and twisted out of range.

Jarvis refused to leave the air above the field. As a target, he proved hard to hit, for he tricked all over the place, and at times it seemed that his plane was out of control.

Howling upside down over the edge of the timber, he let a bomb drop and the explosion put another ground gun out of business and demolished another hangar. Careening along on his ear, he heaved a bomb at the remaining transport, and that plane split up like firewood.

There were Simms and Harkness, skimming the trees, a huge gash in one wing and the fabric flapping in the breeze. Harkness slammed a bomb down toward a spot from which puffs of smoke had just risen. That bomb cleared away considerable timber and another anti-aircraft rifle.

The attack had been sudden, unexpected, terrorizing. Bombs mowed down the timber, spread havoc below, and the reckless maneuvers of the planes out-fought the guns on the ground. Presently there were no more puffs of smoke. Men could be seen in frantic flight.

Gales and McGill, premier sky-eaters, landed on the field and taxied up toward the buildings. Jarvis followed, and the others landed behind him, and with much difficulty, because the field had been torn up by bombs and broken metal lay strewn about.

The birdmen joined together on the field, pulled their revolvers and headed for the ruins of the demolished buildings, led by Gales and McGill. Through the smoking ruins, and up to one of the buildings that had not been touched. And here they found a barred door.

Gales beat upon it with his gun. It did not open.

"Whoever is in there, open up!" he demanded.

No answer. Harkness and Jarvis walked back, caught hold of a beam that lay among the ruins and dragged it over. McGill and Derwent joined them in the lifting.

Then Jarvis—"All ready, boys. One…two… *three!*"

They lunged with the beam, and the blunt end of it crashed against the door. The door splintered, gave way and slammed inward.

A thunder of gun-fire came from the interior, and Harkness sagged and fell away, looking at a bloody hand.

Before echoes had died McGill went through the doorway like a man propelled by a spring. His gun blazed even as other guns blazed, and he felt a jolt in his leg. He keeled sidewise, still pumping his gun.

Gales heaved on the scene, saw the swart, contorted face of Volskoff—Volskoff crouched ominously behind a table, a gun in each hand.

ONE OF those muzzles belched flame, and Gales' flying helmet was laid upon, and it felt as if a club had descended upon his head. But his eyes were on Volskoff, and his gun boomed in his hand.

Volskoff fell backward, opening his mouth in awe.

"Blast my blooming stars!—"

That was Jarvis shouting and shooting, and hurtling across the room like a man possessed.

In the smoke and the gloom Gales saw General Petrovosk fall across a table. There were other faces, wide-eyed, fierce with lust or horror—Major Plitz, shorn of his monocle, one hand upraised, fright congealing the features on his face. Other faces that Gales had never seen before, and the faces of his own men.

Men sweeping and slashing about the room. Guns blazing and the thunder of their reports, and screams and curses.

Gales tried to yank himself out of the daze into which that shot had thrown him.

Through the murk he saw the twisting, gyrating bodies of two men. Volskoff again! Volskoff tearing at McGill, with a knife in his hand. That knife was slashing downward—

Gales leaped and crashed against Volskoff. Volskoff reeled backward, snarling out bitter oaths. He made to throw his knife, but a gun boomed close beside Gales' head, and Volskoff pitched backward with a wild scream.

"Got that blighter!" snapped Jarvis. "I say, Gales, we're wiping up the bloody General Staff. Rather!"

A sudden hush descended upon the room. The men from the air stood around breathing heavily, smeared with sweat and blood. Six gray-clad officers lay on the floor, and not one of them breathed.

Gales came out of his daze. Blood was dripping down his cheek, and he pulled off his helmet.

"Gawd, Bill!" cried McGill, leaping to his partner's side.

"Nothing, Mike. Just a scalp wound. Look here, boys. Now that we've mopped up, we'll see where the wireless outfit is. There's one, I'm sure. How's your hand, Harkness?"

"Rather blotto," grinned Harkness.

"See what I can do, John," said Simms.

They were casual, these men from the air.

CHAPTER XV

FIGHT'S END

GALES WENT outside, put his hands on his hips, and cruised his eyes upward. He espied an aerial strung above a small house on the other side of the square.

He strode toward it, entered, and found a pretentious wireless set. He sat down and clamped the receivers to his ears. Wiping the blood from his face, he looked at a chart, and spun some dials. His fingers played with the instrument, and he listened intently.

Then he bent forward, his eyes steadying. He had picked up the War Office in Canton. He ticked off what had taken place, reported that the seat of the New Empire had been demolished and the General Staff wiped out, one and all. Then he listened.

The others began trailing in, and stood around smoking cigarettes. Finally Gales took off the ear-phones and swiveled around. He lit a butt and gushed smoke through his nostrils.

"Things have happened. Canton is safe, has not even been visited by the enemy, as I supposed. Six planes swooped down on Nanking at dusk yesterday. At the same time two regiments were out and fighting to the death with an army of rebels that tried to take all the government offices by storm.

"The three Chinese planes at Nanking had been joined by an English civilian plane, and these rose to meet the enemy. The enemy managed to drop only one bomb. The four Nanking planes carried the fight away from the city. In one hour of air combat the six enemy planes were shot down, and three Nanking planes. The Englishman, badly wounded, crashed his plane in landing. They found seven bullets in him. But Nanking was saved and is now under martial law.

"The big unit of three two-motored bombers and six two-seaters approached Shanghai at the same time. There were ten defense planes originally at Shanghai, but half of them were almost obsolete and unequal to the enemy. However, four crack Japanese planes showed up, and that made the odds almost even.

"The bombers got in some work at the west end of the city, but the defending planes drove the fight away from the city, and it kept up for two hours. Both sides lost heavily, but every enemy plane was shot down, and four defending planes landed safely. Marines, sailors and Chinese regulars managed to hold the uprising in hand.

"Canton is still on guard, however, and we've been asked to hurry back. I think we can make it before dark, if there's any more fuel left around here."

They found a storehouse with plenty of petrol still untouched, and while some of the men refueled the planes, others went out, gathered up the bodies of the two dead Chinese, and put each into the fuselage of a separate plane.

Gales had bandaged McGill's leg, and the red-head was limping about and looking over the old *G-M*, which still stood where they had last seen it, minus its prop. Gales joined him, and McGill said:

"I'm going to come back for this old crate, Bill. I'm kinda sentimental about it."

"Same here, Mike. We'll come back. But now—let's breeze. There's Jarvis revving up."

THE PLANES winged high over the savage wilderness. Hour followed hour, and then towns began to appear.

Canton emerged out of a gray mist—ancient walls and temple spires, and countless houseboats. Gales swooped down over the city, crossed the Foreign Settlement, saw troops encamped on the river front. He wheeled off and rose over the flying field, and the other planes swept after him.

He looked down and saw a mass of people gathered around the field. Handkerchiefs and flags were being waved.

He leveled off, shoved the stick forward and shot downward. He throttled down, and the motor died to idling speed. The wings swayed gently, and the wind whistled mildly through the wires. He dropped down over the edge of the field, pulled back on his stick and struck the field with scarcely a jar.

Gales climbed out of the cockpit and helped McGill out of his. The Field Superintendent was there, and reached up his arms to receive McGill.

"Oh, it's you!" clipped the red-head.

"I say, by-gones, and all that sort of thing, sir!"

"Now I'm *sir!*" chortled McGill. "Hot diggity!"

McGill was brought safely to the ground, standing on one foot. Gales joined him and McGill hooked onto his partner's arm. Jarvis came stamping up, a broad, tight grin on his face. The others joined the group, and special policemen had to break a path through the crowds. Cheers and shouts thundered in the flyers' ears. Flowers showered upon them.

Outside were palatial limousines, and into the first went Gales and McGill, joined by the Field Superintendent. A liveried chauffeur sat at the wheel, and the car started off. Two other cars followed, and a third, a touring car, carried the brass band, which burst forth into *Over There,* and followed it with *Tipperary,* as the procession swept through the streets. Crowds cheered by the way, and many other cars fell in behind.

Gales and McGill were astounded. They kept looking at each other, grinning jerkily. The Field Superintendent sat straight and very dignified and very pleased with himself.

"Say," chuckled McGill, "this is hot stuff!"

The Field Superintendent seemed touched. "Rather topping, what! I arranged this procession, y' know."

"You're hot stuff, all right!" said McGill.

"Thought it the proper thing, y' know, after I'd treated you so beastly, sir."

"For crying out loud, don't call me *sir!*"

"Very well, sir."

Flags and banners were waving in the Foreign Settlement. Ladies flaunted gay parasols. Military men abounded. The cars stopped, and a bemedaled lieutenant saluted and helped McGill out.

The doughty red-head, limping on one foot, grinned from ear to ear. Gales joined him, lean and rangy, and covered with smiles. Jarvis, laughing shortly, butt drooping from one corner of his mouth, was set upon by fellow officers.

In a great room, decked with many flags, stood Mr. Smith, a radiating smile on his face; and there were many officers, diplomats, and military attachés.

McGill muttered, "Gosh, Bill, look what we got into!"

"Grin and bear it, old tomato!"

Smith was saying, "We are deeply indebted to you, gentlemen. In securing that document, in solving the meaning of it, you saved China from civil war. You prepared us for the attack, and we have repulsed the enemy at all points. Your leadership of our fighting unit was remarkable. You met what, was likely the squadron destined to destroy Canton and you demolished it.

"We are your servants—and I speak for all the powers in Canton and for the Chinese government. The city is yours. We shall fete you and your gallant comrades in a manner befitting to heroes and gentlemen. And the powers will join in presenting each of you with a purse as a token of their esteem and thanksgiving. No doubt you are weary, and in need of rest, and the crowds appall you. And some of you need medical attention.

"We have arranged for suites at the best hotel, and anything is yours to command."

HOURS LATER the two partners sat in a sumptuous suite of rooms at Canton's leading hotel. McGill's leg had been treated and bandaged, and he was able to hobble around. Gales lounged in a chair with a long drink and a fifty-cent cigar. There was a banquet going on, but McGill had used his wound as an excuse not to attend, and Gales would not leave his partner.

There was a knock on the door, and Gales said, "Come in!"

The door banged open and in strode Captain Jarvis, smartly uniformed. He flung his visored cap into a chair and smacked his hands together.

"Cheerio, fellows! I left that party, you know. Lot of women messing about, and one Spanish charmer I was frankly afraid of. So much so that I escaped in self defense. If you want to marry an heiress or a title, there's a flock of 'em down there. Rather!"

"Catch us!" chortled McGill.

Jarvis said, "I say, there's an American game I like—stud poker. I've a deck here and—"

"Sit right down, brother!" grinned McGill.

Gales mixed a drink, and they gathered around a table, using matches for chips.

The huge banquet went on, down below in the ballroom. The band played and exquisite women danced with soldiers, diplomats and military attachés. Wine and champagne were drunk, tall tales were told, and charming women asked here and there about the whereabouts of those two wild-cat Americans Gales and McGill—and that striking English Captain Jarvis.

The two sky-eaters—and the striking English captain—sat around in shirtsleeves, smoking excellent cigars, talking man talk—about fighting planes and tricks of combat and all the warp and woof of that hard-bit man's game. And playing poker—which is a man's game too.

HIGH-FLYING HIGH-BINDERS

A fortune in jewels... Gales looked at McGill, and McGill grinned at Gales. They serviced their battered old crate, and watched for a gun-toting green biplane on the hurry hop to Bangkok.

GALES AND McGill, flyers of fortune, were sitting at a table on the *terrasse* of a café near the Hotel de la Marine, in Saigon. Two days before they had flown their ramshackle crate down from Canton, and since they had been instrumental in thwarting a civil war, the authorities at Saigon permitted them to land, but quite grudgingly.

For the time being the partners were treated with some measure of civility, but there was about this civility an air of watchfulness, of guarded suspicion. For it was alleged, as you well know, that whenever Gales and McGill turned up, trouble followed as the night follows the day.

Said McGill through a cloud of excellent cigar smoke, "I never liked this dump anyhow."

"Don't call this joint a dump," said Gales. "They might even arrest us for that. By the way, did you see that flying-boat out in the stream this morning?"

"Yup. I hear it came down river, from back country. Nice bus. There's another one up now."

There was a drone overhead, then a green biplane swooped over the city, banked and rose and loafed about.

A man, sitting at the table, had been eying the partners for the past half-hour. Now he suddenly rose and came over.

"I beg your pardon," he said. "You are *Messieurs* Gales and McGill."

"Brother, we are," said McGill. "Park your hips."

"Thank you. I am Captain Henri Blondeau."

He sat down and asked if they would drink, and when they said that they were on the water wagon he ordered a *fine* for himself. He was a small, dark man, very thin, with small, quick eyes and a thin spiked mustache.

"I have been wanting to approach you since early this morning, when I saw you at the hotel. You are quite famous by name. They say that your integrity is unquestionable. That is why I have finally approached you. What prompted me was—" he looked aloft—"the plane that just flew over. I—flew that flying boat in yesterday."

"Nice crate," said Gales.

"Yes. But I am in some difficulty. I am employed by Mr. Fu Poy, of Bangkok, and I have been back country. Now I am here—and in danger. I wish to hire you men."

"What for?" asked Gales.

"A very small job that will pay you a thousand dollars. I want you to fly to Bangkok."

"Is that all?"

"Not quite. I want you to carry a small metal box to Mr. Fu Poy."

"What's in it?"

"Jewels. Eighty thousand dollars' worth of jewels that I brought in from the farther provinces."

GALES SAT back and lit a cigarette. His blue eyes narrowed speculatively. He clamped them on Blondeau.

"What's the catch?"

"That green plane you just saw flying past. I have a very great suspicion that the man in it is after the jewels. He was back country too, and he knows that I came out with the jewels. Is it not significant that he should arrive here five hours after I did? You see, the jewels are not mine. I was commissioned by Mr. Fu Poy to secure them. That man in that plane has a machine

gun which he can mount whenever he chooses to. I have none. Mr. Fu Poy would not permit."

Gales said, "And since we carry a machine gun you want us to fight this man?"

"No—a thousand times no. I want you to carry the jewels to Bangkok. He will never suspect that you are carrying them. He will be watching me. And I shall stay here until Mr. Fu Poy wires me that you have arrived safely. But first I must get in touch with him to explain my plan. What do you say?"

"Sure—take him on, Bill. I like Bangkok better than this burg anyhow."

"All right," said Gales.

"Very well. I shall telegraph immediately. Let us go to the hotel."

They went, and Captain Blondeau sent a wire to his employer. There was a reply a couple of hours later, and he showed it to the partners. It read:

> Under circumstances favor your plan have heard of Gales and McGill none better await their arrival in Bangkok.
>
> Fu.

They went up to Captain Blondeau's room and he showed them the small black metal box which they were to deliver to Fu Poy. It was packed with precious gems, and when the partners had feasted their eyes, Blondeau locked the box and put it away.

"In the morning," he said, "you will call for it. I shan't leave my room, naturally, since that might cast suspicion on our connection and ruin everything."

"Okey," said Gales. "We'll pop in at six."

"Very good. I shall give you Mr. Fu Poy's address—though that seems hardly necessary, since he is perhaps the most famous jeweler in Bangkok. But—*voila*—at six!"

The partners went around to their own room.

McGill scratched his head. "It takes years to get a reputation like that, Bill?"

"Like what?"

"Well, being trusted with eighty thousand berries in jewels."

"Yeah?" grinned Gales.

McGill frowned. "I don't like the tone of your voice, handsome."

"Too bad, half-pint." He walked away, still grinning.

McGill was perplexed.

THE BATTERED red monoplane crouched in the dawn. Gales and McGill came out of the mist, and Gales carried the black box under his arm.

Up in Canton they had fitted the plane with light pontoons as well as wheels, since, in their vagabond career, they were never certain of the next landing field. Here in Saigon they had been fortunate enough to find a likely bit of terrain. On the flanks of the plane was the legend *G-M*—which stood for nothing more or less than *Gales-McGill*, though a Hongkong wiseacre had once said it stood for "General Murders." Whereupon McGill had hit him, on general principles.

It was a dual control crate. They put on lightweight coveralls, and Gales climbed into the rear cockpit, closed the radiator shutters, pulled out the choke, and advanced the throttle slightly.

"Ready, Mike!" he yelled.

"Okey, big boy!"

McGill grabbed the prop and heaved hard on it several times, in order to get a fresh charge of gas in the cylinders. Then he shouted, "Contact!"

Gales switched on the ignition and called back, "Contact!"

McGill heaved on the prop and the OX5 started with a roar. Gales pushed the choke back into place and let the motor warm up while McGill went around inspecting the flying wires and the empennage. Finally the motometer showed a temperature of 160 degrees, and Gales opened the shutters, pulled back the stick to keep the tail down, and proceeded to rev up. The motor howled and Gales kept his eyes on the instrument board. Oil pressure 50 pounds; and the tachometer showed 1450 r.p.m.'s. He looked out and nodded to McGill, and then throttled down.

The red-head withdrew the chocks and climbed into the front cockpit, behind the Vickers machine gun, which now was covered with a waterproof hood. He pulled his goggles down over his eyes, looked back and grinned and waved his hand.

The plane's nose was up-wind. Gales opened the throttle, and the old crate lunged forward. The motor bellowed. Controls in neutral, air speed at forty, she cleared the ground and pounded up over the edge of the field. At five hundred feet Gales went into a bank and turn and then climbed higher. At fifteen hundred feet he leveled off and headed westward. Saigon swept below them, dim beneath the mists of the morning.

The OX5 was knocking off 85 miles an hour. It was a noisy old motor, noisier than any motor had any right to be. The plane itself was something of a tramp, a battered veteran of the skies, pocked with bullet marks, patched and nondescript.

But the birdmen liked it, as men like old and familiar things. It had taken them through storms and danger, had romped its devil-may-care way up and down the China Coast. Sometimes it had been beaten, but against great odds, and it always had taken new courage and tried its wings again. A rattlebox, which some men called a flying joke, but it somehow got where it wanted to go.

THE SUN, flaming up on its tail, drove the mists away, and the wilderness spread beneath them. The wind drove from the west, a keen, blustering wind that hooted down the fuselage and screamed in the wires. The instruments showed that everything was working normally.

Gales pulled back on the stick and climbed to three thousand feet, then leveled off. He gave the controls over to McGill. He took out a map and spread it on his knees. He had marked out their course, indicating towns and landmarks that would be easy to place. A flight of approximately five hundred miles. They had built spare petrol tanks into the wings, streamlining them carefully, and this brought their cruising range up to about eight hundred miles.

The air trail was moderately smooth that morning. There were few up-drafts or down-drafts, and the *G-M* droned along complete master of the sky, swaying gently at times from side to side, but generally maintaining a level keel. McGill thought the job was a snap. Captain Blondeau had paid them a thousand dollars in advance, and they would have a gay fling in Bangkok, then maybe loaf on down to Singapore for a while. And since Mr. Fu Poy was a big shot in Bangkok, it would be well to know him.

After a while Gales took the controls back, and McGill, to pass the time away, got out his binoculars and looked the country over. A wild, tangled country, with few towns and with lots of rugged ridges, lone lakes and thin ribbons of flashing metal that were in reality rivers.

McGill was happy—but then he was always happy when they were on the wing. In town, on the ground, he became restless. Once on a time, a long while ago, he used to drink a lot and get himself into a heap of trouble, but Gales, the headier of the two, had finally succeeded in breaking Mike of the habit, and now McGill rarely drank—merely a cocktail at times, or an after-dinner liqueur. No two brothers had ever been closer together, despite the fact that these two were always flinging jibes at each other.

It was McGill who spotted the plane behind them.

It was far behind, merely a speck in the blue, but recognizable, with the aid of binoculars, as a plane. He squinted hard for a long moment, then gesticulated to Gales. Gales flung a look over his shoulder, saw the spot, and then looked at McGill. McGill's lips were moving in a curse.

Gales drew back on the stick and hit the air trail for altitude. It was nothing out of the ordinary to see another plane in the sky, but it was safe anyhow to attain some altitude.

McGill was still twisted around his cockpit, the glasses glued to his eyes. And he saw that the plane was growing in size. He took down the glasses and said a lot, though the racket of prop and wind were too much for Gales to hear. But he could tell that McGill was mad.

Then McGill turned front and removed the hood from his machine gun. Having done this, he again studied the following plane. Gales kept looking back too, and he could now see it clearly with the naked eye. It was a biplane, and a green one.

It was the plane which they had seen loafing above Saigon— the plane which Captain Blondeau had feared.

THE *G-M* did nothing—merely kept to its course. Gales' face was set in grim, taut lines, and McGill's eyes were two narrowed pin-points of hard challenge. There was no getting out of it—these two birdmen attracted trouble as a magnet attracts chips of metal. If they did not start it, somebody else did, and they were drawn into it as a matter of course.

The green biplane was creeping closer. It was a single-seater, but armed with two synchronized guns, against the *G-M's* one Vickers. Its prop was a shimmering disk, and suddenly its two guns were red, smoking eyes.

Lead whanged through the after part of the *G-M's* fuselage. McGill spat and cursed. Gales kicked right rudder bar and wheeled off, and another burst from the green biplane missed the *G-M's* tail. Gales rose mightily, biting into the wind, and the plane vibrated in every fibre. The biplane swung off and climbed too, and they met at ten thousand feet.

The *G-M* roared toward the other, and for the first time McGill's gun talked. He put a line of shots through the biplane's struts, but most of them were wild, and the biplane yawed off, then stood on its tail and howled for altitude.

Gales shot beneath its tail, drew back on his stick and zoomed. The biplane was turned above when McGill slammed a hot burst into its green belly.

But the biplane came out of the turn in good order and dived head-on for the climbing *G-M*. Its guns spoke. Lead came down like an avalanche of death, ripping through the *G-M's* wing fabric, chipping the struts and snarling through the wires.

Gales pulled out. It was too hot, and he had to pull out. The green plane shot past them, and for a split-second they saw a hooded and goggled head, and a fixed smirk. Gales turned his plane on one ear for a fast corner, and looking down, he saw that the green plane was turning the other way.

Again they met and charged toward each other, and Gales and McGill crouched low in their seats while lead banged around them. One corner of McGill's windshield was ripped away, and splinters of steel and glass lashed Gales' face. Blood trickled down his cheeks. McGill's gun was hammering violently.

A quick jerk of the stick on Gales' part averted a crash, and the green plane shot by close overhead, flame streaking from its exhaust. Again they rose, each plane fighting to get on top. And again they leveled off at ten thousand feet.

But Gales swung quickly to the right, dived beneath the green plane, then zoomed and executed an Immelmann that brought him out on the green bird's tail. It was a quick, dangerous maneuver.

McGill opened fire and sent his lead screaming through the biplane's empennage. The biplane ran for it. It had been caught nicely in a trap, and its pilot opened everything wide and burned the wind in a frantic attempt to shake off that deadly fire. Down he went in a mad dive, straining his wings—down toward the jungle, which brooded below, tangled and dangerous—down like a bolt from the blue.

And Gales after him—Gales with everything wide, too, wondering at what precise moment his wings would be torn off by this reckless power drive. And McGill, his jaw set, his eyes keened—McGill pumping his gun with deadly precision, thinking not a whoop about the wings and caring less.

BUT THE biplane pulled out of the dive—and not soon. Its wheels seemed to graze the tops of the trees, and it streaked along like a frightened bird, then zoomed mightily. The *G-M* went after it prop digging resolutely into the air. Up they went, these two warring eagles—up to the region of the clouds, and through the clouds. Through gray fog that smoked and swirled about them—and then out into the white sunlight.

Gales looked around. The green plane was not in sight. He circled about, keenly on the lookout. Then the green plane smoked out of a cloud and came plummeting toward them. Gales hit the throttle hard with his right hand, kicked left rudder bar and shoved his stick to the left. It was a bad skid, and the wind hit them like a sledge-hammer. But it helped, for the biplane's fire went wild.

Gales pounded off, saw a cloud ahead and plunged headlong into it. The gray mist billowed over and around them, and they tore out into the sunlight again with mist-streams trailing from their empennage. Then Gales zoomed and hovered above.

The green plane shot out and zoomed too, and Gales dived for it. The green plane cut short the zoom and wheeled off to the left, and McGill's lead hammered the trailing edge of its lower wing.

The biplane straightened out and tried to zoom again, but Gales cut it off, and McGill's gun hammered, and the biplane banked sharply and ran for it. Gales followed, his throttle wide open, while the biplane circled swiftly and rose while it circled. Then it swung about and headed for the *G-M*.

The two planes charging toward each other, and lead ripping from McGill's one gun and the enemy's two guns. Lead hanging and tearing about them, and the wind hooting and booming.

McGill saw that shimmering prop coming toward him, and he saw the red muzzles of the two guns. And he worked his own gun savagely. His teeth were clamped, his eyes staring fixedly....

There was a blinding flash straight ahead—a sheet of flame that made McGill blink his eyes. Gales blinked too, but his hand was quick on the stick—so much so that in that hair's breadth of time he avoided disaster.

The biplane, a mass of flame hurtling through the air, almost touched the *G-M's* uplifted left wing. Gales thought he felt the furnace heat of the doomed plane. All happened in less time than it takes to tell it, but to Gales it seemed like a large and ghastly chunk out of eternity. He did not see the pilot—saw only that torch of flame which but a moment before had been a plane driving toward them and hurling lead upon them.

He leveled off, eased up on the stick and cruised around. He could see the burning plane tumbling downward, trailing smoke and flame and charred ashes. It crashed, what was left of it, in a thick growth of forest. There was no use going down to look for remains. That pilot's doom had been sealed in mid-air.

GALES SHOOK himself. He might have shivered—just a trifle. For death on the wing in flame is not a pleasant thing to watch. He throttled down still farther, and McGill looked around at him.

"Well, Bill, that's that," he called out.

Gales nodded, his lips compressed, his eyes thoughtful behind his goggles. And loafing about, high above the earth, he reflected and cogitated. Then he yelled at McGill: "We're going back to Saigon!"

"Saigon! Why?"

But Gales shook his head. He could not have explained above the racket of plane and wind. A man can only hurl brief, simple exclamations at another. But as he turned, his eyes were suddenly arrested at sight of another speck in the east, and for a moment his face was a blank.

McGill, who had been on the point of putting the hood back over the Vickers, changed his mind. Gales immediately poked upward for greater altitude and kept cruising in wide, lazy circles. The speck grew larger with the minutes, and presently McGill was able to define it as a plane—a white plane—a flying-boat. He shot this information back to Gales, and Gales nodded, and continued to loaf.

The flying-boat drew nearer, gaining altitude as it covered distance. Mono-winged, it was fast but not particularly flexible. Its motor was above and to the rear of the control cockpit. McGill kept watching it through his glass, and soon he could make out the name *Gull* on its flank. It was Captain Blondeau's plane.

Inquisitive Gales dropped off some altitude and went down to look around. The *Gull* had slowed down. It had not changed its course, but the altitude of its flight hinted that the man at the controls was spending some little time to deliberate. Gales edged closer toward it, and then he saw a hand wave, and McGill recognized Captain Blondeau.

Gales worked his controls and fell in beside the *Gull*, and thus the two planes flew in the general direction of Bangkok. But Blondeau was gesticulating—pointing downward. It occurred to Gales that Blondeau wanted to land, and that was all right by him whenever they found a negotiable place upon which to land.

McGill got Blondeau's drift too and began looking downward. About half an hour later they saw a lake. Gales caught Blondeau's attention and pointed to it, and Blondeau nodded and waved and forged ahead. Gales fell in behind.

When they were over the lake, Gales rose a bit, and Blondeau began taking his *Gull* down. Gales circled leisurely until he saw that Blondeau had made a safe landing; then he gave his motor in short burst, eased up on it and drifted downward. He struck the water at the head of the lake, and spray dashed up over them, and the plane rocked—then steadied.

Gales gunned the motor and the light pontoons slushed over the surface. The *Gull* was lying well out toward the center of the lake. The *G-M* was moving toward it. McGill had undone his belt and was perched on the coaming. Gales was at the controls.

As they drew up alongside the *Gull*, Captain Blondeau grinned and waved.

"Well, *messieurs*, so it happened!"

"Yes," shouted Gales, looking slightly puzzled. "How did that bird get away?"

"Ah, he must have suspected. But I followed."

"So I see."

Blondeau was sitting on the coaming of his cockpit. "I am very sorry, but at least you are alive, and that is good. And—you should be happy—you will not have to fly to Bangkok. I can very well take the box on myself."

"But, brother, we're aching to go to Bangkok," said McGill.

"Splendid. But, anyhow. I can very well take the box. One of you can step upon the nose of my plane—and so." He made a gesture with his hands.

"Okey," said McGill. "Bill, give me that box."

Gales still looked puzzled, but he gave McGill the box and McGill climbed out, stretched for the nose of the *Gull*, and stepped on board. He crawled up toward Blondeau, and Blondeau held his hand out. He took the box, and McGill crouched, grinning.

Then suddenly Blondeau's right hand appeared from behind him. In it was a gun. The barrel banged down on McGill's head.

IN A flash Blondeau swung toward Gales, swinging up his gun. But Gales had been puzzled, and a little wary. He ducked and three shots snarled past his head—then two more shots that ripped open the padded coaming. He was pulling out his gun. He was thinking about McGill—poor old Mike clouted on the head. He had seen his partner drop into the water. Mike would be drowning.

He gripped his gun hard, fired once in the air haphazardly. Two more shots smacked the side of his plane, and then he jumped up and fired point-blank—twice. His shots were wild, but he had had no time to aim. At any rate they made Blondeau duck.

And Gales saw McGill's face in the water, and McGill's arms working feebly. He saw his partner sink. He forgot everything and dived. And as he came up, he saw McGill swimming, a little stronger now.

"Mike!" he shouted anxiously.

"I'm all right, Bill. Look out for that guy!"

They kicked with their feet and went under, and came up against the *Gull's* tail. For the time being they were out of range of Blondeau's gun.

Gales said, in a whisper, "I'll swim under water on the off side and try to come up by the nose. Pretty soon he'll start back here. You make some noise, then dive out of sight. How are you?"

"Pretty rocky, Bill, but the old head's clearing fast. This palooka is out to finish us."

Gales nodded, then went under the water. Opening his eyes, he could see faintly the hull of the boat. He groped his way forward, and then came up. He was at the bow on the off side.

For a brief moment he listened. Then he saw Blondeau crouched on the top of the fuselage, creeping aft inch by inch.

Very quietly Gales drew himself up over the nose. Blondeau was concentrating on the stern. The motor was still idling. Gales reached the cockpit. He stopped. He was unarmed. He had dropped his gun before jumping overboard.

Only one thought had filled his mind then—to rescue McGill. Now the same thought was paramount. Blondeau was well aft, and McGill was still in the water—and even if the red-head dived under, Blondeau could get him when he came up.

Gales eyes alighted on the black metal box. It was heavy, and the only thing he saw that could serve as a weapon. Eighty thousand dollars in jewels! But what mattered that when McGill's life hung in the balance?

He picked up the box, steadied himself. He raised it over his head, held his breath, then flung it. It caught Blondeau on the back of the neck. The Frenchman cried out and pitched into the water.

Gales dived after him and struck the water only a moment later. When Blondeau came up, Gales grabbed him with one hand and struck him with the other. He knocked him well-nigh senseless. Then he looked around and saw that McGill was swimming toward him. And McGill was grinning.

"Great work, big boy," he said.

"Give me a hand, Mike. We'll drag this guy aboard his own crate."

THIS THEY did, and dropped Blondeau into the two-seater cockpit. Then they sat on the coaming and waited for him to regain consciousness. He came to slowly, and blinked. Then he blanched.

"Well," said Gales, "what the devil got into you?"

"Yeah, brother, ain't you the nice guy!" said McGill.

Blondeau rubbed his head. Gales pointed toward the water.

"And your nice little box went down."

"What!" cried Blondeau.

"Why, down," said Gales. "You were out to kill my partner and that box was the handiest thing lying around. I don't just know what this is all about, Blondeau—but I suspected something crooked from the start."

"The box is lost," said Blondeau dully.

"It was strange," said Gales, "the way that green plane picked up my trail. It was strange, too, the way you popped up. And when you tried to brain Mike here—well, that settled you. Mister, we are all going to Bangkok and see this friend of yours, one Mr. Fu Poy."

"What—after having thrown the box away!"

"Exactly," said Gales. "This thing isn't finished yet."

Blondeau shook his hands in the air. "No—not that! I was a fool. I was told that you intended to rob the jewels, and that is why I took up the pursuit."

McGill spat, "Listen, bud. If we was going to rob any jewels, d'you suppose we'd come down when you signaled?"

"I did not know. But I was very excited."

"Ha" chortled McGill. "In the words of Shakespeare, that's boloney!"

"But I cannot face Mr. Fu Poy now, after the jewels are gone. I am disgraced. I was a fool, I admit, but give me what you call the break. Let me fly off."

"Not yet," said Gales. "I'm going to see this thing through. You're going to Bangkok, and that's that. Mike, we'll tie this bird up. I'll fly this crate to Bangkok, and you fly the *G-M*.

"Something tells me Mr. Fu Poy is being gypped. His wire said that he depended on us. It's no more than right for us to go there and tell him how the box was lost. Our name's been smeared up too much in the country by gossip. It's not going to be this time."

"And how, big boy!"

Blondeau struggled and cursed and implored them to let him go, but Gales was adamant. He was determined to face Fu Poy in Bangkok and tell him the whole story. When finally they had bound Blondeau and strapped him in the safety belt, Gales settled down beside him at the controls and McGill jumped into the water and swam back to the *G-M*.

Gales roared the *Gull's* motor, wiggled the controls, got the feel of the stick and the rudder bar. His eyes ran over the instrument board. He looked at Blondeau. Blondeau was like a man in a trance.

McGill took off first. When he was well aloft, Gales gunned his motor hard and started down the lake. The water roared and sprayed. Then the float lifted and the plane pounded upward, trailing drops of water that flashed in the sunlight. At two thousand feet he leveled off, got out his soaked map and looked at it.

Then he waved to McGill and, advancing the throttle, hit the air trail for Bangkok.

MR. FU POY, jewel baron, stood behind a mahogany desk in his sumptuous library. He was a large, leathery-faced old Chinese, with a kindly eye. He wore dinner clothes, and held a cigar in one of his jeweled hands.

"Be seated, please," he said.

Gales sat down. McGill sat down. Blondeau seemed not to have heard.

Mr. Fu Poy put his large head on one shoulder. "Captain Blondeau, you may sit down.

Blondeau dropped into a chair. Then Mr. Fu Poy sat down and sighed.

"So the black box was thrown overboard," he said.

"Yes," said Gales. "I flung it at this man because he was out to kill my partner.

I realized what was in it, but at the moment that didn't seem to matter."

"Ah, yes," sighed Mr. Fu Poy. "And you, Captain, whatever possessed you to strike this man and then shoot at the other?"

"I told you, I lost my head," muttered Captain Blondeau.

"And the jewels are gone," sighed Mr. Fu Poy.

"Yes," breathed Blondeau.

Mr. Fu Poy suddenly laughed. He looked at Gales and McGill. "Gentlemen, I thank you for bringing to me a thief and saving me jewels worth eighty thousand dollars!"

Captain Blondeau lost color. Gales looked at McGill and McGill looked at Gales.

"How come?" said McGill.

"Simple," said Mr. Fu Poy. "When Captain Blondeau wired me suggesting that you bring the pearls down, I naturally agreed, knowing your worth. But I sent another wire to a secret investigator in Saigon requesting him to watch Captain Blondeau.

He did. This morning he said that Captain Blondeau had put in a safe deposit vault in the bank a certain black box. Gentlemen, you were not carrying the jewels. You were carrying—well, a black box that might have contained anything to give it weight."

"Jumping cripes!" exploded McGill. "The pair of highbinders."

Gales said, "I was suspicious, but I couldn't lay my hands on anything. I was even going back to Saigon to face Blondeau."

"But you brought Blondeau to me—and to the law," said Mr. Fu Poy. "He was very clever. I have reasoned it out this way. He wanted to impress me with the fact that you were carrying the jewels. The man whom you thought was his enemy was in reality his accomplice. The investigator saw them together in Saigon this morning, directly after you two men left.

"It was arranged then—let us say—that his accomplice was to shoot you down, having two guns against your one.

"Then he was to crash his own plane, and Blondeau was to come on here and show surprise that you had not reached me. The jewels were not to be found. Your plane, having crashed, was found in ruins by someone and the jewels taken away. Later, of course, Blondeau and his accomplice would have rejoined and split the loot. Is that not right, Blondeau?"

Captain Blondeau wilted but said nothing.

Mr. Fu Poy rose, said: "My dear Gales—my dear McGill, you must have dinner with me. I shall reward you with a sum of three thousand dollars and I shall make it a point hereafter to employ men whom I can trust—such as you. I am frequently in need of men to gather gems for me. The police will be here for Blondeau.

"The jewels are safe in Saigon. Gentlemen, again I thank you."

The partners stood up.

Gales smiled. "Glad to help you out any old time, Mr. Fu."

"And how," said McGill.

"And how what?" inquired Mr. Fu mildly puzzled.

"Uh—just and how!" said McGill.

Mr. Fu let it go at that, and ordered refreshments.

SIREN OF THE WIND

Skullduggery shatters the sky partnership of Gales & McGill. On two trails instead of one, the cloud hurdlers take to the blazing air.

SAIGON IS sometimes a place of witchery. To begin with, it has about it a subtle touch of Paris, but added to this is the warm dark lure of the East and the haunting mystery of yellow lights and temple bells at dusk. Strange men and stranger women drift past its sidewalk cafés, and the ten commandments have been cut to three, and some say less.

Gales and McGill, cloud hurdlers of chance, had flown their nondescript crate *G-M* from Bangkok, with an idea in the back of their heads of pushing on up to Canton and looking for something that in a mild way might lead to adventure. There was rumor around the cafés that the Emeralds of Tsin had been looted from the Tsin Lo Palace beyond Pnom-Penh, in upper Cambodia—six emeralds that had been handed down through the centuries in the family of Tsin to the present Prince Tsin Wei. But rumor is always rife in Saigon, and many took this latest with a grain of salt.

Having finished some brief letter writing at their hotel, Gales went out to look for McGill.

Tall, bronzed, clean-cut, Gales cut a fine athletic figure that drew the eye of more than one coquettish *mademoiselle* of the terrace cafés. And at one of these cafés—quite naturally—he expected to find his red-headed partner. Gales usually spent most of his ground time either keeping his partner from going astray or looking for him after he had gone. For Mike McGill,

having red hair, and being mostly Irish, was incorrigible and as hard to keep track of as money in a fan-tan parlor.

So Gales cruised the cafés, overlooking not one. The night was liquid warm there was music drifting through the scented shadows, and the cafés were gay with that gaiety which is only French. Gales was about to give up his quest, when he spotted his partner sitting at a little round table with a slim, dark woman who looked as dangerous as she was pretty.

"H'm," muttered Gales. "Just as I suspected."

He turned into the terrace and approached the table. McGill was so taken up with the ravishing beauty that he was totally unaware of anything else.

"Ahem!" coughed Gales.

The woman looked up, and then McGill looked up.

"Uh… hello, Bill. Sit down."

Gales sat down and removed his rakish Bangkok straw. McGill looked flustered for a minute, and then he said, "How about a drink, Bill?"

"No, thanks. I just popped around to pick you up, since we're getting an early start for Canton tomorrow."

"Who said so?"

"I made up our minds about an hour ago."

McGill regarded the end of his cigarette. "Uh… Bill."

"Yes?"

"Uh... *Mademoiselle* Le Blanc, this is my partner Bill Gales."

"It is a pleasure!" she cooed.

"It is indeed," said Gales stiffly. "I hope you don't mind my butting in and collecting my friend."

"Ah, well!" she laughed softly.

McGill went into a huddle. "You see, Bill, it's this way. *Mademoiselle* Le Blanc has been telling me about her brother Andre. He's—um—lost in the jungle, and she was wondering if we'd go and find him."

"I'm very sorry to hear that," said Gales.

Mademoiselle moved her head, shoulders and hands in a despondent gesture. "It is so, *Monsieur* Gales. I fear for Andre.

"Your friend has been good enough to say that we would go."

"We?"

McGill said, "Yeah, Bill. *Mademoiselle* and you and me."

GALES SAID, "Why, Mike, how could you have said that when you know we have an important engagement in Canton?" And he punctuated this with a hard blue eye on McGill.

McGill's mouth fell open. "We—"

"You know we accepted that offer in Canton, Mike."

McGill gulped and colored. This was news to him... but there was something dangerous in the cold eye of Gales as he kept it clamped unwaveringly on his partner.

McGill said to the women, "You'll pardon me, *Mademoiselle* Le Blanc? I'll see you here in an hour."

"I will be waiting," she said. "Yes, I will be waiting." And she favored Mike with a beautifully devastating smile.

McGill got up and walked with Gales out into the street. He shot Gales a mean, wicked look. "We'll go back to the hotel, big boy."

"Intended suggesting that, Mike." Back in their hotel room, McGill slammed the door behind them and jammed his freckled fists against his hips.

"Now, what," he snapped, "is the idea?"

Gales was unperturbed as he lit a cigarette. "You should thank me, half pint, for getting you out of the clutches of that vamping female."

McGill's sandy brows bent downward. "You go easy when you talk about her, brother."

Gales laughed. "Fell hard, didn't you?"

"We're going to make that flight with her," snapped McGill.

"Not while I'm conscious," said Gales. McGill took a swift turn up and down the room, his hair bristling. "What you got against her?"

"I don't like her. I don't like her type. One of my main missions on earth is to keep you sober and out of the hands of designing women. And if you ask me, she looks crooked."

"You cut that out!" howled McGill. "She's a wonderful woman!"

Gales pumped a cloud of smoke through his nostrils. He stood spread-legged and dropped his eyes gently on his partner. "Mike, use your head. I'm only doing it for your own good. Stay away from her. We leave"—there was finality in his tone—"for Canton tomorrow morning."

"We do not!" his companion clipped.

The bitterness in McGill's voice startled Gales. "Mike, old tomato—"

"Can it! We're going to take that girl and look for her brother!"

Gales thought for a moment, and then said, "We've always been partners, Mike. I don't like to bring this up. But—remember that my money is in that plane."

"You would say that, wouldn't you?"

"I'm merely trying to—"

"You can go to blazes!" barked McGill. "Keep your plane. I've got some money. I'll charter one. And as for you—well, go ahead to Canton!"

McGill was mad. He was blazing mad. Without another word he began packing his hand-bag. Gales looked on, a little shocked, a little meditative. They had, like all good friends, had many arguments in their day, but never one like this. Never an argument that terminated so abruptly in a complete break.

"Mike, old boy, listen to reason."

"I've listened to you all I'm going to. I don't need you to wet-nurse me. You give me a popular pain in the neck."

He slapped on his hat, picked up his hand-bag and yanked open the door. "I hope," he said, "you have a nice flight to Canton."

The door banged. McGill was gone.

Gales stood looking gravely at the closed door. He felt very unhappy. He sat down heavily on a chair and stared at the floor. This could not be true. And yet it was. McGill had packed up and left him.

HE WAS shaving at nine next morning when he heard a drone overhead. He went to the window and looked out and saw a blue biplane circling for altitude. A second sense told him that McGill and the woman were in that plane. He sighed, watched the plane disappear in the west, and then returned to the bathroom and continued shaving.

He was having breakfast when an annamite servant came in and said that a man wished to see him. Gales nodded, and a few minutes later a tall, dark man entered and bowed.

"I am very sorry to disturb you," he said. "I am Louis Cartier of the Secret Police."

"Sit down," said Gales.

The man sat down, laid aside his hat and stick, and regarded Gales keenly.

"Did you notice a plane leaving Saigon?" he asked.

"Yes."

"That is what I came about—that plane and one *Monsieur* McGill, who is its pilot—and about the woman *Mademoiselle* Le Blanc."

Gales showed sudden interest. "What about them?"

"I have been shadowing the woman for the past few days. When I saw her with your companion last night I was ready to assume that your plane the *G-M* would be used for a flight. I see I have been partly wrong. But your companion has hired another plane and is now winging westward."

"I still don't see the point."

"You will presently. *Mademoiselle* Le Blanc, we suspect, is connected with a ring that loots hill temples and palaces. You have heard, no doubt, of the Emeralds of Tsin, which have been stolen from the Palace of Tsin.

"A month ago two men, Andre Du Bois and Rene Vavin, left here in a plane for the farther reaches of Cambodia.

"They were seen with the woman before they left. We have word that the two men who looted the Palace of Tsin arrived there in a plane and left when they had gotten the loot. It is my contention that they were forced down somewhere and in some manner got in touch with the woman and instructed her to try sending out another plane to rescue them.

"I came to warn you that a prison sentence is awaiting those in any way connected with the looting. In other words, your companion has gotten himself into a bad tangle."

"By George!" exclaimed Gales. "I wonder if I can catch him!"

"I can give you a route map to the palace, but Du Bois and Vavin are reckoned to be somewhere between here and there."

"Give me the map," said Gales.

"I shall be glad to," said M. Cartier. "Er—whatever happened between your companion and you?"

"Need we go into that?"

"No," smiled M. Cartier.

Armed with the route map, Gales drove out to the flying field. And all the way out he cursed McGill for a scatter-brained fool. But even so he was determined to make some effort toward saving his ex-partner from a malignant conspiracy.

The battered old *G-M* was standing beneath a shed which the officials at the flying field had lent him. He recruited a couple of mechanics and they rolled the crate out upon the field. Gales climbed into a suit of lightweight cover-alls, hopped into the front cockpit, closed the radiator shutters, pulled out the choke and advanced the throttle slightly.

A man standing by the prop yelled, "Switch off!"

"Switch off!" yelled back Gales.

The man grabbed the prop and pulled down several times, to shoot a fresh flow of gas into the cylinders. Then he stepped back and shouted, "Contact!"

And Gales shouted, "Contact!" and turned on the ignition switch.

The man grabbed the blade, heaved, and the OX5 burst to life like a clap of thunder. Gales shoved the choke back into place and warmed the motor up, listening with a practiced ear. When the motometer showed a temperature of 160 degrees he opened the shutters, drew back on the stick to keep the tail down, and then started to rev up. The oil pressure went up to 50 pounds and the tachometer showed 1400 r.p.m.s.

Presently he throttled down, climbed out and walked around inspecting the flying wires. Then he climbed back into the cockpit, pulled on his goggles, and nodded to the mechanic. They pulled away the chocks, and the *G-M* lumbered forward.

GALES TAXIED down to the farther end of the field and swung the crate around into the eye of the wind. He waggled his controls, settled himself firmly, and gave her the gun. The old red plane snorted and plunged ahead. The motor hooted and then roared steadily. With the controls neutralized, and the air speed at forty, it shook its wheels off the ground and droned up over the edge of the field. At five hundred feet Gales banked and circled aloft, then flattened out and stuck the red bird's nose into the west.

This flight to him was not the same as others that had gone before. He somehow felt very much alone. Usually he flew from the rear cockpit, with the old familiar head of Mike McGill in front of him—and sometimes that freckled face turned round in a wide, careless and happy grin. Now he was alone, alone in this ramshackled old tramp of the air that had carried Mike and himself through a score or more of high adventures.

He wondered if Mike were repenting the hot-headed impulse that had so suddenly disrupted their long companionship. He wondered, even, if he himself had not been a little headstrong. But this he knew: he knew that what he had done had been for Mike alone, he had distrusted that woman at sight, and he well knew that Mike was a fool in the face of a charming and clever woman. She had bewitched Mike; there was no other explanation.

The OX5 was doing ninety miles an hour, and making a lot of noise about it. The wings creaked, the fuselage creaked, the wires creaked. No sleek young bird—but a scarred old man of the wind trails rumbling along at three thousand feet, swaying, bumping, jerking savagely through adverse air currents.

He followed the general course of the Mekong River. The plane was equipped to alight on either land or water, and since the terrain was not inviting, it was wiser to stay within gliding radius of the river; and anyhow, this did not take him off his route. M. Cartier had given him a makeshift map with landmarks conveniently tabulated, and with the mileage reckoned after the manner of a crow's flight.

The wind was on his starboard quarter—not a wind that blew steadily, but one that blew in fitful gusts and caused the plane to yaw widely. Up- and downdrafts were numerous, and Gales was continually bouncing in the cockpit. At times he drew out his binoculars and scanned the skyscape ahead. But McGill had had a two hour's start to begin with, and the *G-M* was not particularly fast.

What gave Gales something to worry about was when a troop of dark clouds marched up the sky in close formation and swung ominously by overhead. The sun was blotted from sight, and presently he began to see quick needles of lightning knifing the murk; and then he heard, far distant, the low lazy rumble of thunder. Beginning afar, the thunder gradually rolled close at hand, like heavy artillery swinging into action; and soon the air about him began to split with reverberating crashes.

The wind blew with a greater velocity; it seemed to become possessed of the growing anger of lightning and thunder, and changing its thrust, now drove from the south. If you can imagine how a ship slogs its way in a cross-sea, then you can imagine how the *G-M* began to ride in that blustering beam wind. To make up for the drift, Gales had to point the nose of his ship obliquely across the river's course, while actually he followed that river toward the deeper wilderness.

Then came the rain—great sheets of roaring water cascading from the solid roof of clouds. Gales tried to get above the storm area, but could not do so. In chagrin, he slapped the crate downward, realizing that he had lost sight of the river. He cannoned down through a wet screaming void, watched his altimeter kick off altitude. It was dangerous business, but he had to find the river.

At five hundred feet he leveled off, and saw nothing but the shaggy wilderness. Figuring that the wind had blown him off his course, he swung the nose of the crate into it and bored through the smoking rain. Presently he saw the river—kicked right rudder bar and swung his stick to the right, and took a blast of rain in the face as he skidded on the turn.

He spat the water from his lips, wiped it from his goggles, and rocked along five hundred feet above the river.

HE FOUGHT with the storm as a man might fight with another man. For the elements seemed possessed of mighty arms that swung and tussled with the battered veteran of the skies. They struck as a man might strike with doubled fists, and the *G-M* staggered, shuddered in every fibre, swayed and sliced the rain with its screaming prop. It too became in some measure a thing of life, for life was at the stick—that brain and the spirit of a man inspired it to carry on.

And Gales felt a great kinship for the ramshackled crate. He had confidence in its roaring motor, in its broad scarred wings. And the concentration he exerted toward keeping it aloft shut out in great degree the chaos that ran rampant about him. He was only dimly aware of the howling wind, the cannonading of the big guns of thunder, the long vicious stabs of lightning that crackled in a lurid pattern against the wet murk and thrust blades of vicious fire at the reeling plane. Man and plane became one unit against the demoralizing onrush of the elements.

The storm was a thing of frenzy, and like frenzy was of short duration. Gales fought with it for an hour. The *G-M* fought doggedly under his guidance, and together they won. The rain fell off. The thunder rumbled away, becoming fainter and fainter, and the lightning paled. The clouds broke up and retreated in tattered formation, and the sun broke through, reclaiming the day.

The dripping wings of the *G-M* began to dry. The wind lost much of its gusto, and Gales followed the river easily. He got out his binoculars, clamped the stick between his knees, and glued the glasses to his eyes. He was in a wild country now and impatient for sight of his wayward partner. And he was in the vicinity where M. Cartier had calculated the lost Du Bois and Vavin should be.

Gales loafed about, crossing and recrossing the river, flying low over the wilderness, scouring the country with his glasses. Then he came back to the river and followed it deeper into the wilds. About ten minutes later he saw a dot rising against the blue beyond. It seemed to come up from the river, and he reached for his glasses and stared through them intently. It was, indeed, a plane circling for altitude.

He put away the glasses and advanced the throttle. The thing to do now was signal Mike in the plane and tell him to land. It was imperative that he prevent Mike from piloting that plane back to Saigon, or anywhere else. Their argument was nothing more than dead limbo. He would make Mike listen to reason.

He pulled back on his stick and hefted the *G-M* up to a couple of thousand feet. He leveled off and cut his throttle and tramped around waiting to see what course the blue biplane would eventually take. He was near enough now to make out its color, and he could see that it was a flying boat.

It occurred to him after a few minutes that the biplane was doing nothing more than loafing about and probably waiting to see what he himself intended doing. That would be a characteristic attitude of McGill's—never to run away.

So Gales advanced his throttle, kicked left bar and slapped the stick to the left. The right wing came up and the plane veered around to the left, whistling keenly on the turn. The wings did some rattling and the wires creaked. Gales poked along with his stick slightly back, rising toward the blue biplane. He circled it and gesticulated for it to descend.

The biplane suddenly gathered speed and zoomed mightily. Gales had not expected this. He looked up after it, his brows bent. He saw the biplane come out of the zoom, wheel around and then plummet toward him. Instinct prompted him to gun his motor, heave up his right wing and go screaming off on one ear.

Looking back, he saw a machine gun spitting from the rear cockpit. The lead fanned his tail. His scalp contracted beneath his helmet. Was McGill crazy?

Gales zoomed. He hurled his plane up toward the sky with the throttle as far forward as it would go. He pulled out of the zoom at seven thousand feet to find the biplane grinding up behind him. He swished his tail around, dipped his right wing and flung himself toward the rising biplane. His synchronized Vickers was ready before him, but he was reluctant to use it. His plummetlike dive caused the biplane to veer off, but Gales sliced after it. One hand on the stick, he took his binoculars in the other and clamped them to his eyes.

THERE WERE three persons in the plane—two in the front cockpit and one in the rear. Three faces turned toward him. Not one of them looked like McGill.

His heart missed a beat, and then the blood surged through his veins. The biplane's machine gun cut loose, and Gales heard the vicious snarl of lead somewhere in the fuselage. He kicked left rudder bar and heeled over in a screaming turn away from the enemy.

His thoughts were suddenly scattered. He was sure that McGill was not in the plane. Then what had happened to him? Where was he? Alternate waves of heat and cold swept over his body. Had they killed McGill?

Gales found that it was neither the time nor the place for concentration. The blue biplane was after him, avalanching down on his flank. He dived—stuck his nose toward the tawny jungle, a mile and more below and hammered the wind on the way down. He heard the enemy's lead whanging into the fuselage behind him.

He fish-tailed at five hundred feet, pulled back his stick, flattened out and went howling over a low, rugged hill. He shook off the following lead in a wide, ear-splitting turn; jerked back his stick and zoomed and leveling off at eight thousand feet, flew for a brief moment on a level keel and then streaked downward.

For the first time his gun spoke. Its dark muzzle became a red-winking eye, and the wind snatched violently at the rapid puffs of smoke. He fired low, snarling his lead among the enemy's pontoons. He was in something of a dilemma. Since there were three in the plane, one of them must be a woman, and he had not yet attained that case-hardened stage where he could fight a woman, much as he believed she had tricked his partner.

He cut his fire short. He blazed past the climbing plane so close that their wings almost touched, and in that split-second of time he was certain he caught one fleeting glimpse of the woman's face. And as he passed, their lead beat a tattoo on the flank of his plane. He yanked back on his stick, brought up his nose, kicked left rudder bar and began to climb again before the turn was completed.

He cursed. If only that woman were not in the plane, so that he could swap lead with those birds in the hard-boiled manner to which he was no tyro! His own thoughts fought among themselves. If they had done away with Mike, then he had every right under the sun to make them pay, woman or no woman. That was logic—the logic of an eye for an eye. And yet Gales could not bring himself to hurl his bullets into the biplane.

He might cripple it. He might try to get on its tail and smash its empennage to smithereens. But that was no easy matter. First you had to get on their tail, and the biplane was remarkably agile.

As it happened during the next moment, he had to concern himself again with getting out of a tight corner. The biplane was swooping toward him, coming down on his starboard bow. Its gun was talking, and its lead was slamming across the *G-M's* cowl. The lead crept aft and rang on the frame of his windshield.

In desperation he turned away, dropping his right wing way down and sweeping his tail toward the diving biplane. He heard the lead biting into his own tail assembly.

THE BIPLANE swept past, downward. Gales whipped around and pounced after it in a mad power-dive. His wings strained, his wires howled, in the blast of the wind.

He gained. He cut loose with a shower of lead that banged into the biplane's empennage, and he kept after it, creeping closer. The biplane fish-tailed wildly, and the man in the rear cockpit was looking upward and firing intermittently.

Gales hammered another burst after it. He saw the gunner twist away from the gun and toss frantically in his cockpit. Gales held his fire. He had hit the man. One of his stray shots, aimed at the tail assembly, had raced forward and put the gunner out of the show.

The woman saw it. She must have told the pilot, for the latter threw one look around, and then turned again to his controls. Gales flung another shower of lead at the biplane's tail and clung to it on the way down.

The biplane was streaking toward the river. The pilot had evidently lost his nerve, along with part of his tail unit. Gales slowed down when he saw the man was attempting to drop the biplane down onto the river. The biplane in rocking from side to side and apparently the pilot was in a bit of trouble.

Gales hung back, cutting his throttle way down. He saw the biplane's pontoons smack the surface of the river and fling up a shower of foam. For a moment he thought that the pilot had fumbled his job, for the foam almost completely obscured the plane. But a moment later he saw the biplane slugging upstream.

Gales shoved forward on his stick, gave his motor a short burst and then retarded the throttle. He dropped to the river, put his pontoons upon the water with a sharp, business-like slap and heard the foam hiss against the under part of the fuselage.

The biplane was still in motion, slicing up the river, and Gales went after it. He reached in beneath his coveralls and drew out his revolver. The *G-M* swayed and threw aside sparkling ribbons of foam, and the wilderness shore sped by. Advancing his throttle, Gales lifted the pontoons off the water and howled along just free of the surface. He gained rapidly, and then put the pontoons back on the water again.

Out of the tail of his eye he caught sight of a strip of beach, and on the beach a plane. Beside the plane was a man, leaping up and down and waving his hands.

It was McGill!

Gales felt like shouting out loud. He felt like giving up the chase, joining Mike on the beach and dancing around with him.

But he was determined to overtake the biplane. He waved once to McGill and then kept on, in the very wake of the blue plane. He fired a warning shot, but they paid no attention. They kept on, apparently unable to rise because of crippled controls, but still trying to get away.

Gales crept closer, up past the tail. He saw the pilot fling a look at him. He saw the woman raise her arm and then there was a spurt of flame.

THE BULLET smashed Gales' windshield, and glass showered in his face, streaking it with blood. Gales raised his own gun and fired at the pilot.

The pilot slumped sidewise. The tail of the biplane swished around violently, and the plane headed toward the shore at full speed. Gales saw the woman wave her hands frantically. Then she stood up, climbed out and jumped into the water.

Gales kicked right rudder bar savagely. The *G-M* swerved around in a cloud of snarling water. The biplane crashed head-on into the trees that walled the shore, and its wings crumpled. Gales headed for the shore, then cut his throttle. His pontoons glided onto a spit of land and the plane jolted to a stop.

The woman was swimming for the shore. Gales climbed out of the plane, walked along the spit of land and reached the shore, where he calmly waited for her. In fact, he walked part way into the river to meet her. He was greeted with a string of abuse in French. He took hold of her arm and said:

"Now be quiet!"

By way of reply she tried to claw him, until he gripped her other hand and with steady persistence dragged her up to the shore. With the same persistence he dragged her out on the spit of land. He forced her into the rear cockpit of the *G-M* and fastened the belt around her waist.

"Now be quiet—please!" he snapped. "You've caused enough mischief."

At that moment a figure came running along the shore. It was Mike McGill, and he was covering ground considerably fast. He cut out toward the *G-M* and Gales was waiting for him, determined to be quite stern.

"Hi, Bill!" called out McGill.

Gales waited, very silent. McGill reddened as he drew up, looked at his partner, then at the ground, then around toward the plane that had crashed into the trees. Without a word he turned and headed for it. When he came back, ten minutes later, he was carrying a small leather pouch.

"Them guys are dead," he said, and then hefting the pouch in the palm of his hand, added, "There's six emeralds in here, Bill."

"H'm," said Gales. "So they tricked you."

McGill fell silent. Presently he looked up at the woman sitting in the cockpit of the *G-M.*

"I thought," he said, "that guy was your brother."

She turned her back on him.

Gales said, "I told you so, you red-headed half-pint."

McGill reddened again. Then, "Are you going to stand there and rub it in all day?"

"No," said Gales, still unsmiling. "We're going back to Saigon as fast as we can get there and turn those emeralds over to the authorities. They were stolen from the Palace of Tsin by Du Bois and Vavin, and the woman was in the ring."

"Yeah," nodded McGill glumly. "I know now. Them two birds ground out a bearing and they were carrying a wireless and they sent a message in code to her. I brought her to the place where they were. Then I was bushwhacked." His jaw tightened. "Well, let's get going. The government'll have to send a plane back for the bodies and the planes here."

Gales said, "Yes, we'll take off. And you can sit beside *mademoiselle* on the way back."

"No! You—"

"You'll sit beside her, and maybe after this you'll listen to reason."

THEY RAISED Saigon when it was getting dusk, but it was still light enough to make an easy landing. Gales brought the battered *G-M* down in a three-point finish, and rumbled across the field toward the hangar.

M. Cartier was there to meet them. With him were two other police officials, in uniform. *Mademoiselle* Le Blanc was quite subdued, and bowed her head as the officials took her off. Gales and McGill went into an office with M. Cartier, and Gales, looking at his partner, said:

"Hand 'em over, Mike."

McGill, still looking very glum, drew the pouch from his pocket and laid it on the desk. M. Cartier picked it up, opened the drawstring, and poured six emeralds into his hand. His eyes sparkled.

"Ah, *messieurs,* that is good!" he exclaimed. "There is, you know, a reward of an amount equal to one thousand American dollars."

McGill was not impressed. He lit a cigarette moodily, turned and walked out.

After a few moments Gales went out with M. Cartier and drove to the heart of the city. He dropped off at his hotel and proceeded to his room. He did not see McGill, and at eleven he turned in. At midnight he was awakened by a telephone.

"Uh... hello, Bill."

"Hello, Mike."

"Uh... how about shoving off to Canton tomorrow?"

Gales grinned. "Okay by me, Mike."

"Eight o'clock?"

"Sure."

"All right, Bill."

Gales asked, "Where are you?"

"At a café. I'll sleep here tonight on a bench."

"You will not. You'll come right up to our room."

A pause; then, "Well, all right. Thanks, Bill."

Gales hung up and jumped out of bed, whistling. He went about mixing two long, cool drinks.

McGill wandered in like a lost soul and quietly sat down in a chair. Gales carried over one of the drinks.

"Have a drink, Mike."

"Thanks, Bill."

Gales took one himself. They clinked glasses. They looked at each other, and then both began to grin.

"To you, pardner," said McGill.

"To you, pardner," said Gales.

WINGED SALVAGE

Birds of prey on a lawless coast... and Gales and McGill tackle odds to defend the code of "Finders, Keepers!"

THEY HAD crossed the Perhentian Islands and were loafing casually down the Trengganu Coast when McGill, sitting in the front cockpit of the battered red monoplane, lifted his binoculars and clamped them against his eyes. Into his line of vision came the edge of the jungle and the lean strip of white beach where the surf creamed. Then that which he had dimly seen with the naked eye he saw clearly now with the aid of his glasses.

A plane, riding on the long ground swell about a mile from shore.

He twisted around in the cockpit, caught Bill Gales' attention, and pointed ahead. Gales craned his neck and squinted his eyes, then raised his own glasses and steadied them against his eyes. When he lowered them he looked at McGill. McGill shrugged. Gales shrugged, then gunned his motor. The old *G-M*, vagabond of the Oriental skies, roared and leaped through the air. The wind rose to a keen shrill note in the wires and struts, and the slipstream stormed down the lean-flanked fuselage.

The air trail was moderately smooth, and the two birdmen had been enjoying the lazy southward flight. They had come down from Bangkok in easy stages, spending a week en route.

Nothing had happened. But a District Agent in Kota Bharu had said that now that the two flying tramps were on the Malayan Coast, something was bound to happen—adding, maliciously, "something of an unsavory nature."

Whereupon McGill, running true to form, had hauled off and knocked that District Agent for a ground loop. And Gales, the younger but headier of the two, had spent two hours apologizing for his partner's behavior.

As the *G-M* bored down the wind, Gales saw the other plane grow larger with the passing minutes. At first only mildly interested, that interest was now intensified as he saw that nobody was on the plane. It looked very much like a derelict. Shoving forward on the stick, he cannoned toward it, passed low over it, saw its big wings swaying gently to the rise and fall of the ground swell.

It was a two-motored job, and he saw at a glance that it was one of the freight planes used in the Singapore-to-Bangkok service. He drew back on the stick and rose in a number of spiral turns, then throttled down and let his crate glide toward the mirrored surface of the sea.

The pontoons struck with a loud smack that sent a shower of spray foaming up against the fuselage. The *G-M* rocked drunkenly, then steadied and drove forward as Gales hit the gun for a burst of power. He headed for the bow of the big flying boat, and McGill shoved back his goggles and swung one leg over the coaming. As they drew nearer, McGill climbed out with a line and tied one end to a pontoon strut; then leaped to one of the freight plane's big floats and fastened the other end there.

Gales yelled, "Hey, Mike, we'd better drop the anchor. Tide's moving in and it'll carry the whole shebang on the beach."

"First let me get a look, Bill," said McGill.

He swung up to the cockpit in the nose, forked the coaming and peered in. There was a roomy cockpit, the forward half open, the other half covered and ending against a bulkhead that separated it from the freight compartment. McGill climbed in, peered around, then stood up and looked over the coaming.

"Not a soul here, Bill," he called down.

"That's funny, Mike. What the devil's this crate doing here without a pilot?"

"Search me. These boats usually carry a pilot and mechanic, but it just looks as if they got up and walked out across the sea."

"Well, we'd better drop an anchor anyhow."

McGill nodded and went about lowering the freight plane's anchor, which served both planes. Gales came on board, climbed into the roomy cockpit, sat down and waggled the controls.

"They feel right, Mike."

McGill, sitting on the coaming, lit a cigarette and looked toward the beach. Nothing was there—nothing but palms and casuarina trees nodding in the breeze. And no sound but the soft cadence of the surf moving on the beach and gleaming diamond-pointed in the sun.

"Funny, Bill… funny." Smoke drifted from his nostrils.

"Mike…" Gales was bent over the stick.

"Huh?"

"Mike, it looks like blood on this stick."

McGILL LEANED down. "Blood? But how did the crate come down? It couldn't have fallen. Where are the guys were in it?"

"There are pirates along this coast, Mike.

I wonder if an open boat could have tricked these guys into coming down and then finished them and let the plane just drift."

"Maybe. But there's freight in the back, and if these here now pirates got them down, heck, man, they'd want the freight. Look through that slot in the bulkhead. You'll see freight back there."

Gales moved back to look through the slot, then turned and shrugged. "Maybe they were carrying bank-gold, and if they were, they'd have carried it here in the cockpit with them. By George, old tomato, there's something rotten here somewhere! As far as we can figure, two men—pilot and mechanic—left either Singapore or Bangkok, and they've disappeared en route."

"Maybe they took the gold themselves—landed near the shore—waded to the beach and let the plane drift on."

"But the blood on the stick, Mike!" He shook his head. "No, something else happened. But anyhow, old kid, this crate is in the salvage class. We found it, and there's nothing to do but try starting the motors and taking it to Singapore."

"Okey, Bill. You take her up and I'll tag along on the *G-M.*"

"Neither of you is going to take this plane up!"

Gales, who was in the control cabin, started—spun about. Framed in the small slot in the bulkhead was a gun's muzzle.

McGill did not budge. He still sat on the coaming, his cigarette half-raised to his mouth, his lips slightly open.

"If you move," went on the voice, deadly cool, "I shall kill you." The threat was directed at Gales, upon whom the gun was leveled.

"Who are you?" he asked, motionless.

"That does not matter. I have been drifting for several hours in this plane. I stowed away in Singapore and I intend to get out."

"Why didn't you get out long ago?"

"I can't. I discovered that the doors open only from the outside. You will remain as you are while your friend opens one of the doors. Then both of you will go into your own plane and I shall not come out until I hear the sound of your motor."

McGill snapped away his cigarette. "I can't open those doors, you fool. They're locked when they leave and unlocked when they arrive. D'you think I go around lugging a skeleton key or something?"

"You will find some way of opening it or I shall kill your friend."

Gales said, "As you no doubt killed the pilot and mechanic.

"It is up to your companion, whether or not you die."

McGill's blood was beginning to pump fast. From where he sat he could not see the slot in the bulkhead, but the cool deadliness of the unseen man's voice carried a promise of certain death for Bill.

Gales said nothing. His face was a little white, and he knew that since this man had obviously done away with two others, he would not hesitate in doing away with a third.

McGill thought fast. He was not the man to give in easily, but he realized the danger of the situation as regarded his partner, and he would have released all the murderers in the world if Bill's life were at stake.

He clipped, "I'll see what I can do."

HE DROPPED back to the *G-M* and hunted through the tool bag. He found a hammer and a chisel, climbed back to the freight plane and crept down along the wing. He reached the footrest beneath the starboard door, inserted the chisel alongside the lock and began hammering.

He worked fast. He ripped and tore at the metal around the lock. He swore and perspired but he kept on hammering. He kept telling himself that Bill's life depended on getting that door open.

The steel of the chisel bit in slowly. He pried with it and jabbed with it, held it in every position possible and whaled the head of it with the hammer. The lock became possessed of some stubborn personality. It seemed to defy him. The echoes of his blows skipped out across the water.

He stopped, breathing jerkily. He snapped sweat from his forehead.

He yelled, "You okey, Bill?"

"Okey, Mike," came Gales' steady voice. "How's it coming?"

"Lousy. 'At stumblebum still got his gat on you?"

"Yup."

"Well…" McGill clamped his jaw, cocked a malignant eye at the lock, braced the chisel against it, and socked the chisel, with the hammer.

At the end of half an hour the door was a wreck. It creaked open. McGill climbed back to the control cabin and leaned on the coaming.

"She's open," he said.

Gales had slightly more than an ordinary amount of courage, but he was only human, and he loved life—wherefore a faint breath of thanksgiving drifted up from his lungs.

The voice of the stowaway was saying, "Now. You will cut away with the anchor so that the plane will drift to the shore after you have left."

McGill was becoming exasperated. It was not his nature to kowtow to anybody. This hidden man was, apparently, a murderer, and he certainly had gotten the jump on them. Muttering diatribes under his breath, the red-headed gypsy cut away the anchor and returned warmly to the edge of the cockpit.

"It's done," he said. "Now try taking that gun away, bud."

"Not yet," replied the stowaway. "This is what you will do. You will get into your plane and take off while I still hold the gun on your friend here. After you have taken off, your friend will dive into the water and start swimming away. You may then go about picking him up, while in the meantime this plane will have drifted ashore, allowing me to jump onto the beach. Is that clear?"

Gales, noted for a close mouth in times of danger, forgot himself and rapped out, "Blast you, what the devil do you think we are? Mike cut the door open. He's done everything he could. You louse, you murdered two other men—"

"And I will murder a third, if I am not obeyed. I command the situation. I am the sole arbiter of your fate."

"You're an ache in the neck!" snarled McGill. "But I suppose we got to do your song and dance. All right, Bill, I'll take our crate up and then pick you up."

"No, Mike," said Gales, grimly, "We've stood for enough of this. Let this egg shoot—"

"Use your head, Bill. You're forgetting yourself, big boy." McGill was swinging away. "I'm taking the *G-M* up."

IT WAS hard for the red-head to give in, but there was nothing else to do, since Bill's life hung by a thread. He cut the *G-M* free of the freight plane, gunned his motor and slogged off. It gathered speed quickly, sliced through the water, lifted its dripping pontoons and rose mightily.

At three hundred feet McGill began to go into wide circles. He watched the freight plane below, saw it drifting toward the beach. He circled round and round, waiting eagerly for sight of his partner.

It was quite by chance that he saw, far distant, a plane moving bug-like across the panorama of sea and sky. Instinct caused him to pull back on the stick and go clawing for altitude, but a moment later he remembered his partner, and looked down.

He saw Gales on the wing of the freight plane. But Gales gave no indication of leaping into the water. For a brief moment McGill saw him looking toward the third plane that was creeping up from the south, wheeling high over the jungle coast.

McGill tried to think fast, tried to figure out what attitude should be taken toward the third plane. The freight plane below meant money to them. It was salvage. They had found it adrift and by returning it to its rightful owner they would collect a pretty penny. And they needed money. Business had been on the decline for weeks. The *G-M* needed a new coat of paint and a general overhauling, and they themselves needed money upon which to live.

It was something of a dilemma to McGill. Two trains of thought were pounding through his head. He had no idea what Gales was up to, and he kept looking down, squinting his eyes, pursing his lips. Now he saw Gales moving aft on the wing. It certainly looked as if Bill had other ideas besides jumping overboard.

The third plane, now recognizable as a black biplane, was drawing nearer and keeping to an altitude of about four thousand feet. McGill, still in perplexed indecision, power dived toward the freight plane and went roaring by no more than twenty-five feet above the water. Gales, crouched on the wing with a gun in his hand, looked toward him and waved his arm toward the oncoming plane. To McGill this meant that Gales was urging him to keep aloft.

McGill screamed the *G-M* over the jungle, banked at two hundred feet and climbed powerfully out over the surf. He drew farther back on the stick and thrust the nose of the plane skyward. He skyrocketed to four thousand feet, leveled off and, cutting his motor, loafed in circles above the freight plane. He squinted toward the black plane and then looked at his Vickers.

The biplane came toward him on a bee-line, then lifted its left wing in an easy bank and swerved off. Its wings leveled for a moment; then the right wing came up and the plane paced McGill around the circle on the outside.

He could see two heads, and from the after cockpit jutted a Lewis machine gun. The plane had no visible markings. It looked shoddy, but it appeared to be fast and seemed to have no trouble at all pacing the vagabond *G-M*.

McGill did not know what to make of it. He kept circling around, and the other plane paced him all the way. It began to occur to him that word might have been radioed up and down the coast that the freight plane was long overdue at its destination. This led him to wonder if perhaps that black plane were not out after a salvage job too. The fact that it kept pacing him round and round was more than a little provocative.

Added to this was his worry over Bill. He was too high to see what was going on below, and after a few more circles, he shoved forward on the stick and cannoned seaward. He flattened out at a thousand feet, cut his gun and idled downward, wheeling low over the freight plane, which now was lying in the surf.

What he saw was Gales crouched by the open door with a gun in his hand. He cursed. He reflected that Bill was always giving him long fatherly lectures on how to attain a ripe old age, and there was Bill now shoving his own head into danger!

HE PULLED up sharp and hedge-hopped over the jungle, then rose mightily and saw the black biplane burning the wind no more than a hundred feet above the freight plane. Those fellows probably had been perplexed by the state of affairs, too. But as McGill rose, they followed, and when McGill leveled off at three thousand feet, the black biplane did likewise.

"Cripes," muttered the red-head, "is this going to be another merry-go-round!"

The black plane showed a sudden, and significant burst of speed—shot well ahead of the *G-M* and swung across its bow. McGill had a fleeting glimpse of the Lewis gun swinging toward him. His teeth clicked together. He saw puffs of smoke, heard the vicious, deadly spatter of lead in the cowl.

With a bitter oath he kicked right rudder bar, gunned his motor hard and went pounding off on one ear. His blood, his mad old fighting blood, cascaded through his veins. He knew what was up now! There was salvage below! Word must have trickled up and down the coast. Those two in the black plane were flyers of fortune also, but they had no right to butt into another man's game.

McGill got mad. With Bill's fate still uncertain below, and with two birds of prey winging after him above, he found himself in one of the worst mental conditions of his life. Thoughts bounced around so fast in his head that they got all tangled up and left him a tight bundle of nerves and bitter rage. His lips flattened back against his clenched teeth. His eyes shot sparks behind his goggles. His hand tightened on the stick. He flung it to the left and roared on a fast, skidding turn. The wind, jumping over the cockpit, hit him like a sledge-hammer.

He cursed the wind. He heaved the crate out of the skid, gunned his motor hard, and found the black biplane storming down on his quarter. He swung to the right as a hail of bullets slammed through his empennage. Another burst stormed in the rear cockpit and he heard the crackle of shattered glass.

What about Bill? Even in that tight corner, with lead snarling behind him, he wondered about his partner. He flipped up his tail and plunged into a short dive, flattened abruptly, kicked right rudder bar and whanged into a howling turn. The black plane streaked by his tail. Bullets crashed into his fuselage.

He zoomed and flung violently out of the zoom, with every strut and wire straining. The black plane had turned and was heading for him, but instead of swerving off, McGill advanced his throttle and thundered toward it, crouched low in the cockpit.

His guns talked. For the first time they belched smoke and lead in the wind, the harsh echoes stammering past his ears. He saw the flashing prop of the black biplane screwing toward him, but he refused to turn off. His guns hammered violently, his own prop was a shimmering disk in the blazing tropical sun, and while still in the back of his head thoughts of Bill kept stabbing through a whirling fury of other thoughts.

He had a quick, kaleidoscopic vision of the other plane hurtling past. It seemed to graze his right wing. It was a black streak against the white sunlight—a black streak and a burst of thunder and two faces that seemed merged into one. It was gone as fast as a flash of lightning, and then McGill banked sharply, his right wing heaving up and slamming against the wind.

He twisted his head, saw the plane swinging around. He hit his motor for every last ounce of energy it possessed, knifed the wind like a keen blade of vengeance, drove headlong for the enemy's flank. The black plane's Lewis gun wheeled toward him. Its muzzle flamed. McGill heard the lead ripping through metal. His own guns pounded.

THE BLACK plane swung off under McGill's devastating fire. It kicked up its heels and dived, and McGill dived after it, javelined seaward, ripping the wind to shreds with all his power in play. Those old wings had something to contend with. Even above the hoot and roar and bellow of the wind he could hear the creaking of his wings.

The black plane screamed low over the jungle, wheeled madly and shot out over the white beach, out over the blue sea, out and upward in a powerful zoom. McGill went after it, sweeping past the freight plane. He looked overside. He did not see his partner!

Where was Bill? The thought burned through his brain. Where was Bill? What had happened to Bill? He writhed in his cockpit. He lifted one clenched fist and shook it at the universe. The force of his emotion drove sweat to his face. The thunder of his thoughts well-nigh blinded him with an all-consuming rage.

And then he discovered that the black plane had turned and was plummeting toward him. His stick went over to the left. His right wing flung up. He saw the black plane shoot by, saw the flashing of its gun, heard the clatter of lead behind his neck and thought they'd got him. He shook his head. It felt all right.

They met again at four thousand feet, with McGill taking the offensive and driving toward the enemy's port bow. His overwhelming rage had ebbed. He felt cool, ominously cool, his face set hard as granite, a numbness in his heart, a tightness in his throat.

And through his head, a reverberating question, beating with the powerful monotony of a jungle drum: *What about Bill?*

True, McGill was just a little dazed. And he laughed to himself—but it was without humor. It was a tight, brittle little laugh, clicking against teeth.

His guns blazed, and his lips twisted in a grim, fixed half-smile. He heard lead banging about him, but he did not duck, did not budge a fraction of an inch. His eyes were narrowed and burning coldly on the enemy plane, and his guns were snapping viciously.

The black plane swung off, showing him her wheels. He cut his own motor and turned to follow. And then he saw that the enemy was gliding downward, and that her prop was moving more slowly. And he saw the men gesticulating excitedly to each other.

"She's conked," McGill muttered.

The black plane was volplaning downward on a dead stick, and the two men kept looking back up at the following monoplane. But McGill held his fire. They were heading for the beach. McGill circled away from them and then dropped his plane toward the sea, figuring to come within easy reach of the freight plane.

Looking downward, he saw a figure standing motionless on the beach. His old heart missed a beat. He clutched at his binoculars and raised them to his eyes. He gave a shout of joy. The man on the beach was Bill Gales! He dropped the binoculars and waved a hand.

Then he slid his plane rapidly toward the water and brought the pontoons neatly down beyond the surf. He gunned the *G-M* over the shallows, then shut off the ignition and stood up as the prop moved slower and more slowly. He dropped the anchor in three feet of water, a stone's throw from the freight plane.

AS HE leaped into the water and sloshed shoreward, he saw the black plane rolling down the beach toward Gales. Gales stood spread-legged, with his pistol in his hand. McGill hopped through the low surf and reached the beach as the plane came to a stop. He drew his own pistol and ran up behind.

Gales had the men in the plane covered. "You just climb down," he said, "and watch how you move."

"Hi, Bill!" shouted McGill.

"Hi, partner! That was a corking fight. Watch these eggs."

The two men jumped down from the plane and stood with upraised hands, their eyes jumping from one to the other of the men with the guns.

"Who are you birds?" asked Gales.

"Why worry about that?" shot back the pilot.

McGill said, "A couple of wisenheimers, if you ask me."

"What was the idea of starting this fight?" Gales went on.

The gunner sneered. "Why d'you suppose?" He nodded toward the freight plane. "Salvage. The news is all over the coast that that crate's lost. We know you guys. We knew the plane the minute we saw it. We're looking for graft too."

"Frisk 'em, Mike," recommended Gales.

McGill went over and relieved the men of their guns.

Gales said, "I'm glad you know us. But you two birds are just a couple of rats. We found this plane, and it's our job, and nobody but Mike and me are going to collect the salvage money. And you had one rotten nerve to bust in on our game."

"Yeah?" sneered the gunner. "Say, everybody knows you guys are on this coast, and as soon as word got out that the freight plane had disappeared, they said, 'Get Gales and McGill.'"

McGill snorted, "Yah, they would say that!"

"Never mind, old tomato," cut in Gales. "You keep your gun on these wiseacres until I tie 'em up. We're going to get that confounded freight plane to Singapore come hell or high water!"

He bound the men with strips ripped from their own shirts, and then tied them to the landing-gear of their plane.

"You ought to be able to work free in a couple of hours," he said, "and then you can go wherever you please, so long as you don't cross our trail again. The trouble with you guys is that you think you're as good as we are. You're not the first."

He turned away and McGill joined him. "Say, Bill, you had me scared for a while. I didn't see you—"

"Oh, that," chuckled Gales. "Well, you see, old Mick, I didn't think that guy deserved getting away, so I fought it out with him. I kept firing and drawing his fire until I figured his gun was empty. Then I took a chance and went in, counting on getting to him before he could reload.

"I did. I sort of belted him all around, and it took quite a while, because he was raving mad and fighting for his freedom. I don't savvy what it's all about yet. Don't know who he is, why he was in there, and why he killed the guys that brought the plane from Singapore. I've got him trussed up now. Well, the thing now is, to get this crate up. She's not carrying much freight."

THE BIG plane was swaying to the rush of the surf, and they went to work in an effort to turn it around so that its bow would point seaward. In this they succeeded, after half an hour's work and under considerable abuse broadcast by the two captives.

Then McGill went into a huddle with the controls and Gales swung on the starboard prop. After a few hiccoughs it started with a roar, and Gales actually beamed. He repeated the process with the port motor. It too roared to life. The captives upon the beach cursed dejectedly. They had hoped the motors would not start.

But the motors turned over smoothly, and Gales and McGill listened to them and smiled at each other. Then McGill climbed down and stood in the surf beside Gales. They looked at the slow-turning props.

"I'll take her down, Mike," said Gales. "And we stop for nothing. This is the last straw. The crate has caused us enough trouble already, and once she's up, she stays up until we reach Singapore."

"Okey, Bill. I'll take the *G–M* up first to get outta your way. Hope you have a nice buggy ride."

McGill was circling aloft when he saw the freight plane push out ponderously across the water trailing a sudsy wake.

Gales was taxiing well out to make an up-wind take-off and to get away from the shore. The wind was from the south, and when he was two hundred yards from the shore he ruddered the plane about. He gave her the gun and she lunged through the water, a motor roaring behind each of his ears. Those motors dragged the big plane up from the water and lifted it mightily toward the sky.

At two thousand feet Gales leveled off and looked around and saw the *G–M* driving along on his starboard quarter. He flung up a hand, and saw McGill's hand fling up too.

The two planes droned southward at ninety miles an hour. Off the Pahang coast two white Waco scouts appeared and circled around them and made motions for them to land. But they did not even alter their flight. Gales kept resolutely to his course, and McGill clung to his quarter.

The Waco scouts kept flying above and below them, and one of them fired a short burst of lead across the *G–M's* bow.

BUT MCGILL paid no attention to it. He saw that the planes were Army scouts and he had an idea that they would not shoot to kill. When they crossed the islands off the eastern Johore coast the two Waco scouts were joined by a two-place monoplane sent out by the line that owned the freight plane. This plane was promptly ignored along with the others.

Gales knew his way about. He cut across the southern tip of Johore and came droning down over Singapore as the sun was setting in a riot of color. McGill followed him. The other three planes followed McGill.

Gales also knew the basin used by the commercial air line and lowered his charge neatly to the water. Sampans drove for shelter. The big plane plowed contentedly down the channel.

Then a launch came curving out to meet it, while Gales, having shut off the ignition, sat on the coaming, lit a cigarette, and watched the other planes come down. McGill drove the *G-M* up close to the freight plane and waved to his partner.

Running true to form, they had come through....

It was the president of the line himself who entertained them that night. He was a big, fat, bluff man.

"It was great work, boys," he said, "and I want to apologize for the way we at first suspected you. But I will say this: I will say that if you had not brought that murderer back, we might still suspect you.

"His own confession absolutely clears you. He murdered Captain March two days ago, and the police were looking for him. Somehow he managed to stow away on the plane. After the plane was in flight he crept forward and stuck his gun through the slot in the bulkhead and ordered Howe and Monrose to land.

"Howe tried to knock the gun from his hand and was wounded, Monrose brought the plane down. When he had done this, the killer ordered both of them to sit on the side of the cockpit—one on each side. They must have known that he was deadly—and crazed with fear. And they forked the coaming.

"Then—according to his own confession—he killed both of them and they fell into the sea. He had thought that after that was done he could break out. And that was his error—he couldn't break out. So—you will get salvage money, and you will also get the reward that was posted for the return of the murderer. Rather fortunate, eh?"

McGill said, "Yeah—it was Bill did it. It was Bill waited that killer out and got him and so cleared us."

"It was Mike," argued Gales. "Mike did the real fighting."

"It was Bill," said McGill.

"It was Mike," said Gales.

But the president broke that up by passing around the cigars.

SOUTH OF SAIGON

*Introducing Gales—in
person! Strange adventure
beckons... out of the sea
flies a mystery plane... and
McGill goes wild.*

T HIS FLIGHT is all about my partner, Mike McGill, and once in a while I have something to do with it, in an incidental way.

We'd been having a pretty good time in Bangkok taking up a lot of folks for spins over the city at five bucks a head, and spreading ourselves in the best restaurants at night. But Mike got gay one day and tried to see how close he could come to the pinnacle of a temple.

He knocked the pinnacle off, and when he brought the old *G–M* down they tried to mob him. We got out of that, but the authorities advised us to leave. They got rough. Mike hauled off and knocked a Siamese big shot for a ground loop, and then we *had* to leave. You know these Siamese!

That's why we came to Saigon, and that's how we came to be sitting on the terrace of a café one day around noon doing ourselves well with *aperitifs*. As I remember it, I was shooting off my mouth about Chinese politics while Mike, running true to form, was parleying with a *mademoiselle* that had It—and also How. I spend most of my ground time trying to keep Mike out of trouble, and since woman in the East is a synonym for trouble, this time was no exception.

I was trying to make my talk go over big when Mike tapped my arm, said, "Pardon me, Bill," and pushed back his chair. He got up—he stands five-feet-eight—put on a lot of dog and swaggered over to that *mademoiselle's* table like he owned the place. He was wearing a swell Panama, and he swept that off with a bow that would have made D'Artagnan look like a bohunk.

The next thing I knew he was leaning on the table with his arms braced down straight from the shoulders and getting chummy with a lot of Irish grins and a lot of his old blarney. The *mademoiselle* was smiling with a lot of white teeth. I was hoping she'd give him the gate, but he has a way with women and planes that's nobody's business. They were getting on great, and he was just about to sit down when a big fat man with a big black mustache and a solar topee zoomed up and made a noise with his throat.

The *mademoiselle* stopped smiling at Mike and looked kind of scared. Mike straightened up and looked at the man with the mustache. The man looked at Mike.

The man said, *"Monsieur,* will you about face and take your departure?"

And Mike said, "Will you go places and pick yourself some dandelions?"

"Monsieur," said the man with the mustache, "I have not the great sense of humor."

"No," said Mike, "but you have the great big mouth. Take it out of here before I push it so far down your throat your stomach will talk."

"Monsieur!" snapped the man.

"Horse feathers!" popped Mike.

I saw the Frenchman's face get all hot and bothered, and I saw Mike's freckled face start to tie up in a way that prophesied trouble, and not at a late date. I stood up and started toward him, and then I saw the Frenchman raise his stick. I don't think he meant to strike Mike, but Mike is like a New York cop I used to know—he socked first and made enquiries afterward.

He took a poke—Mike did—at the man's stomach, and the man said, "Ooh!" and doubled up and then sat down. A lot of people jumped up. I jumped and got Mike by the back of the neck.

"Look here, you crazy Mick!" I growled in his ear.

"Leggo!" he shot at me.

A couple of waiters came on the double-quick and started waving their hands. I thought Mike was going to poke one of them too, so I grabbed both his arms and planted a knee in the seat of his pants.

"You cut it out!" I told him.

The Frenchman was getting up with a lot of wheezing, his hat way over on one ear and a bad light in his eyes. He started for us, with a gun that only Mike and I were able to see.

I SHOVED Mike behind me and got between them.

"Monsieur," I said, "there's been a great mistake. My friend misunderstood you."

"Yah," said Mike behind me, "in a pig's fat neck I did!"

I held up my palms in front of the Frenchman and said, "I apologize for my friend's mistake, *monsieur.*"

He puffed, "And who, *monsieur,* are you?"

"My name is Gales, and my friend's name is McGill."

The Frenchman looked surprised. Anger fled from his big swart face and his fat eyes gleamed. He put away his gun, raised his arms, flung them around my neck and hugged me like I was a long lost son.

"Monsieur, this is providential!" he cried.

"This is darned embarrassing!" I said, fighting free.

He grinned all over his face and for a minute I thought he was going to cry for joy. He clasped his hands and wrung them under my nose.

"You are just the men can help me! Come! Come to my hotel! Quick, *messieurs!* Ah—*la-la!* Gales *et* McGill! *Voila!*"

He got between us and hooked an arm in either of our arms, and before we knew it we were being swept off the café terrace.

I looked over my shoulder and saw the *mademoiselle* standing up, stamping her foot, and looking peeved.

I said, *"Monsieur,* the lady—"

"Ah, that is nothing!" he cried. *"Mademoiselle* will wait."

"Hey," said Mike, "what you doing? Wait a minute! Hey, what is this?"

"Messieurs, the argument was most fortunate. Come! We must not delay!"

We wound up in a swanky suite at a swanky hotel, and the Frenchman had a boy bring up some drinks, and there was a box of Romeo and Juliets on a console. He said his name was Jacques Crillon, and that was all right by us. He got us into a huddle and began spouting:

"Messieurs, you are at leisure?"

"Until we get something to do," said Mike.

"Good! I have something for you to do, and it will not be very difficult. Attend. There is a vessel bound from Singapore to this port. It is at this time within twelve hours steaming distance—about a hundred and eighty miles, one might say. The vessel is named the *Coronet.*

"Upon this vessel is a friend of mine, one M. Ragenau. We are in the bond business, the two of us, and it is necessary that he be here before the day is out in order to affix his signature to a very important document. If he is unable to do this, we stand to lose a matter of fifteen thousand dollars. And that is a lot of money, is it not, *messieurs?"*

"Nothing to sneeze at," said Mike.

"Exactly!" said M. Crillon. "We have been in touch by wireless, and he has asked me to try to get the services of a plane. This plane would fly to meet the *Coronet,* alight on the sea, and the *Coronet* would stop long enough to permit my friend M. Ragenau to leave the ship and board the plane. Is the point clear?"

Mike said, "I don't even need glasses."

"And is the venture agreeable to you, *messieurs?"*

I said, "And the matter of payment—"

"Ah!" he broke in, rocking on his heels. "I will give you three hundred dollars."

"In advance?" asked Mike.

M. Crillon demurred. When he did that, Mike and I began to look uninterested. Then he shrugged in the way the French do, and said:

"But certainly, *messieurs!*"

"Okey," said Mike.

And I said, "Sure."

M. Crillon said, "Then I will wire my friend," and he began counting out the equivalent of three hundred American dollars.

Then he said, "Since your plane is only a two-seater, which one of you will go?"

Mike and I tossed for it. Mike won and poked me in the ribs, and that didn't make me happy.

We lost no time in grabbing a cab and going out to the field. The only flying equipment Mike needed was a white helmet and a pair of goggles, and he was all pepped up and raring to go.

The old *G-M* stood at one end of the field. She had pontoons and wheels and she wasn't pretty to look at. She was all scarred from the many sky brawls we'd been in, and a lot of guys kept saying that some fine day the old OX engine would fall out and leave us parked on a cloud in the blue.

Mike was always used to riding in the front cockpit behind the Vickers when I was with him, and rode that way too when he was alone, for the *G-M* was dual control. He climbed in.

I went around to the prop. He yelled. "Switch off!" and I grabbed the prop and heaved on it a couple of times to shoot a fresh charge of gas into the cylinders. Then he yelled, "Contact!" and I took a good heave and jumped back as the motor cut loose with a roar.

While he warmed her up he kept grinning at me, and I tried to look unconcerned, though I was sore as the devil because I wasn't going along. When he waved his hand, I pulled away the chocks and stepped back. He waved at me, gave her the gun, and the old crate lunged down the field.

I stood with my hands on my hips and watched him take her up neatly and circle once over the field. Then he dipped one wing as a parting salute and plugged away.

Now because I know Mike as well as I'd know a brother if I had one, because I know how he'd react under certain circumstances, and because I read his report in the Consul's files, I can give you the lowdown on what happened.

MIKE HAD clear sailing from Saigon to the sea. He took the *G-M* up to fifteen hundred feet and slammed her along at ninety miles an hour. The hot white furnace of the sun was directly over his head, and he followed the river to its mouth, when he swung the crate out over the sea, dropped to a thousand feet and struck a course due south.

The sea beneath him was as smooth a carpet as you'd want to find anywhere. The sun was reflected on its surface in broad glittering sheets of metallic radiance. The wind was lightly on his tail and there were no bumps to speak of. The old engine made a lot of noise, which you'd do too if you'd gone through what it had, but like an old glove it wore well and strutted its stuff smartly down the coast.

Mike went down to look at a ship that was steaming northward, but it was not the *Coronet,* and after circling it once at a hundred feet, he yanked back on the stick and lifted the crate to twelve-hundred. He passed a four-masted schooner and a barkentine, and because he felt in good humor he dropped down to give 'em a wave.

During the first two hours he made a hundred and seventy miles, but then he ran into a mess of cross-currents and up-drafts that raised the devil with him, and the old crate slopped along like a drunk for an hour, making only sixty miles. After that the air cleared again, and the *G-M* pillowed along like a darling.

And it was a little later that Mike spotted a smoke and headed for it. Soon he could make out a ship, and he hung to his course, screaming the *G-M* down the wind. As he neared the ship he dropped to five hundred feet, and when he got nearer still he went down to a hundred and howled past, looking through his binoculars. He could see the word *Coronet* on the bow, and he saw some men making motions from the bridge. Then the ship stopped making a wake and he knew it was lying to.

He cut his gun and slipped down the air. The sea was a pretty sight to look at, and he brought his pontoons against it with hardly a smack, and throttled down his motor. He was lying then about fifty yards from the *Coronet*.

A boat was being lowered, and after a while the boat began pulling toward him. He had forked the coaming of the front cockpit, and saw a man in whites and a topee sitting in the stern. The man waved and Mike waved back, his cigarette bobbing, as I knew it would, in one corner of his mouth.

The small boat came up to the *G-M,* abaft the wing, and shoved its stern toward the pontoon. The man in the topee had stood up and was holding a suitcase, and Mike grabbed this, heaved it on board and stowed it in the fuselage. Then he helped up M. Ragenau, who was a small, wiry man, with a small trick mustache and the blackest, most piercing eyes that Mike ever saw.

"Ah, so you came!" exclaimed M. Ragenau.

"Yeah, me and my shadow," grinned Mike. "Get comfortable there and then don't forget to hook that safety-belt."

"Indeed—indeed!" laughed the man. "I have flown before, *monsieur!*"

"You have never flew a crate like this," said McGill.

And Ragenau laughed as he buckled on the safety belt. The officer in the boat waved and shouted good-bye, and both Mike and Ragenau waved back.

When the boat had drawn away, Mike gave the *G-M* the gun and began sliding across the water. The spray hammered up against the fuselage, but he lifted the pontoons in short time and howled the crate up into the blue.

He rose in a number of banks and turns until the men on the bridge of the boat looked very small, and then he straightened out and stuck his nose northward.

He was feeling great. He hadn't had such good flying weather in a long time, the motor was fine, and there was nothing to do but sit back and drive the crate home to Saigon. He said he had an idea in the back of his head of looking up that *mademoiselle* again and dating her, no matter if Crillon didn't like it. He looked back several times during that first hour and found Ragenau smiling and looking very pleased with himself.

It was when he had gone about a hundred and twenty miles that he suddenly felt a bump against the back of his head. He looked around—

And found himself making goo-goo eyes at the black muzzle of an automatic that didn't by any chance look like a toy.

RAGENAU WAS smiling, but with one of those white fixed smiles that are supposed to have been originated but not copyrighted by the devil.

As he looked past the muzzle at that fixed smile, Ragenau reached forward with his other hand and passed Mike a note. When Mike bent to read it he still felt the muzzle of Ragenau's gun bumping against the back of his head.

The note said:

> You will remove the joy-stick. I will fly this plane with the stick in this cockpit. I will also blow off the back of your head if you don't obey. For remember, I can fly a plane.

Mike cursed an indigo blue streak and looked around with his lips snarled savagely over his teeth. He was never a tame bird, and that command sent the blood steaming through his veins like a high-pressure boiler. He raised one fist and shook it violently, but Ragenau kept on smiling in his devil's way and kept training the muzzle of his gun on Mike's head.

Then Mike had to look front suddenly to get control of the crate, which was slipping downward. He yanked back on his stick and hung up two thousand feet worth of altitude, and then he looked around with another snarl and a lot of righteous abuse. But the gun was still looking at him, and now Ragenau's smile had faded and there was a dark malignant glitter in his eyes.

Mike looked front again, shaking with rage. He was thinking of his ship, and—he was frank about it—he did not want to have his head blown off. While he was writhing in the throes of indecision, he felt the tug of the rear cockpit stick on his own, and with a hot oath he drew out his own.

He figured that he would bide his time, try to concoct some scheme to outwit Ragenau, and he figured too that he ought to find out just what Ragenau intended doing.

When Ragenau had control of the crate, he swung in from the open sea and headed up the jungle coast. He flew it pretty well, though at times increasing up and downdrafts worried him, and the *G-M* swayed and stumbled uncertainly. Meanwhile Mike boiled all by his unmerry lonesome, glaring straight ahead of him with the fixed and glassy intensity of a man at war with impulse and reason.

The Cambodia coast was a wild one, and there were not many towns, but Ragenau clung to it, and whenever Mike looked around to glare at him, Ragenau raised his pistol and smiled thinly. A little later Ragenau shoved forward on the stick and went down to look at a bit of beach that was near the mouth of a river.

He circled it, and Mike thought he was going to land, but apparently the beach looked bad, and after a few looks Ragenau yanked back on the stick and climbed to a thousand feet. He continued northward, but with the motor throttled down, and Mike knew he was looking for a place to land.

The next thing that surprised Mike was the sight of a plane bearing down from the north. He looked at it through his binoculars, and saw that it was a white seaplane.

When he turned around to look at Ragenau, he saw fright written all over the man's face. And Ragenau cursed and waved his gun at Mike.

THEN THE Frenchman gunned the motor hard and high-stepped for altitude, almost tearing the heart out of the old OX. He leveled off at six thousand feet, then kicked left rudder bar and wheeled in over the jungle. When he straightened out, his nose was pointed due east, and he hit the gun to the last notch.

Mike looked back and saw that the seaplane had changed its course and was coming hell-for-leather after the *G-M*. And every time he looked at Ragenau that man waved his pistol furiously. Mike struck fist to palm and cursed loudly.

He kept jerking around angrily in his seat. He thought of leaving the plane by way of his chute—but he did not want to leave the plane. It was his companion—had been for years. It was like an old dog—nothing thoroughbred about it, nothing high-toned—it was an old mangy mongrel of a plane, but to him it was precious. That was Mike all over. He was one of those men who treasure old familiar things with a true male sentimentality.

He saw that the seaplane was overtaking them. He writhed in that seat like a bound man watching his buddy being shot. The wind was mad thunder past his ears, the plane was vibrant beneath and around him, straining its lungs out.

He swung around and shook both fists at Ragenau. And he saw Ragenau's face, contorted with fear and horror and a fierce madness that he knew might at any moment send a bullet into his brain.

Now the seaplane was close behind the *G-M,* and gradually it began to creep abreast of it. There were two men in it, and the one in the rear cockpit, who looked over a lean machine gun, made a motion for the *G-M* to return to the sea and alight.

For answer Ragenau kicked left rudder bar, slapped his stick to the left, and sent the *G-M* screaming off on one ear.

It was a bad turn. Mike felt the wind leap across the right side of the coaming and bang him viciously against the head. Then Ragenau was diving, diving like a fool, almost straight downward, with every ounce of juice behind the motor. Mike expected the wings to be ripped off. He expected anything to happen. He hung on, with the motor pounding furiously and the wind screaming past like a thousand devils.

At five hundred feet Ragenau pulled out of the power-dive, went thundering straightaway. And Mike, looking back, saw the seaplane sweeping after him.

Ragenau kicked right rudder bar and made another bad turn, and the plane trembled in every fibre. The seaplane shot past its tail, and a burst of lead smacked around the *G-M's* empennage.

Mike turned and yelled, "You fool! You lousy fool! This is my crate—*mine!*"

Ragenau's lips moved rapidly, his eyes blazed, the gun shook in his hand. He fired, and the shot skimmed the top of Mike's head and clipped the top of his windshield. He ducked down and admitted that he almost swallowed his throat.

Ragenau's next move was to zoom mightily. The seaplane seemed to loaf around a while and then it picked up his trail again and chased him toward the clouds. The *G-M* ripped through a low cloud and Mike heard the hard spattering of moisture against the plane.

Then they were out of the cloud, diving wildly, with the seaplane plummeting after them. It shot past them, and the man in the rear cockpit made another warning gesture.

Ragenau raised his pistol and took a pot-shot at him, and the seaplane veered off. Ragenau veered in the other direction and hit out for altitude again, but the seaplane wheeled in a wide gaining circle and then broke the circle to come streaking for the *G-M's* bow.

Mike ducked, raving like a madman. He heard the lead smacking the *G-M*, snarling through the cowl. He saw part of the padded coaming ripped open—saw then the pontoons of the seaplane shooting by close overhead.

RAGENAU SWUNG to the right, standing the plane on one wing and driving along that way for almost a minute. Then he fell back to a level keel, pulled back on his stick and zoomed with the throttle wide open.

The seaplane came after them at eight thousand feet and raked their tail with a business-like rain of lead. Ragenau shoved forward on his stick and dived, and he must have been getting all hot and bothered, for Mike left the plane stumbling, and he punched the coaming and yelled for Ragenau to snap out of it.

When Ragenau straightened out he almost hit the top of a tree, and the *G-M* went hedge-hopping over other trees. Mike's breath was in his throat, his jaws clamped down tight. His breath shot out when Ragenau rose slowly and then gathered speed on the getaway.

But the seaplane was waiting for him, and with a burst of power it lined out for his left flank. Mike saw its machine gun spit and again he heard the bullets hammering in the fuselage. He groaned, because he knew this could not last many minutes longer. He was in agony because he had to sit there and witness his plane being riddled to pieces.

Somehow the *G-M* won through that burst of gunfire and climbed the air trail like the sturdy old mongrel it was. When it leveled off at eight thousand feet, the seaplane was a thousand feet beneath it but climbing fast. Ragenau's eyes were wild with dark mad fire, and his hand was knotted on the pistol, as he watched that sleek seaplane climbing.

Mike was at the end of his tether. His nerves were strained to their utmost, and he was seeing red—nothing but red. The crisis had come to him. He was playing tag with Death, but in that frantic moment he did not care.

He unbuckled his belt to give him greater freedom. He gripped the joy-stick which he had taken from the socket under threat of death. He twisted in his seat, and in less time than it takes to tell it, he sprang up and whaled that stick down across Ragenau's head.

He said that Ragenau's eyes blinked just once and that Ragenau sank way down in the cockpit. Then the wings wobbled and the crate began to fall. Mike sank back into his seat, got the stick into the control gear, and pulled the crate out of the beginning of a tail spin.

The men in the seaplane had seen that something was wrong, and loafed around watching. When Mike got his ship back on a level keel, he took a look around and had to stretch his neck to see just the top of Ragenau's head.

He cut his gun and cruised along idly toward the sea, and when the seaplane swooped toward him, he made motions with his hands. One of the men was looking through binoculars, and when Mike pointed ahead, indicating that he intended to drop the *G–M* down on the sea, the man lowered his binoculars and waved.

Then Mike picked up speed, and the seaplane paced him across the wilderness. From time to time Mike looked back and found each time that Ragenau was still slumped down in the cockpit.

When they came out over the coast, the seaplane rose and circled slowly above. Mike took that as a hint that he should go down first, and he did, dropping the pontoons neatly to the smooth surface of the sea. When he had done that, he left the motor idling, stood up in the cockpit and looked at Ragenau. Ragenau was still out, and there was a tracery of blood on his cheek.

Mike forked the coaming and sat there. He lit a butt and waited while the seaplane, which had come down, moved toward him. When their wings almost touched, he waved and grinned cheerfully. One of the men in the seaplane waved back and called:

"Did you enjoy the combat, *monsieur?*"

"Now be funny!" laughed McGill. "What I want to know, what is it all about?"

"It is about M. Ragenau."

Mike spat at the end of his cigarette. "You better take that guy before I ruin him."

"We saw you strike him, *monsieur*. It is still a mystery."

"Oh, is it? Well, look here, buddies, I was hired in Saigon to take this louse off the *Coronet*. I did it. Then after we've gone about a hundred miles or so, he pokes a gun at me and takes control of my crate. Maybe I laughed out loud, eh? Maybe... but I didn't!"

The man in the seaplane said, "Ah, now it becomes clear, *monsieur*. I will ride with you back to Saigon. My companion will take M. Ragenau. We are of the police."

I WAS at the field when the planes came home. I saw the seaplane making to drop on the river, while the *G-M* circled over the field. Mike brought it down beautifully on a three-point landing and I ran out toward it with a lot of officials.

He bounced to the ground with a tight grin on his face and a windy look in his eyes. The gunner of the seaplane jumped down after him and we all ganged around both of them. A pompous official elbowed me aside as I was making to grip Mike's hand and said:

"Now! Now what have we?"

The gunner replied: "Everything is all right, *monsieur*. M. Ragenau is in the custody of Lieutenant La Croix, who has taken the jewels from M. Ragenau's person. *Monsieur* McGill is entirely innocent. At great risk he knocked M. Ragenau unconscious so that he might regain control of his plane, which M. Ragenau had taken from him."

When everybody had stopped talking and shouting at each other, I grabbed Mike and steered him across the field.

"What about these jewels?" I asked.

"Oh, them," he said. "It was this way. Ragenau was traveling on the ship with a jewel merchant from Singapore named Farley. It was all arranged that Ragenau should kill Farley during the voyage and get the jewels. Crillon is his buddy.

"The ship was supposed to make a stop down the coast, but it turned out that it didn't have to. Ragenau was going to get off. He'd made up to Farley and spent a lot of time in Farley's room. He poisoned him so that it looked as if Farley was only drunk.

"Then when the ship steamed past the point where it was supposed to stop, Ragenau knew that his game was up unless he could get off the ship in some other way—before it reached Saigon. He did—by getting in touch by code with Crillon.

"A steward found Farley in his room just after we left. He'd seen him lying on his bunk an hour before but thought he was sleeping. This time he looked closer. The captain wired Saigon. And there you are…. Now I want to find Crillon, that big two-timing bum!"

But he never found Crillon. Nor did the authorities. That left Ragenau to take the rap—and he got it.

On the café terrace that night I said to Mike, "You see what happened because you tried to make that *mademoiselle?* That's what started it—a woman."

But I was talking to deaf ears, because at that moment Mike was trying to make another.

I ask you!

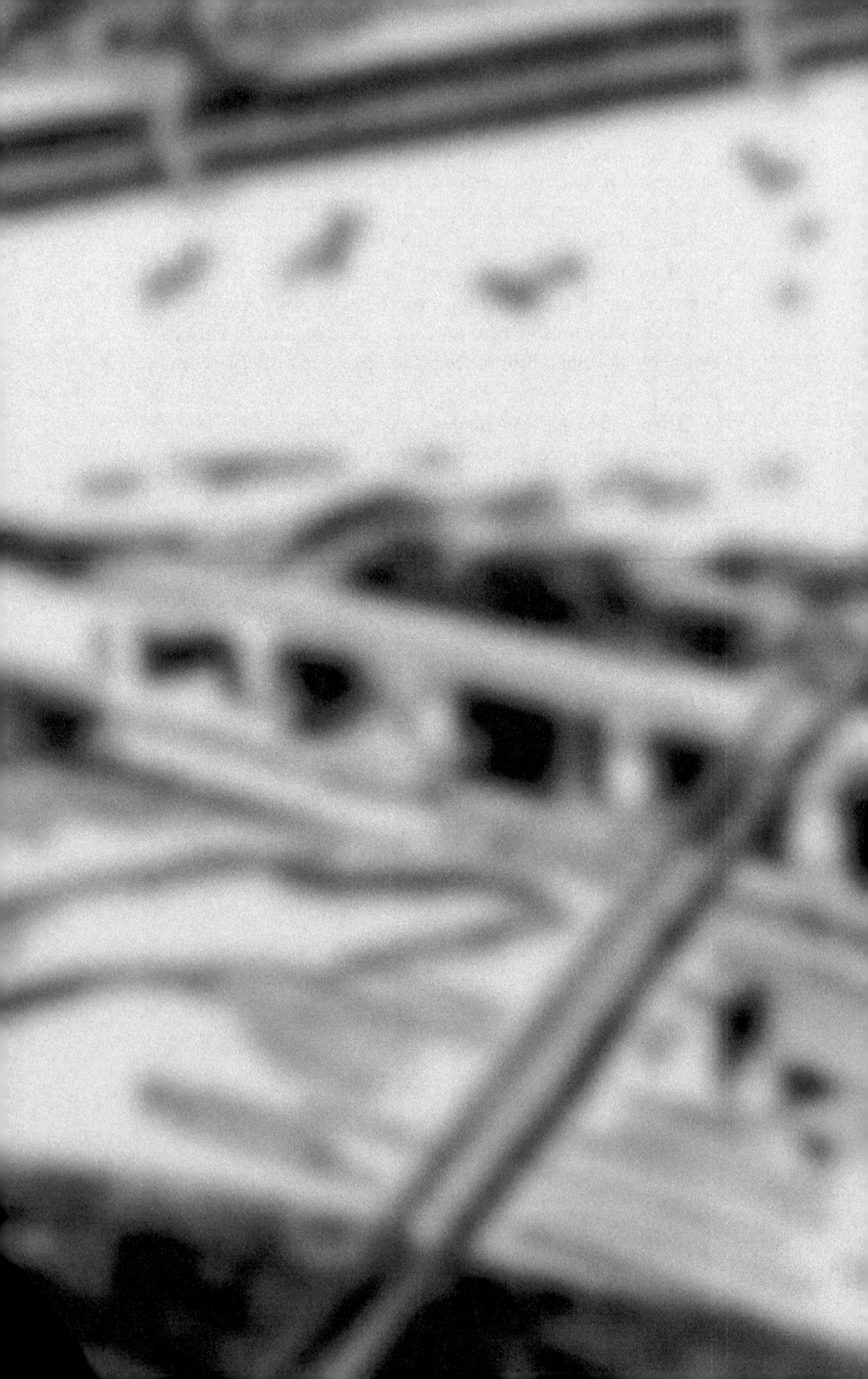

BLOOD-HOUNDS OF THE SKY

The Sky Hawk struck... the China coast clamored for the best in air... and into the circle of death flew the black sheep of the cloud lanes, ranking freelances of fortune—Gales and McGill! You know these two sky-hooters, and you've met K.O. Pike and his Straits Agency boys. Here they fight wing to wing—against a menace that many men had seen in its swoop, and none had lived to describe!

THE INCREDIBLE had happened!

At first no one believed the papers, said it was all a hoax, a monumental joke on the part of some cock-eyed newspaper correspondent. But the newsmen, all of them, guzzling whisky-stengers in Oriental bars, swore by all that was saintly, including the beard of the prophet, that it was so.

Foreign office men heaved great sighs, wagged heads dolorously, predicted the worst. Military attachés preened their mustaches and said it was a downright outrage. Pompous mandarins singsonged that no man would enjoy any privacy thenceforth. And lesser voices of the outer islands, stretching as far as Port Moresby on the dark island of New Guinea, joined in the general denunciation.

But K.O. Pike, head of the Straits Agency, pioneer flying detectives of the yellow and sinister East, roared back that he had chosen on merit and that anyone who disapproved could go places and do things.

The incredible had happened. Gales and McGill, most famous free lances of the wing east of Suez and west of the International Date Line, had linked their names with the Straits Agency. It was done. K.O. Pike had done it.

Said he to a visiting newsman. "Tell 'em this! Tell 'em, those that yap the loudest! Tell 'em that it's my business and not theirs! Has anyone ever touched the *Sky Hawk?* A lot of you mealy-mouth back-biters try to laugh it off and say the *Sky Hawk* is

a figment of the imagination, a nightmare that a half crazed sailor got on belly-wash gin. But don't you believe it! What happened to the *Princess?* What happened to the *King's Castle?* What happened to my flyers, Cooke and Bliss, who went sashaying off to find this *Sky Hawk* and never came back? Answer me that! No, you can't! Nobody can! You all sit and twiddle on your thrice-blasted thumb, ignoring the fact that there's a sky pirate that has a cruising range of three thousand miles or more."

"Well," the newsman said, "don't take my head off."

"Then get out of my office! *Get out!*"

The newsman got.

K.O. dropped back into his chair, dragged a handkerchief from his pocket, mopped his sweaty brow.

The lean and soldiery Bill Gales turned from the window and said, "Maybe we'd better not join up, boss."

K.O. glared. "What?"

"He didn't say nothin'," chimed in Mike McGill, sitting on a chair tipped back against the wall.

Gales was reasonable. "I mean, boss, I don't want to put you in a bad light. We've got a pretty notorious reputation—"

"Do you or do you not want to fly for the Straits Agency?"

"Of course I want to fly—"

"Then no more of this nonsense!" boomed K.O.

McGill said, "He gets ideas that way, Bill does. Don't mind him, commodore—"

"I'm not a commodore. K.O.'s my name. Plain K.O."

McGill looked at the ceiling. "As you were sayin' before that dish-faced palooka came in?..."

K.O. heaved out of his chair, took a pencil and crossed to one of the walls on which was spread a huge map. McGill got up and Gales joined him on the way over. K.O. pointed to the map. The point of his pencil leaped and jabbed an X in the South China Sea, due west of Brunei in Borneo.

"Here is where the *Princess* was last heard from. She asked Singapore for weather reports by wireless. She did not acknowledge the reply. While Singapore was trying to get in touch with her one word came through—plane. That's all. The *Princess* was never heard from again. Strange you never heard of these atrocities."

McGill said, "We took a trip back to the States to vote for the Democrats."

"I ought to hold that against you but I won't," K.O. shot back. "To go on: Lots of people, even the wireless operator here, thought a mistake must have been made. Nothing was done. Two weeks later the *King's Castle*, Singapore to Canton, was reported overdue. A week after that a man was picked up on a reef off Palawan. He gibbered. He mentioned the *King's Castle*, screamed about a plane the size of a dreadnaught with a hundred motors that came out of the sky, bombed the ship, landed on the sea, sent men aboard; took off one hunderd thousand in gold and scuttled the ship. He died two hours after he screamed this yarn. Of course, he exaggerated, but still he remembered things—in a mad hazy way.

"China and Island Transport, owners of the two vessels, hired us to see if there was any truth in the matter. I sent off Cooke and Bliss in a Waco equipped with a wireless set. They hedge-hopped up the Borneo Coast, taking their time, looking around. Two days later a southbound P.&O. boat reported receiving a strange message, to wit: *Plane is the Sky Hawk of ten tandem motors*. That was all. They must have shot Cooke and Bliss down before my boys could report any more."

Gales asked, "Where were they at the time?"

"About a hundred miles off the coast of British North Borneo."

McGill made a clucking sound, said, "This sure needs lookin' into, K.O. We'll take our old wagon and look in."

K.O. shook his head vigorously. "Not that rattlebox you came down from Mandalay in! Not on your natural! You'll take our new seaplane, *Miss Mermaid*. She's the sweetest Vought that ever came down this way.

"She's armed with a Lewis gun, and I've added another fuel tank, giving her a range of a thousand miles."

Gales said nothing. He was the younger, the quieter of the two. A slim young man, clean-jawed, good looking, the brains and the boss of the two-man partnership. His blue eyes traveled slowly over the map, rested on the X's that marked the places where the two ships had gone and where Cooke and Bliss were last heard from. His blood warmed in his veins. He saw a long sky trail ahead of him mile-stoned with danger. He and Mike had been called in to attempt something in which others had failed.

He said, "Okey, Boss."

"Ten thousand bucks if you clean up, besides your regular and special salary of fifty dollars a day each."

Mike said, "I always knew there was a Santa Claus."

Gales was staring transfixed at the map. A plane with ten tandem motors.

CHAPTER II

S.O.S.

I N A way of speaking, the city of Singapore turned out next morning to see the notorious partners off. Not really every soul in the city, but police officials, embassy whatnots, military brass hats, newsmen, cameramen.

The two partners appeared on the Agency's white wharf wearing ordinary white suits and Panama hats. Cameras clicked and McGill, jabbing Gales in the ribs, said:

"Those babies are prob'ly thinkin' it's our last appearance. There's the dish-faced bad news come in yesterday. I wouldn't charge him a cent to change the shape of his mug.... Hello, K.O. You left some egg on your lapel."

"Hello, boys. I didn't expect a crowd like this."

Down below in the basin grease-monkeys were obeying the Vought. She was a sweet-looking crate, riding on her pontoons, pale blue like the tropic skies and the shallow seas, with the legend, *Straits Agency*, painted on her flank, and beneath this legend, *Miss Mermaid*. A special job powered with a 300 h.p. *Whirlwind*, radio-equipped.

Behind the rails the crowd grew, natives chattering, white topees of big timers flashing in the sun, moving about. From time to time movie cameras clicked. The partners were very much in the limelight, but they had been in and out of the limelight for four years, until their names were almost legend, and they did not blush.

"Now, boys," K.O. said, getting them into a huddle, "you'll hit for Sarawak, add more fuel to your tanks there, then proceed north carefully, watchfully. If necessary you will go as far as Negros in the Philippines, then west across Palawan. Report to me every two hours, either direct or through relays."

Gales was attentive. "Right, boss."

K.O. was grave now, not blustering. "This is dangerous, don't think it isn't. It takes courage, and I'm back of you, and don't you give a rap about what people say or think about you. I'm banking on you. God be with you, boys!"

He shook their hands and they turned and went down the ladder to the big square float. The grease-monkeys had started the plane and one of them was revving it. At a sign from Gales he got out of the front cockpit, and Mike climbed in, put away his Panama and yanked on a white helmet. Gales climbed in the rear cockpit, donned a similar helmet. They put on goggles.

Water and emergency rations were in the fuselage. Two thousand rounds of machine gun bullets. Two Winchesters. Two Colt's automatic pistols. A dozen grenades. In the rear cockpit was the radio set slung from rubber shock-absorbers. The Lewis gun was hooded.

McGill howled the *Whirlwind*. Scattered cheers broke in the crowd on shore. A few hats waved. A few parasols. Wireless keys were clicking up and down the coast. Operators on ships in transit were getting the news. Gales and McGill had stopped freelancing and were flying for the Straits Agency. Gales and McGill were taking it on their shoulders to solve a sinister mystery.

The mooring lines were loosed. The Vought began floating away. A deep-toned siren boomed, warning sampans to get clear. The *Whirlwind*, idling for a few minutes, gathered speed and thundered. The Vought rocked. Her floats sliced the water. More hats waved; K.O. and the entire staff of the Agency waved.

McGill gave her the gun hard. The water began to streak past, to snarl whitely around the floats. The wind began to whistle, to hum in the struts. Sampans, junks, schooners flashed by. The floats lifted, trailing sheets of water. No longer the water snarled. The plane was climbing, boring into the wind, leaving the city and safety behind.

Out over Singapore Roads she roared laying a course for Horsburgh Light. Out over greenish-black mud flats, leaving the ships and the junks and the sampans behind, with a short red-head at the controls and a tall, dark-haired man in charge of machine gun, radio and navigation in the rear.

TO BILL GALES it was another adventure in a long series of adventures. Youth was his—bright, adventuring youth—and the never-ending thrill of high trails and a plane's wild sound. Rounding thirty, life had not bored him once because he had chased life as far back as he could remember. He had found it full of new scenes, new faces, new dangers, new victories.

Gossip had put a blot on his name; but no man, if called on the carpet, could swear to any one of the off-color deeds which malignant rumor tacked to his name. That was why neither he nor Mike McGill paid any attention to the wholesale slander. In their hearts they knew they were right and that was all that mattered. And K.O. must have known, too, else he would not have taken them on.

Soon land was behind. Beneath—beyond—the wide carpet of the sea spread, running in gulf streams of blue and emerald, bright-faced beneath the rising furnace of the sun.

McGill drove the crate at two thousand feet, sitting back in his cockpit, taking his pilot's life easy. It was the first time he had driven it. He listened to the sound of the motor, eyed the many dials on the dash, heard the whining and sometimes the mad clap of the wind; rode the occasional bumps like a veteran, offhand, unconcerned. The waggish, wisecracking—sometimes fiery-tempered—Mike McGill, eight years a side-kick of Bill Gales in good times and hard.

He picked up the inter-cockpit speaking tube and buzzed Gales. "Hello, big boy. How are you?"

"Okey. How's she feel?"

"Honey couldn't be sweeter, brother. She's the answer to a pilot's prayer. We'll have our pans in the movies."

"That's tough on the movies."

"That sounds like a bright sayin' of children."

"I'm busy figuring the wind drift. How's to sign off?"

"Signin', sweetheart."

McGill dropped the tube, cut his gun and sloped down to fifteen hundred feet, then leveled off. Gales put on the radio earphones, called the Agency, reported:

"Two hundred miles east. All well."

He left the earphones on, the key open and continued figuring on his chart. When he looked up again he saw a plane bearing out of the east. He reached for his binoculars, clamped them to his eyes, adjusted the lenses.

A tri-motored job. One of the Garrison Airways passenger planes.

He got in touch with the radio man on board, asked, "How's the weather from here to Sarawak?"

"Jake. Good luck, boys."

"Thanks."

The planes drew nearer. A hand waved from the passenger plane's control cockpit. The partners waved back. They could see curious faces pressed against the window panes of the cabin. Then the tri-motored job was on the port quarter, then astern.

Gales left his earphones on. Messages came to him, not intended for him—ship talking to ship or to land; broken messages, snatches of orders, questions, crackling through the air from unseen sources. Four hours out of Singapore he sent his second report: "Strong headwind. All well."

McGill was poking his way higher, trying to find better conditions. No danger in the wind, but it offered a lot of resistance, burned up fuel. He was unsuccessful, and finally chose a three thousand foot level, blasting his way eastward.

Then Gales' eyes narrowed, became intent. He pressed the phones against his ears tightly.

"S.O.S."

HE GOT his key working. "Straits Agency plane, *Miss Mermaid*, standing by."

A silence—seconds that seemed like an eternity.

Then: "Yacht, *Wildway*, four degrees and ten minutes north; one hundred seven degrees and five minutes west. Strange plane similar to rumored *Sky Hawk* bearing down from north with escort of two very small planes. Anything may happen."

Gales clicked off, "Report every two minutes." He picked up the speaking tube. "Mike, head due north. There's trouble."

McGill did not ask for details. He kicked left rudder bar, pushed the stick to the left. The Vought heeled over, banked and turned.

Came the *Wildway's* report: "The big plane is white. It has ten motors in tandem. It is coming down. The escort planes are circling above."

Gales sent his message clicking through space: "We are heading for you. Continue to report."

The Vought was doing a hundred and twenty miles an hour.

The *Wildway's* operator came through with: "The big plane has landed. It is the *Sky Hawk*, a tremendous flying boat. She is off our port bow. A man has appeared on the wing and commanded us to heave to. We are heaving to."

A pause; then: "A trap door has opened in the plane's flank. A small boat with eleven men has slid out into the water and is making to come alongside. Machine guns on wing and flank cover us and the two small planes are hovering. This may be all. The *Wildway* is the property of Stephen J. Manners. He is not on board. We are taking his daughter from Saigon to Singapore. The small boat is alongside. Armed men are coming up the pilot ladder. This is—"

That was—all.

Gales squirmed in his seat, tried futilely to regain communication. But the yacht's key—or its operator—was dead.

Gales grabbed the speaking tube. "Step on it, Mike! The yacht, *Wildway,* owned by Manners, the tin magnate, has been boarded about a hundred miles north by men from the *Sky Hawk!* Hit the gun for all she's worth!"

"Okey, Bill!"

Gales' blood tingled. He called the Singapore office and reported. They ordered him to report every half hour, to take no unnecessary risk. He signed off, left the earphones on and twisted to take the hood off the Lewis gun. He loaded it and fired a short burst to test the mechanism.

The Vought was a blue streak in the white blaze of the sun. Every last ounce of power was hurling her through space, driving her athwart the hard-fisted wind. McGill did not relax now. He was alive to his controls, part of them, his squinted eyes glued on the horizon, his lips tight against his teeth.

Gales could do nothing but wait. Yet he clung to his earphones, hoping against hope that another message, however brief, might come through. What was happening now? Was there fighting on board? What did the pirates from the air want? Surely the yacht carried nothing of great commercial value. Not like the *Princess*—nor yet like the *King's Castle.*

Gales reported to Singapore: "Heading north at one twenty miles an hour in strong beam wind. All well."

He signed off, took up his binoculars, stretched his neck and peered hard, sweeping the glasses in slow searching arcs. He could almost picture in his mind's eye the pirates on board, grim men heavily armed herding the yacht's complement on deck. Was there fighting? Was there bloodshed? What did the pirates want of a pleasure yacht?

The sky was empty of anything but puff-balls of cloud. The sea was empty. There was a lone reef where waves broke hugely and dazzling foam cascaded. The Vought hammered over the reef.

They thundered over the spot before they realized it.

GALES YELLED into the speaking tube. McGill cut the gun and banked sharply, began loafing. Gales saw through his binoculars bits of wreckage on the face of the sea, and as McGill circled downward Gales could see patches of oil.

But no lifeboats—nothing but bits of chaff and blotches of oil.

McGill took the Vought down low, skimming the swells round and round, back and forth. But they saw no lone survivor. They cruised in a ten-mile circle, hoping to find a life boat. But they found none.

Gales informed Singapore, and incidentally, the entire coast, that "Yacht *Wildway* destroyed by *Sky Hawk*. No survivors in vicinity."

Grim faced, he picked up the speaking tube. "Okey, Mike. Sarawak."

"We're gonna get those babies, Bill!"

"I wouldn't fool you, brother!"

CHAPTER III

MR. LEE GOY

KUCHING, THE capital of Sarawak, had the disastrous news by the time the two partners dropped their crate down on the river. They tied up at the Garrison Airways wharf, tipped the watchman to keep an eye on their plane, and went up to town after reporting their arrival to K.O.

They took a room at a modest hotel, washed up and shaved, and went down to the restaurant for dinner. They finished the meal with a liqueur and topped that off with a couple of cigars. They sat back like lords of the earth, and word buzzed around the restaurant as to their identity. Feminine eyes regarded them from many quarters, and Gales went so far as to return a smile here and there.

McGill cautioned him. "Look out for the janes, Bill. Janes don't do a man no good. I got my lesson in Saigon last year."

"And up until that time," Gales said, grinning, "I had to spend all my ground time keeping you away from petticoats: Why the sudden change of heart?"

"I tell you, old tomato, I learned me a lesson. Janes are dynamite. Stay clear o' them. There ain't no good in janes."

"You'll change that tune at the first blonde gives you the wink."

"I can't help it if I attract them, but I'm through with them."

Gales wagged his head. "Of all the conceited—"

"Now lay off!" McGill shoved back his chair. "Let's go."

They went to their room, intending to turn in early and be up at the crack of dawn. Their room was a large one, with two windows overlooking the street. Against the rear wall was a large mirror stretching almost to the ceiling, and about five feet wide—such a mirror as Gales had seen in many a Parisian hotel.

He pulled the shades up, opened the windows wide, and took off his white coat. McGill sat on the edge of the bed thumbing a dog-eared magazine that someone had left behind. Gales went to a writing table in the corner beside one of the windows,

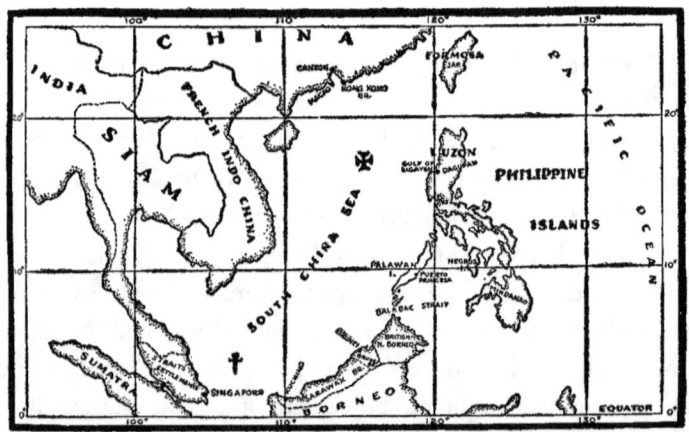

The cross marks the point near the Equator where the yacht *Wildway* was sunk. The dagger indicates the point where Gales and McGill found the schooner *Homeward*.

sat down and got out his navigation chart. He began mapping out the course they were to take tomorrow unless new word from K.O. should change their plans.

McGill lay back on the bed, arms upstretched, hands gripping the magazine, eyes squinted at the print.

Half an hour later, when Gales was absorbed in his map, McGill in the magazine, the sound of a shot split the silence. Almost simultaneously there was the snarl of glass. McGill scooted off the bed and grabbed his pistol from the chair. Gales pivoted on the chair, saw the shattered mirror, glanced at the window, saw a hole in the screen.

McGill switched out the lights.

Gales said through the darkness, "Someone saw my reflection in the mirror, thought it was me!"

McGill snapped, "There's a roof across the way even with this window. I'm on my way, sweetheart!"

The door flung open. McGill dived out. Gales stumbled through the darkened room, found his gun, went lunging into the corridor. Three persons had come out of rooms, shouting. Gales saw McGill bounding down the stairway. He bounded after him, and the two partners raced through the lobby, out into the street.

The place across the way was a novelty shop, still open. They could see an alley on the side.

Gales said, "You go in the shop, up to the roof. I'll take the alley."

McGill sailed into the shop, saw a man behind a littered counter, saw a staircase beyond. He said nothing to the man. He scaled the counter and went bolting up the staircase.

Gales plunged into the narrow alley, into darkness that was black as pitch. The alley led him to another street, and after a look up and down, he turned and retraced his steps, hugging the walk.

He saw a dim shape appear in the alley and head swiftly for the street on which the hotel was located.

GALES DID not shout. Nor did he shoot. He ran faster and reached the street and saw the man running toward the waterfront. He gained, and the man, looking back, saw him and darted across to the opposite side of the street—suddenly disappeared. Gales discovered his method of disappearance; another alley similar to the first. And though the alley was so black he could see nothing, yet he heard pounding feet not far distant and he blasted his way into the alley.

He did not want to kill the man, even though the man had tried to kill him.

He wanted to get the man alive, to find out what the man knew; if need be, to choke the truth from him. Gales' blood ran hotly through his veins, pounded at his temples. This was luck of a sort, unexpected. He was certain he was on the trail of one of the enemy's agents.

The alley emptied into another street—dark, deserted. And the fleeing man was a dim shape in the distance, the sound of his flying feet made staccato echoes in the warm night.

Now Gales yelled, "Stop—or I'll shoot!"

But the man did not stop. He must have known his way about, for again he vanished into one of those murky alleys. Gales did not run pell-mell into the alley, but ran to within twenty feet of it, then hugged the wall and crept forward. He did this because he did not hear the running feet.

He stopped a foot short of the alley. His breath was pumping from his lungs, and he was bathed in a hot running sweat. His hair had become disheveled and clung wetly to his forehead, and the palm of his hand was moist against the gun's butt. Where was the man? Just around the corner, waiting with leveled gun? Or had he chosen to move more slowly and with less noise? If he had, then he would be moving farther away each moment Gales waited there in the tense indecision of a man who is on the brink of failure or possible success.

Gales looked around. He was near a door of the house that stood on the corner of the alley. He moved back and tried the door. It opened. He entered the hallway and followed it until it terminated. Here was another door. He tried it and opened it softly. He heard a man snoring. Beyond he saw a window, opening on the other angle.

He closed the door softly, tiptoed across the room and reached the window. The window was open. He looked out. Not five feet away, between the window and the end of the alley, waiting for him to come into the alley from the street, was a man crouching with a gun.

Gales gripped his automatic hard, put one leg over the sill, stepped out. A loose stone crunched beneath his foot. He tightened his muscles. The crouching shape whirled with a cry of surprise. A gun boomed and flame shattered the darkness. Gales felt the bullet brush by.

There was only one thing he could do. He did it. The muzzle of his gun belched flame. There was a hoarse scream that died in a choked rattle, and there was the sound of a body falling, an abandoned gun clanging down.

For a moment Gales stood rigid, tense. Then he went forward and bent over the motionless shape. He lit a match.

Dead eyes looked up at him. Dead eyes in a yellow Oriental face.

Quickly Gales went through his pockets, found spare ammunition, and a wallet. He lit another match, held it in one hand, laid the wallet, open, on the ground, and drew out its contents. Some Straits money, three picture postcards, a leaflet of steamship sailings, and a dozen small cards held together by an elastic band.

Gales took the band off and looked at all the cards. On each was inscribed:

> Mr. Lee Goy
> 24 Sun Foo Street
> Canton

That was all.

Voices were babbling from windows now. Half a dozen men appeared at the entrance of the alley. They carried guns and their actions were businesslike.

Gales called, "All right, police!"

McGILL SAID, "Well, big boy, what do you make of it?"

Gales was standing spread-legged in the center of their hotel room, staring transfixed at the shattered mirror. "I was just thinking what a lucky guy I happen to be. The manager's shedding tears over his mirror. He said a French countess gave it to him."

"I'm weepin', too."

"So I notice. Yeah... so am I!" He turned and stared at McGill. "Mr. Lee Goy, Mike, of 24 Sun Foo Street, Canton. I tried to get him alive, but I couldn't. It was either the Chink or me, and I think I rate a few more years with mechanical wings instead of the other kind. Mr. Lee Goy. He wanted to kill one of us. He was an agent of this mysterious air pirate. But in bumping him off, we learned nothing."

"Except," put in McGill, "his home address."

Gales pulled a packet of small white cards from his pocket. "You know what I did?"

"What?"

"Something irregular. I kept the cards. The police don't know who he is?"

"Why'd you do that?"

"Because," Gales said, "they would have gone ahead and wired for instructions regarding the disposal of the body. And the home folks no doubt would have changed their address."

"You mean now—"

"I mean, brother, that if we got to number 24 Sun Foo Street—"

McGill did a backward somersault on the bed, came out of it sitting calmly with his back against the wall.

Gales regarded him. "What's that vindicate, lame brain?"

"Approval, my *dear* Mr. Gales!"

"If we're going to be formal about it," Gales said with dignity, "how's to get your dirty feet off my bed?"

CHAPTER IV

DRONE OF DOOM

S O THE partners were already on the spot—marked for death. And since his first attack had come so suddenly, and so unexpectedly, it was reasonable to suppose another would follow. Somewhere. Sometime. And when they least expected it.

Next morning they reported to K.O. and K.O. complimented them, assured them that he was certain now he had chosen the right men. News said that Manners, owner of the lost *Wildway,* was alternately rageful and despondent. His daughter was gone. She was only twenty-two, in the flower of youth, and she had met a horrible fate.

He nor anyone else could conceive of any motive behind the brutal sinking of the *Wildway* with all hands. No motive other than a bestial lust for blood.

Who was the fiend? All the newspapers were interrogative. And Manners offered twenty thousand for information leading to the whereabouts of the *Sky Hawk.* The caldron of the East boiled to overflowing. Cruisers left Saigon, Hongkong and Singapore—to get the *Sky Hawk.*

Gales and McGill left Kuching after having spent an hour with the officials on the matter of the killing of the mysterious—and "unidentified"—Chinese. Gales was cleared easily enough, and nine o'clock found the two birdmen of fortune roaring their crate down the wilderness river that led to the sea. The sun was steaming in the mists when they soared over the delta at the river's mouth, past the lighthouse on the headland, north on the raw primordial coast.

Their first stop was to be Kudat, on the northwestern tip of Borneo—roughly, seven hundred miles. McGill did not loaf along, but stepped his wagon at a hundred and twenty most of the time. Winds were favorable, and they stayed far enough off the coast to avoid the updrafts and downdrafts characteristic of a coast sprinkled with river mouths, deltas, bays, flats and headlands.

Canton was their ultimate destination —by way of Kudat, Puerto Princesa, Dagupan, Laoag, and then across the China Sea to Hongkong, a city out of which they had been kicked more times than one. The intervening stretches of sea-waste, of sprawling islands and snag-toothed reefs, had been to date the hunting ground of the mysterious *Sky Hawk*. No one knew their route. No one knew their destination.

The flight up the Borneo coast turned out to be a joy hop, and at three-fifteen McGill put the crate down in the harbor of Kudat. By three-fifty they had refueled, tuned up their motor, and were on the wing, leaving dark Borneo behind. They hurtled across the island of Banguey, across the Strait of Balabac and then Balabac Island, and raised the southern tip of the island of Palawan, droned up its east coast over the Sulu Sea.

Dusk was falling, lights were beginning to blink, when McGill circled Puerto Princesa, cut his gun and took the Vought down. They refueled before turning in that night, and were on the wing again at six next morning.

Fortune in the way of weather smiled on them, and at eleven o'clock they dropped down on Lingayen Gulf, refueled to capacity, grabbed a hot meal and were on the wing at a little past noon. Gales, instead of proceeding up the coast to the tip of the Philippines, laid a course northwest from Dagupan for Hongkong. Land was left behind. Beyond them stretched the South China Sea—a long and dangerous flight over wide waters of seven hundred miles.

"Hongkong before dark," McGill swore.

"You voice my sentiments," Gales said through the speaking tube.

McGill held the crate to three thousand feet. The last headland of the Philippines vanished in the distance behind, and the bloodhounds of the wind were alone over the sea and beneath the wide sky.

In these waters, and farther south, the *Sky Hawk* was known to have pirated.

AT FOUR o'clock, Gales, peering through binoculars, picked up a two-masted schooner dead ahead, showing no sails. He conveyed this to McGill by means of the speaking tube, and McGill craned his neck and knocked off a thousand feet of altitude. Soon he too was able to see the schooner, with his naked eye.

He knocked off more altitude, and when they neared the schooner they saw that she was deserted. No one was at the helm. No one moved about the deck. Yet they saw shapes on the deck that looked like men lying down.

McGill eased up on the throttle and said through the tube, "Wanta go down?"

"Let's get a closer look first."

McGill pushed the stick forward, dropped to five hundred feet, and loafed leisurely over the schooner. Gales could see through his binoculars that men were lying on the deck, some with their faces turned to the sky. He shuddered. He was about to pick up the speaking tube when he saw a person emerge from the after deckhouse, stop and look up at them.

Then Gales grabbed the tube. "Go ahead down, Mike."

McGill went down. Slapped his crate on a long low swell in the lee of the schooner. The solitary form on board the schooner had come to the lee rail and was watching them. Gales clamped binoculars to his eyes. He saw a head of hair that was a girl's—bright gold in the sunlight. She wore a black blouse or jumper, he was not sure, and she neither waved nor called.

McGill gunned the motor a bit and drove toward the schooner's lee. Then he throttled down until the motor was idling, and the Vought drifted toward the schooner's scarred hull. Gales climbed out to the wing, reached out for the pilot's ladder, caught it and swung from the wing. He went up the ladder, swung a leg over the rail and sat there forking it and looking at the girl.

Now he saw that she wore what looked like a black sateen pilot's suit. Her gold hair was bobbed, and she looked at him with a blank fixed stare. An uncannny feeling crept in upon him, and he took his eyes from the girl and looked over the deck.

His throat tightened. Dead men lay about. Blood spattered the deck, and the halyards clicked against the masts like old dead bones. The rail on which he sat had the imprint of a bloody hand that had rested there.

He started when the girl came toward him, her hand out-stretched. He looked at her. Her wide blue eyes were fastened on his, and her face, lovely at another time, was strange now because of the weird expression it wore. She walked with slow steps, and her out-stretched hand touched Gales' arm, gripped it. Her hueless lips parted and a long-held breath rushed out.

She choked, "Who—who are you?"

"Gales," he said, shrinking much against his will. "Gales of the Straits Agency."

She sobbed, "Oh!" and fell back a step, put a hand to her forehead, toppled and slumped to the deck.

In a bound Gales was beside her, his arm beneath her head. He saw her lips quivering, her throat throbbing. Her eyes were closed. He stood up and jumped to the rail.

"Stand by, Mike," he called. "This girl's fainted."

"Okey, Bill."

GALES RETURNED to the girl, lifted her in his arms and started across the deck. He had to step over the body of a dead man to get to the cabin companion. He went down with her into the cabin, and the sunlight pouring in through the ports showed him a man sitting on the settee. At first he started. But then he knew that the man was dead, chin on chest, arms slack at his sides.

He found a bunk and laid the girl on it. He saw a bottle of brandy on the table and some glasses and a jug. He tried the jug. It contained water. He tore away part of his shirt, soaked it and laid it on the girl's forehead. Then he washed one of the glasses, poured in some brandy, returned to the bunk and forced the brandy between the girl's hueless lips. Then he refreshed the cloth with water, washed her face, patted her forehead. Gradually—over a space of twenty minutes—she came to.

"How are you now?" he asked, smiling.

"Weak. But all right. I was a fool to faint. But all I'd seen— all the bloodshed—and the dead men lying around. It was frightful! Horrible!"

"Who are you?" he asked.

"Gwen Manners. I—"

She stopped short at sight of the look in Gales' face.

"What's the matter?" she asked.

"Nothing. But—you're Gwen Manners?"

"Yes. What seems to be the trouble?"

"You were aboard the *Sky Hawk*—and got off?"

She sat up and put fingers to her hair. There was a vacant look in her eyes. "Yes, I was aboard the *Sky Hawk*. Ever since it first came out of the sky life has been a frightful nightmare. Even now, it all seems like a horrible dream and yet—"

Her eyes stopped on the dead man on the settee. She covered her face with her hands.

"Please," Gales said earnestly, "try to pull yourself together. I know it must have been terrible, but come—pull yourself together. My partner and I are on the trail of the *Sky Hawk*. The tragedy of the *Wildway* is known up and down the coast. Your father thinks you are—dead."

"No. They spared me. But every other soul went down when they blew the yacht up. They wanted me. For ransom. They were planning to ask a hundred thousand, but were biding their time. Before they took me on board they blindfolded me. I've been blindfolded ever since. I know we've been on land since. I walked on land, but I never saw anything. Always somebody led me, and I remember the voice of their leader, soft and purring—an Oriental voice, the voice of a Chinaman. Once I felt his long fingernails on my arm." She shivered and stared into space with horrified eyes.

"How did you get here? How did you get away?"

She relaxed, smiled wanly. "It was strange. While I was blindfolded one of them came to me. He said he knew me and respected me, that he was one of them because of circumstances. He did not tell his name. But he planned my escape. We were in flight then, after we'd left land. He said we were looking for a schooner that carried a pearl-buyer and fifty thousand dollars in pearls. When the men boarded an overhauled ship they all wore uniforms like this. There's the helmet over there on the table, with the mask attached. He said that at the last moment he would get me, and I would put on his uniform, go aboard with the others—and not come back. He would hide on the plane, don another uniform, and mingle with the others when they returned. He said I had once done him a kind service.

"Everything worked perfectly. He took me to a dim chamber on the big plane, and helped me on with the uniform. I never saw his face. I joined the others in another dim chamber, got into a boat with them. When the plane landed, a door in its side flung open and the boat slipped into the water. I saw sunlight—and the schooner. He'd said they would not sink the schooner. They boarded the schooner, got the pearl-buyer, got his pearls, and then simply shot every man down. In the confusion I hid in the hold until they had gone. And here I am."

"And the boss hadn't decided on the ransom?"

"No. My benefactor told me that the ransom would be collected but that I would not be returned."

"How long ago did they leave?"

"About two hours ago."

"And when they find you're not on board?"

She shuddered. "My benefactor said that after I had gone he would open one of the big ports. This would indicate that I had chosen to jump to death from the plane."

Gales stood up, fists clenched, eyes narrowed. "I hope to God they don't find another solution—or suspect the guy got you free!... Come on. We can jam you in the rear cockpit. It will be uncomfortable, but we'll get you to Hongkong."

She rose and went with him toward the companion. "They have two other planes, you know. Very tiny ones, single-seaters, armed. Each one hangs from either tip of the big plane's wing and is released by some sort of mechanism while in flight. If I'd been told that such a tremendous plane existed I wouldn't have believed it. It's tremendous!"

As they came on deck Gales stopped short, stiffened. Then he ran to the rail.

In the West he saw, far off, a plane against the blaze of the sun.

McGill was yelling, "Hey, Bill! Hey, Bill!"

CHAPTER V

THE WINGED DECOY

GALES GRIPPED the girl's arm. "They've found out! No plane but one like that could make such a noise!"

The girl looked at him, white-faced, tense. No fear was in her eyes. Her lips were setting in a grim line.

She said clearly, "Then we're trapped after all. If you've got an extra gun I'll do my bit."

Gales felt like gripping her hand, pumping it man-like. She'd said that like a man—like a brave man. And yet she was all woman, one of the loveliest he had ever laid eyes on.

"Hey, Bill! What the devil! You fallin' for a jane already?"

Gales took her hand and led her to the rail. He glared down at McGill. "It's the *Sky Hawk*, Mike!"

"That ain't news, brother! Of course it's the *Sky Hawk!* What did you think I thought it was?"

Gales thumped the rail with his fist "For Lord's sake, Mike, cut out wisecracking! This is Miss Manners! *Miss Manners!* You get me?"

"Gotcha, pal. What next?"

"They're coming back for her. She escaped and was hiding here, and they're coming back. We can't take off because they've got two single-seater fighters, and with Miss Manners crammed in the cockpit we couldn't fight 'em."

McGill sat up straight, his face suddenly serious, a bitter light in his eyes. He snarled, "We'll fight 'em!"

"We can't, Mike! We can't."

"I know, Bill. I know. I'm sorry I acted like a slob." He ground his teeth together. "But—dammit—we've got to fight!"

Gales knew him. Gales knew the wild reckless blood of him, the hard fighting heart, the nerve that no enemy, however great, could break. Nor was Gales backward when it came to danger and the chance of sudden death.

But he had the girl, and common sense told him that with the three of them in the plane they could not fight. And he knew Mike was a winged acrobat. Alone, Mike could fly rings around any pilot in the East.

He yelled, "One chance, Mike. You've got a fast crate there, and it's up to you to fool 'em. Take off. They'll think the girl is in the crate and they'll take after you. Wait a minute."

He ran into the cabin, came out with the black helmet and mask. He went among the dead men, chose two of the thinnest and lightest and dragged them to the rail. He got a length of line, lashed it about their waists and lowered them over side till they reached the water.

Then he climbed down the ladder, got aboard the plane's wing, and McGill, seeing what he was up to, came out of the cockpit to help him. They placed the bodies in the rear cockpit, and Gales fastened the black helmet on one of them.

"Now go to it, Mike. They're about three miles off."

McGill was serious. He gripped Gales' hand. "I hate leavin' you, Bill. I hope this'll work. If it don't, if they do you in—I'll get 'em, one by one, if it takes ten years."

"You've no soft job yourself, partner. Get to Hongkong. Give 'em our position. Luck, Mike!"

They released hands, looked at each other for a brief moment.

McGill laughed brokenly. "Hell, we're gettin' sentimental! So long, old sock. And mind what I told you about janes."

Gales laughed too—kind of hollowly, with no heart—and climbed back to the schooner.

The next moment McGill was foaming off, his motor howling.

The girl asked, "Is that the famous Mike McGill?"

"That," said Gales grimly, "is the best pal a man ever had." Then he shook off the low mood, gripped her arm. "Come. We'd better stay out of sight."

"Will he make it?"

"The old boy always comes through."

They went down into the cabin, stood silently and listened to the oncoming drone of the great air pirate.

Now the girl was gripping Gales' arm. She could feel the taut muscles beneath his sleeve.

"You men are doing—this—for—me," she breathed.

Gales said nothing. He was thinking of Mike McGill.

McGILL WAS thinking of Bill Gales. The red-head had the Vought up to five thousand, and the huge pirate plane was off his starboard bow. Suddenly he saw the two small planes drop from the goliath's great wing, their props flashing. McGill was almost ready to disbelieve his eyes. Was this possible?

It was, for the two planes were leveling off beneath the *Sky Hawk,* and the latter was banking hugely, turning toward the Vought. The small planes, mono-winged, the one gray, the other brown, were rising rapidly now on either side of the *Sky Hawk* and forging ahead of it.

McGill did not change his course. He had his throttle forward to the last notch, and the Vought was doing a hundred and forty, every fibre of her straining. Even above the racket of his own motor and the wind, McGill could hear the dull thunder of the *Sky Hawk's* ten motors. He could see the glitter of her ports, and when he raised his binoculars he could see guns jutting from her flank, from her tail, from streamlined hoods on the top of her mammoth wing.

But the small planes were beginning to frolic in a manner that hinted at trouble. McGill put away his binoculars, grabbed his pistol and kicked left rudder bar. He knew now that anyone on board the *Sky Hawk,* using powerful glasses, could see the shapes in the rear cockpit. McGill wanted them to. He wanted to get close enough so that the shapes could not possibly be overlooked.

He reasoned he had done that, and now he was ready to lead the chase. First, being a game bird, he tried out the speed of the other planes.

He made a stab at the brown monoplane, then banked sharply and ran for it. He ran in a wide circle, and he saw that the monoplane could not overtake him. It might best him in maneuverability, but not otherwise.

The gray plane came at him on the port quarter and tried a burst of machine gun fire. It fell short, and McGill fishtailed by way of showing his contempt, and then tacked on more altitude. He followed that by making a headlong dive.

It was a crazy stunt, but McGill had more nerve than one man should have. He howled past the tail of the mammoth *Sky*

Hawk, saw a streamlined turret there and swung his tail around violently to escape a hail of machine gun fire the turret slashed at him.

The gray plane was surprised by this stunt. McGill was bowling along at a hundred and forty in the eye of the gray plane's prop. The gray plane heeled over to avoid a collision, and McGill, laughing contemptuously, emptied his pistol. He left two scars on the gray plane's flank. But a moment later the brown plane opened up on his tail. Lead snarled in the empennage. McGill knew it was time to cut out monkey-shines and start going places.

He howled off on one ear, straightened out, yanked back on the stick and hiked for altitude. Over his shoulder he saw that all three planes were after him, the monoplanes ahead of the giant *Sky Hawk.*

His throttle could do more. He had the lead. He figured the *Sky Hawk's* top speed at about a hundred and twenty. And while the smaller planes could match his own, he knew that he carried more fuel, that the small planes would have to refuel from the mother plane. This settled in his mind, he hoped that his motor would not fly to pieces and that the wind wouldn't tear the wings off. And he hoped Bill would not fall for the jane.

GALES, STANDING at the port of the schooner, said, "Blast Mike, it's just like him to take a couple of pot-shots at those birds!"

"But the big plane has turned!"

"Yes. They're after Mike."

"Can he fly faster?"

"I think so. I hope so. Yes! Look—look at him run away from that brown plane!"

The girl gripped Gales' arm. "He's wonderful!" she cried.

They waited, side by side, speechless now. They saw McGill slice dangerously close to one of the small planes, saw the small plane veer off, saw McGill rise and outstrip the other small plane.

Gales said, tensely, "I think Mike's started for certain now." The three planes were falling in behind McGill. Gales raised his binoculars. "Yes, Mike's setting the pace. He's Hongkong bound!"

There was no exultation in his voice. His words came thickly, clogged in a throat where a lump refused to go down. He watched until McGill disappeared, until the small planes disappeared, until the only one visible—and that barely—was the giant *Sky Hawk*.

Then it too faded into the blue, and silence reigned on the schooner—silence but for the slow creaking of her timbers and the slap-slap of the water against her hull.

They turned from the port, looked at each other with wide grave eyes. Then they looked away, and Gales, lighting a cigarette, went on deck. The girl joined him, and for a while they stood by the rail looking out across the desert of water.

"Both of you have been wonderful," she said.

"We're not saved yet. We're adrift. We're over too many fathoms for the anchor to be of any use. If a storm comes—"

He did not finish, but laid his clenched fist on the rail, thumped it slowly. He looked aloft. "In a pinch— By George, we'll have to! If Mike gets through and gives our position, they'll send someone after us—maybe a cruiser. If we keep on drifting—"

"I can steer," she said. "I hope I can. I've sailed a yawl from New York to Bar Harbor."

"Great! Let's get some canvas up. We'll sail back and forth over the spot."

Her eyes sparkled. "Aye, skipper!"

They both laughed, forgetting for a moment their plight.

CHAPTER VI

McGILL COMES THROUGH

FIVE O'CLOCK found the redoubtable Mike McGill still storming along. The motor had not gone to pieces. The wings had held. The three planes were a mile behind. The wind was a fair wind. The sea below was an undulating carpet of emerald, and the sky above was cloudless.

It was five-fifteen that Mike looked back and noted a change in formation. The two small planes were going down. The *Sky Hawk* was banking.

McGill yelled into the wind, "Whoopee!"

He had reckoned rightly. The small planes were running out of fuel. They were going down, and the *Sky Hawk* was going down too, to give them more gas. Everything was—in a word— jake. McGill saw the two planes alight on the water, and his last backward glance showed him the *Sky Hawk* skimming the sea's surface.

He grinned. He shifted in his seat for a more comfortable position, leaned back and began to whistle, even though he could not hear himself. He mused that everything was pretty corking now—except Bill back there with the jane. Bill had passed up many a good-looker during their exploits in the East. But McGill had always figured that when Bill finally got the bug, he would go into a tail spin and fall hard.

McGill was flying practically on dead reckoning. He did not hope to raise Hongkong first. His main desire was to raise land, reach the coast, then get his bearings. Gales was the navigator of the two. McGill flew by instinct, his compass, and luck.

He raised the islands first—tiny ones. He did not recognize them, but he was flying north-northwest, and he stuck to that course. Then land more solid loomed beyond. He thought at first it was the mainland. But it wasn't. He recognized it and whooped with joy.

He howled over the port of Macao, where six cops had once beaten him up—after he had beaten three. He checked his gas. Could he make Canton? No.

But he could make Hongkong. He was none too popular in Hongkong, either, but that didn't cramp his style. He kicked right rudder bar, shoved the stick to the right, and left Macao behind.

Dusk was falling when he boomed over Hongkong. And when he slapped the Vought's floats on the harbor, lights were beginning to blink on the Bund. Gay city! Romantic city! Many a time Mike had strutted down the Bund with a girl on his arm. He ground his teeth. *That* was before he had met that girl in Saigon—the one who had done him wrong.

As he edged the Vought into a basin between two piers, the motor sputtered, coughed, stopped.

McGill said, "All right, sweetheart," and shut off the ignition. His tanks were empty. But he had come through. A man in much uniform and mustache appeared and yelled down:

"I say, you can't park that bloody thing here!"

"Can't I?"

"No!"

McGill calmly carried a line to the nearest pier, made fast. He returned to the Vought, got out another line, and yelled to the officer on the other pier:

"Grab this, buddy!"

He snaked the line out. The officer, bewildered, found himself catching hold of the line.

"Now hold it," McGill said.

The red-head climbed to the nearest pier, walked around to the one on which the officer stood. The officer was red-faced, sort of steamed up, but he was holding the line whether he realized it or not.

McGill took it gently from him, said, "Thanks," and made the line fast on the pier.

"I—I say, you can't—you bloody well can't make fast here!"

McGill stood up, smiled indulgently, patted the man on the shoulder and said, "There, there, George, I wouldn't take it so hard."

The officer stepped back, towered. "You're under arrest!" He drew a pistol.

McGill was lighting a butt. He spun away the match and the butt bobbed in his mouth when he said, "All right. I'll go quiet, George."

"My name is not George!"

"Do I go this way?"

"Come along with me!" The officer took McGill's arm and led him off.

McGill remarked. "Let's hurry."

SIR IAN MacWHIRR, the port brass hat, exploded, " 'Tis ye, Irish, again! Ah didna think y'u'd e'er come back! Ah dinna ken but what tr-r-rouble's afoot. Weel, Lootenant Talley?"

"Landed his plane, sir, in the harbor and made fast to a pier against orders."

Sir Ian twitched his heather eyebrows. "Weel, McGill—"

"Now give me a chance, brother," McGill broke in. "I was comin' here anyhow. Your boy scout saved me the rikisha fare, and that oughter appeal to your Scotch big-heartedness. At any rate, I've been chased by the *Sky Hawk*—"

"Weel, now! Yis, McGill. G' on!"

"Miss Manners is safe aboard the schooner *Homeward* with my partner Bill Gales—"

"What!"

"For cryin' out loud, listen! Bill and me found the derelict and all hands dead and Miss Manners on board. She escaped from the *Sky Hawk*—don't ask me how—when the big crate cleaned out the schooner. We were about to take her off, when the *Sky Hawk* puts in an appearance. I take off to lead the *Sky Hawk* away, with two dead guys from the schooner to make the big plane think Bill and the girl are with me. I sashay around awhile and get the *Sky Hawk* to follow me. I lose 'em. I arrive. Now get started. I left the *Homeward* in latitude seventeen, ten, and longitude a hundred fifteen and twenty."

"When did ye leave 'em?"

"Four hours ago. Send a cruiser or a destroyer. Or a flock of planes. But send somethin' quick!"

Sir Ian barked, "O' course! Lootenant, send in Major Kief!"

"Yes, sir!"

Talley went out smartly.

Sir Ian bit McGill with a cold Scotch eye. "Weel, Irish, ah dinna ken but what the town's yours."

"Keep your old town, brother. Only get a wire off to my boss, K.O. Pike, and tell him Miss Manners is safe for the time bein'. Don't wire the position. Don't say where she is. The enemy might pick it up."

"Ah c'n do better than that, Irish. Ah weel wire S'pore in naval code and have 'em send a messenger t' your boss."

"That's jake. Any objection now to my parkin' the plane there?"

"None."

"Okey. Then how's to send down some men to take off the dead ones. I'll want to refuel before I hit the hay."

"It weel be done." Sir Ian stood up. "Though ye be Irish, would ye mind shakin' me hand?"

"Sure. Too bad you're Scotch, Sir Ian."

HONGKONG BUZZED, throbbed with the news. Reporters besieged the hotel in which McGill took a room. And be it known that McGill chose the best hotel in town, ate the best dinner procurable, drank the best wine and finished off the best cigar. Then he fled to his room, barred the door, and paced the room worrying about his partner.

The telephone rang constantly. Reporters wanted to see McGill, get his story. He finally told the operator that if the room was rung again he would go down and push in the operator's face. Notes were slipped under his door when constant knocking availed nothing. Fabulous offers were made.

McGill said, "You can all go to blazes! A week ago you were all pannin' Bill and me! Now get!"

The destroyer *Halcyon* was off under full steam to find the *Homeward*, foaming through the night. Planes were not sent because of the darkness and the great distance and storm warnings. It was reckoned that if all went well the destroyer would reach the *Homeward's* last position at noon next day—perhaps before.

McGill spent a restless night, tossed constantly. He was up at the first streak of dawn. By ways that were dark and surreptitious he reached his plane before the sun had risen. Mists were writhing over the water, but McGill was bound to take off.

He started his motor, warmed it up, and then freed the mooring lines. No one was down to see him off. He wanted it that way. He drove the Vought through the mist, almost hit a barge, missed a junk and two sampans by a bare margin, and rising with a roar from the water, almost clipped off the mast of a barkentine.

But he got the plane up. He circled the city, got his bearings, and lit out for Kowloon. Hongkong was lost in the mists. The waters beneath were shrouded, and the wind was a tough, two-fisted wind slamming against the Vought's nose. The plane did some yawing and smacked some hard bumps, but she was doing a hundred and fifteen when Kowloon swept beneath, and then she roared over the mainland and after a while struck the Canton River. The sun was up and the mists were being driven away.

The day was bright when McGill came booming down on Canton. He knew the city, knew it of old: its crooked streets, wayward canals, low murderous dives. He crossed the east wall at a thousand feet, saw the four old forts in the north, the north wall beyond. He saw its junk-littered canals, its west gate, and the neat foreign concession in the southwest corner, where the Pe-Kiang River met the Canton. It was said that eighty-odd thousand houseboats float about Canton and that a hundred and fifty temples lift spires to sun. No one has ever said how many murders are committed between dusk and dawn because nobody knows.

McGill eased up on the gun. The motor quieted. He picked out a likely space of water where the houseboats were fewest and pushed his stick forward. He crossed Respondentia Walk at eight hundred feet, watched the houseboats flash beneath him. He went into a slow bank and turn, eased up more on the gun, and whistled downward. His floats struck. Water spumed up on either side of him, and three yelling natives leaped from a sampan ten yards away.

McGill drove his crate through the maze of crafts, and finally reached a familiar dock. It was familiar because once he had thrown a customs official off it, leaped in and saved him and then spent ten days in the lock-up.

But this time he had papers acquired in Hongkong—signed by Sir Ian himself. There was a small amount of bickering, but McGill got through and ten minutes later found him smacking his heels down Respondentia Walk. In another street he found a bookstore and a map of the city, and after a long search on the map he located Sun Foo Street.

He shoved the map in his pocket, went to a dark corner, looked to his automatic and then stamped out.

HE TOOK a rikisha that took him out of the foreign settlement and into seething, turbid Canton proper, where children squawked and dogs barked and merchants hammered brass gongs. Here the sun beat down mercilessly, and slant-eyed Chinamen plied their trades, and the rikisha coolies trotted tirelessly and yelled endlessly.

Finally he alighted, paid his fare and set off on foot.

He was not a big man. Rather a small one, but put together with whip-cord muscle and shock-proof bone. His blue eyes had the glint of blue metal now and his mouth was set above his small square jaw.

He turned three corners before he came to a street that was narrow, crooked, more like an alley. No tradesmen here. No shuffling throngs. An empty street where the sun did not reach, where the houses were low, huddled, blank-faced. The sounds of more hectic Canton came over the roofs in a muted murmur.

McGill's footfalls echoed. Presently he began to slow down. Then he crossed the street and continued slowly along the housewalls. Finally he stopped and looked at a number in Chinese on a stout door. He knew Chinese numbers.

This was 24 Sun Foo Street.

McGill's right hand went into his pocket, closed over the butt of his automatic. His left hand rose, poised for an instant, then knocked.

A minute later the door moved; opened slowly. A tunnel of darkness lay beyond. On the edge of the door McGill saw yellow fingers of a yellow hand.

A thin reedy voice said, "You want come in, mister?"

McGill went in.

WHEN GALES saw the significant spot in the sky he was standing in the bows of the schooner *Homeward*. His blood froze in his veins. He flung a look aft. Gwen Manners was braced at the wheel, her golden hair blowing in the stiff quarter wind.

Her voice came down the wind, "Is that a plane on the port bow?"

He strode aft swiftly, and the look on his face told her that it was a plane. She tightened her lips a bit and fought the kick of the wheel.

"It can't be helped—yet," she said.

"No," Gales muttered. "It's the *Sky Hawk* coming back. Either they finished off Mike, or Mike eluded them. Either your good Samaritan talked or the *Sky Hawk* is bound for its base."

The canvas clapped and the shrouds hummed. Man and girl stood and stared grimly at the oncoming plane. Soon they could hear the distant hum of its ten motors.

"This is certain," Gales said. "We can't hide. They've seen our sails up, and the sails weren't up when they last were here. They're making a bee-line for us now."

"The skipper of this schooner had some guns below. I saw them." Challenge was in the girl's eyes. "I'm not going to be made prisoner again."

Gales looked at her. "You've got nerve—by George, you have!"

He went below and found a couple of Winchesters. He found ammunition, loaded the rifles, crammed his pockets. He had a Colt's automatic pistol of his own. He rushed on deck with the arms, and by this time the plane was nearer, the motors were droning. The girl and the man stood side by side at the wheel, companions in danger now, drawn close to each other. Gales used his binoculars.

"The small planes are attached," he said. "The *Sky Hawk's* landed somewhere and taken them on. I can see that they're so adjusted that they act as wing-tip pontoons. With a fleet of planes like that any nation could master the world."

"I wonder why the small planes don't take off."

"One guess. The *Sky Hawk* probably has only sufficient gas for its own motors. I wonder—if Mike got through."

Now the big plane was roaring nearer, the sun turning to a red ball behind it. The monster of the air was dropping lower.

Gales spoke rapidly to the girl, giving last minute advice and instruction. The girl nodded, alert, attentive. She kept throwing glances at the oncoming plane. The thunder of the motors was very close, the plunderer was dropping more rapidly now. The girl did not alter the schooner's course.

The *Sky Hawk* struck the water, split the water into twin foaming geysers and came rumbling down on the schooner's port bow. Gales, peering through his binoculars, saw a wide trapdoor in the plane's flank open outward and downward.

A small boat slid out into the water manned by ten men.

Gales saw a big outboard motor and a man stationed at it. He saw the man yank the starting lanyard, saw the motor begin to make a wake behind while the *Sky Hawk* moved slowly toward the schooner, her props barely turning over.

THE SMALL boat was making to head off the schooner, intending to board it while the schooner was bowling along. The wind was on the starboard quarter and everything was perfect for the stunt Gales and Gwen had in mind.

The stunt was almost fantastic, but they knew of no other, and they were game for anything. The small boat was in a position to come alongside and board over the schooner's lee rail. The *Sky Hawk* was lying to.

Gales had his eyes alternately on the plane's tail gun turret and on the man who steered the smallboat. A Winchester was gripped in his hands, and he was standing in a position to protect Gwen.

When he said "now!" Gwen heaved on the wheel mightily. The schooner heeled hugely to port. The wind hummed. The rudder tore water into white foam. At that moment Gales raised his Winchester, drew a bead on the slot in the tail turret and fired. Quickly he swung his rifle toward the small boat and fired. The muzzle blazed and the man at the tiller fell sidewise. The small boat yawed.

The schooner kept swinging, her lee rail almost awash. The men in the small boat fired, but their shots banged harmlessly into the semi-deckhouse. Those on board the *Sky Hawk* must have become aware of the impending danger, for the props began turning faster.

But too late.

The schooner slammed her blunt bow into the plane's tail gear. Her bowsprit tore the rudders asunder. Her masts, leaning way over, carried away what remained of the rudders, carried away the stabilizers.

Then Gwen heaved the wheel to starboard—hard, and the *Homeward* swung clear, caught the full blast of the wind over her quarter and went bowling along with a bone in her teeth. Gales lashed the wheel, took Gwen and the rifles and went into the waist to crouch behind the deckhouse.

Another man had come to the gun in the plane's tail, and was raking the schooner's stern. Bullets clipped the lashed wheel and smacked into the after part of the deckhouse, while the small boat, with a new man at the wheel, was driving after the *Homeward* and cutting loose with rifle fire.

Gales and the girl looked along their rifles—fired. The new man at the small boat's tiller fell away, and the small boat yawed wildly, shipping a sea. The plane had swung broadside and was opening up with her starboard guns. The bullets crashed viciously into the schooner, shattered glass ports, but the schooner kept jogging along.

Gales said, "The plane's helpless without her tail gear. It will take 'em all night to repair it."

The girl pointed. "And the small boat's given up!"

When the plane's shots began to fall short Gales and Gwen rose and returned to the stern, and Gales unlashed the wheel.

The girl braced herself abaft it and twirled the spokes. Her face was flushed.

"We'll just sail on and on," she said.

"Yes," Gales nodded. "I'll get out the charts and we'll steer by the stars."

The sun went down. Dusk flung out over the seas, and the *Sky Hawk* was lost astern. The schooner pulsed to the drive of the wind, and the man and the girl took tricks at the wheel.

CHAPTER VII

THE FIRST CAPTIVE

McGILL WATCHED the yellow fingers on the door of Number 24 Sun Foo Street as he crossed the threshold. He stopped just inside, facing the dim shadow that was a small Chinaman. His hand was tight on the gun in his pocket.

The Chinaman closed the door softly, bolted it, and then lit a match. He put the flame to a candle he held, and when the candle was burning he smiled at McGill with broken yellow teeth and pointed for McGill to proceed.

McGill said, "After you, Chinee boy."

The "boy" was really an old man, with sunken yellow cheeks and one dark glittering eye. He said nothing, but led the way down the corridor. He came to a door, opened it, and ushered McGill into a large handsomely, furnished room. In the center of the room stood a mahogany table ten feet long and three wide. Behind the table sat a scholarly-looking Chinese with horn-rimmed spectacles. He looked up from a sheaf of papers.

"Yes," he said quietly.

McGill heard the door close. He looked around. The old Chinaman with the one eye had gone out. The room was soundless. McGill looked around. He saw no windows. Two lamps burned on the table. At the rear of the room was a closed door. At the left was another.

The scholarly Chinese sat back and said, "Well?" patiently.

McGill did not go to the table. He stood with his back against a blank wall so that he had an unobstructed vision of the entire room.

He said, "I happen to come from Mr. Lee Goy."

"I did not catch the name?"

"Mr. Lee Goy."

The Chinese bent his brows. "I am sorry. I do not know such a man. Could you have made a mistake?"

"I don't think so. He used to live here."

"Perhaps that was before my time. I am an innocent and humble student of medicine but recently moved in here. I thought perhaps you had come for treatment. Some white men do."

McGill snapped, "I didn't come for treatment!"

McGill eyed him keenly. The Chinese sat back comfortably, an innocent look on his face mixed somewhat with bewilderment. Then McGill's ears picked up a sound—faint, muffled by walls. What did it sound like? He listened intently. Then he knew—was positive. A wireless key!

The Chinese sighed and put his elbows on the desk.

McGill snapped, "Keep your hand away from that button!"

"Button, sir?"

"The white button you're looking at and startin' for! Keep away from it or I'll drill you clean!"

"I am sorry. I had no intention, kind sir, of touching the button."

"I'm not a kind sir, and put your hands behind your head!"

"This is extraordinary." The Chinese looked slightly hurt.

Suddenly a voice boomed in the room, as if coming through a loud speaker:

"The *Sky Hawk's* tail assembly is repaired and she's heading for Base 2 to refuel. She will report when she reaches Base 2 and she'll keep an eye out for the *Homeward.* She will also steer clear of the *Halcyon.* She asks to be informed of any new developments at this end. Also she wants to know when the *Mirador* leaves Canton for Bangkok."

The Chinese tensed in the chair.

The voice said, "You get all that?"

The Chinese, eying McGill, picked up a black mouthpiece attached to a tube and said, "Very well." He put the mouthpiece down.

"So you're just a medical student," McGill said. "Easy now! Hands behind your head!"

THE CHINESE was calm again. "This will avail you nothing."

"Says you, brother!" McGill drew his gun from his pocket. "Get up! Come over here!"

The Chinese rose complacently and came toward McGill.

"Turn around!" McGill said.

The Chinese turned around. McGill frisked him, took a small pistol from his pocket. Then McGill hefted his own gun.

"I don't usually do this, but—"

His gun banged against the Chinaman's head. The Chinaman slumped to the floor. McGill dragged him across the room and placed him behind a screen in the corner. Then he stood and listened to the faint sound of the wireless. He crossed to the rear door, opened it and found himself in a smaller room. It was deserted, but the sound of the wireless was more apparent. He opened a door and found himself in a corridor. He saw a short staircase.

He went up quietly, swiftly, and saw light streaming through an open door above. When he reached the doorway he saw a big wireless room and the back of a white man bent over the key. Cigarette smoke curled upward.

McGill entered the room and placed the muzzle of his gun against the man's neck. The man started and jerked around. McGill looked down into a white, pasty face, a slack mouth and sunken eyes.

McGill said, "I guess you're the guy I want."

The white man's mouth hung open.

"Up, baby," McGill said. "And we'll go out."

"Why—I—I—"

"Now never mind the song and dance. Get up!"

The white man staggered to his feet and as he did so McGill took away the gun that jutted from the man's hip pocket.

McGill said, "The quickest way out, brother—and the safest. Lead me into a trap and I'll blow you apart."

"What—what do you want with me?"

"Dumb-bell, you're goin' to tell the world what you know about this dirty racket. Get!"

He drove the man out into the corridor, down the stairs—held him up at the bottom.

"We're not goin' out the front way," he said. "Find another— and make it snappy."

The white man choked and stumbled down the lower corridor. He opened a door at the very end, looked into a room beyond. It was a storeroom. McGill drove him across it.

Bells began ringing.

The man cried, "That's the alarm!"

"Fast, brother!"

A DOOR opened and a big rangy Chinese came in carrying a revolver. He cried out and swung his gun toward McGill. Its muzzle blazed. The report was interlocked with McGill's—but while McGill stood erect, the rangy Chinaman crashed to the floor.

The wireless man screamed and turned on McGill, sent a kick at the red-head's stomach. McGill twisted and the foot caught him on the hip. He sidestepped and leveled his gun at the man.

"You fool, get goin'!" he barked furiously.

The man whimpered and turned and fled to the door through which the Chinese had come. McGill was at heels, and then the two of them were racing down a hallway. The wireless man flung open a door and daylight streamed in. McGill could see out into a yard, and he shoved the wireless man out.

The bells were still ringing.

A high board fence walled in the rear of the yard, and McGill drove the man toward it, yelled, "Scale it, brother!" McGill made a flying leap himself, swung one leg over the top and looked backward. He saw a man thrusting a rifle through the window. McGill fell over the fence as the rifle cracked, and the wireless man landed beside him.

"Quick! This way!" McGill clipped.

They started off down an alley, the wireless man coughing and choking. They reached a street and pounded along, soon came to a crowded thoroughfare, where McGill hailed a rikisha and hustled the wireless man in, jumped in beside him and bade the rikisha coolie show his heels.

It was a wild ride to the waterfront, and McGill kept repeating his threats and warnings.

"You act sweet now," he said. "You're goin' aboard my crate and we're takin' a little hop. You act nice at the pier."

"What are you going to do to me?"

"Nothing—except ask you questions later."

They reached the foreign settlement, drove up to the wharf where McGill had left his plane. The wireless man had calmed down, and McGill got him safely aboard the Vought. He handcuffed him in the rear cockpit, then started his motor and drove the Vought howling past the houseboats. He took off in a smother of spray, left the river behind and thundered up over the city.

He had what he wanted. He had one of the enemy's men. He had not chosen the scholarly Chinese because he knew that the man had sand and would die before revealing a secret. This white man was softer stuff—a wreck to look at. He would crack up.

McGill leveled off at two thousand feet and hit the gun for a hundred and twenty miles an hour. He was Hongkong bound.

MAJOR KIEF had seen service in Palestine, British Africa and North India. He was a sun-bitten rugged man of forty, and Sir Ian MacWhirr had put him in charge of affairs relative to the *Sky Hawk*. Kief was in his office when McGill came in lugging the wireless operator.

"By Jove!" exclaimed Kief. "What's this?"

"Take a look at it, Major," McGill said, tossing his captive into a chair. "Take a long look and then wash your eyes out. The boy friend goes by the name of Wardle."

Kief peered hard. "I say! He has a blacked eye, a welt on his cheek, and a cut on his jaw."

"He tried to run away after we landed," McGill said. "I tapped him a few times…. Put him aside for a minute, Major. What news of my partner?"

"The *Halcyon* wirelessed an hour ago that it had reached the vicinity. Finding no schooner, it is cruising now in a wide radius, in the hope that your friend and Miss Manners are still about."

"Well," McGill said. "I got a little inside dope. I figure Bill got away okey with the schooner. Somethin' happened to the *Sky Hawk* because she was down on the sea for repairs."

"Where did you hear this, McGill?"

"This," said McGill, indicating the wireless man, "is the Canton contact man. He operated the wireless. I heard the *Sky Hawk* reportin' but I thought you might ha' got more news. I skipped right out of Canton and now you can order someone there to clean out number 24 Sun Foo Street. That's their Canton Headquarters."

Major Kief stood up, put his hands behind his back, swelled his chest and laid a withering eye on the wireless operator.

"Wardle," he said, "what does this mean? Who is the leader of this abominable organization? Speak, man!"

Wardle gulped. "I—I'm only the wireless operator."

"I know you're the wireless operator," Kief ripped out hotly. "Therefore, being what you are, you must know much of the details. What is the strength of the organization? What is its mad purpose? But mainly"—Kief shook his fist—"who is the master mind behind it all?"

Perspiration gleamed on Wardle's face. He twisted his mouth, gnawed at his lips. "I—I don't know who is behind it. I tell you I'm only the wireless man. I received messages and sent them—at the commands of others. I was hired in Canton, picked out of an opium dive, given a big salary and told to keep my mouth shut. I didn't even know what organization it was until—later."

"And yet you continued to work for it?"

"Yes. I was warned that I was in the net, that if I tried to escape I would be killed."

Kief snarled, "Spineless jellyfish that you are!"

McGill cut in, "Mind if I speak a minute, Major?" And when the Major nodded McGill turned on Wardle.

"I was listenin' when you spoke through the loudspeaker to the Chink in the office. You said the *Sky Hawk* was headin' for Base 2. Now, where is Base 2?"

The man squirmed. "I tell you I don't know!"

"Putrid liar!" boomed Kief.

"I don't know!" cried Wardle.

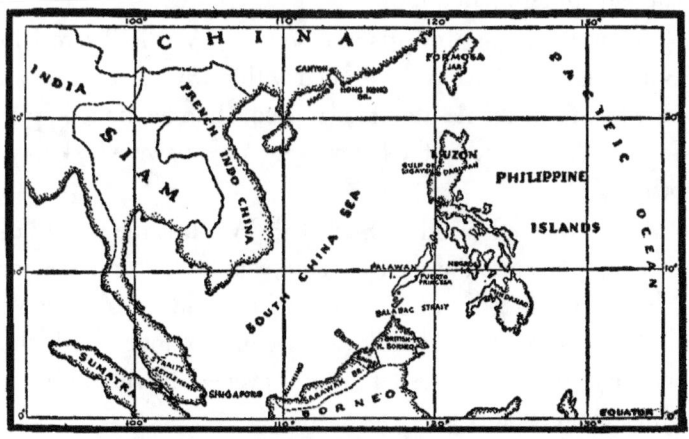

Where the *Sky Hawk* ranged. It was due south of Hongkong, and due west of Dagupan, on the island of Luzon, that McGill picked up the unsuspecting *Mirador*. Then the South China saw a fight.

Kief took three fast steps, laid a hand on Wardle and yanked him to his feet. "Wardle," Kief said grimly, "you will talk and you will talk presently. These outrages cannot go on forever. You are as much a murderer as the rest, and the penalty for you will be just as severe… unless, Wardle, you speak. In which case I shall try to minimize the charges against you."

Wardle's knees buckled. He drooped from Kief's powerful arm, the sweat dripping from his face. Kief's face remained grim and hard as granite. He was a relentless man, a man who had been hardened on raw frontiers.

Wardle cried, "Honest to God, Major—I don't know! I'm only the wireless man. I know nothing about their plans. I've never even seen the boss. I tell you, I've never been out of the house in Canton since the day I walked in, a month ago. I know there are wireless stations in Shanghai, Saigon and Singapore, and I know there are secret agents in many cities. But I don't know their addresses, and I don't know where the stations are. I know there are three bases—called One, Two and Three—but, honest, I don't know where they are."

Kief's face was dark with contempt. He flung the man from him, muttered an oath, and stood making a face as though the man had contaminated him.

"What a crawling bit of slime you are, Wardle! Were I in frontier camp I'd have you whipped with rawhide to within an inch of your miserable life!" He snorted. Then he looked up at McGill. "Well, it seems the fellow is merely a pawn who knows nothing."

McGill was red-faced with chagrin. Was this the reward of his having gone into the enemy's camp, shot his way out, brought with him a man whom he had thought would reveal valuable information? With Bill still adrift, still in danger, with the solution of the mystery as far away as ever—McGill felt bitter against circumstances.

And yet a thought clicked in the back of his head.

"Look here, Major!" he said warmly. "There's somethin' this palooka does know! They were usin' code—secret code—in their messages. *By hell, he knows the code!*"

CHAPTER VIII

SHIP-WRECK

AT NOON of the day on which McGill brought Wardle to Hongkong, Gales and the girl Gwen Manners were sailing the schooner *Homeward* toward the west under light following winds that hardly disturbed her canvas. At dusk of the night before they had triumphantly eluded the *Sky Hawk*. They had sailed by the stars, and now, at noon, Gales shot the sun and thereby got an idea of where they were.

"We must be a couple of hundred miles east of the island of Hainan," he said. "But if the wind doesn't pick up we're going to be calmed. And I wonder if Mike got through."

Gwen was leaning against the wheel. "I pray God he did." She went on, "I wonder if the *Sky Hawk* has made repairs and is on the wing again. I wonder where it will strike next." Her eyes roamed the horizon.

They did not know that the destroyer *Halcyon* was looking for them. They did not know what McGill had done in Canton. The long hours aboard the *Homeward* had drawn them close together, and their only hope was to reach land or sight a coasting steamer. That—and the hope that McGill was safe.

That afternoon the dead calm locked them in its passive grip. The sails hung limp, and the sea was a burnished plate beneath the sun. Gwen made a meal in the galley. Gales had drawn the ten dead men into the bows, covered them with a tarpaulin. Now he stood by the wheel, running his binoculars around the penciled horizon for sight of smoke or a sail.

The day dragged by and night came, but the dead calm held. The darkness was relief from the sun and from the possibility of being picked up by the *Sky Hawk* again. But the heat seemed to remain like an invisible hot blanket flung over the schooner. Man and girl stood watches, four on and four off, but all through the humid darkness no light appeared on the dark horizon. Dawn came, and then the red sun—but no breath of breeze.

The sun had not been up two hours when a breeze sprung up, suddenly, ominously. Clouds came over the rim of the sea in great black masses, and soon the sun was blotted out. Thunder began to rumble. When Gales had set the sails the schooner bowled along rapidly, the wind grew in velocity, began to whine in the halyards.

The storm broke at noon. It seemed to burst overhead, and rain came down in great torrents, lightning crackled and speared the clouds. The sea snarled and broke in huge rollers, and the wind became a gale, banging in the canvas. The schooner heaved and lunged drunkenly, and Gwen clung grimly to the wheel while Gales kept after the sails. Time and time again he was knocked down by boarding seas, until Gwen screamed for him to come aft and stay out of danger.

"You can't do a thing!" she cried.

He was not a sailor. He was a birdman. But he tried his best, even though his best was no match for the storm. He fought his way aft to the wheel, relieved Gwen and tried to hold the schooner's bow into the storm. He had some success in this, though before half an hour was up the wind ripped the canvas from the sticks, the boarding seas lifted the dead men in the bows and carried them off. Gales could see nothing but spume smoking. The wind and the rain had torn off his shirt; it blinded him, the salt spindrift got down his throat, choked him.

Then there was a terrific jar. Out of the tail of his eye Gales saw Gwen flung against the bulwarks, yelled madly for her to hang on. He leaped from the wheel, reached her, held her, while the schooner heeled way over, a wave hammered them to the deck, tried to tear them away from the rail.

For a moment the schooner seemed to stand motionless, then lunged, bows tunneling another wave that swept the deck fore and aft. The bows lifted hugely, the water boiled down the scuppers, and the schooner went staggering on.

Gales, breathless, said, "We've hit something!"

"Yes! I felt it!"

THEY WON back to the wheel, and both gripped it, Gales on one side, the girl on the other. Soon they noticed a slight list to starboard, noticed that the seas were boarding the starboard rail easily.

"We struck a reef!" Gales bellowed. "There's water in the hold."

"What shall we do?"

"Nothing. Nothing but hang on. Look! The clouds are breaking in the north!"

What could they do but hang on? There was a lifeboat, but it could not be launched in such weather. And they were certain now that the schooner had sprung a leak. They could see the bows burying lower each time the waves struck. Half an hour later the fore-deck was awash, and the schooner was logging sluggishly, a broken skeleton doomed to go down before long.

But suddenly the wind abated, the rain stopped. The racket of the storm died like a whistling breath, and only the running seas remained.

"We've got to get off in the small boat," Gales said.

He slushed knee-deep in water to the galley, got a jug of Water and some hard-tack, came aft and stowed them in the small boat. He freed the tackle until the small boat was adrift and then drew it alongside by means of a lanyard. Gwen went down, and Gales followed, and she was swinging out an oar even as he sat down beside her to take one himself. They pulled off, and were less than half a mile away when the *Homeward* went down.

Gales said grimly, "Another mark against the *Sky Hawk*. Gwen, I'm going to bring those birds to justice if it takes the rest of my life!"

She heaved on the oar, smiled and said, "Do you know you called me Gwen?"

"I'm sorry," he said, missing a stroke.

She laughed. "Don't be sorry, Bill."

An hour later the seas calmed down. And two hours later they sighted smoke in the north. Both yelled the news to each other at the same time.

"Oh, I'm so happy, Bill!"

"In plain words, Gwen, you've been through hell. You just go ahead and yell for joy all you want."

RUSTY-PLATED, WITH a single cigarette funnel well abaft the beam, the *Mirador* lay to and her master, leaning in the lee wing of the open navigating bridge, yelled down:

"Just take it easy comin' alongside, mister. Mr. Willey, you at the pilot ladder?"

"Aye, sir."

Mr. Willey, the third mate, flung a lanyard down to Gales, and Gales made it fast to the small boat. Then Gwen went up the rope ladder and Gales followed, and a curious crowd of passengers—no more than a dozen—gazed at them.

The captain met them on the bridge deck and shifted a black cheroot to say, "Wrecked, eh? Well, I've seen worse castaways in my time."

"This is Miss Manners," Gales said. "And I'm Bill Gales of the Straits Agency. We've been aboard the schooner *Homeward* for a couple of days. She went down about three hours ago. I was—"

"Well!" exploded the skipper, rocking on his heels. "So it's Gales, is it? Many's the tale I've heard of you, Gales—and that partner o' yours McGill. And Miss Manners! This is a pleasure. I'll see you both get good bunks."

"Where are you from?" Gales asked.

"Hongkong to Bangkok. We left Hongkong yesterday afternoon much against the warnin' o' the Admiralty. Huh. This

Sky Hawk business again. Rumor had it your pal McGill kidnaped a secret agent and found the *Sky Hawk,* if such there is, was plannin' to raid us. I—"

"Wait!" Gales broke in, gripping the skipper's arm. "You say—McGill is safe in Hongkong?"

"Was when I left, though folks say he won't be for long."

Gales began laughing jerkily, happily; and not knowing what to do for a moment, he shook the skipper's hand, then shook Gwen's hand, saying, "I—I knew the old boy would get through. How far are we from Hongkong, Captain?"

" 'Bout two hundred fifty miles, I'd say. And our first port o' call is Saigon. Huh. The way them fellers worried about the *Sky Hawk!* I ain't worryin'. I been fightin' off Chink pirates for twenty years on this Coast. I ain't worryin'. Besides, I got me some machine guns on board."

When Gwen had gone to a stateroom, Gales got the skipper in the cabin and talked turkey.

"Listen, Captain," he said grimly. "Miss Manners has undergone an awful experience. Put into the nearest port. Her father is one of the richest men on the Coast, and he'll reimburse you. I'm sure o' that."

Captain Skinker was amused. "What? Worryin' about that *Sky Hawk* business?"

"Yes. I don't care if you have got machine guns. I'll bet you haven't the men to handle 'em. Besides, this *Sky Hawk* is armed to the teeth, and it carries bombs. I tell you, man, I've seen it!"

"Mr. Gales, my first port o' call will be Saigon. Have a drink?"

Gales thumped the wicker desk. "Captain, please listen to reason. I want to get the girl ashore. I want to get her out of danger. I tell you, you can't lose financially. Her father—"

"I'm sorry, Mr. Gales. I'm a day behind schedule as is." He downed a tot of Scotch neat. "You'll have to go to Saigon with us. I'm very sorry. I'm carryin' a valuable cargo o' Chinee silk for the King o' Siam, and he ain't a patient chum."

"You were a fool to put to sea!"

"Eh? Suppose I hadn't? You'd still be in the open boat. I bid you good-day, Mr. Gales."

Gales glared at the complacent old skipper. Then he said, "Well, this you can do. Wireless Hongkong—the American Embassy. Tell them to send McGill after you. Don't say anything about Miss Manners being on board. Mike will come. Will you do that?"

"I can do that very well."

"Thanks."

Gales went out very much on his dignity.

Five minutes later the wireless operator was talking with Hongkong.

CHAPTER IX

THE EAGLE FLIES

McGILL WAS like a hound on a leash, waiting to go places, but having no place to go.

The *Halcyon* was steaming back to Hongkong after having battled her way through a terrific storm. She had been unable to locate the *Homeward*, find any trace of it.

Wardle had come through with the secret code after several hours of grilling the day before, and Major Kief, bound to make use of the code, had given out dispatches that Wardle was near death after refusing to give up any secrets of the enemy. This, Kief thought, would stop the enemy from changing to a new code.

"But I gotta do somethin'!" McGill ripped out, pacing the Major's office. "Where's Bill? Where's the schooner. Ah-r-r, they probably got Bill, and sunk the schooner! Listen—if somethin' don't burst soon I'm just goin' places anyhow. I gotta do somethin'! I can't sit here waitin'. I can't!"

"I know, McGill. I know how you feel. But try to wait. Don't run into danger. Don't be like that skipper of the *Mirador*, putting to sea in the face of all our warnings. You're too valuable a man to lose on a foolhardy pointless flight."

"But, Major, I just gotta go places—"

An orderly came in and laid a message on the desk, saluted and went out.

Kief leaned over what looked like a hodgepodge of meaningless words:

Npwf dboupo cbtf up bnpz xf bsf mfbwjoh cbtf pof opx up nffu njsbepo.

McGill went around the desk to look over his shoulder.

"This is a message from the *Sky Hawk*," Kief said. "I spot the word *Mirador*. Let's see now. According to Wardle, it is merely a matter of shifting one letter forward in the alphabet. That is, the B in the message means A, C means B, and so on until we come to A again, which is Z. Now let's unravel this."

He picked up a pencil and began working. To change the code message into readable English, he had to replace each letter by a letter alphabetically preceding it. The result was this:

Move Canton base to Amoy. We are leaving Base One now to meet Mirador.

"There!" Kief exclaimed. "I knew it. The *Mirador* is to be raided."

"And it says 'meet,' Major, which oughter mean the *Sky Hawk* is headin' from some place south."

"I must wireless the *Mirador* immediately."

He was about to summon the orderly when the latter entered with another message saying, "This was forwarded from the United States Embassy, for Mr. McGill."

McGill grabbed it, tore it open, read:

Proceed immediately to overtake us. Urgent. Explain later. We are in latitude eighteen north; longitude one hundred thirteen east.
John Skinker, Master,
S.S. Mirador.

McGill tossed the message on the deck and said, "Get a load o' that, Major! I'm goin' places for sure now!"

The Major read it. "Don't be foolish, McGill! This message is absurd!"

"There's somethin' in it. I'll be seein' you sometime."

To the orderly Kief gave a scrawled note. "Have this wirelessed immediately to the *Mirador*.... McGill, don't be a bloody ass! I tell you—"

"I got a hunch, Major. The hunch says, 'Go, Mike, and ye shall find.' I'm pilgrimin' south pronto. *Adios!*"

He grabbed up his topee, went out of the door like a blast of wind.

HE DID not bother going to his hotel. He hailed a rikisha, threatened to break the coolie's neck if he didn't break a couple of world sprinting records, and jumped in. He rode the rikisha like a cowboy, and if no records were broken to the waterfront, McGill figured there was something wrong with the world.

His tanks were full. He had everything in readiness. He started his motor and warmed it up impatiently. He got his mooring lines free and was climbing back into the control cockpit while the Vought drifted clear. He taxied out into the roadstead, swung the crate around to put it into the wind, and then opened everything wide.

He lifted the Vought low over the Bund in a thunder of great-lunged power. He howled over the city of Hongkong, got the altitude he wanted, then leveled off and opened the throttle wide. He tooled the crate south in a bee-line for Hainan, and thanked his stars that he had some excuse for starting.

Not much of an excuse, to be sure. The *Mirador's* message was silly, yet there was something cryptic about it. Under ordinary circumstances McGill would have pitched it in the basket.

But there was a chance that something vital lay behind it, and he knew the *Sky Hawk* was heading for the southbound vessel.

What could he do if he met the *Sky Hawk* on the wing? Logically, nothing. As a matter of fact, he had no plan figured out. He was going blindly into a danger and in a vague way he realized it.

But he did not care. He had visions of meeting the *Sky Hawk*, getting close enough to it to heave a couple of grenades, or chasing it to one of its bases. Absurd again. But if he foresaw doom the moment he sighted the air plunderer, he would be licked before he started. He chose to anticipate success for himself instead of the enemy, thereby keeping his nerve at high water.

He got a wild ride south of Hongkong. Atmospheric conditions after the storm were unsettled, erratic, and the Vought hit some queer bumps, got in the way of some freakish drafts. The plane staggered, wheeled, and once its tail whipped from side to side violently.

McGill took the best with the worst, and two and a half hours out of Hongkong he roared low over the northernmost tip of Hainan, changed his course to southeast, and left land behind. Luck came his way in the shape of a smoother air trail, and the sea looked calm below.

When he figured he was near the position reported by the *Mirador* he began using glasses. Of course, he had a hazy idea of where he was, but by no means could he have steered to the exact position. The electrical storm had cleared the air considerably; hence with the use of his binoculars, considering his height above sea-level, McGill figured that he would be able to spot a ship within a radius of twenty-five miles.

He cruised at about eight-hundred feet circling and at the same time working his way southward. He used up half an hour doing this and began to get sore. If only he had Bill along. There was a guy could take a chart and a lot of gadgets and lead you by the hand to a spot a thousand miles away.

McGill cursed.

Then he stopped cursing.

There was a dot on the horizon. He kicked right rudder bar and turned on his ear, straightened out and opened his gun. He kept the binoculars glued to his eyes, and soon he saw the dot grow bigger, saw a smudge now above it.

"Come on, baby!" he yelled to his plane.

MINUTES CLICKED past. The dot grew in size, took on the semblance of a ship. McGill became restive in his seat. Yes, it was a ship, and as the minutes sped by McGill could pick out more details. It was the ship he had seen steam out of Hongkong.

It was the *Mirador*.

She was still steaming along, kicking up a white wake.

Out of the blue bolted McGill and his White Vought. He sloped down over the *Mirador's* stern, bent around her bow to give them a full view of the words Straits Agency painted on the plane's flank. Rising again, he saw that the wake was growing smaller.

He eased up on the gun and let the Vought have her way about going down. The plane smacked the water to the lee and twenty yards ahead of the vessel, and then McGill gave the motor some juice and headed for the pilot ladder hanging down from the rail amidships.

Who was the fool waving his arms and standing on the rail? The sap would fall overboard if he didn't look out. Who?—By cripes, it couldn't be! Was it? It looked like him, and yet— Great guns, it was! It was Bill!

McGill yelled, "Bill, Bill! Hey, Billy boy! Doggone you! Dog—"

He pushed the throttle up a little more and the plane moved faster. Then McGill retarded it until the prop was barely turning over and making a slight swishing sound.

"Hi, Mike!"

"You—you old horsefly, you!"

Gales came down the pilot ladder, stopped on a rung near the water and leaned out catching hold of the plane's wing.

McGill threw him a line, and Gales fastened it temporarily to the ladder, then climbed out on the wing and grabbed McGill's outstretched hand. Now that they saw each other alive, they pretended to take it all lightly, though in their hearts was the ache after the long suspense.

"Well, Mike, I've seen you bring a crate down better than that before."

McGill poked him in the chest. "Ah, you. What you been doin'—cruisin' around with the jane? Forgettin' you got a job? Leavin' me in the lurch? Ah, janes, Bill… they'll get you yet."

"I mind a time in Saigon when you said one of God's most wonderful creatures was girl. The only thing better, you said, were two girls."

McGill got slightly crimson. "If it's all the same to you, let's talk about the weather. The skipper get the warnin' from Hong-kong?"

"Yes. And it happens the destroyer *Halcyon* is steaming this way too, to escort this wagon to Saigon—just in case. The skipper expects to raise her any minute."

"How about the *Sky Hawk?*"

"No sign of her yet. Say, Mike, would you like to come up and meet my fiancée?"

"Your"—McGill gulped—"which?"

"Gwen Manners and I have decided to hitch up some day soon and raise pilots. Come on up."

McGill's jaw hardened. "Nix. I got no use for dames. If you're still flyin' with me say your farewells to the petticoat and come on. Besides, I don't like rope ladders."

Captain Skinker demanded, "What do you men intend doin'?"

"Get goin', Bill," Mike said. "Remember, you're still workin' for the Straits Agency, and though we get the reward for savin' the jane, you're still workin' for the Straits Agency and you're not through yet."

FOR A brief instant Gales looked hurt. Then he said, "Of course I'm going with you. I planned to take Gwen with us and strike out for land. But she'll be safer on the ship, now that the *Halcyon* is coming to convoy it to Saigon. You and I'll loaf aloft until the *Halcyon* arrives. I'll be right down."

"Okey. Neck the jane and snap on it."

Gales clipped, "Listen, Mike, you go on talking like that and I'll crack you in the mouth. She's a wonderful—"

"Go ahead, big boy. Go up and then come down and smack me." McGill dropped back into the cockpit and sulked.

Gales went up on deck and explained matters to the captain. He spent a minute with Gwen in her stateroom. Her arms were around his neck.

"God be with you, Bill, and bring you back to me."

"I'll come back, Gwen. You've been wonderful through all this. I'll be lonesome."

"So will I, Bill—awfully. Be careful, dear. Don't take chances."

One last embrace—and then Gales was striding out on deck, down to the head of the ladder, over the rail and down to the waiting plane. McGill sat grimly in front puffing on a cigarette. Gales loosed the line and coiled it up, stowed it away. McGill didn't look at him. Gales muttered an oath and climbed into the rear cockpit.

"Okey?" McGill called over his shoulder.

"Shoot."

McGill took off in a smother of foam, almost wrecked the plane. He was seeing red. He was mad. Mad at Bill and mad at himself for being mad at Bill.

Was a jane going to bust up a hard-flying comradeship that had lasted eight years through good fortune and bad? One of these society dames.

Well—he mused—as soon as she got back to civilization and safety, maybe she'd forget all about Bill. That would be jake. And yet—tough on poor Bill.

CHAPTER X

WING BUSTERS

THE *MIRADOR* moved ahead at reduced speed, its lookout watching and waiting for the first glimpse of the *Halcyon*. Another lookout kept an eye peeled for the dread *Sky Hawk*. The skipper went slushing about deck with his monumental unconcern. He cracked jokes about the *Sky Hawk*.

The Vought loafed at five thousand feet, McGill tooling it gently back and forth or in lazy circles. Gales rarely had his binoculars away from his eyes. He was looking for both the *Halcyon* and the *Sky Hawk*.

He saw the *Sky Hawk* first, coming out of the south. He picked up the speaking tube, buzzed McGill.

"*Sky Hawk,* Mike."

"Where's she?"

"Due south."

McGill used his glasses. "Yeah. I see her. We'll go right after her."

"Let's."

Gales took the hood off the machine gun, fired a burst to test the mechanism. McGill took another thousand feet of altitude, then straightened out and opened the throttle wide. He hunched himself in the cockpit, ran his eyes over the dials. Everything was all right. He looked over his safety belt. That was all right.

He yelled back through the tube, "You in tight, boy?"

And Gales replied, "Real cozy, Mike. I figure she'll drop off her two planes any minute. We'll blaze right through them first and put a scare into the big baby. I'll heave a grenade if you can get close enough."

"I'll scrape her paint with the pontoons, brother."

They left the *Mirador* behind, their aim being to keep the fight away from the vessel as long as possible. They saw that the *Sky Hawk*, now recognizable, was not altering her course a bit. She was intending to plow right through, no doubt. She was still about three miles off when she dropped her two single-seaters. The small planes compared as crows to an eagle in size. Yet they were dangerous because of their maneuverability.

Soon the thunder of the big plane's motors were heard above the thunder of the Vought's. The small planes were about a quarter mile ahead of the *Sky Hawk*, flying close together. McGill held his course in a bee-line for the *Sky Hawk*, Gales was ready at the Lewis gun.

The small brown plane opened fire first, her synchronized Vickers snapping lead through her shimmering prop. The lead spattered the Vought's wing.

McGill ground his teeth, held resolutely to his course, aiming to go between the two planes. The gray plane cut loose with a burst that snarled in the Vought's landing gear. Grimly McGill clung to his course. Grimly Gales waited with his Lewis gun.

At exactly the right instant, when he was almost between the two planes, McGill yanked back on the stick. The Vought leaped upward. The gray plane, veering inward, cut loose with a burst that went well beneath the Vought's pontoons. Gales swung his Lewis downward, let fly.

The gun vibrated. Its lead ripped a gash in the gray plane just aft the headrest fairing. The gray plane almost did a barrel roll getting out of danger. The brown plane banked sharply, and Gales swung his gun around at it, let fly with a burst that tore through the plane's wing, started fabric flying in the wind.

Now the *Sky Hawk* was dead ahead—five hundred yards ahead, ten props thrashing, ten motors roaring. There was the gun sticking from the bow, the gunner tense behind it.

Behind the Vought came the small planes.

McGILL'S HAND was gingerly on the stick, his eyes fixed on the *Sky Hawk*. When it seemed the two planes must crash head on, McGill drew back on the stick. At the same instant the *Sky Hawk's* bow gun opened fire. Lead snarled through the under part of the Vought's fuselage.

The Vought was roaring low over the *Sky Hawk*. Gales raised his arm.

The arm went outward and downward. A grenade smacked the top of the *Sky Hawk*, bounced harmlessly off. A dud!

McGill zoomed, and while the Vought's nose was sticking skyward, Gales swung his gun down and opened fire on the tail gun even as the tail gun sent lead into their empennage. Gales silenced that gun. Two guns placed on the top of the great wing opened fire, riddled the Vought's wing. The two small planes were zooming too.

McGill leveled off abruptly, then made a sharp turn, opened his throttle wide and went screaming off after the brown monoplane. The gray plane swooped to head him off.

McGill promptly turned on the gray plane, wheeled away from its prop, and Gales started lead singing through the wind. That stream of lead opened the gray plane's cowl, carried away its windshield. The gray plane swung away for cover, and McGill whipped the Vought around until he was storming head-on toward the brown plane.

Suddenly he shoved forward on the stick, dived beneath the brown plane, slammed the throttle into the last notch and headed after the *Sky Hawk*.

Creeping up on the big crate, McGill began to tack on altitude until he was a thousand feet above it. He passed over it, passed over machine gun fire from its wing guns, got ahead of it. Gales took a look through his binoculars at the *Mirador*, a mile north.

Beyond the *Mirador* he saw a cloud of smoke coming over the horizon. His blood leaped. That must be the *Halcyon!*

He yelled this information to McGill through the speaking tube. McGill waved his hand.

The *Sky Hawk* must have seen that smoke, too, because she was reducing speed, beginning to turn. The two small planes, in hot pursuit of the Vought, saw the *Sky Hawk* turning and turned with it. Gales, looking at the *Sky Hawk* through his glasses, saw a man standing up in the nose cockpit and waving two flags in the wind.

Signals to the small planes! What sort of signals? Retreat?

The small planes were going round and round the *Sky Hawk*, and the big plane had turned completely around and was moving southward at a low rate of speed.

The small planes took a position to protect her tail. Gales and McGill went after them. The two planes saw them coming and turned to fight. The brown plane took the initiative, headed for the Vought. McGill kicked right rudder bar and banked sharply, then advanced his throttle and started around the brown plane.

The gray one moved to protect the *Sky Hawk*, and McGill swung left and started around it. At four thousand feet, he shoved forward on the stick, sliced the wind in a terrific power dive that carried him well ahead of both small planes and set him on the *Sky Hawk's* tail again.

Rising powerfully, gradually, he had the Whirlwind pulling the crate to the last ounce of speed. He got up under the *Sky Hawk's* belly, so close that neither port nor starboard guns could reach him. In order to remain there he had to reduce speed, and this would allow the small planes to catch up with them.

But it gave Gales time to get a line on the *Sky Hawk's* empennage, and his lead slashed viciously through rudders and stabilizers. Then he swung his gun upward and pounded lead into its hull.

BUT THE small planes were drawing near. McGill saw this and shoved forward on his stick again, power-diving to five hundred feet and then leveling off and getting away in a straight hard run that carried them well beyond the *Sky Hawk's* range. When they were five miles ahead of the *Sky Hawk*, and at four thousand feet, McGill roared into an Immelmann, swung out of it nicely, and headed for the brown plane, which was about four hundred yards ahead of the gray one.

The brown plane's Vickers began to hammer out lead and the lead walloped the underside of the Vought forward. Gales waited another split minute and then started the Lewis going.

His first burst tore open the brown plane's cowl. The second burst demolished the windshield. The third burst sent the brown plane into a sheet of flame, and the Vought howled past so close that Gales felt the heat—and flying metal rattled against the Vought's white flank.

Then the gray plane was directly ahead. Beyond it, the mammoth *Sky Hawk*. Instead of bearing against the gray plane, McGill kicked left rudder bar and wheeled away, drawing the gray plane after him. He led it away steadily, until both planes were two miles on the *Sky Hawk's* starboard bow.

McGill made a short turn, skidded, and the wind howled into the cockpits. Flank to the gray plane, Gales opened fire, and kept the lead going until the gray plane turned away and began to climb. McGill did not climb after it. He dropped lower and began cruising at two thousand feet, and Gales pointed his gun skyward and waited.

The gray plane stopped climbing at six thousand feet, circled warily while the Vought circled below. Apparently the gray plane couldn't resist the temptation. She stuck her nose downward and power-dived. Her Vickers began spouting before she was within range. Gales waited the fraction of a minute, then opened up.

It was a case of dog eat dog. Gales saw his windshield disappear. He saw McGill's headrest fairing ripped apart, saw part of his own cockpit coaming gashed open. But he kept his gun working, drove lead into the diving plane.

Two hundred feet above, the gray plane flattened out, its motor seemed to diminish. It started upward faultingly, stalled, wobbled, flopped over and began tail-spinning downward. McGill heard the *Sky Hawk* approaching with a roar. McGill took one look and sloped off on a full throttle.

Gales saw the gray plane smash to the sea, saw steam rise. The *Sky Hawk* banked hugely over the crashed plane, circled once and then thundered on its way—south. McGill, hovering afar, came back and saw only oil on the water. He banked, opened his gun wide and took up the trail of the *Sky Hawk*.

Now dusk was settling, laying its first broad shadows over the sea. Gales put the wireless headphones on and got in touch with the *Mirador*.

He said, *"Two small planes downed. We are following the Sky Hawk southward."*

The operator on board the *Mirador* replied, *"We are proceeding for Saigon under convoy of the Halcyon. Miss Manners sends love."*

Gales grinned to himself.

THEY WERE half a mile behind the *Sky Hawk*. The big plane did not choose to turn and fight it out. Her two planes had been demolished and she was no doubt heading for one of her bases. The way she clung to her course indicated that she was certain she could outstrip the Vought merely because her fuel would last longer.

When darkness came down McGill crept closer until the sound of the *Sky Hawk's* motors could be heard. Gales checked their gas and found they had enough to fly another two hundred miles. They were doing ninety-five miles an hour in the big plane's wake, and the big plane was little more than a shadow until the moon came up.

Half an hour later they were surprised to find themselves on the edge of land. The *Sky Hawk* was now flying in a southeasterly direction down the coast. An hour later Gales saw a beam of light spring up from the shrouded coast. McGill eased up on the throttle.

The *Sky Hawk* began to knock off altitude, and the beam of light swept the sky, then went out. Next, a luminous glow appeared on the coast. Then the big plane dropped lower and lower, and Gales peered hard. He was certain now that the big plane was going down, and the lights that had sprung up indicated that this was one of her bases.

The *Sky Hawk* flew low over the darkened earth, then appeared above a small inlet illuminated by floodlights. McGill edged closer, and Gales saw the *Sky Hawk* alight and foam through the water.

"Her base," Gales said through the speaking tube.

"Yeah. Should we drop in for a drink?"

The floodlights went out. The coast was dark again.

McGill tooled the Vought on a low throttle, cruising out over the sea. He drawled through the speaking tube.

"Well, we can't go far, boy. What's your idea?"

"Poke along, Mike. We'll have to go down at any rate."

McGill advanced the throttle a bit and continued down the coast. He dropped the plane lower until they were droning along at three hundred feet.

Gales picked up the tube. "Looks like a lagoon, Mike! Get over it and I'll drop some flares."

McGill pulled back on the stick, curved over the coast and came back to the small inlet. He flew low over it, and they saw that it was deserted, with trees growing to the water's edge.

"We'll try it," Gales said.

McGill rose and Gales dropped a parachute flare, watched it and got an idea of the wind velocity.

"Out to sea a little more, Mike."

McGill banked slowly and followed instructions. He cut his gun and Gales started three flares downward. He saw the wind carrying them toward the coast. McGill banked again, pointed his nose downward.

The flares drifted past the mouth of the small inlet. One snagged in a tree but kept burning. Another landed on a sandbar. The third reached the inner shore and burned there.

Mike dropped lower carefully. The water was faintly illumined. Enough to afford visibility, but care had to be taken. McGill tightened to his job. The plane crossed the inlet's mouth. McGill drew back slightly on the stick. The plane was level when the pontoons struck. But the pontoons struck hard.

Water banged up against the fuselage, sprayed over the men, hissed on a hot motor. The plane heaved mightily, scooping up water with its left wing, yawing around.

But gradually it settled, and the motor was still turning over. McGill headed the plane for the flare that burned on the inner shore. Near it, he shut off the ignition, and the plane drifted slowly. Its pontoons slushed into soft mud, and the branch of a tree flicked McGill's windshield.

Gales climbed out, carried a line ashore and made fast to a tree. McGill forked the coaming and lit a butt as the flare went out.

Gales said, "All right, Mike. Come ashore."

WHEN THEY stood on the shore, Gales got a light from McGill's butt and puffed up. It was dark as the pit among those great-trunked trees—and silent. The water lapped softly against the muddy bank, and moonlight shone from time to time on low ripples.

"Creepy joint," McGill said. "I'll get a flashlight."

He returned to the plane, got a pocket flash and carried it ashore. He stood beside Gales and swept the beam among the silent trees, up through the branches, then down again.

Gales said, "I have no idea where we are, Mike. Won't be able to figure out our position until noon tomorrow, when I can shoot the sun. Gosh, if I knew where we were I could wireless the *Halcyon!*"

"It looks," said McGill, "like we poke through the woods tomorrow and give this base the once-over."

The next instant he leaped back, cried out. His flash went out as glass splintered, and he yelled:

"Duck, Bill!"

Gales flopped down to the soggy earth, drawing his pistol. McGill had his own drawn. He fired blindly, and mingled with the echoes was the faint sound of footsteps speeding off on the wet rot.

"What was it, Mike?" Gales asked, breathless.

McGill said, "A blowpipe dart, Bill. It socked the flash and put it out. The guy shot it aimed for my stomach!"

"Which means," Gales said, "that they had a scout stationed here! Stay down, Mike! Don't budge! There may be another—and in this part of the world a blowpipe dart is poisoned!"

McGill growled, "Would I be shakin' like a leaf if I didn't know that, sweetheart!"

AN HOUR after the mysterious blowpipe dart had almost killed McGill, the two partners rose and stood side by side against a huge tree.

Gales said, "If you ask me, Mike, that guy *was* an enemy scout, stationed in this inlet to warn the enemy if anyone put in here. He must have heard us talking about the *Halcyon*. Now

I'd say he's gone off to warn the enemy, and if we stay here all night they're liable to spring a surprise."

McGill was not hopeful. "We got enough gas to fly a hundred miles. That ain't far."

"At least," Gales said, "we'll have to move. The sea's calm. We'll just run the plane out and drive down the coast a bit without taking off."

"You're the doctor, Bill. Come on."

They started the motor, swung the plane around, and chugged out of the small inlet. They went slowly down the coast for a matter of three miles until they found another inlet, smaller than the other but quite as dark. They had no trouble gaining entrance, and instead of tying up at the shore they dropped an anchor in the middle of the inlet and planned to stand watches.

This much they had accomplished since joining the Straits Agency: They had saved Gwen Manners, daughter of the tin king. McGill had crashed the Canton wireless station of the enemy, had run off with the wireless operator who had subsequently come across with the secret code. They had protected the *Mirador*. They had dealt a severe blow by downing two of the enemy's planes. Now, for the first time, they were near one of the enemy's three secret bases, but they had not sufficient fuel to be effective.

Their next move—Gales figured—was to get close to the base, minus their plane, and try to find out who was the mastermind behind the *Sky Hawk's* depredations. As yet, this was the deepest and darkest mystery of all. Who was the man? What motivated his brutal deeds? What was his most vulnerable spot?

He said, "One of us goes, Mike. The other stays with the plane. Let's toss. Heads I go. Tails you go."

"Toss it."

Gales tossed a coin, caught it in his open palm. "I go, Mike. You stay with the plane. Keep your eyes peeled for a ship, and if you see one, take off and overhaul it. You may be able to get some fuel. If not, maybe they'll haul the crate on board."

"And suppose you get caught tryin' to bust into the enemy's camp?"

"That's a chance." Gales lit a cigarette. "Get some sleep, Mike. I'll wake you in four hours."

AN HOUR after sunrise Gales was pushing his way north on the coast—alone. He carried his Colt's automatic, plenty of ammunition, and two hand grenades. There was no trail, but he managed to keep within sight of the sea, and sometimes he found beaches where the going was easy.

When he reached the inlet where he and McGill had first brought their crate down, he became cautious, and after scouting around for half an hour he found the spot where he and McGill had stood when the blowpipe dart came out of the darkness. Here he found footsteps other than he and McGill had left. There were many imprints, as though men had come during the night.

He had been right then. The unknown man who had sent the dart was an enemy scout. He had gone off and reported to the enemy, and some men had come to the inlet during the night to surprise the partners. When the partners were not there, the men must have returned to their base somewhere on the coast.

Gales found their trail. It was a narrow trail, but easy to follow. It appeared that many times a man or men had trod it. It did not follow the coast closely, but went inland, hardly ever turning. Foliage canopied it, and the sunlight pierced the foliage only at rare intervals. No breeze stirred, but insects were plentiful, and the ground was soggy with wet rot that had never dried out.

Gales wore only an undershirt, white pants and a topee. Each hip pocket bulged with a grenade, and his other pockets were crammed with cartridges. He carried his gun in his hand, ready to use it on a moment's notice. He carried water in a flask hung from his belt, and used it sparingly. He plodded through the heat of morning, through the greater heat of mid-day, and his white pants were muddy to the knees, water sopped in his canvas shoes, and his shirt was soaked with sweat.

The trail began to rise gently, then more abruptly, and he thought he saw a clearing beyond the trees ahead. He knew he was climbing a headland, and soon he saw the sea off on his right. He approached the edge of the timber, and he could see a bay beyond, and he knew then that he was nearing the enemy's base. When he reached the crest of the headland he stopped and leaned against a tree. Yes, there was the bay, with the neck in the bottle entrance.

AT FIRST glance it looked deserted. In fact, he had to search intently before he saw the first sign of life. He saw the shape of a man moving among the trees on the northern bank. Then, farther in, he saw a wide platform built out over the water. This platform was covered with leaves and branches and vines, and only by keening his eyes could he see the nose of the *Sky Hawk* beneath it. The hide-out was hidden from the sea by the headland. A plane flying above would mark down the platform as natural jungle growth. Nothing was visible.

After a while Gales moved along the crest of the headland toward the platform, and soon he heard the sound of a motor. Not a plane's motor, but possibly a gasoline engine. And he heard a sound that was like metal being struck by metal. He stopped when he saw nearby the flash of sunlight on something bright. He peered hard. It was one of the big floodlights near the water's edge. Possibly the engine he heard was the one used to generate electricity.

Gales thought he had gone far enough for the time being. He hid in thick bushes and waited for darkness. He longed for a smoke, as much to settle his nerves as keep away the droves of insects. But he dared not light up.

When the darkness came he saw a few lights begin to glow in the trees, far back from the shore. He got up and moved toward the lights. He passed within twenty yards of the edge of the big camouflaged platform. The base of it extended well over the shore. He saw several lanterns beneath it, and in the lantern-light he saw half a dozen men and the tail of the big plane. They were working on her stabilizers.

He pushed on into the darkness of the jungle and came to three big shapes set deep in the trees. They were boxlike, about twenty feet tall, constructed of metal plates. He did not have to guess a second time to know they were fuel storage tanks. Still farther on were the lights.

They were the lights of a small group of houses constructed of boards with thatched roofs. Gales counted six in all, three of them showing lights. The sound of the big gasoline engine was nearer.

Gales no longer walked erect. He was down on his knees, and he muscled his way through the outlying bushes cautiously. Soon he crouched behind a tree near one of the smaller buildings. He could see the heads and shoulders of six men. They were seated at a table. They were white men, and he heard the sound of dice rolling on the table.

He moved away from the building, crawled through the bushes and crouched outside another. Through the window he could see one man sitting at a table, three standing and looking down over the man's shoulder. They were white, too—but they spoke in a foreign tongue.

After a few minutes Gales pushed on until he drew near the third lighted building, which was the largest of the lot. Here he had to work his way to within ten feet of a window. He heard voices, and then he saw a man sitting back in a chair and smoking a cigarette through an ivory holder at least a foot long.

This man was large, fat, and he wore a white suit, rimless spectacles. He was a Chinese and about him was the air of authority. Standing near him, and looking at him, were three men—one a slim Chinese, the others white. All were well-dressed.

The fat man was saying, "I think it advisable that we abandon this base. Although we have landed safely, and although the confounded Straits Agency plane left the inlet, still there is a possibility that these men Gales and McGill may be able to find our Number One Base."

The taller of the white men spoke—"Impossible! They couldn't have known where they landed. Why give up this base?"

THE FAT man was placid, purring on, "I have given my reason, Crag. We must take no unnecessary chances. Remember, we have just lost two planes and two excellent pilots. It is not the time to be headstrong. It is the time to be cautious, to bide one's time, to strike again when the opportunity presents itself."

"That is so," nodded the smaller of the white men, preening his dark mustache. "We must abandon this base, fly at sunrise to Base Number Two, and bide, as you so aptly put it, our valuable time."

The fat man said, "Count Pohly agrees with me, Crag. So does my eminent secretary Mr. Song Gow."

The young Chinese dropped a monocle from his eyes, smiled with an even row of white teeth, bowed. "Yes, sir."

Crag shrugged, scowled. "All right, if that's how you feel about it. But I didn't think we were going to be so la-de-da. We've lost the Canton wireless station. We've lost two planes and we didn't succeed in raiding the *Mirador*. We lost the girl and a nice fat ransom of a hundred thousand—and now we're crawling off to lick our wounds. Bah!"

The fat man smiled indulgently. "You were ever a headstrong man, my dear Crag. As I said, we abandon this base tomorrow morning. Wardle must have given up information despite the Hongkong reports to the contrary. They knew we were planning to raid the *Mirador*. Well, the new code goes into effect tomorrow. Gentlemen, one month from today I retire, my vengeance complete, great fortune in my coffers—and in yours. I return to Peking and become a mandarin, live out my years in peace. And none will know that my motive has been revenge. When I return to Peking, none will know that the illustrious Tai Yut has been a—pirate."

Tai Yut! At sound of that name a chord of Gales' memory was twanged. Where had he heard the name before? He'd heard it—somewhere sometime—during his four years in the yellow East.

There, sitting before his lieutenants, smoking a cigarette, was the mastermind behind the sinking of the *King's Castle*, the *Princess*, and the killing of two Straits Agency men. There was the man who had held Gwen captive, who had raided the *Homeward*.

Gales' hand tightened on his gun. He raised the gun, his jaw set. Then he lowered it, and fresh sweat burst from his pores.

He had a better idea. He crept back into the darkness of the jungle, worked his way through the thickets until he came within sight of the *Sky Hawk*. Here he sat down, mopping his face, to think his plan out in detail.

And the name of Tai Yut kept echoing in his brain....

CHAPTER XI

FLIGHT—AND FIGHT

AT **MIDNIGHT** the entire settlement lay in darkness. Gales could see a guard on the outer edge of the platform. Sometimes the guard paced back and forth, but mostly he remained seated. Gales was hiding behind a tree at the shoreward edge of the platform. He waited until the guard sat down again. Then he got down on hands and knees and crawled forward. He found a series of steps that led down the bank beneath the level of the platform. The steps ended at a footbridge that extended out over the water and beneath the platform. Now Gales was out of sight of the guard, and he stood up on the footbridge and took cautious steps. The tail of the giant plane was above his shoulder. He walked along its flank until he came to a door. He opened the door gently, climbed in, and closed the door behind him. He was in Stygian darkness.

The thumping of his heart against his ribs seemed to echo throughout the plane. He was, in a way of speaking, inside the enemy's stronghold. He could have shot down Tai Yut tonight, but what would that have availed him in the end? The others would have run him down, since they were no doubt familiar with the country. And if Tai Yut were killed, would not the others carry on? It was obvious that the loot was not stored at this base, else they would not abandon it so swiftly. Where, then, was Base Two?

Gales shoved his gun in his belt and put his hands out ahead of him, feeling his way through the darkness. He wanted to reach the rear of the plane. Presently he stubbed his toe, realized he had come to a stairway. He followed three steps upward and felt his way through a door. His hands found a table and some chairs, and he groped around the compartment for five minutes before he found another door.

Next he was in a corridor. He felt his way past four doors on left and right, and then went down a flight of four steps to another spacious chamber. He found another door in the rear, and then a corridor, and after a matter of a dozen feet he climbed a flight of six stairs and entered the tail gun cockpit. He heard, faintly, the guard pacing.

He returned down the stairs, paused at the base and felt around until he found another door. This was smaller than the others, and when he had opened it he had to bend way over to get in. He got down on hands and knees. He felt coils of rope, many wooden cases, parachutes, and other odds and ends. He was in a store-room. He was satisfied. He chose a corner behind the cases and sat down.

When the first glimmer of daylight came through the single small port, Gales heard distant voices and the sound of movement on board the plane. He looked at his strap watch. It was six-thirty. He heard feet tramping past the storeroom door, heard a man laugh. A door somewhere banged and there were no more footsteps nearby.

Then there was the burst of a motor, several backfires. Then the burst of other motors starting, all joining finally to make a deafening roar beneath the platform. Gales could feel the slight tremor of the plane. Looking through the port, he could see nothing but brackish water and the underside of the platform. Someone was revving the great power plant. The *Sky Hawk* rocked a bit.

After a while the roar decreased to a low rumble, and Gales knew the motors were turning over slowly. He saw a sampan go by with two Chinese in it. He saw them unloose the bow lines, then paddle back again. It was seven o'clock.

At seven-ten the motors roared again. The huge plane rocked and Gales saw the water flowing past. Suddenly bright sunlight struck the port. They had passed from beneath the platform. The motors quieted again, then roared a moment later, and the *Sky Hawk* mashed the water and wind began to whistle. Then the wind struck a shrill, keen note, the plane rose laboriously.

Gales saw the mouth of the inlet sweep beneath. He was on the port side of the plane, and when the plane banked gently the white sun blinded him. The plane leveled off, the sun was still in the porthole. Gales reasoned the plane was flying southeast. He looked back and saw the coast dropping behind. Mist veils writhed over the sea below.

Now the motors made a smooth roar, and the plane was as steady as a dread-naught on a calm sea. Hour after hour she thundered over the empty reaches of the sea, never banking, never turning, but sticking rigidly to a course she had taken in the beginning.

At noon, land was still somewhere beyond the horizon. Gales swallowed some water from his flask.

AT TWO o'clock Gales felt the plane slant. She had put her nose down a bit. He stumbled to the port and looked out. Far ahead he saw land. The plane leveled off again, and was driving toward the land. Then Gales saw mountains rising in the distance, Where were they? He remained by the port, and at two-thirty he saw surf breaking on a long reef. Beyond the reef was a raw jungle coast, and beyond the coast low foothills that attained the dignity of a minor mountain range farther inland. Something familiar about that coast and the mountains!

"It's Borneo!" Gales said aloud.

He expected to feel the plane slant again, to alight on one of the inlets. But he was mistaken. At about two thousand feet, the *Sky Hawk* crossed the jungle coast and roared over the wilderness. Then the plane slanted, but upward. They were taking on altitude to cross the hills! The motors were working harder, thundering.

Gales spun away from the port as the compartment was flooded by light.

A voice said, "Take that coil of rope there—" then stopped.

Two men were in the room, and both of them saw Gales.

The two men snarled and streaked for their guns. Gales streaked for his, and the muzzle of it belched flame. One of the men staggered.

The plane banked, and Gales lost his balance and was thrown toward them. The second man fired, but he was off balance, and his shot went wild.

The wounded man fell against the bulkhead, raised his gun and fired as Gales pitched into the other. The shot missed. Gales twisted and shot from one knee, and the man dropped his gun and slumped down. The other man evidently wanted to get Gales alive, for he took a vicious swing with his gun at Gales' head. Gales saw the blow coming out of the tail of his eye, ducked, and got the blow on his shoulder. It was severe enough to floor him, but as he went down he caught the man's leg and yanked him down too.

They heaved toward each other, and Gales found his gun hand imprisoned in the other's left hand. He cut loose with a left jab that crashed against the man's mouth, but the latter was tough, and he held on with his left hand and walloped his gun barrel against Gales' head.

Lights spattered in Gales' brain, and his stomach seemed suddenly empty. He fell awkwardly against the man, reached frantically for the man's gun hand—got it in a grip of steel. He remained thus, marking time until his head stopped spinning. His opponent writhed and heaved beneath him, but Gales was beginning to see clearly again, and he worked his knee up and jammed it against the man's stomach.

In a flash he released the man's gun hand. A split-second later he drove his fist between the man's eyes. That did the trick. The man groaned and relaxed, and Gales was able to free his own gun hand easily. He stood up. The plane banked again and he fell down. He sat there for a moment, getting his breath and gathering his wits together.

These men had come in for a coil of rope. Someone had sent them. When they failed to return, others would come. Gales knew he could hold the compartment against any attack while the plane was on the wing. But when it alighted he would have little chance.

He rose and went to the porthole. He looked out and saw a lake ahead. The lake was on the top of a mountain, and the plane was slanting down toward the lake. As he looked he saw a mast rising from the roof of the trees, and at the top of the mast was a wind-cone.

This was Base Two!

HE SPUN from the porthole. He was trapped! He would have to fight it out here in the compartment until they got him!

His eye lighted on the parachutes, in racks against the bulk-head. His eyes keened. He set his jaw, crossed the compartment, and removed one of the 'chutes. He strapped it on, loaded his gun to capacity, and looked out into the corridor. No one was in sight. He stepped out, walked a few steps and then ascended a flight of six stairs. As he climbed he smelled fresh air and heard the wind more clearly. Near the top, he paused. He saw a man in the tail gun cockpit, leaning over the side of the coaming.

Gales crept upward, reached the cockpit and stood up as the man turned. He saw Gales—but he saw Gales diving at him. One well-aimed blow, and the gunner collapsed. Gales watched him sink to the floor of the cockpit.

The motors diminished a bit, and the right wing tilted. Gales looked out and saw the lake almost beneath them. The plane crossed the lake and curved over the wilderness beyond to get into the wind.

Gales forked the coaming, took one look downward, and then dived head first. He dropped a couple of hundred feet before he yanked the rip-cord. The silk ballooned, and the harness bit into his flesh. He swung like a pendulum, and then when he saw that the wind might carry him to the lake, he spilled the wind from his 'chute and plummeted. When he released the cords the 'chute ballooned again, and he was skimming near the tree-tops.

Going down—

He struck hard, crashing through branches, and for a moment he could do nothing but hang on to a limb and choke for breath. Then he unbuckled his harness, left the 'chute in the trees, and climbed down to the ground. He took to his heels, running pellmell away from the trees where the 'chute was tangled.

CHAPTER XII

McGILL GETS SORE

K.O. **PIKE** looked up when the door opened and dropped pencil, pipe, and a whisky-stenger.

"Hell, your nerves are in bad shape," McGill said.

"Where did *you* come from?"

"Commodore, that Vought you gave us is a lulu. I just made a non-stop flight of a thousand miles, and I plank the old boiler in the harbor and have a pint o' gas left. You got egg on your tie this time."

K.O. thumped the desk. "Where's Bill?"

A shadow crossed McGill's face. "I don't know."

"Then why are you here?"

"Listen here, big shot, I ain't deaf!"

"Well, then blast my stars—"

"Ah, blast 'em yourself. Give your ears a chance. If I knew where Bill was, d' you think I'd be lookin' you in the face? You got the dope up until the time we downed the two planes, didn't you?"

"Yes. The *Halcyon* shot all that in."

McGill sat down and laid palms on his knees. "Okey. Bill and me foller the *Sky Hawk,* and it gets dark, and the *Sky Hawk* goes down at one of her bases. We're almost out o' gas. We light ten miles down the coast, and we're crackin' jokes on the shore o' the inlet when—*wham*—my flash blows up, and there's a dart stickin' it. So we shift to another inlet, and in the mornin' Bill slopes off for the base. That's the last I seen o' him."

"Why didn't you go with him?"

McGill cocked an eye. "Are you intimatin'—"

"I'm intimating nothing, and mind your lip. I'm boss here, and if you get gay I'll slide you out on the seat of your pants!"

"Oh, yeah?"

"Yeah!"

"And what am I goin' to be doin' while you're tryin' to slide me out?"

K.O. leaned forward. "Forget it. Go on with your story."

"Sure. Next mornin' I see the *Sky Hawk* way out over the sea. I'm still low on gas, and no ship has come in sight. So when the *Sky Hawk* disappears I take off and head for the base. I got enough gas for that—it's only fifteen miles. I circle around and see nobody. I slop the crate down and still see nobody. I go ashore and there ain't a soul. There's houses there, and a dynamo for the floodlights, and some fuel tanks. So I load up with gas."

"Is that all?"

"Well, before I take off, I blow up the fuel tanks, the houses, and I wreck the floodlights. When I take off, I see there ain't much left. I'd say Bill's on the *Sky Hawk*. Maybe he's a captive. Maybe he sneaked on board in the night and is plannin' things."

K.O. said, "You did remarkably well."

"I should hope to tell you we did!"

"Yes. Miss Manners arrived here this noon. She arrived safely in Saigon and took a Garrison Airways plane here. There's great rejoicing in the Manners household."

"There won't be when that jane hears Bill has pulled a fade-away again?"

"What do you mean?"

McGill made a face. "Ah-r-r, they're nuts over each other. Poor Bill. If it ain't the *Sky Hawk*, it's the jane…. Well, when I last seen the *Sky Hawk*, she was headin' southeast. I want a man who can run the Lewis gun and fiddle with a radio, and then we'll be takin' off and lookin' for the bums again."

"Hogan's the man. And I'll send another plane with you. The Waco. When you've washed your face, my stenographer will take down your entire report from the time you left here."

"If she don't like my face, she can go places. I'm ready now."

McGILL WAS summoned that afternoon to the Manners estate. He was informed the Manners limousine would call for him. He road down Connaught Drive in style, dressed in crisp clean whites, a dazzling topee, and a sky-blue tie. The limousine entered a pebbled drive, followed a serpentine course a matter of two hundred yards and drew up before a big white mansion. Two men in livery came out to meet the car and followed McGill up the broad veranda.

Gwen came rushing out. "Oh, Bill is gone again!" she cried, and McGill saw that she had been crying. She gripped McGill's arm. He froze, intending to be very severe.

"You must find him," she went on passionately. "You must! You can't realize how utterly desolate I feel. Oh… my poor Bill!"

"I'll get him," McGill stated. "What was I wanted for?"

"My father wants to see you."

Manners received McGill in an elaborate study. Manners was a tall, hawk-nosed man, and he had a keen eye, an ambassadorial air.

"Hello, Mr. Manners," McGill greeted. "How you feelin' today?"

The familiarity didn't go over at all. Manners was holding a check in his hands, looking down at it.

"This," he said, "is my check for twenty-thousand dollars. You and your companion have done well in returning my daughter to safety. I want to thank you very kindly." He held out the check and McGill received it.

A little puzzled, McGill said, "It's tough, though, that your daughter and Bill got all tangled up with each other."

"Just a passing fancy, I imagine."

"Yeah. I hope so. I can't imagine Bill married to your daughter a-tall."

"Don't worry," Manners put in coolly, "It will never take place."

"I don't know, Mr. Manners. Bill's pretty set on it, and so is the ja—I mean, your daughter."

Manners sighed. "No, I'll see it doesn't take place. You men have been paid for what you did. Of course—it would be— er—impossible for my daughter to—er— Well, after all, your friend is a wild sort of bird, with a scanty background, and— Well, I wish you luck, Mr. McGill."

McGill's left eye narrowed and glinted. "I ain't in no hurry, chief. Do you mean to stand there and hint that my partner ain't good enough for your daughter?"

Manners frowned. "I did not put it that bluntly, but—"

"Yeah, I got you, buddy," McGill said. "You don't have to dress the facts up in fancy words. Well, let me give *you* a load of somethin'. Your daughter ain't nowheres good enough for Bill, but if he wants her, well, he'll get her."

"Really, my dear McGill—"

"My dear, my eye! No matter how you slice it, it's still boloney to me! He ain't good enough, eh? Ho! Don't that tickle me!… Well, you pipe this, sailor: I was against Bill stoopin' to marry that flap. Ain't good enough, eh? But now I'm all for him. I'll be seein' you sometime when I can't avoid it. Thanks for the pin money."

He pivoted on his heel, swung out of the house with the light of battle in his eye. Gwen nailed him on the veranda, but before she could say anything he gripped her arm and growled:

"You want to marry my pard?"

"Yes, of course. I—"

"You love him?"

"Why, certainly—"

"Foller him to the ends of the earth, or somethin' like that?"

"Indeed, Mike—"

"Nothin''ll stop you from marryin' him?"

"Nothing! Nothing!"

"Okey, sister. I'll get your sweet man back if I gotta bust a dozen crates doin' it. And if you don't treat him right, sister, I'll bust your neck! Get that: I'll bust your neck!"

He left her standing like a woman stricken. The limousine purred off with him, and his face was red, and he kept cursing a blue streak on the way back to the city.

CHAPTER XIII

DEATH SENTENCE

GALES WAS surrounded. He could hear men all around him, and he knew they were closing in. He crouched, in a thicket, drenched in sweat, and gripped his automatic in his hand. How many could he down before he was himself riddled at close range? It didn't matter, because he knew they would get him in the end.

Things had worked out badly for Gales. What a stroke of bad luck that those two men had entered the plane's storage compartment! The flight almost over, no one suspecting his presence aboard the plane... and then misfortune. He was a man alone now, very near the end of his tether. He had tried heroically to undermine the sinister enemy. But he might have known that one man could not do it. It seemed he had nothing more to do but meet his end.

Hunched in the thicket, he thought of Gwen, and how wonderful she was. And he thought of Mike, and the good times they'd had. It was pretty rotten to die when you had so much to live for. A lump rose in Gales' throat. He did not want to die.

After a few minutes he took one of the small hand grenades from his pocket and looked at it. Then he took out his handkerchief. He rolled up his left trouser leg and placed the grenade against the hollow on the back of his leg just above the calf. He lashed the handkerchief around it, knotted the handkerchief below his knee. He took the other grenade and buried it. He rolled down his trouser leg and looked around.

Sounds of his trackers grew nearer. Twigs crackled, and he could hear low whispers—everywhere.

Then a voice called, "We have you surrounded. You'd better come out."

Gales drew in a long breath, rose and stepped out of the thicket. He held up his hands. Men appeared—a dozen of them, and closed in around him. One took away his gun, searched his pocket and removed the spare ammunition. He was a big man, dark-skinned with a scar on his chin.

"I've seen pictures of you," he said. "You're that guy Gales."

"I'm that guy," Gales said.

"So you tried to pull a fast one, eh?"

Gales said nothing. He looked around at the men. A mongrel lot—some of yellow Asia, some with the stamp of cross-breeds.

The leader said, "All right, Gales. Get going."

They started off through the jungle, and an hour later they reached the shore of the lake. Gales saw a platform similar to the one at the other base. The *Sky Hawk* was beneath it, and several men stood on the platform. The little band marched along the shore toward the platform, and then entered the woods and came to a group of three thatched huts. Outside the largest stood a group of men in white suits, and they began talking when Gales marched up before them. Crag was there. And Count Pohly. And the Chinese secretary, Mr. Song Gow.

"So it *is* Gales," Crag said.

The man with the scar on his chin said, "Yeah. He surrendered."

Mr. Song Gow placed his monocle over his eye. "This is a great surprise."

Crag said, "We'll take him in."

HE GRIPPED Gales' arm and marched him into the hut. Inside, it was no longer a hut, but a comfortable dwelling. And in a large room, reclining in a Hongkong chair, was Tai Yut, smoking a cigarette through his long ivory holder.

"Here he is," Crag growled.

Tai Yut smiled sweetly. "And is he the notorious Mr. Gales?"

"Yes. It's Gales."

"Ah," breathed Tai Yut. "This is an extraordinary pleasure, Mr. Gales. Accept my humble hospitality. Deign to be seated. And my dear Crag, have the servant bring Mr. Gales refreshments. He looks rather haggard."

Scowling, Crag left the room, and a moment later a servant appeared with decanter and glasses.

Wearing an insidious smile, Tai Yut said, "Please be kind enough to mix refreshments to your own taste, Mr. Gales."

"Thanks," said Gales, and mixed a gin-sling. He took a long drink. "Tastes good," he said.

"I am infinitely happy," smiled Tai Yut. "Cigarettes are in the sandalwood box."

Gales lit up and sat back.

Tai Yut went on smiling, and gently caressed the back of his left hand with the palm of his right.

"What a pity," he said, "that you are not one of my men. Believe me, Mr. Gales, I am aware of your stupendous record. You would be a most valuable flight commander. What a pity that, instead, I must put you to death. You have no idea how it grips my heart with remorse."

"Yes," said Gales. "I imagine it does. You look very pained."

"I am, to the nadir of my humble being." Tai Yut put fingertips beneath his chin. "How brave of you to attempt such a thing. I mean, of course, trying to break up my organization."

"It was fun while it lasted."

"Yet now it seems a pity that you must pay for your fun. You have indeed made marked inroads against our progress, but we expected a little opposition. Your companion did well by ferreting out our Canton wireless station. But we have changed the code, and although you have downed two of our planes, we have two more coming from Amoy, and they will join us at a designated rendezvous. Our next victim will be the great liner *Majesty*, of twenty thousand tons. Ah, what a glorious prospect."

Gales showed polite interest. "What do you hope to gain by this?"

"So far we have realized a total of six hundred thousand in loot. Six hundred thousand of your American dollars. We have destroyed thousands of dollars of shipping. And why do I do this?" His eyes glittered. "An eye for an eye, Mr. Gales. Once I was a merchant prince. And a combine of mercantile companies and financial wizards joined to boycott me and drive me from business. This is my revenge. Every ship I have raided and sunk was connected with that combine. The great Manners also used his influence and money against me. And now—I am paying them back. And the fools do not know who is behind the *Sky Hawk!* That, my dear Gales, is priceless! Is it not?"

"Since you ask me," said Gales, "I think it's a crack-brained idea. You can't win."

"But I am winning. For a year I planned this. I chose my men, and we established three bases. A great aircraft designer, exiled from his native land, built my *Sky Hawk* in secret. All the loot I realize goes to my men. I do not want, do not need it. It is vengeance that soothes my nerves. Only one of my men was unfaithful. He once was a servant in the Manners household. He helped Miss Manners escape. That man was thrown from my plane, along with a time bomb that exploded mid-air. My third base is a rocky island in the China Sea, uninhabited until we claimed it. There our loot is taken, stored, and there come the junks to bargain with us and take it off."

"I still think you can't win."

Tai Yut chuckled satanically. "No matter, Mr. Gales. You will be shown a bed now, while my men and I think up a choice way of snuffing out your life." He leaned forward, rubbing his hands together and wearing now a fiendish smile. "I usually think of the most exotic method of killing a man. My aides usually cheer me."

HE CLAPPED his hands. A servant appeared, and Tai Yut spoke in Chinese. The servant went out, and a moment later two armed men came in.

"Show Mr. Gales to his room," said Tai Yut. "Treat him as you would a great visiting potentate. Wine. Tobacco. The best of food. I fancy having my victims die on a full stomach. Am I not droll, Mr. Gales?"

Gales stood up, bit the Chinese with a wintry eye. "You're a conceited old idiot—and because of that you'll crack up when you least expect."

"It is a pity," chuckled Tai Yut, "that you have not the well-known American sense of humor. Escort Mr. Gales out, men."

Gales turned on his heel and went out between the two armed guards. The guards turned him over to Crag, that saturnine man, and Crag showed him into a room in one of the small huts that had no windows. A lantern was lighted, and a guard posted at the door. Crag pitched in some old magazines.

"Enjoy life while you may," Crag chuckled. "The boss is wrecking his brain for a new way of killing you. He gets really swell ideas. It amuses him. Take the skipper of the *King's Castle*. We hanged the guy in mid-air from the wing-tip. We made the wireless man walk out on the wing and then—I was at the controls—I went into a sharp bank and the poor guy slid off. He had a good idea about that Manners broad, too. After we got the ransom we were going to stage a mock marriage in the air, with Song Gow as the groom. She was a swell broad and I aimed to buy her from Song—"

Gales streaked across the room. His fist whipped up, caught Crag on the point of the jaw, lifted him, and sent him flat on his back. The guard leaped in and jammed his gun against Gales' stomach. Gales backed up, his eyes blazing with rage—not at the guard, but at Crag lying motionless on the floor.

Crag was out. He remained out, despite administrations, for one solid hour. Tai Yut was highly amused and chuckled to himself, poked fun at Crag. Crag wanted to take a whip and lay it into Gales, but Tai Yut was against it, saying that the prisoner must be in good condition at the time of his impending death. "So that he will struggle longer," Tai Yut supplemented. "So that he will realize more clearly that he is dying. Anticipate, my dear Crag! Anticipate!"

While Gales sat in the small lantern-lit room, elbows on knees, head in hands, wild hopes assailed him. A hope that McGill had flown away from the wild coast, reached a ship and taken on fuel. A hope that Gwen was safe. A fantastic hope that McGill would have a dream in which McGill would see the location of the *Sky Hawk*, would come storming down, wipe the place out, rescue him.

He still had the grenade. He could blow himself up as a last resort. Of course he would blow himself up when the inevitable approached. Blow himself up and several others with him—preferably that smiling satyr, Tai Yut, the mastermind of the blood-thirsty clique.

As another piece of irony, Tai Yut sent in clean underwear, socks, shoes, a tailored suit of white drill, shirt and tie. And a Chinaman to shave Gales. Gales dressed, accepted the shave. Then a tray of food was brought in. Wine. An excellent cigar. A choice of liqueur.

Then darkness fell. A change of guards.

Gales waited, unable to sleep, unable to remain seated. He knew that death hovered, felt that the end was not far off. He paced the floor like a caged animal. He prayed. He swore. Every time he heard footsteps he stopped, and his breath stopped, and he bent over a bit, ready to snatch the grenade from beneath his trouser leg.

MORNING CAME. And breakfast. And a hint of things doing.

Song Gow, the monocled secretary, came in, smirked, said: "Your presence is desired, honorable sir."

He waited, and Gales scowled at him, went out and was escorted by two guards into the big hut. Tai Yut smiled and said it was a lovely day. He remarked about how sweetly the birds sang and added that life was a great and glorious adventure. Gales stood in silence, shaking with rage.

Then Tai Yut said, "We are about to take off, Mr. Gales. My new planes are on the wing, and the *Majesty* is out of Saigon for Hongkong. Mr. Song Gow will take you on board the plane and show you about. It should be interesting."

Mr. Song Gow would be delighted to show Gales around. They boarded the great plane, climbed to the wing, and Song Gow pointed out the motors, and the four gun cockpits atop the wing. He pointed out the gun in the nose, and then showed Gales into the big control cabin. There were two sets of controls, side by side, two compasses—a magnetic and a periodic, a tachometer, an altimeter, an inclinometer, a rate of climb gauge, and an artificial horizon. Seen through a glass-covered aperture in the floor was the wind and drift indicator. Aft of this compartment, was the radio room. Mr. Song Gow explained everything proudly.

He showed Gales the port and starboard gun slots, showed him the water-tight compartment where the small boat was kept. Showed him small state-rooms used by the leaders, and a large compartment containing twelve bunks, used by the crew. Tai Yut's private stateroom was amidships, handsomely furnished. On the deck were eight French phones giving direct communication with control cabin, wireless room, chief engineer, port gun crew, starboard gun crew, wing gun crew, tail gunner, and observation post.

"This room is soundproof," Song Gow said. "Ports are of the strongest non-shatterable glass. Between the inner and outer walls of the hull is a substance made from a secret formula that closes over any chance penetration a bullet may make. It also slows down the speed of a bullet eighty per cent. Fuel is stored in the wings and in compartments aft. Ah, here comes the illustrious master! We will take off presently!"

Tai Yut entered with a fat portfolio. He was very cheerful. Opening the portfolio, he laid a roll of maps on the deck, removed his topee and sat down. He unrolled the maps and picked up a pencil.

"This may interest you, Mr. Gales. You see, here is Base One, which we have temporarily abandoned. Here is Base Two— where we are at present. You see, we are seventy miles east of the Borneo coast. And here, of course—here is Base Three, latitude fourteen north, longitude one hundred fifteen east. This is the calculated position of the *Majesty* at eight this morning. Right here, one hundred miles south of Base Three, is where we shall meet our two planes from Amoy. They reached Base Three last night, refueled, and will join us at noon today. Interesting?"

"Very." Gales fists were knotted at his sides.

"Be seated, Mr. Gales. Feel that you are my guest."

Song Gow remained in the room, twirling his monocle. Tai Yut picked up one of the phones and spoke with the chief engineer. A couple of minutes later there was a muffled roar, and the plane trembled.

TAI YUT lit a cigarette and bent over his papers, wearing a studious frown. He did not look up when the plane began moving. He puffed indolently. Gales saw trees flashing past the ports, heard the faint drone of the motors. Tai Yut sighed and made notations. The plane was off the water. The tops of trees dropped beneath the level of the ports.

Tai Yut grew more interested in his calculations. He picked up one of the phones and spoke with the wireless room; picked up another and spoke with Crag, who was at the controls.

Then he looked up at Gales. "Should you want refreshments, the steward will be summoned."

The plane banked a bit. The chair in which Tai Yut sat, creaked. Gales saw clouds through the ports. A white light blinked on one of the phones. Tai Yut raised the instrument, listened.

"Yes, Crag," he said. "Cross the coast at eight thousand feet and maintain an approximate speed of one hundred miles an hour. That will be quite sufficient."

Tai Yut leaned back, regarded Gales with twinkling eyes. "I know," he said, "that you are eager to know what manner of death we have chosen." He chuckled. "Again I have set forth the most appropriate idea. I'm sure you will approve of it. A man of your stature, your accomplishments, your fame, should of course be the recipient of a quite novel method of extinction. I think I have chosen wisely. In fact, my able secretary heartily endorsed it."

Sun Gow bowed and then adjusted his monocle with elaborate care.

Gales bit Tai Yut with an unwavering blue stare.

Tai Yut went on: "It is this: We shall bind you hand and foot. Fastened to the inside of your trouser legs will be two fuses, the cuffs of your trousers securely strapped and a quantity of gunpowder to supplement the fuses. As a second supplement, to make the experiment more glamorous, your clothes will be saturated with petrol. A parachute will be strapped on, and several of my men will take you on the wing, pull the cord so that you will execute what is known as a pull-off. Just before you go the fuses will be set off, will ignite the powder, and as you are going off, your saturated clothing will catch flame, and you will have eight thousand feet in which to play the part of a torch. Crag, who for once approved of my plans, says that before you have dropped a thousand feet you will be enveloped in flames, that one by one the parachute ropes will break, that when you have dropped three thousand feet all the cords will break and you will be a plummeting skeleton. Then, of course, you will not have to worry about how hard you strike the sea. Now tell me, Mr. Gales, is that not a brilliant idea?"

"And when," muttered Gales thickly, "will this take place?"

"In about an hour. Come, join Mr. Song Gow and me in a cocktail. Be a sport, my dear fellow."

Gales' voice was clogged, but he said,

"Okey. Make mine a Dry Martini."

CHAPTER XIV

THE SECRET STATION

McGILL, RETURNING from the crackling interview with Manners, spent an hour in a famous bar taking on long cool drinks to settle his anger. Tomorrow morning at daybreak he would take off for the north, hoping against hope that Bill was alive, that he would find him, that he would wipe out the *Sky Hawk*.

The long cool drinks did not help much toward cooling him off. He had been violently against the Manners jane on general principles. Now he had to be all for her because the old man was against Bill. He had to stand up for Bill, and that meant he had to sanction Bill's taking this jane for a wife, if Bill ever lived long enough to do it. He'd be a fog-eyed hoot-owl if old Manners could put on the high hat where Bill was concerned!

McGill left the bar with his rage all bottled up. He strode with his fists clenched. He glared at anybody who happened to meet his eye. He wished somebody—anybody—would haul off and pass a wise remark so he could haul off and knock the guy flat. It was that kind of anger, eager for something to pop that would release the old safety valve. He remembered K.O. had threatened to slide him out of the office on the seat of his pants. Suppose he hunted K.O. out and said, "Come on big boy—begin sliding." But no. K.O. was a good guy.

Weaving his way through the crowd, glaring about, his breath stuck in his throat when he caught a glimpse of a familiar face passing beneath a light on the opposite side of the street. Where had he seen that face? One instant he asked himself this question. The next instant he answered it.

The scholarly looking boy friend! The guy he had seen in the Canton wireless station! The guy he had socked on the conk for a quick fade-out!

McGill crossed the street. His first impulse was to run up behind the guy, get hold of him and begin some serious mopping up. But a quick thought curbed that impulse. In Singapore was a secret wireless station still to be located. Surely this man knew where it was. Just as surely, he was connected with it. Follow him!

So McGill followed him, tipping his topee well down over his eyes. Now he forgot his anger. He tightened up, was prepared to watch his step. This was a break! By George, it was! Follow this man. Find the secret wireless station. Then—

He saw the man enter a waiting black automobile. McGill stepped out to stop one of the new taxies, climbed in and said:

"Follow that black car."

They wound through the city and finally struck a boulevard where many cars purred. The way led out of the city, past large estates, past trees where the wind rustled in the branches. The road became lonely. Fewer cars passed. Plantations rolled by. Then the black car left the highway and took a woods road.

"Keep goin'," McGill said. A hundred yards farther on he told the driver to stop. He got out, paid his fare, walked back on the highway and turned off into the woods road. It was dark, and he kept to the shadow of the bushes.

Fifteen minutes later the road ended and he saw a large rambling structure, stacks of sawed timber. He saw a couple of lights, but the night was bright enough for him to see that this was a sawmill. Creeping nearer, he saw an open door, saw a man shoveling coal into a furnace. He could see smoke rising from a stack. Faintly he heard the sound of a dynamo.

His blood quickened when he saw the black car parked in the shadows. He worked his way around through the bushes and came out behind the mill. He found no way of entering. He remembered the open furnace room door. He drew his gun and crept around toward it. He saw a coolie clearing out ashes.

He moved softly forward.

He leaped swiftly, struck quickly. The coolie sank without a sound. McGill bound him hand and foot with strips of hemp he found, and put a gag in his mouth. He threw the coolie in the coal-bin.

Opening a door, he was faced by a narrow wooden staircase.

HE CLIMBED the stairs and came into a vast room full of belts and saws and the smell of saw-dust. At the farther end was a sliver of light. He moved toward it through the darkness and found a door slightly ajar. Creeping up to it, he peered through the crack.

He saw a wireless-room. In it were the scholarly looking Chinese, a Chinese in a chauffeur's uniform, a Latin-looking white man leaning on a stick, and a short fat man—white or crossbreed—at the key. All were standing except the operator. All were silent, wearing expectant faces.

Presently the operator turned from the key, took off his headphones.

He said, "Tai Yut has arrived safely at Base Two. They found Gales on board. He stowed away from Base One, cleaned up two men, jumped with a chute, near Base Two. But they got him, haven't killed him yet. Tomorrow morning the two planes will join the *Sky Hawk* a hundred miles south of Base Three, and they'll go on to raid the *Majesty*. Tai Yut said we should endeavor to cripple any planes slated to take off from here. If possible, to kill McGill." The operator unrolled a map and held it up. "They plan to raid the *Majesty* here."

The man with the cane said, "Very good. We must endeavor to cripple the Agency planes tonight."

McGill's forefinger curved around the trigger of his gun. He kicked the door open, leaped in.

"Raise 'em, buddies!"

The three men spun. The operator dropped the map. The man with the stick started a hand toward his pocket.

"No you don't!" McGill snapped.

The man raised his hands.

McGill's eyes were watchful as a hawk's. "That map," he said. "I want that map."

No one moved.

"You," he barked at the operator, "pick it off the floor!"

The operator bent over and picked up the map.

"Now throw it here," McGill said.

The operator threw it, and the two Chinese sucked in sibilant breaths. On the wall near the door was an array of electric switches. Two of them were flush with the wall. Six stuck out. McGill tried one of the latter. He saw lights outside the door spring up. One by one he threw the switches until the entire mill was lighted.

"Now the three o' you stand facin' the wall—and keep all hands up."

When they had done this he looked at the map. Several quick glances showed him blue circles around three different spots. One was in Borneo. One was on the Indo-China coast. A third was on the South China coast. He put the map under his arm.

He raised his gun and fired a shot into the wireless board. Glass flew. He fired another shot.

Then he said, "Now I ain't got time to rope you guys in. I got what I want. I'm goin' out now, and I'm closin' the door, and it ain't gonna be healthy for any guy to open it inside of three minutes. Take a tip, boy friends."

He backed out, closed the door and backed away. He passed one of the big saws. The door was still closed. He stopped beside a heap of shavings and saw dust. He took some old letters from his pocket, tore them, laid them on the floor and lit them. He sprinkled on some sawdust, watched the flames take hold. He saw the door open on a crack. He raised his gun, and the muzzle belched. The door banged shut. The flames were crackling.

Then he turned and ran, went down the staircase, through the furnace room, out into the night. He found the parked car, jumped in and started the motor.

As he was swinging the car onto the dirt road he heard the bark of a gun. A bullet tore into the metal of the car. Another broke a window.

But then McGill was out of range, stepping on the throttle.

WHEN HE turned onto the highway he looked back and saw a faint glow in the sky. They would never use that wireless again!

He had a hard time finding K.O. He located the Agency chief finally at a club, and they went to a room.

"I got it!" McGill said. "Boy, I got it!"

"Got what?"

McGill produced the map. "I found their wireless station here and set the place on fire. I ruined the wireless set. I got it here! Look! Here's Base Two, where the *Sky Hawk* is now, where Bill is. Here's the base they abandoned. Here's Base Three. Here's where they're gonna raid the *Majesty* tomorrow. Here's where two new planes are gonna join the *Sky Hawk* before they raid the *Majesty*. Now—first—send some men down to guard our planes. They may still try to cripple us. Then I'm gettin' set for a night take-off. I can't reach Base Two in time to get the *Sky Hawk*, but I can get to the *Majesty* or I can get to the spot where the two planes aim to join the *Sky Hawk*. And—pipe this—the main cheese is a guy named Tai Yut. He's on the *Sky Hawk* now."

"Nonsense!" said K.O. "Tai Yut arrived in Singapore yesterday from France by way of Suez. He's at the Metropole Palace. He used to be a big shipping man."

"I tell you, they got orders from Tai Yut at Base Two!"

"I tell you he's in town. He arrived on the Magnetic yesterday. And I'll prove it. Everybody knows Tai Yut. There's a picture in the paper of him."

It took five minutes to prove that Tai Yut was in town. He was host at a banquet at the Metropole Palace. Among his guests was the skipper of the ship that had brought him from Marseilles after a tour of the world.

"Anyhow," said McGill, "I'm takin' off. Hogan—get Hogan. And get Butts and Allenkamp for the Waco. This is hot news, and by God if I can't save Bill I'll wash out this *Sky Hawk* outfit!"

"Of course, of course," nodded K.O. "I was only saying you're wrong about Tai Yut."

"All right. Have it your way. But I'm not wrong about the *Sky Hawk*. I was there when the news came in over the wireless. I got the map. All I need is a plane and a guy to navigate. For the love of cripes, get Hogan—get Hogan!"

K.O. had to call six bars before he located Hogan. Hogan was playing Russian Bank with a cashiered subaltern but he chucked it and headed for headquarters.

Butts and Allenkamp were summoned from a gay house-party. They barked into headquarters wearing evening clothes and pulled on overalls. K.O. paced the floor and shot out instructions, while grease monkeys were already warming up the two planes.

K.O. went down to the wharf with the four pilots, and a couple of guards were pacing up and down in front of the gate. The planes had full tanks, ample ammunition and half a dozen bombs each. The floodlights were turned on the water. The siren boomed as a warning to any night-prowling sampans. Allenkamp would pilot the Waco. Butts would handle the gun and the wireless.

The party was complete.

McGill and Hogan climbed into the Vought, and McGill waggled the controls while the mooring lines were hauled in. Hogan had the map in the rear and was already planning their course. Last minute reports said the weather would be fair.

The Vought took the lead. McGill opened the throttle, and the pontoons flung up spray that glittered in the bright floodlights. The motor thundered, the water drummed beneath. Then the pontoons were clear, the plane shot up out of the radius of the floodlights, plunged into the darkness above. Out over the harbor climbed the Vought, out over the twinkling ship lights.

At a thousand feet McGill leveled off. He looked back and saw the Waco rising, and he throttled down until the Waco joined him on the windward side. Then McGill opened the throttle wide, and the Vought wheeled beneath the stars, boring in the wind. The Waco paced it.

Gradually the lights of Singapore faded behind, The sea was hidden by the darkness. In the reflection from the flashlight. McGill's face was grim, set, and his eyes were narrowed points of blue flame.

Beyond the darkness and the dawn, he knew, they would meet the *Sky Hawk*.

A DRY martini—and then.... Death.

The fixed smile of Tai Yut, the drowsy eyes of him, contained all the guile and subtle malevolence of an artist in the profession of murder. He was like some big fat cat which, having glutted itself, was inclined to dally with its victim at leisure. Take that monocled son of Satan, Song Gow, grinning joyously, his monocle glinting in his eye.

Said Tai Yut, raising his drink, "Well, Mr. Gales, to your health."

Gales raised his glass, kept his blue eyes fixed on the yellow face of Tai Yut. "To yours—which won't be good for long."

"I do not catch the significance."

Gales emptied half of his cocktail. Tai Yut sipped meticulously. Likewise Song Gow.

The big plane swayed a trifle, and shredded clouds whipped past the ports. The motors sounded faint and far away to those inside the soundproof room. Gales turned and looked out of one of the ports. Far below—more than a mile—was the coast of Borneo. Ahead lay the dim floor of the sea. The sun was bright.

And Gales was slated to die in less than an hour. He finished his Dry Martini and set the glass down on a console. This big room was more like a luxurious stateroom on board some palatial ocean liner. Gales dropped into a fan-backed wicker chair and started a cigarette. The room was fireproof. The chair creaked faintly to the motion of the great plane.

Tai Yut picked up one of the eight phones and buzzed Observation.

"Any ships in sight?... No? Very well. Do not relax your vigil for a moment."

He hung up and spoke to Gales. "This great liner *Majesty* which we are going to send to the bottom of the sea, is one of three such ships that will go down similarly. They are operated in these waters by the Yokohama Transport Syndicate, a Japanese combine. They too combined at one time to drive me from the mercantile trade. The *Majesty* is carrying British gold to Kobe—twenty-five thousand pounds of it. We shall order the crew and passengers to the boats under threat of bombing. My men will board the ship, take off the gold. We shall sink the ship. Then we shall go after the small-boats and while away half an hour sinking them."

"You scum!" Gales gritted. "You depraved—"

"Now," broke in Tai Yut, "I think I shall have you prepared for your death. Mr. Song Gow, go fetch three sturdy men, the fuses, the powder. You can saturate Mr. Gales with petrol outside my cabin."

"Very good, sir."

Mr. Song Gow started for the door. Gales raised his left trouser leg with his left hand. With his right hand he caught hold of the grenade. He sprang to his feet and raised the grenade.

"Stop!" he barked. "This is a bomb! One move out of either of you and I throw it! It will blow all of us up and blow the side of this plane out!"

Song Gow was looking over his shoulder. Tai Yut lost his placid good-humor, and his eyes narrowed, his lip lifted in a wolfish snarl.

He said, "Put that down!"

"When I put it down it will blow all of us up. Raise your hands, Song Gow! You, Tai Yut, keep your palms on the desk!

Now, Song Gow, get away from that door. Stand by the desk. Quick!"

Tai Yut cried, "By all that is sacred to Buddha, where did he get that bomb?"

"I—I do not know, sir," quaked Song Gow, standing by the desk.

GALES CROSSED to the door, eying both men, and locked it. He crossed the cabin to the rear door and locked it. Now the three of them were bottled in the cabin, and in his hand Gales held death for all of them. He knew he would have to use it eventually. He would have to kill them and himself. But doing that, he could save hundreds of lives on board the liner *Majesty*. This, then, would be his farewell gesture.

It was bitter medicine, for he would leave Mike behind, leave Gwen behind—the only girl he had ever loved—and leave the bright good world behind. He stood spread-legged, ten feet from the two Chinese, holding the hand grenade aloft. Song Gow's knees were shaking.

"Tai Yut," said Gales grimly, "you will call your control cabin and tell Crag to shift his course. The *Majesty* is not to be raided. Have a course laid for your Base Three."

"Nonsense!" fumed Tai Yut.

"I warn you," Gales said, "you cannot raid the *Majesty*. Just as soon as she's sighted I'll blow this plane to pieces. Pick up that phone! Do as I tell you!"

Tai Yut buzzed the control cabin and said, "Crag, shift immediately from our chosen course. Go to Base Three.... Do not ask questions! You have my orders!"

Fear gripped the two Chinese now. They saw the desperate look in Gales' eye, the fierce determination. The full realization of his power seeped into their brains. They saw a man who was slated to die, but when he died they knew that they would die also. Song Gow's lips were quivering, his knees were knocking together.

Thoughts no longer flowed through Gales' mind coherently. He was on a hair trigger, ready to heave the grenade at the first false move either man attempted. In the ratio of values, his death, he reasoned, would be justified in that it would save the lives of the men, women and children on board the *Majesty,* and it would save other lives.

It would wipe the *Sky Hawk* and Tai Yut from the skies, make the sea and the coast once more safe for shipping. In his upraised right hand he held—Destiny.

Song Gow stammered, "Master, c-can't we m-make an offer?"

Gales snapped, "None of that! I'd never get a break. I tell you, both of you, that I am ready to die. And you will die with me. In this closed room, the force of the bursting grenade will blow out the walls, blow the ship in two. And"—he clenched his teeth—"you will never raid another ship, kill another man, woman or child. You hear me! Both of you will die!"

Song Gow's legs gave way. He whimpered as he sank to the floor, his teeth chattering. He groveled and crawled on hand and knees. Gales had to kick him back. Song Gow lay flat on his stomach, clawing at the floor. With an eye on Tai Yut, Gales bent down and removed the pistol from Song Gow's holster.

"Fool!" cried Tai Yut. "Worm of no courage, woman of a man!"

Song Gow leaped to his feet, staggered to one of the big ports, opened it and crawled half-way out. But he hadn't the courage to jump. He fell back in, sank to the floor and—fainted. Gales knocked the port shut.

Gales laughed harshly, said, "Well, Tai Yut, why don't you talk about the beauties of life now? Lost your tongue?"

"I am thinking of making you a proposition."

"What is it?"

"I will land you safely on the Borneo coast."

"And then before I can get away your men will shoot me down. No, Tai Yut. There's no way out for either of us. We've both got to die together."

"I will give you my word—"

"The word of a murderer like you means nothing."

Gray color seemed to be creeping into Tai Yut's face. Fear had reached his heart, was closing around it.

"I swear I will see you off safely!"

"What? With all I know? I know where your two remaining bases are. I know you have loot stored at Base Three. No, Tai Yut. You wouldn't let me go once you were out of danger."

The light on the phone marked Observation blinked. Gales nodded. Tai Yut picked up the instrument. His eyes started, his left hand clawed at the desk's surface. "Very good," he choked, and hung up.

Gales was suspicious. "What was that?"

"Two planes have been sighted!"

"Your two?"

"No. They are from the south." He reached for another phone.

Gales clipped, "What are you going to do?"

"Crag must be told—and the gunners!"

"Not a bit of it! Leave that phone alone!"

Two planes! What two planes? Thoughts began clicking through Gales' head. McGill? Could it be McGill?

Tai Yut was breathing thickly, his fingers clawing. He wanted to get at the phones. His eyes bulged and his teeth showed between writhing lips. Sweat broke on his face, and his mouth opened wide as if he were gasping for breath.

THE BIG plane lurched violently. Gales was thrown backward. He tripped over the form of Song Gow and crashed down. Tai Yut yanked open the desk drawer, whipped out a pistol. Song Gow, who had been playing possum on the floor, clutched at Gales. In a flash Gales bit at the grenade, heaved it. It hurtled across the room. Tai Yut covered his eyes and fell down. The grenade struck one of the glass ports, exploded. The cabin was a white hell. The plane shook.

In that split-second Gales had swung on Song Gow, and he felt Song Gow flattened against him, heard the tearing of metal, a man's scream—Song Gow's. The desk crashed against the bulkhead near his head. Glass rained on Gales' face. Was he alive? How could he be alive? The ship swayed. If he were dead he couldn't feel its motion, nor could he see a patch of sky through a jagged rent in the ceiling where the in-driving wind fought the smoke.

He shoved Song Gow off. That proved to him that he was alive. He saw that most of Song Gow's clothes were gone. There was blood. Song's body had shielded Gales from mutilation. Gales staggered to his feet. He saw Tai Yut lying on the floor, tangled up with a shattered chair. Blood was on Tai Yut's head.

This had happened: The grenade had struck the port. Much of its explosive violence had burst through the port, escaped into the wind. Yet there had been sufficient force driving inward to blow a gash in the plane, turn the cabin into a shambles, put Song Gow forever out of his misery of horror.

Through the skeins of smoke Gales could see the forward door splintered and twisted and hanging by one hinge. The door leading aft was still intact. Gales rushed to it, picking up Tai Yut's gun on the way, so that now he had two. He opened the rear door, went into the corridor, closed the door and locked it.

Blood was on his head too. He didn't know it. He didn't notice that his clothes were in rags, that trickles of red were on his chest and arms, his cheek. Still shocked, he was amazed that he was alive, and wounds were of no consequence. And greatest of miracles, the plane was still flying, and from the steadiness of its keel, Gales knew that it was flying well.

He knew where that corridor terminated. It was the avenue to the rear cockpit. He expected to find a man in the rear gun cockpit. He found the man. He loomed up in the cockpit bloody and ragged and terrifying to behold. Well, he was fighting for his life. He had a lease on life that a miracle had extended. He swung both guns in a cyclonic motion, and the awestruck gunner flopped down like a punctured balloon.

Gales saw the open steel trap door that, had it been closed, would have changed his destiny. He swung the trap down with a bang after he had relieved the unconscious gunner of his chute and sent him sliding down the staircase. Now he was alone in the cockpit, alive when by all the dictates of circumstances he should be dead.

Alive! It didn't matter for how long. And he was still in a position to do considerable damage before they got him.

His roving blue eyes settled on the two planes off the port quarter. They were still far away. The lookout must have sighted them with a powerful telescope. Gales couldn't make out their color, nor their design. But they were from the south, high on the wing.

"Maybe," he shouted breathlessly into the wind, "Mike had a dream!"

He turned just in time to see the man in the cone-like observation post aiming at him. Gales dropped. The shot went wild.

McGill? Could it be McGill? No, that was beyond reason.

CHAPTER XV

GUNS OF THE WIND

NOW YOU know those two planes. You saw them leave Singapore in the white glare of floodlights, wheel over the dark harbor, and thunder out to sea at breakneck speed. In one were McGill—the inevitable—and his gunner Hogan; in the other were Allenkamp at the controls and Butts at the gun. Their motors were at 160 Fahrenheit. During the night tragedy had almost befallen them, but Butts had gone out on the wing of the Waco and repaired the leaky fuel line. In pitch dark, mind you, holding a small flashlight with his teeth so that both hands would be free.

Hogan had unbuckled his safety belt and was half-standing, with binoculars pressed to his eyes. Far off, and dead ahead, he saw the *Sky Hawk*. He had first sighted it ten minutes before; had sighted a plane, rather, and was now certain it was the *Sky Hawk*.

"It's it, Mike," he said through the speaking-tube.

"Okey, Jake. If she's runnin', it's gonna take us at least half an hour to overhaul her. Though it's by me, brother, why the bus don't turn and show her stuff."

Positive now that they were in the wake of the sky plunderer, Hogan lowered his glasses and looked to his gun, testing the mechanism and firing a short burst. Butts did the same thing in the Waco, and the two planes flew close to each other and signaled by hand, then drew away slightly, to give each other leeway.

Under full throttle the two planes were doing about a hundred and thirty an hour. The *Sky Hawk* was doing a hundred and fifteen. At the end of half an hour McGill's chance reckoning proved wrong, for they had not overhauled the pirate plane, were in fact still a mile behind. Yet they were gaining—but burning up precious fuel and oil doing it. They had enough left for about two hundred miles of high-speed flight. No land in sight. One advantage lay in the fact that, due to their low weight in fuel, stunting would be more effective in a jam.

McGill had practically given up hope for Bill. A faint possibility that Bill was still alive at one of their bases. McGill couldn't guess that Gales was on board the *Sky Hawk*. McGill knew nothing of the fiendish plan that had hatched in the depraved mind of Tai Yut. Yesterday—tomorrow—seemed strangely detached in the mind of McGill. Only today existed, the very present. Bill was gone. Ahead was the *Sky Hawk*. It would have to fight now.

Slowly the two Straits Agency planes gained—slowly but surely. Soon McGill could make out its ten motors, and when he used his binoculars and saw a queer gash on the topside amidships, he was puzzled. It looked—to him—as if the *Sky Hawk* had already been in a sky brawl.

Hogan, seeing it too, said through the tube, "You see that hole, Mike?"

"I sure do, Jake. What d' you s'pose?"

"I'll stick to cross-word puzzles. You got me, mate."

"Better get down, Jake. Them babies are gonna open fire before long."

"And so am I. Sort of get on her port quarter, and up a bit, and I'll try sockin' some shots through that hole and see if I can make it bigger."

"Okey, Jake. There goes the Waco up now."

The Waco had stuck her nose upward—just slightly, and was tacking on altitude. McGill drew back on his stick a bit, rose and banked a bit. The Waco banked the other way. There was a plane now on either quarter of the *Sky Hawk,* and quite suddenly they were within range.

HOGAN SWISHED his gun back and forth a few times, then steadied it and started things going. The Lewis vibrated and hacked out lead, and Hogan's first burst trimmed off the edges of the hole in the *Sky Hawk.*

Two of the *Sky Hawk's* port gun-slots began snapping out smoke puffs. McGill took a look at his left wing tip and saw fabric flying.

"Cripes, what lousy shots!"

Hogan moved his gun and trained it on one of the gun-slots. The gun coughed violently. *Wham!* A burst from one of those gun-slots piled into the Vought's flank. Hogan felt the impact and gritted his teeth and held his gun on the mark and kept the lead slashing through the wind. One of the gun-slots stopped spitting smoke abruptly. That was a good sign.

He yelled through the speaking tube, "What gets me, Mike, is that tail gun of theirs. Not a peep out of her."

"Maybe Butts gave him the works."

"Nope. Butts is way around and workin' on the flank. As a matter of fact, that gun is stickin' smack up in the air. She's been that way from the first... and I don't like the way that wagon's stickin' to her course."

"Hey!" yelled McGill. "Look ahead there and— Will you pike what's comin', Jake!"

"Huh?"

Hogan squinted. Sure enough, two planes were materializing out of the blue ahead. Hogan grabbed his glasses. Still too far away to make the planes out definitely.

Wham! That was another load of lead ripping across the Vought's cowl, dangerously close to the main fuel tank. McGill yanked back on the stick and zoomed. A thousand feet above the *Sky Hawk* he leveled off, then forged ahead to regain the straightaway distance lost in the climb.

How about Allenkamp and Butts? Those two boy friends were flirting with death off the *Sky Hawk's* starboard quarter. They too noticed the tail gun sticking upward. The most valuable gun to hinder a stern or quarter attack! And yet it was silent!

The Waco was taking and giving. There was no more padded coaming on the left side of the rear cockpit. A couple of wing ribs were showing. Her rudder didn't look exactly like a sieve, but given time and a few more loads of lead, and it would resemble something closely akin to a sieve. The "a" and "i" in the word *Straits* on the flank, had been completely obliterated by a concentrated burst, and a ragged hole replaced the spot where the "A" in *Agency* used to be. Allenkamp, the one-time Australian cattleman, and Butts, an ace of Spads in the war-time R.F.C., were beginning to think conditions were warm—when they spotted the two oncoming planes.

Butts took one keen look and said, "Extraordinary!"

Allenkamp said, "If I ever see Australia again, it will be lookin' up at the roots o' flowers. An' to think I 'ad a career before me!"

Then they saw McGill hiking hell-bent for altitude. Allenkamp banked sharply and dived headlong beneath the *Sky Hawk*, and Butts could not resist piling lead into the *Sky Hawk's* belly. The strange maneuver had its good point. Allenkamp, a flying fool only second to McGill, zoomed when he was scarcely away from the big plane's belly. And streaking upward, Butts wheeled his gun across the tail and ripped lead into the nearest gun-slot, then shifted the Lewis and raked lead across the top of the wing, driving the gunners there to temporary shelter. This was spectacular stuff, and nine times out of ten the plane strutting its stuff would pay for it. But the Waco won the tenth chance and flaunted her tail in a powerful zoom.

The two planes coming down from the north were now clearly visible with the naked eye. McGill saw that they were not little single-seaters. They were planes to match his own. One was red, the other was yellow. Both were monoplanes, and were two-seaters, low-winged; not by any chance were they set-ups, flying stumblebums.

Still neither McGill nor the others of his party knew whether the planes were were friend or foe. No such planes had been known to fly with the *Sky Hawk*. But McGill felt it in his bones that Providence would not be so kind-hearted to make them friends. The way they matched the Waco and Vought for altitude seemed to indicate that they were going to make things hot. Hogan loaded up and waited. The *Sky Hawk* was fifteen hundred feet below, half a mile astern.

The red monoplane dipped her right wing and made a quarter turn. As she did so a machine gun in her rear cockpit started the festivities. Bullets whanged in the Vought's landing gear. Then the red monoplane, having got in the first blow, swept her tail seaward and her nose skyward.

McGill cocked his eye at it, yanked back on his stick and muttered, "Well, sweetheart, the higher you go, the bigger fall you're gonna have!"

TAKE A look at Bill Gales in the tail gun-cockpit of the giant bird of prey. He didn't know why the two Straits planes had suddenly stopped peppering the *Sky Hawk* and zoomed for greater altitude. He had not yet seen the two approaching planes. Necessity forced him to remain crouched in the cockpit. The man in the observation cockpit had almost taken his head off, and the danger from the Straits planes had been obvious.

Now the Straits planes were out of sight, somewhere above and ahead. He remained on the floor of the cockpit looking upward, and finally he saw what he had half-expected. The Chinaman's new planes were in combat with the Vought and the Waco. No doubt the wireless man had got in touch with them, urged them to come on.

Gales felt the big plane tilt, knew it was rising. A quick look showed him the wing guns pointing skyward. They were all going after the two Straits planes. Gales caught a fleeting glimpse of the observer drawing another bead on him. He ducked just in time. The bullet ricochetted off the machine gun. Gales swore violently. That bird was just waiting to pot him, to blow his brains out.

Well, why not make a duel of it? No danger now of stray shots from the Vought and the Waco. Gales gripped his two pistols. He took another quick look over the coaming. The observer blazed away. Up popped Gales again, with two guns. Both muzzles blazed at the same time. The observer sat in his cockpit, but his chin fell to his chest.

Then Gales saw the wing guns opening fire on the Straits planes. Gales knew the two planes would have little chance when these three planes got to working on them in earnest. Something had to be done.

Gales looked at the machine gun. It was loaded. He gripped it and swiveled it round, pointing forward. He started blazing away, raking his lead back and forth. He silenced one of the guns. The other two stopped a split-second later. Then Gales opened fire again, concentrating on the extreme left motors.

He saw the pusher prop stop spinning. He thought he saw metal parts flying. He kept laying lead into the same target. More metal parts flew. The tractor of the two-in-tandem expired, and then only the wind turned the prop. The *Sky Hawk* began to list.

Driven by rage or imperious orders, two of the wing gunners swung their guns aft and cut loose. Gales got out of sight and crouched while a hail of lead snarled and whanged around him.

The *Sky Hawk* was not climbing any more. She still had a bit of a list and she was fighting for skyway. Remember, two of her motors were dead, broken, useless, beyond repair. She was a big wagon, and the loss of those two motors meant a loss of eight hundred horsepower. Besides, they were end motors. That's why Gales had chosen to demolish them.

Consider the position of Gales. Quite impregnable—for the time being, at least. One man, he held the most valuable position on board the plane. No man could force his way through the trap in the floor. No man could climb aft on the top of the plane without being riddled. If they landed they might get him. In fact, they would—he figured. But while they were on the wing he was securely embattled and could use their own gun against them. In using it, he had equaled the odds above.

The four planes were having it out two miles astern, at eight thousand feet. The *Sky Hawk* was fighting her way from the scene of action on eight motors—maintaining her keel now, but apparently with no little effort. Gales surmised that they were running for Base Three and leaving the two new planes to wipe out the Vought and the Waco.

That meant— Of course, Gales nodded to himself. That meant that they would alight at their last base, moor the plane, and then set about exterminating him forever from this mortal sphere. Well, so be it. He had at least kept the *Sky Hawk* from joining the fight against the Straits planes.

McGill? Gales asked himself. Of course, McGill would be in the Vought. He had acquired a new gunner, and a plane to fight with him. Had he gone all the way to Singapore? And had he come upon the *Sky Hawk* accidentally or had he rooted out important information? Gales remembered McGill's brilliant work in Canton. Maybe the glorious little red-head had repeated history.

Gales would have liked to see the fight through. But gradually the four planes disappeared astern. The roar of the eight motors deafened him. He was trapped again, but again he had evened things. An eye for an eye. He had a chute, but there would be nothing gained by leaping into the sea. He might try putting a couple of more motors out of the show and thus force the plane down shy of her base. But he did not have to look to know that the wing guns were leveled in his direction, marking time.

"Well, Mike," he said aloud, "you tried your best."

CHAPTER XVI

FLAME IN THE CLOUDS

HAD THERE been reporters and cameramen around, this fight in the blue would have made history. As it was, there were no eye-witnesses.

The planes became almost human in their dives, climbs, barrel-rolls and wild skids. Coming out of a bad tangle at ten thousand feet, when the two enemy crates almost smacked into each other, the Waco was diving away from a tail fire and McGill and Hogan found themselves on the outside track. Let it be said here that during the last five minutes the Vought had lost part of her rear windshield, that a strut had been splintered and was likely to give way any minute.

Also, had you been around, you could have looked through a hole five inches in diameter in her left flank and seen daylight coming through a similar hole in her right flank. Her fixed vertical fin had a saw-toothed edge as a result of some telling quarter fire, and there was a six-inch gash in the leading edge of her starboard wing. But now—she had the outside track.

Hogan, whom McGill began to rate as a gunner only slightly inferior to Bill Gales, went into a huddle behind the Lewis and wiped out the front windshield of the red monoplane. This was a good average. His burst before had shattered the same plane's rear windshield to smithereens.

Allenkamp, seeing what was taking place above, braked the plane's dive so hard that the Waco shivered and Butts held his breath lest the wings disappear. But the wings held, and Allenkamp took courage and hoisted his crate up nearer the hot spot of the carnival. Allenkamp should have died ten minutes ago.

That furious hail of lead, streaming over his shoulder, had smashed every instrument on the dashboard. Three gray hairs were added to Allenkamp's head. But then Hogan, in the Vought, had removed the red plane's rear windshield. What a break for Allenkamp! He was just getting over the hot sweat now. But the lad had guts!

Bung-g-g!

That was the yellow plane's lead socking the empty gas tank in his right wing. Thank God it wasn't the left! He tipped the right wing up on the climb, and the yellow plane, diving at him, was shunted off by the lead that blasted upward from Butts' hot Lewis gun. The yellow plane skidded badly and her backwash roared into the Waco's cockpits, her tail whipped down and the men were for an instant so close that they could have thrown wrenches at one another. Roars of the two different motors were intermingled. Then the yellow plane was pulling away on one ear.

A thousand feet above these two were the others: the Vought and the red enemy monoplane, playing tag and leap-frog among the clouds. This was more dangerous than it sounds. They appeared, disappeared, then appeared again, snapping short bursts at each other and then plunging into the streamers of cloud again.

For some reason Hogan had got disgusted with his goggles, then his helmet, and was now riding the clouds without either, his sandy hair a ragged pennant in the wind. Sunlight after the mystery of a cloud, and then the red plane diving from a cloud dead-ahead. McGill kicked right rudder and bent the Vought on a violent turn. The red plane's lead enlarged the hole in the Vought's left flank, and Hogan's gun vibrated as he crammed lead into the enemy's belly.

THIS VICIOUS fighting could not last for long. These planes were out to fight a showdown battle, and they were taking long chances. There was very little sparring. Both sides were taking the offensive. One did not have to force the other to fight.

The Waco and the yellow plane were darting at each other, exchanging fire at short range, wheeling so close that one or the other's prop blast was felt. Butts had chosen a spot just forward of the front cockpit. He concentrated on nothing else. Time and time again he came back to hammer that spot, while the enemy tried constantly to blow off Allenkamp's head.

But the English Butts won his point first. They were close at hand when they saw a thin tongue of flame leap from the cowl of the yellow plane. The pilot ducked, and the plane staggered. The gunner jumped up to the coaming, swung a leg out. The plane yawed and lost speed, and the gunner fell backward over his gun, then out over the side. His chute fouled on the gun, and he dangled. The pilot was climbing out to jump, when the tongue of flame burst into a blinding sheet of white and red fire.

"Ah, the poor beggars!" Butts muttered grimly. He shuddered, and turned his eyes away.

The yellow plane was a torch plunging to the sea below.

And at this time McGill had the red plane running away. Hogan had winged the gunner even as the other plane had burst into flames. Now the red plane saw its plight, and its pilot was bent only on saving his life.

But the Waco was rising swiftly to head him off. The pilot swung to the left, threw a frightened glance backward and saw the Vought turning with him and bearing for his quarter, while the Waco was rising on his starboard bow. Then the Waco turned to fall in on his starboard flank, pacing him, while the Vought edged in on his port flank. The red plane was between two fires. He could turn neither left nor right. He could dive, but the other planes could dive with him. He was in range, but the planes did not fire. They were creeping closer.

Hogan was standing up in the cockpit and waving for the enemy to go down. The enemy kept on driving ahead at full speed. Hogan sent a line of lead into his left wing, again gestured the man to go down. The man obeyed, slackened speed, waved his hand in surrender.

The three planes alighted on the sea within fifty yards of one another, and the Vought and the Waco plowed toward the enemy. The enemy pilot was sitting in his cockpit, his goggles up on his forehead, a tense look on his face. He had a thin black mustache, swart skin, and jet eyes.

The Vought almost touched the red plane's wing, and Hogan, out on the foot-hold, caught hold of the wing and held it while all motors idled. McGill conned the enemy plane. A neat job. A low-wing Lockheed, Whirlwind motored.

Hogan yelled, "Well, Mike, any idea?"

"I'm thinkin'. Hey, you"—to the man in the Lockheed—"crawl out and come over here."

"*Si, senor.*"

"H'm. The guy's a spic," said McGill.

The enemy pilot climbed out of the cockpit, crawled out on the wing. As he swung to the Vought Hogan relieved him of his gun, and then the man reached the Vought's fuselage. McGill told him to climb in the rear cockpit.

"You put up a neat scrap, Spanish. Your boy friend dead?"

"*Si, senor.*"

"Say, can't you say anything else but that?"

"I spik leetle English."

"Okey. Stop swallowin' that way. We ain't gonna bump you off—yet. We got another job. I s'pose the *Sky Hawk* lit out for Base Three, didn't it?"

The man shrugged. "Eet is maybe posseeble. Eet is all ver' strange, de way t'ings dey happen. I do not un'er-stand."

McGill yelled across to the Waco. "Hey, Butts, get that wireless goin' and see if a ship's near us."

"Right-o!"

They waited ten minutes.

Then Butts popped up and called, "Yes, Mike. Ship named *John W. Moss* is about a hundred miles west. Carrying general cargo and drums of petrol and on the lookabout for the bloody old *Sky Hawk*."

"Well, ask 'em if they'll accommodate us by comin' this way and reloadin' our tanks. Tell 'em they needn't worry about the *Sky Hawk*. Tell 'em we're stranded."

Butts disappeared, and five minutes later yelled over, "Coming!"

"That's great." McGill took a look at the Spaniard and said, "How much gas you got, buddy?"

"For to fly posseebly four hundred miles, *senor.*"

McGill nodded. Then, "Hey, Jake. Here's the dope. You and me pile in this red Lockheed. Butts comes over and takes charge o' the Vought and our spic friend. He hangs on the radio and waits for the ship along with Allenkamp in the Waco. You and me take us a ride to Base Three. We'll have to give the stiff a deep-sea burial, and then you look the gun over and we'll take along what bombs we have."

"Base Three, eh? Maybe we'll find some real action there."

"I wouldn't fool you, Jake—not even maybe."

CHAPTER XVII

THE GRIM LAGOON

FIGHTING HARD for skyway, the *Sky Hawk* struck another snag. One of her pusher motors sputtered, coughed, and expired, and the huge plane swayed. Three motors now dead. Seven left to lug her great weight through the air.

Gales embattled in the tail cockpit, did not know. He felt the lurch of the plane, but the death of another motor could scarcely be detected in the roar of the others. He sat on the bottom of the cockpit, out of range of the wing guns. He still gripped his automatics, and his eyes searched the sky for sight of a plane.

But those of the enemy inside the *Sky Hawk* received the news with low mutterings. Crag, that saturnine killer, was still at the controls, swearing, driving his remaining motors to the utmost of their endurance. Count Pohly who had charge of all the gunners, shouted questions in Crag's ear, but Crag only snarled and cursed him away.

Pohly had been the first to enter the shattered stateroom where Tai Yut once sat and jibed Gales on his impending death. Pohly had seen Song Gow dead on the floor. He had found Tai Yut tangled up with the chair. Tai Yut, the master murderer, the inventor of exotic deaths for his victims, the man who had ordered women and children slaughtered in open boats—this same Tai Yut was dead now. Gales had done it. Gales had wiped a fiend from the seas and the sky.

"Why," snarled Crag, "don't some of you yellow-bellies go back and crucify that guy Gales? Hell knows what he'll do next."

"He is in an enviable position," said Pohly. "No one can touch him—yet. But when we get to Base Three, Crag—then we will crucify him."

"If we ever get there!" yelled Crag. "Three motors gone! And a wind pasting us on the nose! We're only doing ninety miles an hour. Don't bother me, Pohly! I've got enough on my hands!"

The gunners argued among themselves. They could tell that the plane was having a rough go of it. Blindly, they blamed Crag. No mechanic dared to go out on the wing and try repair to the third motor. They were afraid Gales would shoot. The remainder of the crew fretted and bickered. With the yellow master dead, they were at odds among themselves. None dared force open the trap that led to the rear cockpit. In their minds Gales assumed gigantic proportions. But there was some balm in the fact that if they reached their base, Gales would be their prisoner, their victim, and they would grant no mercy.

While Gales knew nothing of their shattered morale, he did know that little mercy would be granted him. He didn't expect it. They would surround the plane, close in on him. He would fight with his guns till they wiped him out.

The *Sky Hawk* was flying at two thousand feet. It was impossible to gain a foot more of altitude. And only the full force of her motors kept her at that level.

Presently Crag stopped swearing and keened his eyes. Then he set his lips, and a confident look appeared on his face. Base Three was in sight! The news reached the crew, and they took on heart. They began to devise a choice way of killing Gales. Some laughed. Others bragged. Crag did neither. He watched his dials carefully.

Base Three, at a glance, looked like a jumble of rocks jutting from the sea. Not a tree was in sight. Not a soul. But the jumble of rocks formed a lagoon. And beneath the many overhanging ledges were stored loot, fuel, and other necessities. Under one ledge were an engine and a dynamo that powered the floodlights. Under another, quarters had been built into the rocks. But a plane, passing casually, would see nothing unless it flew very low, and a passing ship would see nothing at all.

GALES FELT the *Sky Hawk* banking, slowing down. He could not see the rocks below because he was hunched in the cockpit. But he sensed that the base was there. He knew by the motion of the plane that it was preparing to go down. But he could see the sky in the south, a bit of the sea when the plane banked. And he saw a shape like a bird in the sky. One. Only one.

Crag saw it too. So did the observer, with his naked eye. But he put his eye behind the powerful telescope and trained it on the spot. He laughed and said to Pohly:

"It is the red Lockheed, alone."

Pohly ran to Crag with the news, and Crag grunted. But he breathed easier. The big ship crossed low over the black crags, skimmed the surface of the rock-bound lagoon, roared a moment later on the water, mashing it into white spume. Half a dozen figures appeared beneath one of the ledges. This ledge extended far over the water, serving as a shed for the *Sky Hawk*, a protecting screen against the sky.

But Crag did not immediately head for this ledge. The *Sky Hawk* came to a stop in the center of the lagoon, and Crag got up, stretched himself. He squinted his eyes at the approaching plane.

"I guess the yellow one went down," he said. "But we had to expect that.... Now we'll run our nose in under the ledge instead of the tail. We'll leave the tail sticking out a bit. Then we can climb to the top of the ledge and look down into the tail cockpit. Gales, damn him, won't have a chance!"

Pohly said, "Hadn't we better do that now, so as to give the Lockheed plenty of room?"

"Yeah. I was waiting for the guys on shore to get that boat out of the way." He sat down at the controls again.

Gales' heart dropped. He could see the plane now, see that it was a red one. He thought of jumping out and swimming. But what was the use? They would pick him off while he swam. Better stay in the cockpit and fight it out till the end.

He saw the red monoplane swoop down over the fringing rocks. He heard its motor dwindle suddenly, saw the plane loaf toward the *Sky Hawk* at five hundred feet. Was that guy going to make a downwind landing?

The plane was almost overhead. Gales saw the man in the rear cockpit lean out. His arm went up—down. An object plummeted, followed by another. Gales threw himself to the floor.

There was a terrific roar. The plane seemed to leap out of the water. Water rushed in on Gales. Gales leaped, losing one gun but hanging on to the other. He began swimming, spitting water from his mouth. He saw the *Sky Hawk* broken in two, the rear half awash, the forward part going under in a cloud of steam. He saw men swimming.

He saw the red plane banking, turning and coming back. He tread water for a moment, shoved the gun in his pocket, and then struck out for the rocks on the uninhabited side of the lagoon.

McGILL TOOLED the Lockheed low over the lagoon. Hogan had his glasses clamped to his eyes. He saw the ledges, and the objects beneath them.

He picked up the speaking tube. "Get close to the ledges, Mike—just over the edge o' them."

"Okey, Jake."

McGill turned the plane, cut his gun a bit and drifted over the outer edge of the main ledge. Hogan threw two bombs that burst on the rim of the ledge and hurled rocks inward. The dynamo stopped working.

The survivors of the *Sky Hawk* reached the rocks, scrambled over them and ran pell mell for cover. With two more well-placed bombs Hogan drove them from beneath the ledges. In a body they ran from the lagoon's edge, scattered among the higher niches and rocks, frightening away nesting sea-birds.

The Lockheed continued to loaf above, and McGill said through the tube, "Well, Jake, no use pottin' them guys. We got what we wanted and them guys are stranded here until a ship comes and picks them up. Wireless Butts and tell him if he's got his gas to come up here with Allenkamp and share it. Then we'll have enough to reach the coast, and you can be wirelessin' Saigon to send a cruiser to pick these babies up—"

"Hold on, Mike!" Hogan was peering down through his glasses. "There's a guy wavin' down there. He's by himself. Get closer, will you?"

McGill cut his gun, drifted down toward the solitary man on the rocks.

Hogan yelled, "By cripes, Mike! It's Gales!"

"This ain't no time for jokes, Jake."

"I tell you it's Bill Gales! Go down!"

Dropping lower, Mike looked for himself, and his breath stuck in his throat. He yanked back on the stick so hard that when the plane leaped upward Hogan fell down in the seat. McGill got the wind on his nose and then scooted downward. His pontoons hit with a resounding smack.

Gales had jumped into the lagoon, was striking out for the Lockheed. McGill left the controls, climbed out to the foot-hold, down to one of the pontoons. He hung there, his eyes shining.

"Bill! Bill!"

"Mike—"

"Bill, you—you old son-of-a-gun! Bill, by cripes— Hogan, it is Bill! It is Bill!"

"Well, I said it was Bill."

The excitement too much for him, McGill slipped and fell into the water, came up spluttering. He trod water and reached out a hand. Gales grabbed it. They shook, and spluttered, and Hogan, forking the cockpit, said, "That's buddies for you."

CHAPTER XVIII

SKY TRAIL'S END

THE NEWS broke, first in Saigon, and later a newspaper was to remark that eighty-five men, as a result of receiving this news, had become inebriated beyond the bounds of respectability. Among them were a brigadier, a visiting colonel, and a captain of marines.

And the news, flying on electric wings in four directions spluttered in Bangkok, Hongkong, Singapore and reached ships at sea whose skippers and mates had been losing sleep. Two cruisers picked up their hooks and lit out for Base Three. An overzealous American banker in Hongkong let his entire staff off for the day and called it Gales and McGill Day.

Down in Singapore K.O. Pike had spent a sleepless night with his radio operator, waiting restively for each report from the two planes after their night take-off. No sleep at all had K.O. Day found him red-eyed and haggard. Then the report from Butts: *"Sky Hawk sighted."* Then the battle, and another report: *"Two strange planes making to attack us."*

At that time Gwen Manners had come, her face ghostly and drawn from worry and lack of sleep. She hadn't said much. Just sat there in a kind of stricken daze, heard K.O. repeat the reports. Then victory for his two planes. And new hope. And then suspense again when McGill and Butts set out for the base in the Lockheed. Finally the news that rocked the coast: *"Sky Hawk bombed and sunk. Men stranded on rocks. Will wireless Saigon to send cruiser."* Gwen had not stirred. Still in a daze. Until, on the heels of that message came another: *"Bill safe and sound."* Gwen had started to rise, crying out but fell back sobbing and laughing hysterically. K.O. roared for joy.

It should be inserted here that certain British Crown Officials, hearing McGill's story of the hidden wireless through the medium of K.O., had tactfully detained the man whom they believed to be Tai Yut. Even Manners identified him, although they were arch-enemies. Still, the Crown intimated that it would be wise for this Tai Yut to remain in his chambers until further notice.

This was the state of affairs when, on the following day, a plane appeared over the roadstead. A grease-monkey, smoking a butt on the Straits Agency wharf, first spied it, jumped up and grabbed a pair of glasses. He took one look, snapped away the butt and sloped into the wharf office, reported to the super. The super took a look through the window, yelped, and grabbed a telephone.

"Hey, K.O.," he yelled, "here comes the Vought!"

Big news has a way of getting around fast. Wherefore, as K.O. came booming down to the wharf, he found newsmen there, and cameramen.

The drone of the Vought came over the harbor. The crate, riddled with bullets, scarred beyond repair, slipped over the city on a tail wind, banked over the Raffles Hotel, and shot out over the harbor again, dropping fast. Spray shot upward when she hit the water. She swung around slowly and headed for the Straits Agency mooring basin.

McGill, at the controls, picked up the speaking tube and said, "Look at the mob, Bill."

"Tough break."

"See you got your tie on straight, pard. And look pretty for the cameras. There's K.O."

"Do you see Gwen?"

"I was expectin' a remark like that. Nope. I guess the jane has gone and fell for a polo player."

Now they could hear the acclaim of the crowd rising above the sound of the Whirlwind. McGill tooled the battered wagon in between the piers, and Gales stood up to catch the lines that were thrown out as the plane moved alongside a low float that passed beneath its wing.

McGill shut off the ignition. On the dock above, the eyes of three cameras were following them. The two partners stepped to the float, and K.O. gripped their arms, shook them.

"GREAT BOYS! Great boys!"

Gales said, "Hello, K.O.," and looked past him for sight of Gwen.

McGill said, "Tch! Egg on that nice white shirt, K.O.!"

The boys climbed the ladder to the wharf. The cameras got close-ups, and the reporters held their pads in hand. Their spokesman said, "Got a little statement, boys?"

"Go ahead, Bill," McGill muttered.

Gales said, "Well, there's not much to say. I've had a rough time of it, and by a stroke of luck I wiped out the master-mind behind all these killings and sinkings. But if it wasn't for Mike here, I wouldn't be alive to tell it. He saved my life at a time when I thought it was just about to end."

There was a woman's cry. Gwen came rushing through the crowd crying, "Bill! Bill!" Gales saw her and the grim look left his face. Gwen flew into his arms, flung arms around his neck, sobbing on his chest. The cameras clicked, and the newsmen wrote rapidly. McGill shifted from one foot to another, half-smiling, half-scowling.

By dint of much effort K.O. and McGill and Gales and Gwen fought through the crowd to a waiting limousine. The limousine carried them the short distance to K.O.'s office, and the office force gave three rousing cheers. In K.O.'s private sanctum, the chief had to say:

"Now, Miss Manners, please let Bill alone for a minute so we can talk things over." He grinned good-humoredly.

Gwen, flushed to the roots of her hair, said, "I've been a wild little fool, but I don't care. Oh, I'm so awfully happy!" She turned on McGill and threw her arms around him. "And so thankful to you, Mike, for bringing Bill back!"

"I—uh—m-m-m—now, Miss Manners—"

Did McGill flush to the roots of his hair? Why, his face was so red that you could not tell it from his hair!

"You adorable old red-head!" cried Gwen, releasing him.

The door burst open and Manners strode in, battle in his eye. He leveled an arm at his daughter.

"Gwen, I warned you not to come down here! Please get out of this office immediately!"

Gwen put hands on hips, tilted her chin. "Father," she said, "I shall come home later. This is Bill, my fiancé. Bill, my father."

"I'm awfully glad—" began Gales.

"Gwen," broke in Manners, "come home—this minute!"

"I am of age, father. I'll be home in a couple of hours."

Manners grew purple. He stared at the girl. Then he stared at Gales. Then he turned on his heel and strode out, slamming the door. Gwen relaxed, made a wry face. It was hard standing up against her father. He was really a fine man, and he worried about her. Gales looked puzzled. Then he began to understand. He bit his lip, and the old challenge came back into his eyes. But he said nothing.

K.O. coughed behind his hand, cleared his throat, said, "Now—ah— Bill."

"Yes, boss?"

"The *Sky Hawk* has been positively sunk, and when you left the base the men were stranded on the rocks with no means of getting off?"

"There was a yawlboat there, but one of Mike's bombs blew it to pieces. There was no other means for them to get away."

"I see. And this master-mind... his name was Tai Yut. Bill, are you sure it was Tai Yut?"

"Yes. He said it was, and his men addressed him that way. He used to be a big mercantile man. It seems certain companies combined to drive him out of business."

K.O. sighed. "Bill, it wasn't Tai Yut. Tai Yut is well known, and he is here in Singapore now, after a voyage from England. All the big shots know him."

Gales thinned his eyes. "I'd like to meet the gentleman. Someone has been impersonating him."

MAJOR SNOW, of the British Intelligence, met K.O. and the two partners in the lobby of the Metropole Palace.

"Ah, Gales… McGill! Right well done, old sons!" He shook warmly with them, twisted his yellow mustache, lowered his voice. "You say the chap was the brains behind this clique called himself Tai Yut? H'm. Rather embarrassing. Yet—well, come along. Meet the old boy."

A personal servant opened the door of the suite on the second floor. Major Snow entered first. Then K.O. and McGill. Gales came last. There were heavy footsteps, and a huge man came lumbering from an adjoining room.

"Ah, Mr. Tai," said the Major.

"Ah, my dear Major Snow. Such an extreme pleasure for this humble soul."

"Not at all," smiled Snow. "Permit me…. Mr. Pike of the Straits Agency. His operatives, Mr. McGill… Mr. Gales."

"It is a profound delight."

Gales stood staring at Tai Yut. It was Tai Yut! The very image of the man aboard the *Sky Hawk!* Yet this Tai Yut did not recognize Gales.

Snow was looking at Gales quizzically.

Gales said, "This man, Major, is a double of the one I knew as Tai Yut."

The Chinese looked amazed. "How very extraordinary! Some fellow of the baser sort assuming my name!"

McGill broke in—"Now hold on a minute. When I was listenin' outside the wireless room at the sawmill, I heard them guys say they'd had a message—by wireless from Tai Yut at Base Two. They called him Tai Yut."

"But my dear Mr. McGill," broke in the Chinese. "*I* am Tai Yut."

Major Snow said, "I have been biding my time until the return of these men. I have got in touch with authorities in Shangai and Peking. I have discovered that Mr. Tai Yut carried a birthmark on the back of his right shoulder. We can settle the matter very easily, sir."

The Chinese looked frightened, then indignant. "Absurd. I tell you, Major—"

"By showing me the birth mark, you will not have to tell me anything. Refusal to do so will necessitate force."

The Chinese took a backward step, his face lowering, a hunted look in his eyes. One by one the men in the room surrounded him. Bit by bit he crumbled.

"No," he said, "I am not Tai Yut."

"I knew it!" yelped McGill.

The Major said, "Then why have you been impersonating him? He is dead now. It does not matter with him."

The Chinese heaved a great sigh. "It was his bidding. I am his cousin. I was a small merchant in the city of Shao-hing. We bore some similarity to each other. One day he came to me and spoke at great length. He wanted to disappear from the world for a year. He wanted me to assume his name for that period. He said he wanted to live solitarily for some psychic purpose. It was very clear to me. He offered me much wealth, a trip around the world.

"I accepted. Then he engaged a surgeon to operate on my face and make it look more like his own. He had me imitate his mannerisms and deportment and speech. Three months we spent together doing this. Finally he left his mansion in Peking, told me to experiment on his servants and friends. It worked admirably. They did not know I was not Tai Yut. When he heard this he rejoiced. Then he put much money at my disposal, and set the date when I was to start on my journey around the world.

"Great mandarins came to see me off, and some illustrious white men. I saw my picture in the newspapers, and underneath each picture the name of Tai Yut. All of China knew that Tai

Yut was voyaging around the world. That is the limit of my guilt. If I have been made a pawn for some ulterior motive, I am very humble, and I am at your mercy, gentlemen."

Major Snow smiled. "No harm will come to you, as far as I see it." He turned to the others. "Now it is clear. Five years ago Tai Yut was practically driven from the sea for his underhand method in shipping. The money of several shipping companies and other companies that used ships for their commodities went into a melting pot to drive Tai Yut out. He was suspected of piracy several times. He had twelve steam vessels and ten junks under his flag. When the *Silas Boone* was raided and pirated off Amoy six years ago, he was suspected. Fate piled his junk *Chong Li* on the rocks north of Amoy, and the loot of the *Silas Boone* was found on board. That was the last straw. The combine of companies drove him from the sea, and through their influence insurance companies refused to underwrite Tai's bottoms.

"And this was his revenge. All ships sunk by his *Sky Hawk* were owned by one of the companies that had aligned against him. You see how clever he was? No one suspected him. Tai Yut as far as we knew, had become resigned to his fate and was traveling for his health. Mr. Pike, you are to be commended for your diligence."

"Rats!" growled K.O. "My boys here. They did it. The guys that nobody believed could do it. The guys that everybody slandered and called dirty names. The guys that—"

"I for one," smiled Major Snow, "am penitent. I fancy almost everybody else is."

THE PAPERS had one more thing to howl about—with delight. On the very next night a plane took off at half-past ten, aided by Straits Agency floodlights.

Next morning the plane alighted on the river at Saigon. Gales and Gwen went ashore followed by McGill. They took an automobile out of town, and entered a white mission building. Fifteen minutes later they came out and drove back to the city, and Gwen was wearing a ring. She sent a lot of wires. Then the newspapers cut loose.

At three that afternoon a wire arrived from Manners. He had resigned himself, wired: *Blessing on you children!*

Gwen was infinitely happy then. Gales was glad the old boy had wired like a man.

McGill still went about in a kind of a daze. He could hardly believe that Bill was married. His partner was gone, and he was alone now, and he knew there would never be another flying and fighting mate like Bill.

Gales and Gwen found him staring blankly out of a window. Mike fidgeted.

Gales said, "Just had a wire from K.O. Mike. He's making me manager of the new Straits Agency branch in Bangkok. He says you will be chief of flight there."

McGill began to grin. He stood up. "That's fine, Bill." He swallowed hard. "Gee, that's great, Bill!"

Gwen asked, "And do you still hate women, Mike?"

Mike crossed the room and picked up his topee. "I'm gonna take a little stroll."

That night Gales and Gwen were strolling up an avenue lined with sidewalk cafés, at which sat bemedalled officers and *chic mademoiselles.*

Gales stopped short, gripped Gwen's arm. "Look!"

"What?"

"Mike. Mike over that—at the café. See him? He's bending over a table and making eyes at that dark-eyed French girl. And will you look at her roll *her* eyes! Gwen, I've got to go over and save Mike—"

She held him back, smiled. "Don't, Bill. I never saw an Irishman yet-and particularly a red-headed one—who couldn't take care of himself. Besides, it's a good sign he's stopped hating women!"

Gales chuckled. "That'll make life easier for you, Gwen."

Arm in arm, they strolled on in the evening cool.

SKY SCRAPPERS

Gales and McGill, tamers of terror, were the top-aces of Tropic air. But in all their flame-shot flights they'd never bucked a play as crooked and as deadly as lay beyond the Border of Lost Men.

THE INCREDIBLE Mike McGill was downhearted.

Many things were wrong. Fifi had chucked him for a dashing naval lieutenant. Bill Gales had gone and got himself married and was now the Straits Agency's brass hat in Bangkok. Insult was added to injury in the form of "Duke" Hannon, the Agency's poo-bah in Saigon and McGill's unrelenting taskmaster.

The forlorn red-head sat at a table on the terrace of a Saigon café, chin in hands; on the table, a half-drunk glass of black coffee and a half-eaten roll. It was seven o'clock in the morning.

Even the sight of Duke Hannon striding wrathfully across the street did not rouse McGill.

"You-four-kinds-of-an-odiferous stink-weed!" rapped out Duke Hannon as he banged his way among the tables.

McGill stared lonesomely at the table.

"McGill!"

McGill sighed and stared at the table.

"McGill!"

"Huh?"

"Where have you been? I said—where have you been?"

The blue eyes of McGill looked up beneath his wiry red eyebrows.

"Says which?"

"Idiot, where have you been? Are you drunk? Have you been riding around all night with that Fifi wench?"

McGill winced. Fifi had done him wrong.

Duke Hannon rapped the table with his swagger stick "Get the lead out of your pants, pilot! The cards say that you are going on a long journey! I've been running all over town looking for you and here you are in a sodden stupor! That Fifi will be the ruination of you."

"First," said McGill, "I was goin' to bust her neck. If you keep on poppin' off, sweetheart, I'll bust yours."

"McGill get up! You're taking the Lockheed to Hongkong with a passenger."

McGill took his time about paying the check and about getting up. He sauntered out of the café unmoved by Duke Hannon's energy.

Hannon was explaining, "Lomis was supposed to make the trip, but he's down with the fever. You'll have to make it, and you'll have to push the crate to make Hongkong before dark. Come on, snap on it."

"Ah, Rome wasn't built in a day."

"Who the sweet suffering cripes is trying to build Rome?"

Hearing the river, McGill heard the sound of a motor warming up. He got a look at the two-place seaplane and then followed Hannon into the little white office.

A small plump man with a black spade beard turned from the window and blinked through rimless spectacles.

"You'll be off in a minute, Mr. James," Hannon said. "This is your pilot, Mr. McGill. McGill, Mr. James."

"Nice day," said McGill.

"How do you do," said Mr. James in a halting un-English accent. "We will take off immediately, no?"

McGill said to Hannon, "How's the weather up the coast?"

"Fine. Light winds from the north. If you push the crate you'll make Hongkong before dark."

McGill lowered his voice. "Who's this guy?"

"James—I told you. Mr. John James."

"I was just wonderin' where he picked up the trick accent with a name like that. Or maybe he picked the name up."

"Don't be a goof!"

McGill picked up goggles and a light flying helmet. "Okey, mastermind."

"And no stunting."

McGill went out and down to the wharf chewing on a cigarette, "How's the coffee-grinder, Jake?"

"The answer to a pilot's prayer."

"I ain't prayed, but— All right, Louie," he yelled down. "Get out and don't leave any grease on the seat. I got to wear these pants on a bender in Hongkong…. Down this way, Mr. James, and in that rear cockpit."

He watched the man go down and took a last puff on his cigarette. His blue eyes were keened. Queer guy, that James. Looked like a doctor. McGill shrugged and swung down and went over the coaming. He buckled on James's belt and helped him with the goggles.

"Remember," Hannon was yelling, "no fancy work, half-pint."

"Go scratch yourself, sweetheart! Who's flyin' this wagon?"

He bounced down in the front cockpit and buckled on his belt while running his eyes over the array of dials on the dashboard. He revved a few times and wiggled the stick. Then he throttled down and yelled to the boys to cut her loose.

THE SLEEK gray Lockheed pranced on the choppy little waves the wharf threw back. The siren to warn craft was howling. McGill yanked his goggles down and squared himself before the controls. He conned the river on either side of the buoys that marked the Agency's channel.

He shoved forward a bit on the throttle, and the plane began to vibrate, her slipstream skimming up a light rain of water. The floats dug in as the throttle went up a little more. The water battled with the floats, roaring, beating furiously, and the wind began to hammer, the prop hummed and the exhaust bellowed. The Lockheed was a gray streak slicing on the surface.

Then it was up, floats dripping, prop boring into the wind, tearing the wind as the powerful crate lunged upward over the river. She was heavy—heavy with fuel in special wing-tanks.

McGill banked gently at eight hundred feet, left the river behind and crossed the city and took his crate droning over the northern wilderness. Northeast his course lay, for Hue on the raw Indo-China coast. Northeast over a half-forgotten hinterland to the coast—four hundred miles of dangerous flying.

He hiked up to three thousand feet and leveled off and watched the airspeed meter till they were doing a hundred and twenty. Everything looked rosy. Wind and motor and prop made a bedlam, but when he looked down there was no sense of speed, for the wilderness seemed to crawl beneath them.

Mr. James took very little interest in the scenery. Nor did he show any uneasiness. Sometimes he looked from side to side casually. Sometimes he read from a book. He looked by no means a novice in the air.

McGill half-drowsed, thinking of wilder, pleasanter days. He had crossed this country before—with Bill Gales. Those were the days!

Fighting. Taking long chances. Running contraband. Barred from half a dozen cities. Flying for the Canton Government. One day the toast of the cities; the next, outcasts. But always together, making a name that was already becoming legend in the yellow and sinister East.

A bump yanked him wide awake.

He tooled the crate out of a bad stagger. He looked at his chart and checked off familiar landmarks. The sun rose higher and was hot. The smell of oil was hot. The endless beat of the motor made a man drowsy. But Hue was reached, the compass checked.

The Lockheed left land behind and soared out over the broad mouth of the Gulf of Tonkin. No landmarks now, and McGill hated navigation.

But Cape Bastion must be picked up.

Below, the sea glittered. Birds wheeled above the plane.

Mr. James said through the inter-cockpit speaking tube, "You will pass Cape Bastion, no?"

"Yeah."

"You will cross Hainan Strait and then you will touch the China Coast just north of Kwangchow, no?"

"You know the road better than I do, mister."

"It is what you will do, no?"

"Yup."

"Thank you kindly, pilot."

Funny guy. Funny accent in a small jerky voice. And the mouth that was inscrutably hidden behind the black spade beard. Like a professor—or a doctor. H'm. Mr. John James.

Well, you never knew. Men were strange out here.

SO IT happened: Hainan Strait, the island of Hainan left behind, and the course altered westward a bit to raise Kwangchow. A cluster of fighting air currents bubbled wildly under the Lockheed, and the plane stumbled violently, its wings whipping up and down.

McGill tussled with adverse currents all the way to Kwangchow. He did not cross the city; merely raised it with binoculars over his port bow and then wheeled away to edge up to the wild coast that straggled north to Hongkong.

The air trail smoothed out. The sun beat down mercilessly. It was warm in the close-cowled cockpits. Rocks gashed huge waves below. McGill was pushing the crate hard, but the motor temperature was too high. He'd have to ease up. His eyes were glued on the dials.

Mr. James's voice came through the tube, "It is interesting to see that we have company, no?'

"Huh?"

"Ahead, and a little inland, there is a plane."

McGill looked up and squinted against the blazing sunlight.

"Two planes," he said. "Mail, prob'ly."

"It is interesting to see, pilot, that the planes are changing their course to wave us good-day."

"Oh, yeah?"

The red-head bent his brows and scowled. Experience had taught him to be suspicious of everything that walked, crawled or flew in the land of poppies and pagodas. He eased up on the throttle and reached for binoculars.

He took a serious look at the two planes. Fokkers. Big babies, too. One yellow and the other brown.

"I may be wrong," he muttered, "but—"

His teeth set. He hit the gun hard and made a long stab for altitude.

"Is something wrong?" shouted Mr. James, and now anxiety quickened his voice.

McGill poked his head out and saw both planes whipping tails downward and props upward.

"I wouldn't fool you," McGill said.

CHAPTER II

THE YELLOW FOKKER

HE **FLATTENED** out at ten thousand feet above a serried cloud bank and looked down and saw the two planes come tearing up through the clouds.

"You punks!" he muttered.

Two-place jobs, big and grim-looking, and both armed, and neither with markings. McGill looked around at his passenger. Mr. James was looking downward, his beard blowing in the wind.

McGill yelled through the tube, "I don't know what those guys are up to, but we can't fight 'em. We're not armed, except me with a pistol, which I might just as well chuck away. But hang on. Maybe we can lose 'em."

He whipped the Lockheed over on one ear and howled away. He could look down and see raised faces framed in tight helmets. He straightened his wings and shoved the throttle up to the last notch. The yellow Fokker came pounding up under his nose.

He looked down and saw a machine gun slanted upward. He saw puffs of smoke but heard no snarl of lead in his plane.

Mr. James screamed through the tube, "They will kill us, pilot, no?"

"Yeah."

"Go down. It is better to go down than to be killed."

"It ain't me they want. It must be you."

"Then go down. I do not know why they want me, but go down! I implore you, pilot, to go down."

"Aw, shut up."

Again McGill looked down. The yellow plane was directly beneath his nose, the brown one back on his tail.

His eyes flicked the dials. That motor was too hot for safety. He himself was sweating, and the smell of hot oil was thick in his nostrils.

He was mad. If only Bill were along—Bill flying this bus and himself at a Lewis gun....

The yellow plane's gun was starting again—quick spurts of smoke that the wind gobbled up. But the lead came through the wind. It rattled through the Lockheed's wing tip. McGill shook his fist. The gunner below was waving for McGill to go down.

And Mr. James screamed, "Go down, pilot! We shall be killed!"

"Listen, mister. You're my passenger. I want to get you out of this, but you've got to stop yellin' at me."

"Yes, I am your passenger. And do you think I want to be shot full of holes? Besides, maybe it is you they want. I do not know that it is I who is wanted. Therefore we must talk with these men. Of what use is it to fly around up here and be shot full of holes?"

"Listen, sweetheart—"

"It is not that I am anyone's sweetheart——"

"All right, all right. But listen! They don't want me. I'm tryin' to do this for you—"

"For me you could do nothing but stop my getting shot full of holes and go down. Is my life not to be considered? Of what use is one who has been shot full of holes? No?"

"Okey, professor. Have it your way. Down we go."

McGill cut his gun and shoved the plane's nose downward. It was not in his grain to give up like this, but there was nothing else to do. His plane was unarmed. It was a valuable piece of property. And Mr. James wanted to go down.

McGILL PUT the Lockheed down well off the coast, where the sea was like a mirror. The yellow plane landed behind and came chugging across the water. The brown plane hovered aloft, its men watching.

McGill forked the coaming and watched the yellow Fokker as it slushed up alongside, its machine gun trained on the Lockheed.

"Wise, ain't you?" McGill yelled over.

The young Chinese gunner stood up and saluted. "You did well to come down."

"My eye! What do you bimboes want?"

"Your passenger."

Mr. James swallowed hard and looked at McGill blankly. "It is me they want?"

McGill dropped his voice. "Hey, you got a gun?"

"N-no."

"Big help you turned out to be."

"We want your passenger," said the Chinese gunner. "He will crawl out across the wing to our plane."

McGill swore under his breath and whipped up his automatic pistol. "Not while I—"

The machine gun blazed and a stream of lead whanged over McGill's head.

Mr. James screamed and huddled in the cockpit.

"I told you we shouldn't have come down!" roared McGill.

"Do not be foolish," warned the Chinese gunner, baring his teeth. "Your passenger will come on board."

Mr. James appeared timidly. "I will go, pilot," he said weakly. "It is a plot. Of what nature I do not know."

He unbuckled his belt. His hands shook.

McGill was grim-faced but helpless. His eyes were glazed with fury as he watched the little old man climbing out across the wing.

"You guys ain't gonna get away with this!" he yelled. "Me and my partner—"

He stopped short. Bill Gales was no longer his partner. Bill was married and had a wife in Bangkok. McGill downed a lump in his throat.

The gunner hauled Mr. James into the rear cockpit and McGill saw him put manacles on the little old man. Then the gunner crowded down into the cockpit and waved.

"Good-bye, my friend," he called, showing his teeth.

"I'll be seein' you, wisenheimer," McGill snarled.

"Discretion is the better part of valor."

"And so is a punch in the snoot."

"Again—good-bye."

The Chinese pilot leered and gunned his motor and the yellow plane started off. It joined the brown plane above and the two headed for the coast.

McGill slumped back into the cockpit. He sat for a moment staring bitterly at the dials. Bill wasn't there to cheer him up. He keened his eyes at the distant planes.

How had they known Mr. James was on the wing? How had they known just where to trap him? Someone who knew the route of the Agency planes had tipped them off.

He gunned his motor and lifted the Lockheed off the sea.

He did not head for Hongkong. He wheeled his crate back over the trail he had taken north, and stopped at Hue for fuel. He took off again late in the afternoon.

Dusk got him over the Indo-China wilds. Then darkness, and he had to pick his way carefully in the night. He got lost and finally found himself at the mouth of the Mekong River, way off his course. He flew low and picked his way up the river.

And at ten-thirty he raised Saigon.

He whipped round and round over the Straits Agency's basin until they turned on the floodlights. He cut his motor down and heard the noise of the warning siren. He slapped his pontoons down on the water and drove the crate toward the wharf.

"What are you doing back here?" yelled Duke Hannon.

McGill said nothing until he had helped make the plane fast. He climbed up to the wharf and Duke Hannon grabbed his arm.

"I said—what are you doing back here?"

McGill snatched the cigarette from Hannon's mouth and took a puff. "My passenger changed planes."

"Your what did which?"

McGill nodded to the office. "You and me have got to go into a huddle."

CHAPTER III

THE COMING OF GALES

THE NEWS stirred Saigon—but not much. The China Coast was never a safe coast, and such things as piracy and sudden death rarely got into the headlines for the simple reason that such things were becoming commonplace.

Whispers of the strange abduction reached the coast cities. But in many a bar or hotel lounge men merely yawned and ordered another drink.

A few of the more curious asked, "Who was this Mr. John James?"

Heads shook and shoulders shrugged in reply. No one had ever heard of Mr. James.

Even McGill echoed, "Yeah, who was he? He couldn't have been no small tomatoes if these guys kidnaped him."

"It seems to me," snapped Duke Hannon, "that you might have got away from the beggars."

"He wanted to go down," growled McGill. "He was scared out of his pants. Besides, you intellectual giant, even if I did sashay around, them babies would have nailed us. They had machine guns. What did I have? Nothin'—except a motor too hot for comfort and an old guy yammerin' my eardrums off."

Hannon bowed with elaborate politeness. "But you forget you are *the* Mike McGill—*the* flying bearcat—*the*—"

"Just a minute," McGill said with equally elaborate politeness.

Hannon glared, tight-lipped.

"You're face is a pretty nice one, Hannon."

"Well!"

"Your teeth ain't false, either, are they?"

"Of course not!"

"Well, you ground-flying son-of-a-so-and-so, I'll—"

He stopped short, listening. He went to a window and looked up.

"Hey," he yelled, "it's Bill Gales' Vought."

"What's he doing here?"

"I hope it's to take your job over."

McGill pivoted and went out like a blast of wind.

Yup—that was the Vought, and she was being flown as nobody but Bill could fly her.

In his excitement McGill struck a cigarette in his mouth and then forgot to light it. He moved restlessly on his feet and kept rubbing his hands together. His freckled face radiated, lost its hardness. He looked boyish—like a kid.

Gales was coming.

Like a bird the Vought flew—graceful, easy, down—down, till the pontoons flicked the water with scarce a splash, and the prop was a whirling disk shimmering in the sun.

"Hi, Bill!"

McGill went scampering down the ladder from the main wharf to the broad moored float below. He caught the wing as the Vought bobbed alongside, and he shouted at Bill Gales, and Gales grinned and waved.

There was another man in the rear cockpit, one McGill did not know. The handlers made the plane fast, and Gales stood up, pointing to his passenger and indicating the way out.

McGill helped the man to the float, and then Gales came— lean and soldierly in an immaculate white suit, replacing his helmet with a white solar topee.

"Hello, Mike, you old roustabout!"

"Bill, you're sure a sight for sore eyes! You sure are, son."

"Hello, Gales." Hannon thrust in. "Glad to see you."

"Hello, Hannon. How's every little thing?"

"Terrible."

Gales turned to his passenger. "This is Captain Ingram, of the British Intelligence. Hannon. Captain, and my old partner Mike McGill."

"Well, well, McGill—this is indeed a pleasure. Oh, hello, Mr. Hannon."

A tall, cool man was Captain Ingram, with merry eyes.

Gales was saying, "Let's go somewhere and talk."

"There's certainly a lot to talk about," complained Hannon.

"You're right, Hannon," Gales said. "There is."

He turned to McGill and pressed the red-head's arm. "Sorry, partner, this had to happen to you."

"That's all right, Bill," McGill muttered. "If it hadn't happened to me it would have happened to Lomis."

"And it's grave, Mike—grave as the old devil."

THEY REACHED the office and filed in. Gales closed the door and tipped back his helmet. Captain Ingram was stuffing a pipe, and he sat down, sighing. Hannon looked troubled. McGill looked expectant.

"Mr. McGill"—Captain Ingram held up a lighted match— "could you describe this Mr. John James?"

"Why—"

Hannon broke in, "He was a short plump man, with a black Van Dyke, rimless glasses, and a sort of quaint accent."

"By Godfrey!" exclaimed Ingram, with a quick look at Gales. "It's the doctor!"

"You were right, then," nodded Gales.

Ingram puffed up quickly, smoke curling around his face. Through it his clipped, pleasant voice came—"Dr. Leopold Jons, the eccentric scientist."

"Who," said McGill, "would want to kidnap an eccentric scientist? And why was he traveling incog?"

"I have heard of him," rattled in Hannon. "Who hasn't? By George, then this is more serious than—than we thought!"

Captain Ingram bit him with a keen glance. "Why?"

Hannon gulped. "Well—well, isn't it? I mean, first—well, no one had ever heard of John James. But—but Leopold Jons! You—you see?"

Ingram said, "Yes," in a vague tone.

Gales suddenly smacked fist into palm. "We've got to get him back! We can't let him—"

"Pardon," said Captain Ingram. "Let me inform these men what has occurred. Dr. Jons is almost a legendary figure. Some claim he is a charlatan. Others claim he is profound. We must assume, for our purposes, that he is profound. Aeronautics has interested him for the past ten years—to the exclusion of almost everything else.

"Oddly enough, he has lived in the East for many years—in Singapore, Peking and Kobe. Let us say that he has become slightly Orientalized—in philosophy only."

"Political philosophy?" McGill asked bluntly.

Ingram shrugged. "He recently completed an invention. This invention, it is claimed, will increase the offensive power of a plane one hundred per cent. It will by the same token increase its defensive power. Consultations have been held with the war departments of England, France and America. I myself do not know what this invention is. Only the secret emissaries of the three Governments know, and they know only the minor details—sufficient, however, to make his kidnaping a grave affair.

Ingram frowned.

"But someone else must have found out. General Kwang Gow, the Chinese warlord, said to have the largest private army in the world, has ambitions. He hates all other Chinese generals, but most of all he hates all white men. He once made the boast that he would overpower all China, burn all the French, American and English settlements—drive us into the sea, those of us he did not kill. It is suspected that General Kwang Gow may have a hand in this. If so—and if he works out this invention, there will be wholesale slaughter."

McGill asked, "But why was this doctor travelin' incog?"

"No one knows. Probably in an attempt to avoid being noticed. There was to be a meeting in Hongkong of the White Powers. You see the importance of this? General Kwang Gow has been a potential menace for the past three years. He has boundless wealth—the loot of a hundred cities. He has secret agents throughout the East. He has power—and satanic ambition. I tell you, gentlemen, every white man in the East has cause to tremble in his boots!"

"It's that bad?" asked Gales.

"Quite," affirmed Ingram.

Gales said, "There's nothing for us to do but get him back."

"That's no small job," cut in Hannon. "It's a job for all the Powers—not for a flying detective agency."

"It's our job, too—a moral obligation," objected Gales. "We let him get away."

"Yes, your bright partner did."

McGill flushed.

Gales said, "He couldn't have done anything else. There were two armed planes."

"What I'm wonderin'," McGill growled, "is how they knew where to head us off."

"I said before," Ingram put in, "that General Kwang has agents all about us. The thing is, we are not sure General Kwang is mixed up in it. We only venture to say that. It must be proved."

Hannon snapped, "All right. I'll attend to it personally."

"I forgot to say," Gales said, "that K.O. Pike wired me this morning. Instructed me to leave Moberly in charge at Bangkok, take Mike here and see what we can see."

"Hot dog!" McGill beamed.

Hannon flared, "I guess I'm capable. This thing happened in my territory. I don't see—"

"You'll have to complain to K.O.," Gales said. "Orders are orders. Lord knows I'd rather stay in Bangkok with my wife."

"I'll wire K.O. immediately," barked Hannon. He went out banging the door.

"Um," murmured Ingram, concealing a smile.

"Hannon's all right," Gales said. "Just a bit touchy. He takes his job seriously."

"Don't I know it!" exclaimed McGill.

"You'll find me at the Hotel de Sud," Ingram said.

When he had gone Gales and McGill looked at each other.

"Bill, this sure is a break."

Gales nodded soberly.

"It's the biggest thing we ever stacked against, Mike."

"Horsefeathers! It's just about our size."

But Gales had a wife in Bangkok.

CHAPTER IV

THE YELLOW WARLORD

THE PRESS blazed with the news that Dr. Leopold Jons had been abducted.

John James was nobody. But Dr. Jons was a name to conjure with, a name to make news.

Few knew what important secret he had. But many conjectured. The newspapers concocted all sorts of fantastic reasons why he had been kidnaped. None of them was right, though a few came near to the truth without perhaps realizing.

Why had he assumed an alias? And why, under this alias, had he taken passage by plane from Saigon? The press asked these questions of stars.

The press also made much of the fact that the notorious partnership of Gales and McGill was again in action. This roused interest in many a hotel bar. The names of Gales and McGill tacked on to any strange venture doubled its interest.

There would be trouble, gossip said. Trouble could not be avoided if some scheme was headed by the notorious pair.

"It's like old times, Bill," McGill said. "Son, we're like a two-man vaudeville team. Alone, we ain't nobody. Together—well, it's like two live wires meetin' and causin' a lot of spark."

There was work to be done. The Lockheed was drawn out of water and overnight turned into an amphibian. It was Gales' contention that Jons had been taken inland. If so, it would mean long flights over rough terrain.

McGill reminded him that the two Fokkers had had only pontoons. Gales admitted that perhaps they came from some lake or river inland.

"But we don't know where that is," he went on. "Hence we need two kinds of gear."

Duke Hannon was in a perpetual tantrum. He had wired K.O. Pike and K.O. had wired him back tartly. Hannon's vanity was hurt. He got it into his head that Gales was trying to show him up, and when Gales good-naturedly scoffed at that, Hannon maintained that McGill had connived to get Gales to Saigon.

McGill took a swing at the super, but Gales dragged him off.

Then Gales threatened to refuse any participation in the hunt, and K.O. wired that he'd come up and mop them all over the place. While the Lockheed was being turned into an amphib, the Saigon division of the famous Agency was in an uproar, with McGill and Hannon always ready to fight on sight.

Then the Lockheed was ready. It was finished during the night, and Gales kept McGill away from Hannon until morning. But morning found both of them still in high heat.

"It's a dirty lousy contemptible shame!" roared Hannon. "I can run this shebang here—as well as either one of you guys. I've got a mind to chuck this job. But—no, I won't. I'll stick and, by the holy, I'll show you that I'm as good as you—both of you."

"For two cents," yelled McGill, "I'd knock your teeth down your throat."

Gales, always the headier of the pair, jumped between them. His blue eyes flashed.

"Cut it out, Mike."

"Says who?"

"Says me. By George, if you don't, *I'll* take a swing at you."

He whirled. "And you, Hannon, get wise to yourself. I don't say we're any better than you are. But we've been chosen for this job and we're going to do it, and if you hop around here like a blasted idiot I'll have to punch your jaw out of place. The both of you are like a couple of dirty hoodlums, so help me!"

"Hoodlums, eh?" rasped Hannon. "You're the hoodlums! For years you've been outcasts on the Coast. Free lances, eh? Bah! A couple of pirates. A couple of flying freebooters. And I'm not so sure, McGill, that you didn't know Jons was going to be kidnaped—"

"Leggo me, Bill! Lemme at him!" screamed McGill.

Gales had to heave all his lean young strength against McGill. The two partners crashed to the floor, legs flying.

"Now, now, Mike—"

"Leggo, Bill! By cripes, that guy's been persecutin' me ever since I been here! He's always been doubtin' me. I gotta paste him. I gotta—"

Hannon stood his ground, white-faced, fists clenched. "Let him up! Go ahead! I'll drive his head through the wall!"

Furious, Gales leaped up, took one hard swing and sent Hannon flying through the door. Hannon lost his balance, crashed into three coolies. The coolies scattered and screeched.

McGill came sailing out and Gales took one step and dropped him with a blow to the ear.

Hannon was jumping up.

"Beat it!" Gales clipped. "There's work to be done, you fool. Don't get this guy started, or I'll never get him in the air."

Hannon towered in red rage. "All right. But I'll show you! You can't make a monkey out of me!" He swiveled and went off, his dignity outraged.

McGILL SAT up. "What a pal you turned out to be, Bill."

Gales helped him up. "I'm sorry, partner. But I had to do it. You yapping—and Hannon yapping—like two idiots. Buck up, Mike. Forget your grudge. Think of what's at stake. We've got enough fight ahead of us without this dirty little bickering."

McGill grumbled, picked up his helmet and swung down toward the wharf. Gales smiled ruefully after him. It was always the way. Mike would grouch now for hours. And so would Hannon. Both had unharnessed tempers.

Gales went back into the office to get his charts, and when he came out again Captain Ingram was standing on the wharf. The captain looked puzzled, nodded to the Lockheed, which McGill was warming up.

"I tried to talk to him," Ingram said. "He—well—just went by. Y' know?"

Gales chuckled. "Little difficulty. Nothing important."

"All my best wishes, Gales. It may be dangerous."

"We're going to Hongkong first. Refuel there and then inland to General Kwang's base."

"Be mighty careful, old man. It must be proved, you know, that Kwang—"

"We'll try to prove it." Hannon appeared briskly, very business-like, very high-hat.

Gales said, "You can relay our reports to K.O."

"I guess I know that," snapped Hannon.

Gales went down to the Lockheed and swung into the rear cockpit. A new Lewis gun had been attached. A wireless set crouched on rubber shock-absorbers. Gales affixed his charts to the dash and then buckled on his belt, put on his helmet, his goggles. He picked up the speaking-tube.

"Take off any time, Mike."

McGill throttled way down and yelled for the handlers to cut away the lines. He raced the plane down the stretch of water and lifted it savagely into the air. He hauled it up over the city and flattened out at a thousand feet, and after one downward contemptuous look that was meant for Hannon, he swung north and left the city behind.

He scowled for three hours. Gradually he cooled off. When they crossed Hue he was whistling to himself.

After all, he had cause to be happy. He had nothing to do but work the controls. Gales did the navigating. McGill was ready to swear that no one could navigate like Bill. Bill had a flair for it, and Bill was rarely wrong.

They crossed the island of Hainan, then Hainan Strait; and when they struck the China coast north of Kwang-chow, McGill said through the tube:

"Around here is where we got attacked."

"You'd remember the guys, wouldn't you, Mike?"

"One of them."

WINDS LAMBASTED them thenceforth. The Lockheed reeled and staggered, and the sea below broke in white-capped angry rollers.

The sky brooded, and the sun was a bruised white eye behind flying scud. Wires hummed and whistled and great gusts of wind shook the plane violently. But the motor was a smooth roar, the prop a shining disc that carved its way relentlessly through the wind.

At six o'clock they droned over the Bay of Hongkong. McGill put the crate down in the shadow of the Bund and chugged it toward a wharf used by the Agency.

Major Downe was there to meet them, and two marines had been brought to guard the Lockheed. An Embassy limousine took them to a hotel.

"We have agents working here and in Canton," Major Downe said, "and through the outlying cities. We have sent spies into the secret Chinese societies and we are tapping all wireless messages. The Peking Government has offered assistance; likewise the Nanking Government. The Chinese in power are afraid that some ambitious rebel is planning to overthrow them."

Hongkong was agog. Dignitaries of three governments called on Gales and McGill.

Reporters interviewed them and tried to discover their plans. Gales got rid of them tactfully.

They were in the limelight again, their names were on every tongue. The general attitude was that Gales and McGill would find no trouble in recovering Dr. Jons or at least destroying his notes and plans.

There was no peace for the partners that night. Telephone bells rang, telegrams and cables arrived from people they'd never heard of. There were three proposals of marriage—to either one of the aces. There were photographers and special news correspondents.

Until finally Gales barred the door, refused to answer telephones.

Worn out, McGill said, "Whew! Somethin' tells me, Bill, that all these people has heard of us."

"With all this horseplay," ripped out Gales, "we'll draw the attention of our enemies—whoever they are. We'll get bumped off before we start. Why can't they let us alone?"

BUT THE two partners got away next morning. Early though it was—just after sunrise—they found a crowd on the Bund and down around the pier.

Major Downe wished them soft landings, and the guards who had watched the plane during the night reported that no one had been around. Gales went over it, however, while McGill warmed up the motor.

They took the plane up into the eye of the sun, pounding low over an American cruiser and two English destroyers. McGill banked and turned over the roadstead. With the wind on the plane's tail, he crossed Hongkong and headed for Kowloon.

Gales, studying his chart, gave brief instructions through the speaking-tube. McGill tooled the crate accordingly, and when they crossed Kowloon they were doing a hundred miles an hour in a northwesterly direction.

Then Kwangtung Province unrolled before them, and the last glimmer of the sea dropped over the horizon.

McGill felt chipper. No one had taken a pot-shot at them in Hongkong, and the air trail was smooth as velvet. The Wasp had never sounded smoother, and Gales' calm, certain voice, altering or okeying the course, was a benediction. There was no Duke Hannon around to get under his feet, and there was a good possibility of a fight in the near future.

Though Gales was not depressed, he was by no means bathed in a roseate glow. The country was wild below. There was no known landmarks. Their course was purely one followed by calculation. He had wired Gwen last night, had received a wire from her. He missed her, and he knew she was worried.

Way beyond, in the mountains of Hunan Province, was the city of General Kwang, reputed an impregnable stronghold. To it Kwang had built roads, had built a private railway to boot. Cashiered officers from half a dozen nations trained his men.

In his city in the mountains he assembled his own planes, paying handsome sums to experts. Many said he was the greatest warlord China had ever known, and that ages ago one of his ancestors had ruled all of China and the wild Siberian wastes.

To this strange city Gales and McGill were going.

They crossed plains and grim plateaus and flew toward the foothills and over the foothills toward the frowning mountains. Out of the tangled wilderness below they picked lone lakes and tiny rivers. With his binoculars Gales saw a road that had been hewn out of the forest, and later he picked up shining rails of a railway. The mountain air currents tossed them about, but they went steadily over the mountains.

Then Gales saw the city.

First, glimpses of things shining, temples and roofs flecked by the high white sun. A narrow valley and a city built on the slopes of a buttressed mountain that rose from the valley tier on tier.

An irregular skein of shining brightness that was a mountain river, cascading down on one side of the city and crashing into the valley below. Buildings that were new and of metal, topped with stacks that belched smoke. Here electricity was made from the power of the falls.

"This guy's no piker," McGill said through the speaking-tube.

"There's still water off the river—and that looks like a flying field at the base of the mountain. It is. Try the field, Mike."

CIRCLING, THEY could see long barracks and tents, and a dozen planes lined up at one side of the field. McGill cut his gun and loafed down.

Men scattered from the field, but a small group remained at the edge and some of them looked up with glasses. McGill made a three-point landing and rolled the crate leisurely up toward the hangars. He cut the motor out and the crate stopped, surrounded by a dozen men.

"You have come a long way," said a tall, lean-boned officer.

Gales heaved out of the cockpit and dropped to the ground.

"Had no intention of stopping here," he lied. "Just saw your spread and thought you wouldn't mind."

"A long way off any beaten track, aren't you?"

"Oh, yes," Gales said lightly. "We're really on a job."

The lean-boned officer bit his lip indecisively. Then he shrugged. He turned away, but swung back immediately, scowling.

"What sort of job?" he barked.

"It's not important. But—come to think of it—General Kwang might help us. Send up our names. Gales and McGill."

The group stirred. Eyes flashed or narrowed. The lean-boned man muttered to a small dapper Chinese, and the latter hurried off.

CHAPTER V

WHERE IS DR. JONS?

THE HEADQUARTERS of General Kwang stood halfway up a tortuous cobbled street. A military car deposited Gales and McGill in front of a massive stone house. The lean-boned-man went with them.

In a great library sat the great warlord. He sat behind a massive desk. He was a massive man, the fat of him bulging a uniform, great fleshy jowls hanging over his collar, fat eyelids drooping over somber eyes. His nose was a huge bulb in the center of his face, and his mustache was like gray weeds dangling over his thick lips. Maps cluttered his desk.

Three aides, one of them a cast-eyed white man, fluttered around him.

"So," rumbled the warlord. "I have the honor of a visit from Gales and McGill."

"They landed, sir, ten minutes ago," said the lean-boned man.

"Very well, Rupert…. Gentlemen, be seated. The humble hospitality of my household is yours." Behind his humbleness was a subtle threat. "What moved you, gentlemen, to honor me with this extemporaneous visit? Or is it extemporaneous?"

Gales said, "It is well known, General Kwang, that you are a great man."

Kwang started to beam at the compliment, but a split-second later suspicion shifted in his eyes. He coiled his thick fingers into his palms and leaned back. His fat wrinkled eyelids drooped till his eyes were almost hidden—yet a faint glitter shone between the creases.

"You are kind," he sighed heavily. "But what really brings you far from the traveled routes?"

Gales was amiable. "Well—you see, we are looking for a man."

"Ah!"

Gales' eyes jumped around the room. He saw only stony faces, passionless masks.

He went on rapidly, "The man's name is Dr. Jons. We received a mysterious message, unsigned, that said he was being held for ransom on the Yangtze, west of here. We have been instructed by the executors of his estate to try saving him."

"I see," droned General Kwang.

Gales shrugged. "Well, what I thought, General—I thought you might have seen a strange plane in these parts. Happened to think of that just as we were flying above. And I assumed that you'd want to do all in your power to help us—or rather, help this unlucky old man—this doctor."

The General opened his eyes and leaned forward. "Naturally I should like to, my friends. But unfortunately I have not been notified of a strange plane in this vicinity. Was the doctor of some importance?"

Gales moistened his lips. "I believe he was. But we're not concerned with that. We've been given a job and we are trying to carry out orders. You know, General, I'm of the opinion that the information we received was wrong. I don't believe the doctor is up this way at all."

The lean-boned Rupert lifted and lowered his eyebrows. All the other faces remained expressionless, and the men seemed to be holding their breaths. Behind the desk, the great bulk of the warlord was enigmatic but sinister.

"I regret," he said slowly, "that I can be of no material assistance."

"Well"—Gales slapped his knees—"thanks anyhow, General. We'll be shoving off."

General Kwang picked up a pencil and turned it over musingly. "I can tell you, however, that the country north and west of here is dangerous for flying. There are brigands too. I would suggest that you remain here overnight and strike south in the morning toward more hospitable country."

His aides looked blankly at one another and the lean-boned Rupert scowled.

"Thanks," said Gales. "We will."

THE CITY was old. It had little beauty. Centuries had left their hall-mark on the weathered stone of houses and streets.

It was a rugged city, grim, built for refuge, for war. Into it the modern warlord instilled electricity gathered from the great waterfall. Shops had been built where machinery whirred and hammered. There was a powerful wireless station. Great tanks of gasoline were stored in the valley.

Munitions were kept in vast caves in the mountain side, and well-clothed troops filled the town, the long barracks, and the tents. His air force numbered twenty-five planes, of all sizes—and a huge tri-motored air limousine, armed to the teeth.

In the past ten years he had hired out his force and his military knowledge to a dozen different factions of China.

Gales and McGill had been given a suite of two rooms in a house three doors down the hill from Headquarters. From one of the windows they could see the valley and the flying field and the stacks belching smoke into the late afternoon.

McGill clipped, "He knows, Bill—he knows."

"He suspects, Mike."

"Well, that's just the same." McGill squinted around the room. "I figure you and me are gonna do some shootin' to get out of this joint."

"You haven't seen that yellow plane yet?"

"Nope."

Gales lowered his voice, "He can't bump us off, Mike. He wouldn't. We haven't found out anything, so why should he? Those maps—did you see 'em? Well, he's planning something. If he got rid of us, he'd have the whole Agency on his neck, and everybody else too."

"And a fat chance we got of findin' out anything. Anyhow, the doc's probably been bumped off by this time."

"If he has, then these birds have his papers—his diagrams and whatever he had."

McGill shrugged. "Listen, Bill, I'm not gettin' leery. I ain't afraid of the whole shootin'-match here. But you, old sock—you got a wife. If anything happened to you, she'd blame it on me."

Gales laughed. "There's nothing going to happen to me, Mike."

"Ah, slice it thin or thick, partner, it's still boloney. You just watch your step, that's all. Gwen'd never forgive me. Now, well, if I had Hannon along 'stead of you, and he got himself bumped off, that—well, that would be a great break for me."

"Hannon's all right, Mike."

"Kwang's all right, too, in his place—but his place is six feet under. No, sir, Bill, I don't like this party at all. Somebody's gonna dunk in somebody's else's Java—Door!"

A servant came in with tea, went out quietly.

"You see, Mike," said Gales buoyantly, "we are guests!"

"That seems to be another bromide I heard before."

McGILL WASN'T crabbing because trouble seemed imminent. He always met trouble half-way. But he didn't want Bill to get hurt. Bill had a wife. And McGill would have swallowed his pride and given up this mission if in the end Bill would be sent back to Bangkok and comparative safety.

But you couldn't do that now. Bill was in it, and Bill wouldn't leave a thing half-done.

It was McGill who went out alone and picked his way down the steep winding street. He went close by the big sheds where the machinery pounded. He could look in and see belts moving, great wheels whirring. In one of the places they were making their own ammunition. In another place, two planes were being assembled. Mingled with the hum and thunder of machinery was the booming of the great waterfall.

He reached the hangars and drifted about wearing an innocent look. The Lockheed had been drawn up to the side of the field. He wound his way apparently aimlessly, but really with a purpose. He spotted all the planes. But he saw no Fokkers—neither yellow nor brown. Nor did he see any men who resembled the Chinese who had abducted Dr. Leopold Jons.

When he got back to their rooms it was dusk. Gales was not in. McGill paced up and down restlessly, and was about to go out and look for his partner when Gales opened the door and walked in.

"What did you see, Mike?"

"Nix. I'm beginning to think we're all wrong about Kwang. I ain't seen any of the guys was in the hold-up, and neither one of the planes. I cast a vote that we turn in early and leave this funny joint at daybreak."

There was a queer light in Gales' eyes. McGill saw it and squinted quizzically.

"I've been poking around," he said. "Up the street—there's a laboratory up the street. I figure Kwang's technical experts live there. I prowled around a bit and found a way I could get in after dark."

"There ain't nothin' here, Bill. I think we ought to turn in early."

"I've got a hunch, Mike."

"And I'll bet my shirt Kwang has a hunch you got a hunch."

Gales was serious. "It will be easy, Mike. I want to see what's in the laboratory. There may be a model there—or some plans lying around. I'll wait till after midnight. If there's anything here, we've got to find it now. If we come back again, Kwang will get suspicious."

"What makes you think he ain't suspicious now? And what makes you think it's gonna be so easy gettin' away from here?"

They looked at each steadily, silently. Then Gales shrugged and got up.

"If you think we're going to have a time getting away," he said, "then it won't do me any more harm to take a look."

CHAPTER VI

LETHAL HEAT

AT ONE o'clock Gales went out by the rear into a dark alley.

He followed the alley till he came to a street. The street was dark as the alley, and the old stone houses squatted silently.

He saw no moving shadows. He heard no footfalls. The only sound was the whisper of the night wind over the rooftops. Far down at the base of the mountain were lights, and if you listened you could hear the faint sound of the machinery and the sound of the falls, muted at this distance.

Gales worked around to the street in which the laboratory was located. He peered up and saw no lights. Then he went farther up the hill till he came to an alley.

He entered the alley, walked to the end of it and climbed a tree that stood on the corner. He crawled out on a branch and stepped to a roof. Across the rooftops he went on rubber-soled shoes, a moving shadow among shadows that were motionless.

Then he was on the roof of the laboratory. He let himself over the edge of the roof until his feet touched the broad stone frame atop a window. Here he huddled, bending over slowly. He let one leg down, got his knee on the support. Strong arms let him down till his feet touched the sill.

In a minute he had the window. It took him less time to get inside.

He stood motionless in the darkness. Then he lit a match, cupped it in his hands and peered about.

There were vials and glass tubes and all the elaborate instruments of a scientific laboratory. He had to keep lighting matches to see everything. He found a model of a plane on one of the tables.

The model was three feet long and though uncompleted, had a miniature power plant installed. On the top of the fuselage, aft, was a peculiar instrument of tiny discs and tubes and many wires. It looked complicated and fantastic, and Gales, who knew a lot about modern aeronautics, could not imagine what connection this strange instrument had with the plane.

The match went out. He was careful to deposit the burnt matches in his pocket. Lighting another, he crossed to a door and opened it. He found a small room that smelt of new rubber. Then he discovered why.

Floor, walls, ceiling—even the table—were made of rubber. And it was new.

Gales retreated into the laboratory, closing the door. He was about to light another match when the heard footfalls.

He felt his way across the room and flattened back of a tall cabinet. He heard a door open, saw the beam of a flashlight spring into the room. His hand went into his pocket, closed on the gun there. The footfalls were in the room. Gales did not dare look. He could only wait.

He heard some objects moved. He heard the footfalls go back and forth. Then a door closed softly.

After a minute he looked around the corner of the cabinet. One door was open, the door through which the footfalls must have come. The only other door was the one leading into the black rubber room. It was closed.

But Gales remained behind the cabinet. It would mean too long a chance to try going out the way he had come. He remained behind the cabinet for ten minutes. Then he heard quick little footfalls again. They went out of the room, sounded as if they were going down a flight of stairs.

GALES LOOKED out from his hiding-place. The door to the black room was open. He could see the long table, with the model plane at one end. He saw wisps of smoke. Suddenly he stepped out and went swiftly to the room.

There were two model planes on the table, one at either end. The one he had not seen before was small. Wisps of smoke rose from it.

Going closer, he saw that it was made of metal and that it had not the queer gadget on top of the fuselage. He touched the model, drew his finger away with a sharp intake of breath. It was hot!

Quickly he turned. Footfalls again! He sped back to his hiding place. Mixed footsteps came into the room.

A voice panted, "The lethal heat is a success!"

Then there was the soft closing of the door to the black room. Gales trembled. To stay here any longer would spell death. He had caught a clue, but his evidence was still incomplete. He did not know for certain whether Dr. Jons was in Kwang's mountain stronghold. Nor could he swear that such discovery as he had made was in connection with Dr. Jons' invention.

If only he could find Jons! It would be impossible of course to get Jons away. But if he and McGill could return to Hongkong with proof that Jons was here, more drastic action could be taken.

McGill knew Jons. It would be necessary, then, for McGill to identify him. The night would not be long. Day would come and they would have to leave. Gales knew he would have to take a chance on going out the way he had come. He would have to get the window up quietly, close it after him—leave no trail of any kind.

Suiting action to thought, he stepped from behind the cabinet. He was soft-shoeing across the floor when the door to the black room opened. The lean-boned Rupert appeared, rubbing his hands vigorously. In a flash he saw Gales and streaked for his holster.

There was only one thing Gales could do. He beat Rupert on the draw and had him covered.

"Not a move!" Gales bit off tensely as he went toward Rupert.

Beyond, in the room, was a stocky Chinaman in a white coat. Gales covered them both, while his thoughts raced wildly. It seemed so futile to keep them covered. He was caught. He could kill them, but that would not engineer his escape from the city.

Rupert must have sensed this. His thin lips parted in a slow leer.

"Well, Mr. Gales, this is amusing!"

"Shut up!" Gales clipped. "And get this, both of you. I may be in a bad jam, but I can kill both of you."

"And get away?" asked Rupert.

"Don't let that worry you. The fact remains that I can kill you, and I will if you don't do as I tell you. The fact that I'm in such a bad jam ought to make it plain that it's not going to take much to make me kill you."

"Don't be a fool!" Rupert snarled. His hand was tense on his gun.

The Chinaman in the white coat stared dully.

Gales snatched the half-drawn gun from Rupert's hand.

He said, "I'm trapped, but so are you. My chances of getting away from this city are mighty small. So I'm going to make the best of it." His voice lowered ominously. "Where is Dr. Jons?"

The Chinese started.

RUPERT'S JAW hardened. "How do I know?"

"You know. And you're going to tell. So help me, I'll kill you both! And right in this soundproof room. Get back. Back in that room!"

He drove Rupert back in with the Chinese and closed the rubber-backed door. The room was hollow and silent as a tomb. Rupert clenched his hands and his face muscles worked. Beads of sweat began to appear on his forehead.

"Start talking," Gales ground out. "Where is Dr. Jons?"

Rupert clenched his teeth. Gales looked at the Chinese. He went toward him and told him to raise his hands and he pressed the muzzle of his gun against the man's stomach. The man wilted and his eyes bulged. He looked toward Rupert.

Rupert scowled at Gales. "Well, since you've declared yourself, it doesn't matter. It doesn't matter because obviously you cannot get away. Dr. Jons is here. Are you satisfied?"

"No. I want to see him."

Suddenly the Chinaman fell against Gales. A knife flashed. Gales wheeled backward, his sleeve ripped open. His gun belched and the room thundered, and the Chinese collapsed. Rupert flung across the room. Gales sidestepped and struck with the barrel of his gun. Rupert let out a choked cry and smashed against the wall.

Gales' eyes blazed. "Steady, you!" he barked. "I want to see Dr. Jons. Quick, now—or, by George, I'll empty this gun in you! Out that door!"

Rupert went quickly to the door, a little dizzy from the blow. Gales drove him down a stairway and into the street. He kept striking Rupert with his gun. He was dangerous, desperate. There was a shuffle in the street when a shadow emerged from an alley.

Gales held his gun ready.

"Me, Bill!" whispered McGill. "What happened?"

"Enough. Keep going, Rupert!"

Rupert stumbled on, muttering, "You fools, you can never get him out! The house is guarded by a dozen men!"

"Who?" asked McGill.

"Jons," Gales whispered.

Suddenly long beams of light appeared in the street. The partners crouched and Gales shoved Rupert against a housewall. A car swung into the street—toward them—with big headlights shattering the gloom.

"We're cooked, Bill!" muttered Gales.

"Looks like it, Mike."

Brakes squealed and the car's door opened. Rupert dived across the street. Men piled out of the car drawing guns and sabers.

Gales gritted his teeth and shot out the headlights. Darkness plunged upon the street again, and the two partners darted across and up the hill. Shouts and oaths of surprise came from the men who had tumbled from the car. Daggers of flame sliced the night, and a shrill whistle sounded.

"Steady, old pal. We can give 'em a run for their money. I found out a lot."

"And a hell of a lot of good it's goin' to do us!"

"Here—down this alley. Quick, Mike! Listen. Jons is in this burg, Mike. I saw the invention—"

"You what?"

"Well—sort of. I mean I heard a guy say—'lethal heat.' I saw some gadgets up in the laboratory. And I had to put a guy out—cold. I—"

"There they come!"

Men had entered the alley and were shouting. A gun blazed and a bullet chipped stone alongside Gales. McGill turned while running and raked the alley till his gun was empty. He reloaded as he ran.

They heard more whistles blowing and shouts came from near and far. Lights sprang up in windows. The two partners got to the rooftops and worked their way uphill while groups of angry men ranged the streets below with drawn guns.

"Yes, sir, Bill—this is our swan song. It sure is. And nobody ain't ever gonna know anything about it."

"Oh, yes they are, Mike."

"I don't see how."

Gales paused. "There it is now!"

"What?"

"Wireless outfit. See the masts?"

"What about it?"

"That's one place they won't be looking for us. Take a look. See the wireless man leaning in the open window?"

"Yeah."

"He's not going to lean there very long. Come on."

THINGS WERE comparatively quiet farther up the slope. The hunt was being carried on farther down. Someone must have got the idea that the partners might try a getaway by plane.

Gales and McGill dropped back to the street from a low building and gained admittance to the wireless tower by a rear window. Gales had no great hopes of escape.

But he had other hopes. He swore to himself that his and Mike's visit would not be in vain.

Climbing a circular staircase in the dark, he whispered, "Waste no time with this guy, Mike."

Up they went—until they heard a low throbbing sound. Then they saw an open door through which lights poured. And they smelled tobacco smoke. On tiptoes they went—Gales forcing McGill behind him.

The wireless man was leaning in the window, looking down over the sea of roofs. Gales stood in the doorway for only a split second. Then he streaked across the room. The wireless man whirled. His mouth opened. But Gales' gun-barrel struck swiftly and the man collapsed without a sound.

"Listen in the hall, Mike!" Gales whispered. "If anybody comes, warn me. If it's a gang, close the door—bar it—and—"

"We fight a fare-thee-well, eh?"

"There's nothing else, Mike. Take this extra gun."

"Okey, pard."

Eyes shining, lean face drawn, Gales sat down before the vast instrument board and clipped on the earphones. Active bronzed fingers flashed across dials. His head was bent, eyes staring with fierce concentration at nothing. His fingers went to the key.

Here in the vastnesses of China he was trying to tell what he knew to the authorities in Hongkong. He was trying to tell this before he and McGill were overthrown.

They had no hope of getting away with their lives, but Gales could deal Kwang a crushing blow.

It took him five minutes to get a faint reply from Hongkong.

He clicked off his and McGill's names to hold attention. Then he clicked off the news of what had happened, what he had found.

His brown fingers flashed. Sweat poured from him. He gauged the strength of the enemy. He mentioned 'lethal heat.' He informed Hongkong that the model appeared to be a success.

Curtly he explained that he and McGill were trapped and saw no possibility of escape. He advised the Powers to take action in time to prevent Kwang's experts from turning the model into a life-sized machine of destruction.

He finished, "Report this in full to Major Downe and relay a copy to K.O. Pike of the Straits Agency." He added, "Send my love to my wife, Gwen Gales, Straits Agency, Bangkok Division." He groaned when he had clicked off this, and his face looked suddenly haggard.

When he turned from the instrument, took off the earphones, he looked like a man who had undergone a fierce physical exertion.

McGill asked, "Get it through, Bill?"

"All through, Mike." Gales' shoulders sagged. He wiped the sweat from his forehead. He sat in the chair like a man resigned to fate.

One thought burned heroically in his brain. He would die. But he had not failed the cause. He had shot through all the information necessary for the powers to send an armed force to Kwang's mountain stronghold.

"Snap out of it, Bill," McGill said. "We're not done for yet."

"I got you into this, Mike. I'm sorry."

"You got me into it! Horsefeathers! I got you into it."

Gales shook his head. "No, Mike. I-"

"Nix on that song and dance, pal. I ain't told you yet, but it was me wired K.O. on the q.t. I told him to send you up from Bangkok if he expected me to stay on the job. I got you in this, Bill. It was a dirty trick. I wanted to show up Hannon. He was drivin' me till I had to do somethin'. I was a louse to do it, Bill, but I knew there was only one guy who could solve this riddle and—"

Gales got up. "Anyhow, I probably would have come. K.O. would have sent me anyhow. Let's breeze."

THEY WENT down the winding stairway and out through a window into the alley. They almost stepped from the alley into the street when they saw a big motor car draw up in front of the wireless building.

Two men in capes and visored caps stepped out. They were white men—renegades. They stood conversing in low tones while the chauffeur sat at the wheel. Then they entered the building.

McGill gripped Gales' arm. "We lay out that chauffeur, Bill."

Gales set his jaw, nodded.

They separated and approached the car from opposite sides. It was McGill who struck.

The chauffeur heaved once in the seat, groaning. Then the groan died. The partners dragged him from the car. McGill took his visored cap and put it on.

"Okey, Bill," he said. "You get in back."

He started the car and turned it around. He started down the hill, rolling fast, the big headlights sweeping the cobbles.

Soon they passed groups of uniformed men. McGill huddled behind the wheel, his eyes glued on the road ahead. Down the hill they went—down past the smoking chimneys and then along the base of the slope. Many figures jumped out of the way. The barracks and the long rows of tents swept by.

"Where you going, Mike?" Gales called.

McGill half-turned. "Kwang built a road through the wilderness, didn't he?"

"He did."

They saw no more men. The way became dark, and the long road rose upward. The big ear was doing sixty-five miles an hour. Trees leaped past. The car lurched and heaved.

Gales was like a man transfixed. This could not be true. They could not be getting away. He looked back and saw nothing but darkness. Kwang's stronghold was hidden by the low ridge they had crossed. And ahead was darkness, and the leaping headlights, and the wilderness road. And McGill—driving like a madman.

Gales lit a cigarette with shaking fingers. It would be only a matter of a few hours before other cars overtook them. He could see the gasoline gauge going down steadily.

There was no way out.

They would pay with their lives for the information they had sent to Hongkong. The law of averages demanded that.

CHAPTER VII

GROUNDED EAGLES

K.O. PIKE stood glaring through the window at the Bay of Hongkong. Suddenly he whirled, a big vigorous man.

"But this delay—this delay!" he shouted.

Major Downe looked at his pipe. "It takes time, Mr. Pike. The diplomats of the Powers have been demurring. A thing as big as this cannot be put into action by the snap of a thumb."

K.O. slashed his fists through the air. "The Powers didn't demur when Gales and McGill were put on the job. A week ago we got that wireless message from Bill Gales. And still the nincompoops—you call 'em diplomats—still they're demurring.

"My boys went there knowing they had about one chance in ten of getting any information—and if they got any, one chance in a hundred of getting away with their lives. What did your blasted secret agents do? Bah! Sit around in cafés and hotel bars hoping to overhear some chance word. My boys go and give their lives, get valuable information through, and then these guys look at their nails and demur."

"Demur!"

"Look here, Major. I've got six planes. I can scrape up some more, and I can spend my last cent for men. I can go back there in the hills and bust this outfit up."

"That, Mr. Pike, would be frightfully irregular."

"My eye! They kidnaped a man who had chartered one of my planes, I took the responsibility in the first place by sending Gales and McGill. And I didn't demur, either."

Major Downe shrugged. "I'm really sorry, Mr. Pike. As you know, I am only in charge of the investigation. I have no power to act."

There was a knock, and a boy came in with a message. "Wireless from Saigon, Mr. Pike."

K.O. tore it open. It was from Lomis, the assistant at Saigon, K.O. started, swore.

"Eh?" said Major Downe.

"My super at Saigon has disappeared. Hannon. A plane we had there has disappeared too. Our new Vought. This morning. Now what has Hannon gone and done?"

Downe started to exclaim, but raised an ear instead. He rose and went to the window saying, "I think I hear a plane. Maybe your man has chosen to come here."

"He didn't have any orders!" snapped K.O.

Both men shoved their heads out of the window.

"No," said K.O. "It's not the Vought. It's one of your new observation planes."

Downe raised binoculars. "Oh, yes. Looks like one from our Canton Squadron."

They watched the plane alight in the harbor, then turned from the window.

"I wouldn't get excited," Major Downe said. "I think we'll see action at the end of another twenty-four hours."

He returned to some papers, and K.O. glared bitterly out of the window.

Ten minutes later the door swung open and a breathless clerk exclaimed, "Mr. Gales and Mr. McGill—"

K.O. spun violently.

GALES AND McGill drifted in. Their clothes were in rags, their hair was matted, stubble covered their faces. Major Downe went limp in his chair and stared. K.O. was rooted to the floor, his mouth agape.

"Hello, K.O.," said Gales.

K.O. went bowling across the room. "You guys! You guys!"

"For cryin' out loud," McGill said. "Don't bust my hand, K.O."

"But where'd you guys come from?" demanded K.O. "One minute you're dead, and the next you're alive! What kind of hocus-pocus is this?"

"Well," said McGill, "It's funny—it sure is funny. By all rights we should be dead. But there is a Santy Claus.

"We got away in one o' Kwang's automobiles. He built a swell road back in them mountains. It's dark when we get away, and soon we begin to run out o' gas. Then we see the railroad line Kwang built for his own use. There's an engine sittin' on the track. That was ours."

"We ditch the car and clean out the engine crew and then we go sashayin' along on the loco, learnin' to drive her as we go. I stoke and Bill drives and we run her till we reach a river where the line ends. We bum rides on river junks, and then we start overland.

"We reach another run, get in a scrap with pirates, and run off with their junk. We wreck the junk and go on foot, and we're somewhere north o' Canton when that British plane sights us and picks us up. We talk the guy into bringin' us here instead o'Canton. And here we are, yours truly and affectionately. Did I stick to facts, Bill?"

"Mike's story is mine," said Gales, dropping wearily to a chair.

"And I suppose by now," McGill said, "Kwang and his whole shebang has been wiped out."

K.O. shook his head. "No. The diplomats are demurring."

Gales started. "No action yet!" He jumped up, weary as he was. "It's crazy to wait. I tell you they've completed the model and it works. I saw Kwang poring over the maps. Lethal heat—something to crucify his enemies in the air! Why wait? Cripes, did you expect us to lick his whole army and walk off with Dr. Jons?"

The clerk entered bearing another wireless message for K.O. The head of the Agency tore it open, and his face blanched. He looked at Gales queerly.

"What's the matter?" Gales asked.

"Nothing, Bill. Nothing." K.O. crumpled the message and started to shove it in his pocket.

"There is," Gales said.

"No—no. Just something personal—"

"K.O., you just looked at me. You're white as a sheet. What happened? Is it—about Gwen?"

"Bill, it's all right now—"

"Give me that message, K.O. Give it to me!"

He snatched it from K.O.'s hand and read it. His shoulders sank. A groan came from his throat.

McGill gripped his arm. "What's the matter, pal."

Gales gave him the message, and McGill read:

> Have authoritative information that Gwen Gales was in Saigon last night. She is not here now. Fact that both she and Hannon have disappeared along with the Vought may be significant.

McGILL SNAPPED a cool look at his boss.

"What's all this about, K.O.?"

"You read it, didn't you? Mrs. Gales must have left Bangkok and gone to Saigon. This morning Hannon was not to be found. Neither was the Vought."

Major Downe said, "You don't mean to infer that your man Hannon is in league with Kwang?"

K.O. colored. "I haven't inferred anything."

McGill barbed, "By cripes, I am! If Duke Hannon ain't in Saigon, where is he? And where's Bill's wife? Hannon is a bum, if you ask me! Looka here, K.O.—and you, Major! We gotta land on Kwang's outfit. Pronto!"

"I understand," Major Downe said. "But the powers that be are still holding off. Many things must be considered. Nothing can be done, no action taken, until an agreement is reached whereby each and every one of—"

"Now don't go over that, Major," Gales intoned dully. "We know all about that. There's a nigger in the woodpile somewhere. My wife has disappeared. I know she means nothing to the Powers, but she means everything in the world to me. To hell with all your meetings and consultations! Get down to it, you're all afraid to tweak the tail of the yellow dragon."

"That's just it," McGill chimed in.

"And we're not," Gales rapped out. "Kwang has no place in China. He's nothing more than a highbrow bandit. His outfit is not recognized as a government or a principality or a kingdom, He's a warlord without portfolio. He kidnaped a scientist whose knowledge is worth a lot to the Powers. And still you demur.

"Well, go ahead. Mike and I built our reputations as free-lances. We can right now gang together any number of soldiers of fortune. We can send out a call for private airmen. There's loot in Kwang's stronghold. With a dozen or fifteen planes I can wreck Kwang and his mob."

"Impossible!" exclaimed Major Downe, who lived and acted on precedent.

"Huh!" grunted McGill.

Gales, his face flushed with excitement, turned to K.O. "If you've got any money, K.O., Mike and I'd like a room and bath and a change of clothes."

Once in the hotel room, Gales forgot temporarily about the bath and paced the floor grimly.

"I'll never see her again, Mike—never!" he muttered.

"It's Hannon—it's Duke Hannon!" groaned McGill. "He did it, Bill. He sneaked her away. I'll kill him—I'll cut his heart out!"

Gales waved his hands. McGill had never seen him so excited.

"But why," Gales demanded, "did she come to Saigon? Why didn't she stay in Bangkok?"

"Maybe she found out somethin' about Hannon. Maybe she came to expose him and he found it out and took her away. Bill, we can't wait till the Powers act. We gotta have action. K.O.'s behind us. There's only one place Hannon would ha' took her."

"Then we've got to get to work right off the bat, Mike."

"You took the words right out o' my mouth, pal."

CHAPTER VIII

WINGS TO THE WEST

G ALES BECAME fierce and a little mad in his purpose. K.O. promised five planes. Had not Hannon disappeared with the Vought there would have been six.

But even so, the number was pitifully small against the imposing squadron Kwang had. More were needed. And Gales sent wires up and down the coast to vagabond airmen he and McGill knew.

Meantime the Powers came to a left-handed decision. They decided to send an emissary to Kwang and deliver an ultimatum. Dr. Leopold Jons, abducted by agents of General Kwang, must be returned within twelve hours, unharmed, and in full possession of his plans.

While Gales was furiously trying to get help, a tri-motored plane left for the interior an hour after sunrise.

The reply that Kwang sent back was smug and not to the point. He said that if Dr. Jons should come to his stronghold, he would certainly return him. He said that Dr. Jons was not there now. He added that one of his lieutenants had said Dr. Jons was there to save himself from certain death at the hands of a wild and crazed American.

He also added that this American, along with another, had gone off leaving a plane on the flying field and that the plane was waiting to be called for. He felt injured and remorseful that the Powers should suspect him of having abducted Dr. Jons.

"It's a lie!" cried Gales. "He's stalling for time!"

But the Powers wanted to think that over. Gales and McGill—they intimated—might have been wrong. It was recalled that their past was a hectic one; some said, a shady one. There was no proof positive that Dr. Jons was there.

Even K.O. said, reasonably, "That last is right, boys. There is no proof."

Added to that, Gales' enthusiasm about getting a private flying army of his own was knocked into a cocked hat. There wasn't a free-lance on the coast willing to tackle the formidable and notorious General Kwang.

Gales faced K.O. "Then listen to this. The weight of popular opinion is against Mike and me. Now you've turned turtle after a lot of big talk—"

"Shut up!" barked K.O. "I haven't. I have five planes. If you want to take them and bust them up in Kwang's territory, go ahead. Get me, Bill—five planes against Kwang's two dozen. Besides, who's going to fly 'em? I'll fly one of them, but who else is going—"

"All right, all right," Gales broke in, his eyes dark. "It's not your fault. But my wife's disappeared with Hannon. To hell with Dr. Jons and his invention. Let Kwang work it out and clean this coast up, down and across. But I'm going to look for my wife. Mike and I are going. And we're going to collect that plane Kwang says is waiting there. And we want your pet Boeing for the trip."

It had to come to that. K.O. offered the Boeing freely. It was a fast, Hornet-motored biplane, two-place, with special pontoons. Unarmed to the eye, it nevertheless carried two submachine guns in its fuselage, and dual controls.

Gales took the crate up, driving from the rear cockpit. He was no longer a reasonable man. The last twenty-four hours had driven away all his usual calm.

Even McGill was amazed, and it made McGill ponder and look worried. It took a lot to work Bill up; but once started, there was no telling what might happen. And since McGill went off the handle on the slightest provocation, the trail beyond would be no bed of roses.

THE BOEING crossed Kowloon at a hundred and thirty miles an hour. Gales was pushing it for all it was worth, and the wind battled wildly in struts and flying wires, and the whole plane echoed the roar of prop and motor. Air bumps struck them. The new white crate heaved and lunged and galloped in freakish currents—but always it kept onward over the wilderness.

Gales did not navigate consciously. Some inner self did that. His brain was a storm of conflicting thoughts.

It infuriated him that Hannon had disappeared. The loss of his wife was something he still found hard to believe. It made him numb at times—but always behind the numbness was the grinding activity of his tortured brain.

And always, beating in a minor key, was the conviction that Jons was a prisoner of Kwang's—that the model he had seen was *the* model.

Rain began pelting the Boeing. Broken dark clouds crawled across the sky, thunder boomed and lightning flashed in sheets and in white crackling daggers.

Gales toiled his plane upward through a rent in the clouds. But there were more clouds above, black and ominous like oily smoke.

He changed his course and went tearing dead-level through wet dark streamers. Above and below the cloud banks rolled, and the world seemed fantastic and unreal, without earth and without sky. Gusts of rain struck with a loud banging; at times it seemed as though great giant buckets were dumped at the roaring plane. Lightning danced about it fitfully, and time and time again the great banks of cloud were made ghastly by the breaking sheets of white flame.

The plane fought its way.

Bitter thoughts were driven, sledge-hammered into the back of Gales' brain. His eyes straining through smeared goggles for a friendly break in the massed clouds.

He turned on his dash lights to read his dials. With a gasp he yanked back on his stick. Rain poured about him into the cockpit. Dark moisture swirled about his head, and there was a drumming on the wings like hail. Thunder shook the plane violently, and you had to keep your ears to hear if the motor was still going. A roar of wind got under the right wing and slammed the plane on one ear. Breathless, Gales slammed it back to a level keel.

You couldn't dive down through the clouds. Mountains sprawled somewhere below. Gales knew that. You had to stay well up, else a mountain top would meet you head on. Way up—and bludgeon your way through the chaos of the storm. Take the rain and the wind in the face, but keep the plane up.

There were trailing twisted clouds below and then a darker mass. Gales rubbed his glasses.

That darker mass was motionless.

Back went his stick, and beneath his pontoons swept a rugged mountain top. That was close!

Gales spat water from his lips as sheet lightning blazed in his face and the plane seemed to pause and shiver in the detonation of a thunderclap. Then it seemed to stumble on, reeling through the driving clouds.

At last a rent—a bit of blue sky beyond. Gales climbed toward it, through it into a wet grayness.

Below he could see the faint shapes of mountains and lesser hills, and the drumming on the wings was light. Then that stopped, and long needles of sunlight shimmered in the moist air and flashed on the plane's wet wings.

"Whew!" whistled McGill.

As the air cleared, Gales cut his gun and dropped lower. Now he could see sunlight on the terrain below. There was a shining river too. Familiar landmarks presented themselves. Gales breathed easier. He shoved up the throttle again and crossed the river at three thousand feet.

Then McGill turned and shouted and leveled an arm toward the south. Gales turned and squinted. There were dark dots against the sky. His lips moved as he counted them.

He counted a dozen. A cold chill knifed the length of his spine.

The twelve dots were like bugs crawling across the face of the sky—crawling west.

He eased up on his throttle and shouted, "A dozen, Mike!"

"Yeah. What do you figure, Bill?"

Gales shook his head. The natural answer was that there were twelve of Kwang's planes afield. But why? Kwang's reply to the ultimatum indicated that he was killing time, and in order to do so would have been willing to have the Lockheed taken back. If this were his attitude, why had he sent aloft twelve planes?

Oddly enough, the twelve planes did not change their course. They must have sighted the Boeing, yet they kept resolutely on their chosen way. By using his glasses Gales could see that several of them were large, two-motored. They looked like bombers. Others looked like single-seater fighters, and there were at least five two-place jobs. The powers had not acted, hence the planes could belong to no one but General Kwang.

Gales kept his glasses to his eyes. He looked for markings. He could find none. Every one of the planes was painted a dull gray, and all of them looked new. Soon he could hear the combined roar of all of them, could make them out in detail with the naked eye.

Then suddenly two of the single-seaters dropped out of formation and came wheeling toward the Boeing.

CHAPTER IX

THE GRAY LEGION

GALES DID not move his controls. He was doing a hundred miles an hour at three thousand feet. He could see twin Vickers on the brisk little single-seaters. McGill watched them with one hand on the coaming, his jaw rigid. He did not know what to expect. The main squadron kept on its way.

One of the single-seaters came straight toward their flank, twin muzzles seen through the shimmering prop. Then it banked sharply, and the pilot peered hard at the Boeing. He was seen to shrug.

The other fighter had gone over the top and was banking on the other side. He too looked hard. Then he waved, holding his arm aloft stiffly, then slashing it back into the cockpit.

Exhaust pipes hammered, and the two deadly little planes went scooting back to join the main squadron.

Gales throttled down and the Boeing loafed. "What do you think of that, Mike?" he yelled.

"I ain't started thinkin' yet, Bill. I dunno."

Now the fleet of twelve gray planes—gray as a storm sky— took on an air of mystery. Where had they come from? Whence were they bound? Surely they were going somewhere. There was a definite purpose in the formation of their flight.

Gales advanced the throttle and kept to his appointed course. It so happened that his course kept him in the wake of the mystery planes. Yet the squadron did not seem to mind.

After a while one of the single-seaters began climbing, and the others began to follow suit. Some climbed fast, but always four of the smaller fighting planes remained close by the three bombers.

They climbed through layers of gauzy cloud, upward through thicker clouds, until the mountains and the valleys were hidden. Below them lay wide fields of snow-like clouds.

Half an hour later Gales saw a change in formation, a slowing down of all the planes. He cut his gun and hung back. He saw one of the single-seaters turn its nose downward and go plummeting through the clouds below. In a moment it had disappeared, and the other planes hung aloft like buzzards.

Gales studied his chart intensely—and he began to understand. They must be near Kwang's stronghold!

He shouted the information to McGill. He became restless in his seat, and the mystery became more a mystery than ever. Where had these gray planes come from?

THEN THE single-seater came tearing through the clouds, leveled off. Its wings wiggled up and down half a dozen times. That must be the flight commander. Gales was certain that it was one of the two planes that had come to look them over.

Suddenly he saw the bombers going down in slow spirals, again convoyed by four fast fighters. The remaining planes spread out and began following. The clouds took them, enveloped them. Gales gunned his motor and shoved forward on the stick. In a moment the Boeing was plunging through the clouds.

It came out beneath the roof of the clouds with the earth two thousand feet below. There was the city on the mountain side! Kwang's stronghold! There were the gray planes sprinting about.

As if by a given signal a bomb dropped from each of the three bombers.

Gales watched the big deadly objects go plummeting downward. A lump jammed in his throat. Suppose Gwen—

His eyes glazed and his clamped teeth appeared between tight lips. He saw great mushrooms of smoke. The sounds were faint in comparison with what damage he knew they did. He saw three hangars wiped out, and he saw men scampering across the field. At the other side of the field were the barracks and the sea of tents.

The bombers banked and headed for the city. Three bombs dropped half-way up the slope. Smoke and flame and stone geysered into the air.

But where were the planes of Kwang?

None was in sight. Could they all be in the hangars? Three more bombs shot downward. Houses blew into the air.

Gales, using binoculars, saw automobiles racing through the streets.

From several points on the slope blazed anti-aircraft guns. One of the gray planes disappeared in a ball of fire and smoke; the tattered remains of it streamed downward like ashes.

As if enraged, three of the single-seaters whipped over and streaked for the gun-flashes. Their Vickers spat wickedly, and behind them came one of the big bombers. The anti-aircraft guns belched redly. One of the single-seaters was blown to smithereens.

The other two screamed low over the slope, and behind them roared the bomber. One—two—three bombs dropped from it. The mountain thundered with the detonation. Stone, broken guns, part of a tree, burst into the air.

Higher up on the mountain one of the bombers, alone now, had turned and was starting back toward the valley. As it came, it unloaded its bombs. It came down over the city, dropping bombs with regular precision, smashing the houses, tearing up the streets.

The city was on fire. Smoke and flame billowed through its torn houses and shattered streets. The third bomber had accidentally located a munition dump, and the stored shells were bursting furiously. Two more anti-aircraft guns started in, their flashes belching through skeins of black smoke. The troops were demoralized and they fled on foot and in trucks.

Gales was stunned. He could not think any more. If Hannon had brought Gwen here, this was the end. Yet he could do nothing.

He could not help admiring the surprise attack these strange planes had maneuvered. But where were Kwang's planes?

He saw the city razed, so quickly that it was hard to believe. The big factory was in ruins. So was the power plant by the waterfall. There were no more hangars, and the fire burning below would complete the destruction.

Soon the planes would go down. Then he too would go down and find the worst. There would be loot there, for Kwang had great riches stored below. Could it be that these gray planes were outlaws too, eager for nothing but loot?

Gales' tired eyes sprang to life. In the south he saw many dots that grew larger with the seconds. The gray planes must have seen them too, for wings began wiggling, and positions were changed rapidly. The leader started climbing, and the other planes followed. They were going to meet the oncoming planes!

GALES DID not follow. He was in a quandary, but the thought of Gwen pounded uppermost in his brain. Could she be down there among the burning ruins?

He shoved forward on the stick. He chose the lagoon off the waterway, even though smoke was rolling over it. Going down, the smoke choked him, but he slapped the pontoons on the quiet water and drove the plane up beneath an overhanging shelf of land. Here it would be partially concealed from the air.

He cut out the motor and swung up to the coaming.

"She may be here, Mike!" he shouted. "But we've got to work fast!"

They made the plane fast and waded through the water. They groped through the smoke to the shore, and went down along the side of the lagoon. They fell over shattered guns and dead men, and they waded through crumpled stone and between the gaunt walls of broken houses.

But no men appeared.

They found the main street that went up the hill. It was a shambles now, strewn with stone and shattered beams, parts of automobiles, glass, furniture and here and there a dead man. Flames were crackling farther along, and the smoke rolled in great suffocating clouds.

The partners clung to each other. It would be easy to get lost in the smoke.

At last they paused, choking, in a clear space. Gales pointed.

Beyond the field were the warring planes in close and deadly combat. As they looked they saw a plane blow up and become a flaming meteor, earth-bound. They saw two planes crash head-on, saw flame burst and part of a shattered wing spin away; and then the two planes, locked in fire, spinning downward.

They went on, probing the ruined houses, dodging walls that swayed and then fell with a crash. Occasionally planes screamed overhead—always two, one after the other—and the brittle rattle of machine gun fire reached their ears.

But they never paused to listen. They tore their way through the ruins, looking for something which both dreaded to find. Jagged rocks ripped their clothes. Smoke begrimed their faces and made their eyes bloodshot.

Then suddenly they stopped. Through twisting ribbons of smoke Gales had seen a man crawl feebly.

He gripped McGill's arm and pointed. Both crunched over broken stone toward the crawling man.

Only a rag of his shirt remained. His face and arms were smudged black with smoke, and his eyes stared glassily. He was a white man.

The partners knelt down and took hold of him and he hung to their arms, panting for breath.

McGill peered closely. "By cripes!" he exclaimed. "It's Dr. Jons!"

"Jons!" echoed Gales.

The man collapsed.

A big cloud of smoke billowed toward them. They raised Jons between them and rushed through the smoke, and they heard a plane scream by overhead, hidden by the smoke. And another plane—and the mad stutter of a machine gun.

CHAPTER X

THE CRACK-UP

THEY REACHED a ruined house where the air was clearer. Half the roof was gone, and one of the walls. They found an overturned divan which Gales heaved back on its legs, and they let the doctor down gently. He was breathing thickly, irregularly.

Gales ran around looking for water, but found none. When he came back to the divan Dr. Jons' eyes were open, but they looked glassy and blank.

"This guy's gonna cash in," McGill said.

Gales bent over him. "Where is my wife? Where is Gwen Gales?"

The doctor was staring fixedly at McGill, and suddenly he let out a terrified scream.

McGill said, "It's a funny mug, but I don't see no cause for that, doc."

They heard the beat of a motor, and looked up through the gaping roof. A yellow plane drifted by.

"That's it!" McGill yelled.

"What?" asked Gales.

"The plane that kidnaped the doc here!"

Silence, but for the faraway crackling of guns, fell upon the room. Hung for a brief moment. Then the doctor was laughing hysterically, and grinning like an idiot.

Gales shook him. "Where's Gwen Gales?" he shouted.

"Kidnaped!" Jons crackled.

Suddenly the glaze left his eyes. A fire burned there instead—burned with smoldering fury.

"Fools!" he screamed. "Fools that you are! I was not kidnaped. It had only the appearance. You are surprised, no? I thought you would be. But how did you know I was not John James, as I said I was? Eh—how did you know that? No matter. It was known. Only I have wondered how."

"Don't be crazy," McGill broke in. "We want to get you out of here"

"Get me—out of here! That is what you call the immense joke, my friends. I do not go. Besides, I am dying—by the inch, by the fraction of the inch. And my models, the plans of years, have been destroyed—"

Gales said, "You're not going to die. You can start again—"

"Fools, I cannot! I will not. I am going to die. It is agreed between the Fates and me that I shall die. And my lethal heat—bah—it is all gone now. Imbecile, did you think I would give that to the Powers? Ah, yes, they found out—somehow, they found—about my invention. Their spies watched me. Their agents approached me.

"Until finally I agreed to meet the Powers and talk business. But I only agreed, to keep them away, that was all.

"The great General Kwang and I arranged the kidnaping. I assumed the name of John James for my own purpose. Had I gone under my real name, no end of planes would have accompanied me north from Saigon. So I was kidnaped, but I was willing to be kidnaped. It was all arranged. But how did we know that some fool would suspect General Kwang had a hand in it?"

The two partners stared speechless.

Then Gales said, "I saw your model."

"Bah! That one was a failure, but the next one worked. I was ill at the time, and Dr. Gee Fo experimented. But only I could do it with success. General Kwang and I would have ruled all China. He did not offer me money. He offered partnership in a great dynasty! And my lethal heat would have done it."

HE PAUSED to gasp for breath. Gales and McGill looked at each other with shocked faces. This man was mad. He had had illusions of empire.

He was gasping, "My lethal heat, you know? Ah, it was a success. It would have wiped out all enemy planes, crippled railroads, the power plants of great cities, ships at sea. Five years I worked on it. My instrument drew power from the electric currents in the air. Mounted on a plane, it converted these currents into invisible antennae that reached out and entered other planes, through their electric units. Immediately the heat waves swept over the plane, bursting the motor, making of the metal parts themselves a red furnace.

"Our planes would have been immune, due to a unique insulation which I have invented. And these electric heat waves would have crippled locomotives in the same way—and the power plants of ships and of the great cities and all enemy wireless stations. I would have been feared the world over! Tell them—tell them about my greatness! I am a great man. Even dying, I am a great man. My models worked! I—General Kwang and I—we—would have—"

He flung back on the divan, his face flaming red with passion, his chest convulsing.

"But my wife—she was here!" Gales shouted. "Where is she? Is she dead? What happened—"

The loose throaty cackle of Dr. Jons cut him off.

Gales stood throbbing with suppressed rage. You couldn't beat this man. You couldn't beat the truth out of him. Because he was dying.

His cackle became a low whimper, and the red color fled from his face. His fingers clawed, then stiffened, and life left him with a low sigh.

Gales fell back, rubbing his head, muttering. "He must have known what happened to her."

There was a long hooting sound. Then a crash—nearby—like terrible thunder. The roof of the house tottered. Gales and McGill dived for the door and reached the street as the house caved in. Thirty yards away they saw a blazing mass of metal.

"One of them gray bombers," said McGill.

Gales seemed not to hear. Gales' eyes roamed the ruins with fierce intensity. Hope was dead here. But a new hope began to burn.

He had seen some cars heading away on the wilderness road when the fight started. He grasped at this like a drowning man. Maybe Gwen was in one of those cars.

"Come on, Mike!" he shouted, and started down the hill.

More houses had caved in since their climb upward. Going down now, they found great mountains of stone in the street, and the wind that blew carried showers of hot ashes and coals. They were scorched in a dozen places, and sometimes they had to climb over the stone heaps or circle through gaping buildings where flames licked at them.

Somehow they reached the valley, their faces black with soot and their clothes in rags. Gales tore along toward the lagoon, heedless of the fighting planes aloft. But McGill could see that of the original twelve gray planes, only five were left. Five against fifteen now.

He pulled at Gales' sleeve. "You can't go up, Bill! They'll crucify us before we get off the lagoon. There's fifteen up there and they're gonna make short work of the gray babies. All the bombers have been knocked down. Them guys can fight like nobody's business, but they're outnumbered three to one. Look! Count 'em, pal. I—"

ONE OF the little single-seaters sideslipped, turned over twice and came flopping toward them. Something banged into the ground a dozen feet ahead.

Part of a broken propeller! That poor guy was done for. He would crash right in the lagoon.

Suddenly the single-seater whipped over, right side up. It slewed downward, then leveled. Its wheels hit the ground along the edge of the lagoon. The crate bounced a dozen feet in the air, teetered, and came down again, folding up its left wing. Its motor gouged the ground.

A man hurtled out and landed feet foremost in the water. In a moment he was swimming, and both Gales and McGill ran to help him.

They saw he was thrashing wildly. Then he went down. Gales jumped in and caught him under water, dragged him up and toward the shore, and McGill helped haul him up.

He sprawled, choking and spitting out water, and there was blood on his face mixed with the water from the lagoon.

"By cripes!" exploded McGill.

Gales was standing spread-legged, arms jammed akimbo, the water dripping down his face.

"So it's Duke Hannon," he said. Hannon lay limp and white-faced, his eyes closed. Gales bent down suddenly, shook him savagely. Then he stopped. Hannon was unconscious.

McGill was saying, "He was leadin' the flight, Bill—"

"Yes, his was the plane that led. How did he do this? Where did he get those planes?"

McGill muttered, "He was crazy about makin' a name for himself. He threatened he would. It's tough he's losin' out. Look, there goes another gray one! They're done for now. But he'll know where Gwen is, Bill—when he comes to."

"He'd better," growled Gales.

"And there ain't no use tryin' to get away by plane, Bill. You always been accusin' me o' bein' scatter-brained. You gotta listen to reason now. We can't take Hannon up with us. There ain't room. But we can tote him off along the wilderness road and hide out with him—"

"Wait a minute, Mike," Gales said quietly. He was peering toward the east, shading his eyes. "Am I seeing things, Mike?"

McGill squinted, "No, I don't think you are. I see some crates comin'. One—two—I see five crates, Bill."

"So do I."

"Bill, this is anybody's fight. If they're not Kwang's, let's join 'em and give them last gray babies a break!"

Motionless, they waited, and watched.

Suddenly Gales barked. "One of them is the Agency's Loening! By George—I recognize others! Look—there's two of K.O.'s green Voughts and another Lockheed—two of them!"

"They must have got a hot tip somewhere. Let's go, pal!"

"Just a minute. I'm not going to take a chance on Hannon skipping out. Get a hunk of wire out of our crate, Mike. I'll tie his hands and feet. He'll wonder how it happened when he comes to."

The five planes were nearer now, driving in a flying wedge. One of Kwang's planes crashed, and the others began grouping, and signaling to one another.

Three gray planes remained, one single-seater and two two-place jobs. Kwang's planes numbered fourteen, and after some wing-wiggling they spread to meet the new opposition. The three gray planes had scooted for altitude during the brief breathing spell. They hovered uncertainly.

CHAPTER XI

BLAZING SHIPS

McGILL TOOK the Boeing up. He left the water in a low fast climb, intending to come up under the five Agency planes and thereby prevent any of Kwang's planes from diving at him. Gales had hauled the two sub-machine guns from the after part of the fuselage, and his cockpit was crowded with fifty-shot drums.

The five Agency planes were beginning to hike for altitude. Kwang's fourteen planes were climbing fast, spread well out. Eight of them were single-seaters; six were two-place jobs, among the six the yellow plane that had kidnaped Dr. Jons.

All the planes began breaking through light running clouds. Gales and McGill were tagging upward, and the three gray planes were scooting over to mingle with the Agency's. The city below was lost behind the screen of clouds.

The first string of shots was fired at six thousand feet. Both forces sprang, as if each would test the other's ability to take hot fire in the face.

There was a mad tangle of planes when Gales and McGill joined in.

Two of Kwang's single-seaters had got on the tail of a white Lockheed and were hammering it mercilessly. One of the gray single-seaters came hurtling down from aloft through a smudge of cloud, its two guns banging. Death was quick for one of Kwang's planes.

It slid away from the Lockheed's tail and flopped over, paused, hovered and then went into a yawning spin. Below, the clouds swallowed it.

There was the Loening, blue as the sky above the clouds, plowing hugely into a fluttering nest of three enemy planes. Its two guns fired from either side. It went through the nest like a scythe through wheat, and banked beyond.

A green Vought came slicing across its tail to meet the yellow Fokker that had come booming down from aloft. The two planes whipped by so close that their wings seemed to click.

Then the yellow Fokker zoomed mightily and ran into the path of Gales and McGill.

Mike swung toward it as it straightened out of the zoom, and heard lead tearing across his cowl. Gales' sub-machine sprayed into the Fokker broadside. Its lead shattered the Fokker's front windshield as an enemy single-seater screamed by close overhead, followed by a gray single-seater with guns hammering viciously.

The yellow plane teetered away, and McGill was going after it when a black two-place job hove up on his bow and crashed a load of lead through his undercarriage. Gales turned his gun on the black plane and a white Vought slammed by toward the yellow Fokker.

A stream of lead whistled past Gales' head and gouged the fuselage behind. Gales emptied his gun at the black plane's prop, and suddenly the black plane fell away, its prop shattered at the base. It fell drunkenly, and one of its own single-seaters, running pell mell from a gray plane, crashed into the black plane's tail.

Flame burst and ballooned violently, and the gray single-seater burst over the rim of the flame and flashed by in front of the Boeing, missing by inches.

For a brief tense minute four planes were in a mad scramble, their guns silent, their pilots striving frantically to avoid one another and get out of an imminent crash. The wind blew hot ashes into Gales' face, and he grabbed up the second sub-machine gun.

Then they were out of the tangle. And for a moment they were on the rim of things.

GALES TOOK the opportunity of reloading his other gun. And he saw the end of the yellow plane, a thousand feet below, blown up by one of the green Lockheeds.

And even as he looked a hissing, hooting mass of flames came down beside him. He felt the heat of it rush by, saw a gray tail and part of a gray wing swathed in whipping flames.

He looked up and saw an enemy two-seater prancing. He raised his gun and spread lead up and down its belly, hammered the long end of the burst up under the enemy's nose.

Flame flashed, and the enemy's tail swung downward, then spun, and the plane flopped on its side and came down like a red comet.

McGill gunned his motor and headed back for the main body of the fighting planes.

He was doing a hundred and thirty when he roared into the thick of it, and Gales blazed away at a two-seater that was hammering the Loening's tail. McGill jerked the plane aside to avoid a crash, and a black crate whanged past, its gun a popping red eye.

Gales looked back and saw a gray single-seater finishing the crate that was on the Loening's tail, while the Loening was meeting a brown Fokker face to face in a shower of lead.

This could not go on forever, yet each minute seemed like an eternity. Gales flung harried eyes across the sky. What was the count?

His lips moved. There was one white Vought gone. Only one of the three gray planes remained. And the enemy?

So far the enemy had lost six crates since the arrival of the Agency unit. That left them eight. And the Agency six, counting the one gray plane that was left.

Now there was an enemy plane plunging downward, a long stream of smoke behind it. Its two men were climbing out, making ready to jump. But the plane burst into flame.

McGill, sparring for an opening, was suddenly driven away by a fast black two-seater that came storming around on his tail.

Gales swung around with his gun and shot over the tail assembly, aiming at the shining prop of the enemy. He saw lead gash open the top of his fuselage, saw it creep forward.

He ducked down as lead shattered his headrest fairing and McGill wheeled off on one ear. But again lead hammered in the Boeing, and McGill stuck his nose downward and power-dived, hoping that another Agency plane would swoop down to get the enemy off his tail.

They tore through clouds, screaming down over the smoking ruins, close over the roofless houses and the dead ammunition dump. Gales' eyes conned all the destruction below—the shattered barracks, the razed tents.

McGill heaved the crate around violently, close over the ground, and enemy lead poured into the Boeing's flank. The black plane swung to head the Boeing off, and Gales sent a burst of lead into its nose.

The sound of his gun was mixed with a fury of lead pounding into the Boeing's cowl. There was a crash, and then an absence of one sound among the medley of others, and the sudden mad racing of the motor.

Their prop was gone!

McGILL SHUT off the motor as his hair stood on end. The black plane flashed by, and Gales gritted his jaw and pounded the end of his burst into the enemy's flank. He saw the gunner throw up his hands.

Below, the field was skimming past, but slower and slower. McGill was headed for the lagoon, but he knew he could not reach it. Try the river, then!

The Boeing dropped fast. The river was narrow, and he dared not take a chance to turn and drop on it lengthwise. His pontoons smacked the water half-way across the river's breadth. The water roared beneath them, and in an instant they hit the farther bank.

The tail whipped upward, the engine plowed into the bank, and the wings cracked. The jolt knocked the wind out of the two partners, and McGill's head smacked the dashboard.

Three minutes passed before Gales stirred. Still in a half-daze, he unbuckled his safety belt and started to get up. Pain knifed his left leg and he slumped down. He reached down and felt blood on his leg. He was wounded, but he hadn't known till now.

"Hey, Mike!" he yelled.

A dazed and glassy-eyed McGill wobbled up out of the front cockpit.

"You all right, Mike?"

"S-well, pard."

Gales tried again to get out. He succeeded this time, his teeth grinding.

"You all right, Bill?"

"Fine!"

Gales tried his best not to limp.

McGill pointed. "There comes the last gray plane."

They saw it crash among the remains of the hangars.

Gales gripped McGill's arm. "Come on, Mike! I saw something from the air. This way."

He walked stiffly, swiftly, driving groans back down his throat. He led the way through the ruined barracks and up a path beyond. He climbed to a shelf of rock and stumbled to an antiaircraft gun.

"I saw this, Mike! If it works!"

"Let's try it, pal."

McGill loaded, and Gales swung the big rifle upward. The concussion shook the shelf of rock.

"Pile those shells over here, Mike!"

With the gun loaded, Gales watched the sky. Sweat poured down his face, and pain was stamped there. He saw a white Vought come tearing downward, with a big black monoplane streaking after it. He crouched behind the gun. He held his breath and keened his eyes. He let it go. A split-second later he saw the black plane burst red against the clouds.

"Great, Bill!"

"Load her, Mike!"

The white Vought came down low over them, and both partners waved. Someone waved down, and then the Vought flew off to join the main fight.

Presently, as if that Vought had had a hand in it, the fight was drawn over the field. And again the white Vought drew a black monoplane after it and headed for the gun.

Gales picked his plane, followed it as it drew nearer, and then fired. The black plane was blown to pieces.

Gales sank to the ground.

"What's the matter, Bill?"

"Nothing, Mike. I—tripped. Load her up."

With a great effort Gales got back to his feet. His eyes were glazed, and he kept them turned away from Mike. He crouched behind the gun and watched the wheeling planes. Waves of heat rushed over him. His eyes danced, or the things in front of his eyes danced.

"There's one. Bill—get him!"

Gales tried to narrow his eyes, to drive away the vibrating sky. Where was the plane? He heard the roar of motors close by. But darkness was sweeping down on him. Suddenly he reeled away from the gun and sprawled headlong.

"Bill! Bill!"

"'S all right, Mike. You try it. I'm tired."

"Bill, are you hurt?" cried McGill.

"Just—tired. Get 'em, Mike. You got to get 'em."

McGill was beside him. "You—you—it's your leg! Why didn't you say it was your leg?"

Gales mumbled, "And don't forget Hannon, Mike, He knows—where Gwen is. Take care of her, Mike—for old times' sake."

CHAPTER XII

FLIGHT'S END

FOUR PLANES lay at anchor on the river at Kweilin. They were scarred and pockmarked. Many sampans swarmed about them, but the mechanics tuning up the motors paid no attention.

McGill, standing on the wharf, tossed a cigarette into the river, turned and strode away with his jaw set hard. Fierce anxiety

burned in his eyes. He went up through the river town to the hospital.

K.O. Pike met him. K.O. carried an arm in a sling, and there were strips of adhesive tape on his face.

"Well, K.O.?" growled McGill.

"I was just looking for you, Mike. Come on up."

There was a white cool room, and two beds, one at either side of the room. In one lay Duke Hannon. In the other, Gales. Beside Gales, sat his wife, holding his hand.

"Hello, Mike," Gales said.

"Hello, Bill." The red-head almost galloped across the room. "Gosh, Bill, it's great to see you lookin' up again. I sure thought you were done for."

Gales was weak, haggard. He had just come to, was still breathless with surprise because he had found Gwen sitting beside the bed. He looked at her.

"I never expected to find her here, Mike."

She turned red swollen eyes on McGill. "Nor did I ever expect to find him again. It's been terrible."

Gales had not seen Hannon. "Where's Hannon?" he said.

K.O. cleared his throat. "Hannon's all right."

"Glad you're one of us again," Hannon called out.

Gales started. He turned his head and saw Hannon looking across the room at him, Hannon's head was swathed in bandages.

Gales said grimly, "I have a score to settle with you, Hannon."

"Oh, Bill," Gwen broke in, "don't think of that. It was all my fault."

"Your fault!"

"You see," K.O. said, "your wife thought you were dead. Well, reports had it that you were. She went to Saigon from Bangkok and found Hannon fuming. Hannon wanted action. He got the idea into his head that all of us thought he was a weak sister. And Gwen was ripe for action. She thought that she—by herself—could avenge your death by going to Kwang's strong-hold alone and getting the secret plans. Hannon talked her out of that, but offered another idea instead."

"I don't believe it," Gales said.

"It's true, Bill," his wife urged. "When Mr. Hannon outlined his scheme, I was all for it. Neither of us thought that K.O. would listen to it, so we decided to just disappear. Mr. Hannon had been speaking with an agent of the Nanking Insurrection-ists. They had a score to pay off against Kwang, and Mr. Hannon and I came here to Kweilin on a secret mission. Between us we got the N.I. to form a flying squadron. They knew that if Kwang succeeded in putting Dr. Jons' plan into effect, they would be the first to suffer. Kwang had no right to exist. He was a menace to all China."

Gales nodded, still hard-eyed.

HIS WIFE went on. "So the squadron was formed, and a date set for the attack. There was a man in the N.I. who they believed was one of Kwang's spies. They let news slip that they would attack from the south, while they actually intended to attack from the west.

"Sure enough, the spy sent the news through, and I understand Kwang's planes went south to head the N.I. off and keep the fight away from his stronghold. Just after Mr. Hannon and the N.I. planes left, a British scout plane dropped down here, and the pilot remarked offhand that you and Mike were still alive. I got in touch with K.O., and he verified it and said you had gone to Kwang's city. I implored him to get all the planes he could and follow."

Gales fell back, sighing. "Well, if K.O. hadn't come, Mike and I would be among the missing."

"Bosh!" said K.O. "What really won the fight, in the end, was you and Mike at that anti-aircraft gun. We'd run out of ammunition, Bill. Mike says you downed two planes with that gun. He downed two more after you'd passed out. The city is in ruin. We found Dr. Jons' body, and Mike told us what he said before he died. And—yes—we found Kwang's body, too."

"They would have wiped out all of China," Gales said.

Gwen leaned over. "Don't be angry at Mr. Hannon."

Hannon grinned. "I was sore. Boy, I was sore! It was like a punch in the jaw to have you two guys go off on a job like that. I was jealous—sure I was jealous. And I guess I was mad to do what I did."

"Well," McGill said, "I always thought I was pretty nutty, but I guess I ain't no more. You ain't a bad guy, Hannon. Trouble is, you're a Mick. And I'm a Mick. And that's the whole trouble. I always had an idea you were a bag of wind, but, Duke, you went and showed me that you got guts a-plenty."

K.O. beamed "That's talking, boys! That's man talk! You boys are going to get on great from now on."

"Well," McGill said, "that's a question. If Duke goes off the handle and tries to crack wise, I'm gonna paste him."

"Oh, yeah?" glared Hannon.

"Yeah!" barked McGill.

"Well, listen here, half-pint—"

"Now, now," broke in K.O.

Gales said, "Come on, you birds. Zoom out of here. I've got to get used to seeing my wife again."

"Come on, Mike," K.O. urged.

McGill went toward the door, looking at Hannon.

"Just keep that in mind, handsome," he clipped.

"Hey, half-pint, when I get out of bed I'll—"

But K.O. rushed McGill through the door.

THE SKYLINE TWO

Men branded with the skull-and-bones sign set a sky trap for unwary sparrows. Gales and McGill took the bait—and the wind gods of the China Sea made scarlet marks in their pilot's logbook.

AT TEN o'clock of a sweltering Singapore morning Sam Garrison, the hard-boiled head of the Garrison Airways, pioneer commercial airman of the East, received a wireless message. John Hu, his immaculate Chinese secretary, brought it in and began to choke over the clouds of smoke the five-foot-three air boss discharged from the rankest cheroot out of Sumatra.

"Got a cold?" Garrison asked.

"No, sir. Uh—wireless—uh—message—"

"Give me it here—"

"K'choo! Beg pardon—"

"Damn my stars! Sneeze the other way!"

Garrison growled good-naturedly, picked up the message. His ragtag eyebrows bent, his eyes became grave.

John Hu suffered a loss of dignity while his eyes dripped and he dabbed at them with a handkerchief, and still gasped.

Garrison began to puff furiously. John Hu retreated to the door in agony.

"John!" boomed the mighty mite of a man. "Have we a cabin job ready to take off?"

"No, sir."

"What—no cabin job!"

"Beg pardon, no, sir. Your two-seater, sir, and that would be of no use. The Boeing left for Penang this morning, the *Goose* is between Kuching and Macassar, eastbound—"

"This is serious, John!" Garrison scrambled out of his chair, pulled his suspenders up to his shoulders and began, pacing up and down.

It was a message from the *Krag Castle*, two hundred and fifty miles east of Singapore, bound for Borneo ports. The message was signed by George Gault, master. The vessel had a man on board with an acute attack of appendicitis. Could the Garrison Airways send a plane to take the man and his companion off and fly them back to Singapore?

Garrison stopped short, snapped the message across an open palm. "Telephone the Straits Agency, John. Ask them."

John Hu, still gasping, fled from the office. Sam Garrison lit a fresh cheroot from the butt of the old and flung himself back into the chair.

He waited restlessly.

John Hu returned and said, "Beg pardon, sir, but the Agency has no plane available in S'pore. However, sir, they have a plane that left Kuching in Sarawak two hours ago, en route to here, and it should be, sir, in the vicinity of the *Krag Castle*."

"A cabin job?"

"Yes, sir. And light, sir."

"Who's flying it?"

"The illustrious Gales and McGill, sir—"

"Hot dog!" Garrison thumped the desk. "The guy is as good as saved, John! Wireless Gales and McGill!"

"Very good, sir."

THE SIX-PLACE special Vought was not new, but her Wasp motor, veteran of many an oceanic hop, had the heart of a lion. The white crate was riding an air trail smooth as velvet. The sea was empty, blue-green and incredibly smooth, like a vast round-table whose rim was the penciled horizon.

Mike McGill was at the controls, dressed in an undershirt, white pants and canvas sneakers over sockless feet. He lounged well back, scarcely bothering with the controls, his eyelids drowsing.

The soldierly Bill Gales was turned toward the radio set, earphones on, finger poised above the open key. The finger darted, the key clicked. Gales grinned to himself. He was sending a message to his wife in Bangkok, telling her that all was well. Finished, he was about to close the key; didn't. He bent his head on one side, listening. He clicked the key briefly, listened again; his eyes became intent. Dressed in a suit of crisp whites, white shoes, white silk shirt and blue tie, the junior member of the famous partnership looked like a million dollars. His finger dropped, rapped the key smartly. Then he sat back and took off the earphones, jabbed McGill in the ribs. McGill started out of his day dream.

Gales grinned. "Mike, little job on the way home."

"That's tough."

"Nothing at all. There's a ship named *Krag Castle* about fifty miles ahead of us. She's bound east. There's a man on board pretty sick, and his friend. Sam Garrison asked us to pick the guy up. Ship wirelessed Sam."

McGill yawned. "Well, I suppose we'll have to. Where's this wagon at, old pal?"

"I'll get in touch with her."

Gales returned to the radio set and in a couple of minutes was in communication with the *Krag Castle*. He secured the exact position of the vessel and instructed the master to have a smallboat ready. Then he closed the key, took up a chart, did some calculation and set the chart aside.

"She's dead ahead, Mike."

McGill sat up in the seat, squinted, and shoved forward on the throttle. The Vought trembled as the motor roared into a fresh burst of speed. At two thousand feet, she sliced through a light headwind.

Gales raised a smoke on the horizon half an hour later and reached for his binoculars. He pointed and McGill nodded. He held the glasses to his eyes and soon he could make out a vessel.

"I guess that's it, Mike."

The *Krag Castle* looked like a waif of the outer seas. Small, rusty-plated, she had a shallow well-deck forward and her dirty superstructure was bunched way aft and topped by a skinny black funnel. Her Plimsoll line was visible above the water and a scarred small-boat was loose in davits on the lee side.

McGill began knocking off altitude. He whistled to himself, cutting down the motor, nursing the stick. He prodded left rudder bar and the right wing came up slowly, the crate turned to the left and McGill looked down at the vessel. The wind sighed and whistled through the wires as the Vought circled the ship and then coasted down toward the smooth surface of the sea.

The big floats smacked the water smartly, the crate heaved, water gurgled, broke and splashed up against the underside of the fuselage. With the motor cut way down, the prop slopped around sluggishly.

Gales opened the door and leaned out, peering at the vessel.

A SMALLBOAT was being lowered from the *Krag Castle*. A man naked from the waist up, and with a white-topped cap on the back of his head, leaned in the lee wing of the navigating bridge and spat disconsolately overside. He had nut-brown shoulders, a black beard.

The smallboat hit the water and the Lascar sailors began pulling. A mate sat at the tiller, a cap tipped over his eyes, a pipe jutting from his mouth. Near him sat two civilians in white suits, one with his arm around the other.

Gales frowned. "She's a tough-looking wagon, Mike."

"Believe you me she is, pard. The baby on the bridge would never be accused of bein' dainty. Nor that palooka at the tiller. I got a creepy feelin'."

Gales laughed, but not heartily. The mission seemed suddenly strange, yet he could not exactly say why. He watched the smallboat as it drew nearer, watched the motionless, hard-jawed mate at the tiller.

The smallboat drew up under the Vought's big wing and the Lascars rested on the oars. The mate stood up, hitching at his pants. He was barefoot. He flung up a hairy arm.

"Hi, mates! Glad you come along. We'll have these chums on board in a minute."

The sick man was small and white-faced. His companion was big and burly and wore a brown sun helmet. He looked up at Gales leaning in the plane's door.

"You're a godsend, mister," he rumbled.

It was easy moving the small man up into the plane. The mate helped, and when Gales had the man inside the cabin the other passenger swung up two handbags and followed them. He turned to wave to the mate.

"Thanks," he called down.

"That's all right, chum."

The mate spoke to the Lascars and the smallboat began pulling away.

Gales had carried the sick man to a seat in the rear of the cabin. When he turned from the seat the burly man was in his way.

"My name is Brunt," he said. "My friend Willis is in a bad way. We've got to get him to a hospital."

"We'll do that, Mr. Brunt," Gales said. "We'll try our best to get him to Singapore. I'll radio ahead and have an ambulance waiting at the wharf."

"I have the honor of speaking to—whom?"

"Gales is my name. That's McGill." Brunt started, swallowed. "Gales—and—McGill?"

Willis, the sick man, caught his breath and blinked his pale tired eyes.

Brunt coughed behind his hand. "Yes—yes, of course. Well, sir, we certainly have heard of you fellows. We never expected to be honored in quite this way."

Gales smiled, said, "The honor, Mr. Brunt, is ours. Well, we'll take off immediately."

He went forward and dropped to the seat beside McGill. "Okey, Mike," he said. "And go easy on the bumps."

"Everything will be la-de-da, Bill," said Mike McGill. "That guy is lucky in a big way to have me at the controls."

McGill gunned the motor and the crate began moving across the quiet water. The backwash snapped at the water, the prop spun faster. In fifteen seconds the Vought tore her floats from the sea and pounded mightily into free air. Ten minutes later the *Krag Castle* was a dot on the horizon and the plane was doing a hundred and twenty miles an hour.

Gales radioed Singapore, reported that they were on the wing and asked to have an ambulance ready at the wharf to rush Mr. Willis to a hospital. He removed the earphones and was about to turn and see how his passengers were making out when a crack on the head hurled him into oblivion.

CHAPTER II

HIGH HOLD-UP

"STEADY ON those controls!" warned Brunt, handling a flat black automatic.

McGill exploded—"Why, you dirty—"

"Shut up! Watch those controls!" Brunt hefted the gun, his eyes narrowed and gleaming. "And do as you're told!" he snarled.

McGill pulled the ship out of the beginning of a plunge and swore an indigo-blue streak. His eyes skipped over the dials. The good-humor had fled from his freckled red face and his lips were curling over clenched teeth.

Gales was slumped way down, his chin sunk to his chest, a trickle of blood winding down behind his left ear. He hadn't uttered a cry. And the blow had been so swift, so hard, that it had knocked him out completely.

Brunt looked around through the windows. Nothing was visible now but the *Krag Castle's* smoke.

"Listen, you, McGill," Brunt said. "Make a turn north and circle way around out of sight of that ship. Then, head east for the Borneo coast."

"Says you!" barked McGill.

"I'm serious," Brunt threatened.

"So am I, brother! My course is west—for Singapore, and this crate is funny that way—she can't go in any other direction."

"You fool! Do as I say! Turn this ship north or I'll throw your partner out of that door!"

McGill felt the hair stiffen on the back of his neck. But he said, "You can't kid me, brother."

"No?"

"No!"

Brunt turned. "Tod," he called.

Willis was standing in the aisle, holding a gun in his hand. He came forward.

"Open that door, Tod," Brunt said. Willis smiled wickedly. Brunt began hauling Gales from the seat and Willis moved toward the door.

McGill rose half-way, turned and took a swing at Brunt. Brunt fell backward, losing hold of Gales, and crashed to the aisle. Willis crowded McGill back into the seat, striking once with his gun. McGill was hit hard. The crate yawed wildly and Brunt, almost on his feet, fell down again. Willis hung on, however, and jammed his gun against McGill's back. McGill fought the controls and finally leveled the plane off at a thousand feet.

Brunt came forward, glaring, showing his teeth and gripping his gun in a big hand. "Well, sir, does your friend take a header through that door or do you turn north?"

McGill was in a hot sweat. His blood rebelled at this outrage, but he realized that Gales was in a tight spot. These men meant business. McGill's calm had been knocked into a cocked hat by the abruptness of the attack and he was struggling hard to regain it and to think straight.

Suddenly, with a disgusted oath, he kicked right rudder bar and swung the ship toward the north.

"THAT IS very sensible," said Brunt. "No harm will come to either one of you so long as you do as you're told. Just head north until I tell you to turn."

Brunt dragged Gales aft, heaved him into the rear left seat and bound him there with straps from one of the handbags. Willis remained behind McGill with a gun. Brunt came forward again, taking a chart from his pocket. He took the ship's chart from the dashboard, compared the two, and made notations. Then he bent down and held the chart Gales had used before McGill.

"Where I have marked an X—you will land there, McGill."

"Borneo coast, eh?"

"Yes."

"And then what happens?"

"You will see when the time comes. Now you begin to swing east. And mark me, no tricks. I know these waters well, pilot. And I mean what I say. One trick on your part and your partner goes overboard. Be sensible, and both of you will be all right."

McGill was oddly reconciled to the circumstances. This was no time to put up a fight. Gales was unconscious, these men were on some deadly business, and McGill had a valuable crate under his hands and his partner's life in the balance. Still, he was not completely over the shock. He had no idea what lay ahead of him, but he picked Brunt for a canny bird. No knock-down-and-drag-out customer, this big man—but a wily one, intent on his business and fiercely determined to win through.

"Okey," McGill said. "You're top-dog now, mister. But some day I'm goin' to give you somethin' to remember me by."

Brunt made no reply. He leaned over and spoke with Willis. Willis listened. His tired, empty eyes moved vaguely, A thin, dry leer moved across his lips. He nodded. Brunt took up a position behind McGill and Willis sat down by the radio set. He put on earphones and opened the key.

McGill, puzzled, turned and squinted. Willis worked his dry smile and began tapping the key. McGill listened. He couldn't understand the key. Gales was the radio man. McGill kept shifting in his seat, and every time he looked at Willis the little sinister man smiled mockingly. Finally Willis closed the key, took off the earphones, leaned back and smiled up at Brunt. Brunt raised his thick eyebrows. Willis nodded. Brunt grinned.

The Vought droned on across the wide and empty sea, a lone bird of misfortune. The prop shimmered and the motor sang its endless song of power.

McGill was a grim red-head at the controls. Brunt sat behind him, fondling the pistol, peering ahead constantly, eagerness and anxiety in his dark eyes; fierce determination in the set of his jaw.

Willis drowsed. Or seemed to drowse. But you knew that he was alert, watchful—a wan-looking tired man who nevertheless had a certain sinister air about him.

Gales, still unconscious, was slumped in the rear left seat.

CHAPTER III

TAKE-OFF

J OHN HU'S fingers shook. He gulped and his eyes stared at the message the boy had brought from the radio room. He let out a short cry and went quick-footed into the smoky sanctum of his chief.

"Well, well, well?" barked Garrison.

"This—this, sir!"

Garrison snatched the message from the shaking fingers of his secretary.

> Motor balking and smoking. Must go down. Fresh wind making sea choppy. Danger.
>
> GALES—

Garrison jabbed John Hu with a quick stare, snapped, "Where the devil did you get this, John?"

"Why, sir, from Mair, the op—"

"Yes, yes, of course." The little air chief got up, pulled his suspenders over his shoulders. "That means they're down—and in trouble, John! Did Mair try to regain communication?"

"Yes, sir."

"And didn't succeed?"

"No, sir."

"Damn my stars!" Garrison threw up his hands. He sailed out of his sanctum, across the general office, into the radio room. "Hey, Mair, get the lead out of your pants! Wireless all ships between here and Sarawak to keep their glims peeled for Gales and McGill. Wireless the same thing to our *Frigate Bird*. She should be leaving Kuching in two hours. And still try to see if you can regain communication with those two eggs."

Garrison turned and stamped out of the radio room, reached his office and found John Hu on the same spot.

"Any Agency planes in yet?"

"No, sir."

"Where's Mr. K.O. Pike?"

"Rumor has it he is in Hongkong at present writing."

"Ixnay on that rumor racket, Johnny. Call up and see."

John Hu telephoned. K.O. Pike was in Hongkong. Pennant, the regional manager for the Straits Agency, got hot and bothered about the reported misfortune of his ace performers.

Garrison grabbed the phone. "Keep your pants on, Pennant. Those two guys couldn't croak. But I'm worried about the sick guy they took off the *Krag Castle*. He won't even be a hospital case if we don't locate that plane.... I know, Pennant, I know. I'm sorry, but what can you do about it? It so happens that all my planes and your planes are elsewhere. Only keep the old pants on, Pennant!"

He hung up and slapped his palms together, rubbed them vigorously. "Pennant's got the wind up, John. He thinks that if Gales and McGill croak the Straits Agency will go bust as a flying detective unit. Well—they might, b'gosh!"

"Situation is most deplorable, sir."

"Or in a word—lousy!"

The hard-boiled millionaire swooped down on the radio room and again demanded news. Mair had none. Mair had got in touch with all vessels plying between Singapore and the islands to the east and had wirelessed the Kuching station. He reported, however, that no vessel was in the vicinity of the Vought.

"How about that *Krag Castle?*"

"I can't seem to raise it."

"Keep after it. By George, it will come to it that I'll take my Lockheed and go look for them!" He snorted. "Yes, sir, that's what I'll have to do, else Pennant will die of a brainstorm." He gushed smoke through his nostrils. "That sick guy, Mair—it's tough being sick in a downed plane—poor guy."

ONCE GARRISON became attached to an idea it was hard to tear him away from it. Inside of half an hour he was down at the waterfront, his pockets stuffed full of cheroots and a glint in his eyes.

He had telephoned ahead for the mechanics to make his Lockheed ready. It lay in the basin, its motor warming up.

"Who's going with you, sir?" the super asked.

"Nobody. It's solo for me. If I find that plane I want one cockpit empty for the sick man. The *Frigate Bird* can pick the others up. But the *Frigate Bird* is running on schedule and I can't have her skylarking all over the sea, looking for the Vought. If she's afloat, I'll find her and then get in touch with the *Frigate Bird*."

Garrison swung down into the cockpit and wiggled the controls. He clamped a chart on the dashboard. Handlers cast away the lines and the blue Lockheed drifted away from the wharf. A siren blew twice. Garrison gunned the motor a couple of times, then pulled down his goggles.

He lifted the crate over the harbor shipping in a hard climb. He was a strange manner of a man, a stormy petrel whose actions could never be prophesied. He had pioneered in the air all over the East, amassing great wealth but still remaining as cyclonic and as unfathomable as he had been when he started on a shoestring. No one knew his exact age, though it was said he was well beyond fifty.

The Lockheed was perfection itself. By the time it reached and passed Horsburgh Light it was doing a hundred and forty miles an hour. And flying low. That was dangerous, but the hundred-odd pound air boss liked danger. He had let down his suspenders again for comfort and his cigar was a dead wet weed clamped in his mouth. He had the last position of the Vought marked on his chart, and he had it stamped on his memory, too.

It took him two and a half hours to reach the vicinity outlined by Mair in the radio office. He raised binoculars to his eyes and scanned the sea. He rose mightily, throttled down, loafed in a circle. He swooped down with a lump in his throat, but what he had thought was part of a plane was only a stick of driftwood.

He rose again, hurtling the Lockheed up into the blue. He circled, making each succeeding circle wider. Time and time again driftwood made him dive down and look closely. His old heart began to sink. He saw no sign of the Vought on all that wide horizon. An hour went by, and half of another hour found him circling, diving, climbing again, and always peering hungrily through his glasses.

Finally he sank, disgruntled, in his seat, wagged his head. He had made a thorough search over a wide area, had found nothing. He hated to leave a thing undone, but he began to reason that he had done everything humanly possible. And he began to reason, too, that the Vought must have crashed and gone under, leaving no trace.

At last, looking at his petrol gauge, he knew that it was imperative to turn back. He swung the Lockheed's nose toward the west and hit the gun hard. He scowled, muttered to himself.

"Queer," he said. "Queer."

CHAPTER IV

MURDER

THE LOW Borneo coast steamed in the late sun. Greenish mud-bars glinted like metal in the sunlight, and a hot mist hung over the lowlands that swept back from the wild coast. No impressive grandeur here. Only desolation—a sweating low jungle that resented sullenly the approach of any white man.

McGill saw this from afar. Beside him stood Brunt, his eyes burning with a dark eagerness, his hand knotted on the automatic he held. McGill was not a man of great imagination, yet he was able to sense a driving force behind the bulk of this man who had become his enemy. And a madness—a madness that McGill knew would flame against himself or Gales on the slightest provocation.

Quiet-eyed was Gales. Still lashed to the creaking wicker seat, his blue eyes studied Willis, Brunt. He did not shout or swear to himself or strain futilely at the straps that held him prisoner. He conserved his energy, thinking that it would stand him in good stead when the time for action came.

Brunt said to McGill, "Now—follow the coast north."

"How far?"

"Never mind how far. Do as I tell you."

Brunt bent over, gripping the back of the seat beside McGill. He peered intently at the low coastline, scowling. Every minute or so he consulted his chart. He breathed heavily, the sweat shining in metallic streaks on his heavy, dark face.

McGill loafed up the coast on a cut throttle. Sometimes he looked back at Gales. His expression said, "Our time will come yet, old pal." And Gales smiled quietly, understanding his partner, but mystified as to what motivated Brunt and Willis.

"There—there!" Brunt cried out suddenly, pointing. "Beyond that spit of land is an inlet. Go down there."

"Well, big shot, I'm glad you've made up your mind."

Brunt turned to Willis. "Look, Tod—look! That's the place!"

Willis gazed through the windows with his tired eyes. His dry lips parted in a wan leer. He nodded.

McGill nosed the crate closer toward the shore and droned over the arm of land. He saw mud-bars and an inlet, more like a river's mouth, that stretched back into the steaming jungle. He got the offshore breeze on his nose and cut his gun. The motor quieted down and the Vought drifted over the outer mud-bars. The inlet seemed tideless. It was flat and dark like wet metal, bordered by big-rooted trees and marshes.

The floats hit the calm water and echoes cracked back and forth in the hot silence.

"Taxi—keep taxiing," Brunt muttered.

He glared hungrily. Willis had drawn his gun. They became watchful, wary, scanning the shores.

THEN McGILL saw a small settlement—shacks built on stilts. Natives appeared and disappeared uncannily among the dark trees. A white man appeared on the jetty that stuck out from the settlement. He looked short and broad. He wore no shirt and his soiled white pants were rolled up over stout calves. He stood watching with his fists planted on his hips.

Brunt began muttering to himself. His eyes glared and his fingers coiled and uncoiled around the butt of his gun.

"Taxi right up to that jetty," he said.

McGill had a feeling that trouble was about to happen. Yet he could do nothing. The madness he had first noticed in Brunt's eyes seemed greater now. Nor was it the common madness brought on by common anger. Something deeper, more vital, was moving Brunt, bringing that fierce light into his dark eyes.

Brunt muttered thickly, "Tod, you keep your eye on McGill here."

McGill had cut the motor out. The plane bumped gently against the jetty, against a couple of moored dug-outs.

Brunt opened the door, stepped into one of the dug-outs, crossed to the other and then swung up the ladder to the jetty. McGill watched him keenly. Brunt went toward the short, broad man, spoke briefly with him, pointed to the settlement. Both walked up the jetty, struck a boardwalk built on piles and followed to a ramshackle bungalow. They disappeared inside.

McGill looked around at Willis. Willis smiled his dry, mocking smile and moved his gun up and down significantly.

There was nothing to say. McGill turned and looked at the bungalow again. The natives moved among the trees, never appearing in full view. The wet heat of the jungle breathed into the plane. The silence was eerie, freighted with anger.

McGill moved uncomfortably. He had been in many strange places, from Peking to the Isle of Bali, but none had been as uncanny as this.

Gales felt it, too—the air of dark mystery and impending danger. He moved in his seat. Beads of sweat stood out on his forehead, rolled down his cheeks.

A hoarse cry sprang from the bungalow. McGill started. Willis hissed a warning and steadied his gun. McGill settled back into his seat. He mopped sweat on his face.

A shot boomed.

"By cripes!" exploded McGill, leaping up.

Willis, white-faced, tense, snarled like a cat and struck McGill with his gun. McGill crashed to the floor. Gales, swearing for the first time, tussled with his bonds.

McGill heaved around and started up again. The muzzle of Willis' gun hovered in front of the red-head's face. McGill gulped, his face flaming with suppressed rage.

"Take it easy, Mike!" Gales called.

"You'd better!" Willis warned in a voice flat with menace.

The natives had started wailing. Brunt appeared in front of the bungalow, gripping his gun. He stood stock-still, swinging his gun slowly back and forth. But the natives did not rush out. They vanished, wailing, into the deeper jungle. Their cries became fainter and fainter.

"Now it's murder, eh!" McGill ripped out.

"Just beginning," said Willis in his sibilant voice.

Feet rapped the wood of the jetty. Brunt was walking down, looking from side to side, his face aflame, his eyes burning darkly. He had killed the lone white man of the inlet. Why had he killed him? The question crackled in the minds of Gales and McGill.

McGill saw Brunt stop at the end of the jetty. He could see the big man look around again and again. The madness was still there, the madness of fierce determination. But he was gloating now. He took off his brown sun helmet and fanned himself and his eyes glittered wildly. He slapped it on again and began laughing hysterically, thumping his chest.

"I've got it, Tod!" he cried. "It's the place!"

Willis sucked in a slow, hissing breath, smiled crookedly.

Then Brunt stopped laughing. He crouched and looked seaward.

Both Gales and McGill heard the far-off drone of a plane's motor.

WILLIS MADE that hissing feline sound again between clenched teeth. Eyes and face seemed to become drier and peculiarly gray like cigarette ash.

Brunt came aboard the plane by way of the dug-outs. He hung in the door, looking toward the west, heaving from side to side. Then he glared at McGill.

"Go up! Start this plane! Go up!"

McGill smiled tightly, said, "We can't, brother. We haven't got enough gas to clear the water."

"You lie!" roared Brunt.

"Not me. Look at the gauge for yourself. Empty."

Willis hissed, "It's empty, Jabez."

Brunt said, "Oh, my Lord," in a throaty voice. Then he said, "I'll take the bags, Tod. Keep your gun on McGill. We'll beat it."

He went aft, caught up the two bags and left the plane, stumbled across the canoes, won to the jetty.

Tod Willis looked at McGill. "Stay right where you are. I can keep an eye on your pal. If you move I'll drill him from the jetty."

Without another word Willis backed out of the plane. Quick-footed, nimble, he attained the jetty and stopped to level his gun at Gales. But McGill had not moved. He knew a killer when he saw one. Besides, there was no object in moving.

Willis ran off, joined Brunt and the two disappeared in the jungle.

Finally McGill moved—went aft, drawing a clasp knife and severed the straps that held his partner. In a moment Gales was on his feet, flexing his muscles. He produced a key, opened a locker, took out two big revolvers. One he gave to McGill, along with a handful of ammunition.

"Now Mike," he clipped, "were you telling the truth about the gas?"

McGill nodded in decided affirmative. "Absolute!"

"There's the plane!"

It appeared low over the roof of the trees, a big tri-motored job, a flying-boat. About its casual appearance there was something as mysterious as the still lagoon and the steaming jungle. Its props were turning over slowly. The big crate was settling down. The partners could see two heads in the open control cabin in the bow.

The ship struck the water, turning up foam, and more faces could be seen at the cabin windows. It came plowing hugely toward the jetty. Several men appeared on the big wing. They carried rifles and looked toward the Vought. The props stopped threshing, and the plane drifted. A man appeared in the bow with a line and swung down to one of the canoes, up to the jetty, made fast.

A DOOR at the rear end of the cabin windows swung open and a lean, gaunt man appeared there. He studied the Vought. Gales was looking out, and for a moment he locked eyes with the stranger.

"What do you do here?" demanded the stranger tartly.

"Nothing," said Gales. "We're out of fuel."

Several men had gone to the jetty and were tramping toward the huts.

The gaunt-faced stranger said, "You will make your plane fast and we will have a talk."

A man came running from the huts, yelling, "He's been murdered!"

"Oh-oh," muttered McGill.

"Steady, Mike," Gales counseled. "Come on. We'll just have to brazen this out."

They climbed out, made fast to one of the moored canoes and climbed to the jetty. Half a dozen men crowded around them with drawn guns. The gaunt-faced man came up to the jetty. He had small gray eyes, hard as agates. He was immaculately dressed in white.

"He has been—murdered, Herr Baron!"

The Baron said nothing. His thin lips tightened. He walked up the jetty, disappeared in the bungalow. When he appeared again he walked slowly, ominously, and red color was suffusing his brown, thin cheeks. He stopped before the partners, his nostrils twitching, and crossed his arms.

"So," he said. He leveled an arm toward the bungalow. "Go!"

"Now look here, buddy," McGill began.

Gales pressed his arm. "Come, Mike."

Three armed men and the Baron fell in behind them. The two partners followed the creaking boardwalk to the veranda of the weatherbeaten bungalow. They went into a dim living-room. The short, broad man was lying stretched on the floor, his throat bloody.

The Baron lit a cigarette calmly. His gray eyes were frigid in his impassive dark face. He removed his topee, revealing thin blond hair slicked down.

"How," he said, "did you get here? And why did you murder this man?"

"We didn't murder this man," Gales said promptly.

The Baron smiled. "Really?"

"On the up and up," McGill chimed in.

"Your names?"

Gales said, "Gales and McGill."

"So!" The Baron twitched his eyebrows. "Up to your old tricks again?"

"Nothing of the sort," Gales said. "We came here under protest. We had nothing to do with this."

He told the Baron what had happened. He spoke rapidly, earnestly. The Baron remained impassive, wore a cynical smile.

"A very nice story," he said. "And where are the men who made you fly here?"

"They ran off in the jungle."

The Baron laughed. "Likely! Indeed, likely!"

"It's the truth," Gales said. "We have no idea what this is all about. My partner and I have got a dirty deal. We're by no means Sunday-school boys, but on the other hand we're not killers. Look for them. Send some men out and look for them."

Who was this immaculate hard-faced Baron? What connection had his arrival here with the actions of Brunt and Willis and the death of the man in the bungalow? Gales eyed him steadily, frankly. He suspected, of course, that the East, always insidious on these fag-end trails, had brewed another pot of trouble. These men were after something. Brunt and Willis were after something. And none of them looked like a man who would go after small fry.

Murder had been done. But had other murders preceded this one? Here was a Baron, as sinister in his own way as Brunt and Willis were in theirs, in command of fifteen men and obviously the owner of that costly flying-boat. Gales knew that if he could have looked into the past he would have found strange trails that converged to this lonely inlet.

The Baron turned to one of his men. "Send some men into the jungle and look." When the men had gone he turned back to Gales and McGill. "One untoward move and you will be killed instantly."

ONE THING Gales had discovered. Fuel was stored back of the huts—drum on drum of petrol and motor oil. And it occurred to Gales that perhaps this inlet was not the end of the trail but merely a supply station. If this was so, then the Baron had been here before.

They waited on the veranda. Two men were tuning up the motors and two others were busy carrying drums of gasoline down to the jetty, to load in the plane's tanks.

Gales said, "At least, Baron, you might give us enough gas to make Kuching."

"I am not," the Baron said, "a philanthropist. I find you two men here in a plane. I find Gossman murdered. You tell me a wild, fantastic story about taking two men from a ship at sea, I do not believe it. It is too incredible."

"Ah, don't be a horsefly," McGill groaned. "Sure it sounds incredible. Don't you think, guy, that we got a shock when we saw that wagon o' yours come floatin' down? Sure. Say, we been handed a pretty lousy deal as it is, so don't you go actin' up. We're nice guys, mister."

The Baron smiled sourly. "Oh, yes—quite. Let me tell you, McGill. I am not a newcomer in the East. What tales I have heard of you fellows! You are old hands in the business of murder."

"That's a downright lie!" snapped Gales.

The Baron held up a stiff forefinger, barked, "Enough!"

Came a period of waiting.

At the beginning of dusk the searchers came back. Brunt and Willis had not been found. Nor any of the natives. By this time too the flying-boat's motors had been tuned up, the tanks refueled.

The deadly Baron eyed Gales. "What did Gossman tell you before you murdered him?"

"I didn't murder him. In fact, I never spoke to the man."

The Baron took a long whip from a peg on the wall. He cracked it a few times.

"The truth, Gales."

"I told you the truth."

The Baron cut loose with the whip. It snapped around Gales' neck. Gales sucked in a sharp breath and stiffened, but he emitted no other sound.

"You pup!" snarled McGill.

He dived for the Baron and uncorked a hard right. The Baron fell down. Three men jumped on McGill, hammered him to the floor, dragged him up and held him tightly.

The Baron rose, smiling. He bowed toward McGill. Then he turned to Gales.

"What did Gossman tell you?"

Gales was calm. "I didn't speak with him."

Crack! The whip laid a welt across Gales' cheek. McGill tussled with his captors, swearing violently. The Baron was methodical. He timed each stroke. Gales rocked every time the lash struck him. And every time the Baron said, "What did Gossman tell you?" Gales shook his head, said, "Nothing." Blood trickled from the corner of his lips. The lash tore his white jacket. It put cruel stripes on his face. Finally Gales sank to the floor.

McGill bit his lip.

The Baron touched his forehead with a handkerchief.

One of his men said, "Let me take the whip, Herr Baron?"

"Later," said the Baron. "He is in a coma now. Let him come to a bit, so he will feel the whip better. I want to know just how much information he got out of Gossman. If he doesn't tell by morning I shall kill—both of them. You, Dorr—you, Mayer—and you, Wiel, stand guard over them here. Give them no water! Never relax!"

Dorr, the man who had wanted to use the whip, made a sharp bow. "Depend on us, Herr Baron."

The three took guard stations.

McGill fell beside his partner. He swallowed hard, muttered, "When our turn comes, Bill, we'll show these punks, we will."

The Baron was very particular about the angle of his topee. He tapped his thin lips with a handkerchief, jabbed his men with penetrating eyes. Then he turned on his heel and went out with military precision.

The guards relaxed their stiff pace, but their eyes were watchful.

Darkness fell rapidly. Gales came to and found McGill close beside him. His eyes were haggard, his face drawn. And it occurred to Bill Gales, then, that he and his partner were in as tough a jackpot of death and mystery as any they had encountered.

CHAPTER V

THE ATTACK

ONE OF the Baron's guards sat on the end of the jetty with a rifle across his knees. He smoked a cigarette. Below, Gales could see the lighted windows of the big flying-boat, and from time to time he could see the Baron pass by one of the windows, gesticulating. The Baron was addressing some of his men.

There was no moon. The lagoon was like a channel of ink, motionless. Cries of night birds came out of the jungle—croaks, sharp little whistles; and sometimes the swish of wings. The breeze came in from the sea carrying the smell of mud-flats mixed with the tang of salt. The guard smoked many cigarettes. Up in the settlement a lantern was burning in the bungalow. It was past midnight.

The guard on the jetty rose and began pacing up and down slowly, but with a certain nervousness. No doubt he was unaccustomed to the jungle at night. His white suit and white topee made him stand out clearly in the darkness. Reaching the base of the jetty, he raised the cigarette to his lips, held it there, making the red end bright while he stared around at the dark forest.

Suddenly he stiffened, fell backward, tearing at his throat. He reeled off the jetty, and a scream tore through the night. Heavy footsteps pounded. One of the men came lunging out of the bungalow hefting a revolver.

"Who cried?" he called out.

A gun shot cracked sharply. Flame stabbed from the darkness and the man who had run from the bungalow wheeled, fired. Two explosions, two daggers of flame, came from the jungle. The man swayed, stumbled backward and finally crashed to the boardwalk.

Men climbed from the flying-boat to the jetty. The Baron shouted questions. Bare feet, mixed with the sound of boots, sounded on the boardwalk. A pair of white-clad legs moved in the darkness.

"Dorr!" shouted the Baron.

Dorr yelled from the bungalow, "What, Herr Baron?"

"Idiot, what has happened?" demanded the Baron.

Dorr came to the boardwalk and found one of his companions lying on his back. He bent down over the man, muttering, "Wiel! Wiel!" Then he stood up. "Wiel has been shot, Herr Baron!"

"Himmel!" exclaimed the Baron.

Dorr fell into a watchful attitude, crouching way over, his gun cruising back and forth. He saw the white-clad legs dimly on the boardwalk beyond. He tensed.

"Who is there?" he barked. "Answer or I shoot!"

For answer three guns rang out, the echoes hammering violently across the lagoon. Dorr fell to his knees, then to his elbows, groaning.

The white-clad legs came down the boardwalk, flanked and followed by dusky shapes that moved silently.

MAYER CROUCHED by a window in the bungalow. He saw the dark shapes. He raised his pistol and let fly with four shots. Screams burst; there was the sound of a body falling into water. Then a fusillade of shots tore viciously into the bungalow. One or two smacked the lantern on the table. It fell to the floor and burst into flame.

The white-clad legs moved faster. Dark shapes accompanied.

The Baron clipped, "There they are!"

One of his men raised a sub-machine gun, held it clamped to his shoulder, low. The gun rattled violently, lead swept back and forth. Two of the dark shapes toppled and fell into the stagnant water beneath the boardwalk.

Mayer, the only guard left in the bungalow, had reloaded his gun. But he had to turn to the flames. He snatched up a blanket and smothered them.

McGill leaped on him, drove a fast blow to the back of his ear. Mayer went down like a felled log. McGill grabbed up his gun and turned to find Gales standing spread-legged and watching him. Gales grinned through his cuts.

"Old boy!" he muttered approvingly.

They crept to the window.

Panic had broken out among the dark strangers. They were retreating down the boardwalk.

A voice bellowed, "Steady, you—!"

The Baron and his men advanced down the jetty, turned into the boardwalk. The man with the sub-machine gun was first. The gun hammered out lead and brought cries of pain from the darkness.

"After them!" barked the Baron.

Gales and McGill saw the Baron and his men tearing down the boardwalk into the darkness. They saw spurts of gun-flame in various quarters, heard the intermittent mad stutter of the submachine gun.

"I wonder who those strangers were," Gales said.

"D'you think Brunt and Willis could have found some natives to throw in with them?"

"Seems hardly possible. Anyhow, Mike, it's now or never—for us! Come on!"

They slipped out of the bungalow and cat-footed down the jetty. Way off on their right they could hear the cries of men and the explosions of guns. Gales led the way down into the big flying-boat. He wanted a gun. The interior was divided into compartments. A short companionway led up to the pilot's cabin. But the partners did not go there.

"Look for their gun-locker, Mike," Gales said in a whisper.

McGILL HEADED aft on the double. Gales landed in a compartment fitted with a desk. On the bulkhead was a black-board with notations on it in white chalk. On the desk was spread a map. Gales bent over it. To him maps always meant romance and adventure—and sometimes a map was the key to a riddle.

He saw the west coast of Borneo and the east coast of the Malay States and the sea between. Lines drawn in red ink traversed the sea and went northward on the Borneo coast, touching land at intervals. Then a line shot northwest from the coast and terminated in a blue circle at sea.

McGill came into the compartment carrying a sub-machine gun and an armful of cartridge drums.

"Look what I found, Bill!"

"Great, Mike! And look what I found." He had a pad and pencil in hand now. "I'll copy down the position of that blue circle. That blue circle stands for something!"

"There's a storeroom aft, Bill. They've got about a dozen drums of gas there. If we could swipe a couple—"

"We've got to step on it, Mike!"

McGill left the flying-boat and swung across to the Vought with the sub-machine gun and the ammunition. Gales lugged two drums of fuel from the storeroom and met McGill in the side-door. McGill took them and carried them across to the Vought. Gales got two more and as he went with them across the canoes to their plane he saw McGill already loading the fuel in the tank. It would not be enough to carry them far, but at least they might reach Kuching.

"Start her up, Bill," McGill called, "while I finish loadin'."

Gales set the third and fourth drums of petrol down and swung in behind the controls. He choked the motor and worked the starter. The motor backfired sharply. Gales knew the Baron and his men would hear that. He tried again. The prop swished into action and the motor roared.

McGill finished loading, threw the empty drums into the water and swung down to cut the mooring lines. Then he leaped up through the door. He saw men running in front of the bungalow. He grabbed up the machine gun and crouched in the door.

"They're comin', Bill!"

"Okey, Mike."

The Vought was drifting away from the jetty. Gales was revving hard.

Rapid spurts of flame burst from the foot of the jetty. Lead banged into the Vought. McGill bent down and pressed the trigger. The machine gun thumped his shoulder and flame leaped from the muzzle. The men on the jetty retreated rapidly.

Gales had the plane's nose pointed toward the sea, though the sea was not visible from that pocket of the lagoon. It would mean a dangerous run over the dark water.

The machine gun on shore rattled again, stabbing the darkness with its lurid flame. The bullets snarled in the Vought's metal. One burst shattered a window and emptied in a wicker chair.

"Can you make it, Bill?" McGill shouted.

Gales shoved up the throttle. The floats bit into the water and the Vought began slipping through the darkness. McGill braced himself in the door, uncorked another burst of lead to keep the Baron's men off the jetty.

The Vought gathered speed. Gales held his breath, glued his eyes on the dark water. He swung the stick sharply to the left, slammed left foot on the rudder bar. The plane heeled over, missing a stump by a bare margin. Cold sweat leaped to Gales' face.

A scatter of enemy lead crackled in the empennage. McGill closed the door and went aft with the gun, opening a rear window.

GALES DARED not speed up for a take-off. You could not see your way ahead. He could only taxi out, and that itself was highly dangerous. He knew there were mud-bars ahead. He rounded a crooked bank and then saw the wide dark sea beyond. But between the sea and his plane were more mud-bars. He could see them vaguely.

But the shots from the jetty were no longer effective. They were at least out of sight of the Baron now. Once they had the mud-bars behind, Gales could gun the motor hard and take off. He peered intently, so much so that his eyeballs hurt. To jam the floats on a bar would spell the end of everything.

McGill had put down the gun. Now he stood behind his partner, gripping the back of the seat, watching too. He knew what danger lay in those bars.

"Watch that one, Bill!"

Gales nodded.

"I see it, Mike."

Gales roared the motor and heeled the plane way over. Soon they would be in clear water.

"There's not many more now, Bill."

"No, Mike—"

He was cut short by a sudden jolt. He roared the motor, and the plane trembled. He retarded the throttle quickly.

"That's that, Mike."

"Jammed?"

"And I don't mean perchance!"

"Hell!"

Gale shut the motor off. "If we drive on we'll only become imbedded."

"What then, old sock?"

Gales got out of the seat, ran his hand through his hair. He opened the door and climbed down. He stood ankle-deep in water. The bar was just beneath the surface and Gales could feel himself sinking. He climbed back up.

"No chance of getting a foothold, either, Mike, and shoving her off."

McGill had picked up the sub-machine gun again. "It looks like a hot time for us, pard."

"The tide may rise before dawn."

"And those babies might come before dawn, too."

They sat down and waited in the darkness.

Suddenly McGill pointed. "There, kid—look!"

Gales started. They saw a boat in the darkness, standing in the entrance to the inlet.

"Now where'd that come from?" McGill asked.

"Looks like a ship's boat. Be quiet, Mike. They're pulling in this way."

The two partners crouched and watched. The sound of the oars was very faint. The boat was a white smudge on the dark water. It was moving slowly. Where had it come from?

"There's a lot of guys after something," McGill ventured.

"They're coming straight toward us, Mike," Gales whispered.

Soon they could see dark shapes bending to the oars. Then the oars stopped moving, the shapes remained motionless, the boat drifted. A man stood up by the tiller. He had on white pants.

Gales took the sub-machine gun from McGill. Then he flung open the door and leaned out.

"Not a move!" he commanded.

MUTTERS OF surprise rose from the dark men at the oars. The man at the tiller swayed and his arm swung upward. Gales ducked as a shot rang out. Gales opened fire, sent a stream of lead in the water alongside the small boat. The natives cried out. The white man sat down abruptly. The echoes skipped away into silence.

"The next time," Gales said, "I'll mow you all down." He turned to McGill. "Mike, get our mooring line."

McGill ran aft.

The boat crew watched, sullen.

Gales spoke to the boat—"We're going to throw you a line, mister. When you get it, send a native overside and have him make fast to our under-carriage. Then make fast at your end and pull around to the stern—and pull us off this bar."

"You're boss," grumbled the shape at the tiller.

McGill tossed the line. A native caught it and made fast on the boat. Then another slipped into the water, followed the line to the plane, when Gales dropped the end down into the native's hand.

"See you pull hard," Gales said, "or I'll rip you wide open—all of you."

The native below made the line fast to the under-carriage. He swam back to the boat and crawled on board. The man at the tiller muttered a few commands and the boat swung around to the stern.

"I'll climb on the wing, Mike. You get at the controls. When we're free start to taxi. I'll keep 'em covered and climb back in soon as we're out of range."

He swung to the wing and lay down flat. He trained his gun on the boat's crew and ordered them to bend to the oars. The natives needed no urging. They bent to the oars with a will, while the white man sat motionless in the stern.

In a few minutes the plane slid back off the bar and Gales made them pull until the floats were well clear. Then he told the white man to send out a native to cut the line clear of the plane. When the native had done this, Gales yelled to McGill to start going.

The motor burst into a roar. The plane began to move forward. The white man in the boat fired two shots. Gales returned the fire with a string of bullets that tore up the water. The white man dropped to the bottom of the boat.

McGill speeded up. And when the small boat was no longer visible, Gales climbed back into the cabin, shut the door and laid the gun aside. Mopping his face, he sat down beside his partner.

"Who were they?" McGill asked.

"Darned if I know, Mike!"

Soon they were through the mouth of the inlet and a wide stretch of smooth dark water lay before them. McGill hit the throttle hard and the prop threshed into the wind. Water began to boil away from the floats. Wires began to hum. The plane took off mightily and pounded up into the sky.

Gales prodded McGill. "Look there, Mike!" He pointed through the side window.

They saw the dim shape of a ship lying at anchor. She carried no lights.

"That's where they came from," said Gales.

McGill said, "This sure has the earmarks of a free-for-all, partner. There may be an answer to it in Kuching."

CHAPTER VI

THE PARTNERS PLAN

AT **DAWN** a man standing on the wharf of the Garrison Airways at Kuching, the capital of Sarawak, put a cupped hand to his ear. He heard the drone of a plane's motor. Visibility was not clear, and the man was perplexed because he knew of no plane that was due to arrive at that hour.

Then the mists broke and he saw a Vought seaplane dropping down to the river. He rubbed his eyes. "By heck!" he cried out. McGill was at the controls. He slapped the floats down on the water and gunned toward the wharf. The motor coughed and expired, and the prop began to spin slowly.

McGill said, "Well, Bill, there goes the last drop o' gas."

Several figures appeared on the wharf and a line was heaved. Gales, hanging out of the door, caught it and held fast. The men on the wharf drew the plane in.

"Hey, Gales," a man shouted, "is that you, Gales?"

"Hello, Samson."

"Well, doggone!"

The plane was made fast.

McGill, landing on the wharf, chafed his hands and looked around. "Well, where's the band? Where's the cameras?"

Samson was still dazed. "But—but what are you birds doing *here?* Last I heard you were wrecked and dead over toward the Singapore side."

McGill said, "Bill, there's been false rumors about us."

"Hey," Samson yelled, "first thing I must do is wireless Sam Garrison that you're okey. Sam's all worked up. He went out in a plane by himself and looked for you. He got a wireless from you that your motor was bursting up—"

"From us?" broke in Gales.

McGill said, patting down the air, "I remember, Bill. Willis worked the key while you were cold. I couldn't understand. He must have radioed that to leave a cold trail behind. Well, Samson, my son, here we are. As soon as I grub up and shave and we tune that crate up, and arm ourselves to the teeth, certain palookas are goin' to get paid back."

"But, man, what happened?" demanded Samson.

Gales said, gripping Samson's arm, "Will you radio through to Sam and my boss that we're safe? And tell them to wire my wife immediately."

They all went into the wharf office and Samson left instructions with the radio operator. Then Gales told him what had happened, and Samson listened, wide-eyed, unbelieving.

He broke in before Gales had quite finished, "But what are they after, Bill—what are they after?"

Gales shrugged. "I'm darned if we know. But"—he tapped his pocket—"we've got a swell chance of finding out. It's something big, Samson. It looks like one of the biggest things Mike and I ever stumbled into. We'll go up to the hotel. Send over any message you get from Sam or K.O."

AT THE hotel the two partners bathed, shaved and had a meal sent up. Their spirits picked up. The mystery gathered impetus in their minds, warmed their blood. They had been tricked on the high seas by Brunt and Willis. Gales had been beaten horribly by the Baron. Gossman, the lone man at the inlet, had paid with his life—for something. Neither Gales nor McGill was the kind of man who when slapped on one cheek bigheartedly turned the other.

A boy came in with two messages that the radio operator had received from Singapore. One was from Sam Garrison, and the other from Pennant, the Singapore super of the Agency. This latter read:

> Take no further action. Thank your stars you are safe and alive and return to Singapore immediately.

Gales passed it to McGill, said, "Well, official orders, Mike." Then he spread the message from Sam Garrison. It said:

> Do not pay any attention to Pennant. He is a nice guy but has funny ideas. I am trying to get in touch with K.O. Pike who is en route from Hongkong to Saigon by plane. Pennant will not take the job. I want your agency to run down these galoots who have been causing me high blood pressure since you two eggs were supposed to have drowned. I want K.O. to overrule Pennant. So hold everything until you hear from me.

The partners read both messages. Gales shrugged, "Well, Mike, what do you think?"

"Radio Pennant that engine trouble is keepin' us here," McGill said. "Pennant ain't got us straight at all, Bill. If he thinks we're gonna walk out of this scatter and let those babies get away with what they done us, well, old horse, then Pennant is just a guy to be pitied and should have his conk examined."

Gales nodded seriously. "I know, Mike, but we're flying a Straits Agency plane, not our own."

"Oh, yes? Well, did you ever see me worry a hoot whose plane I was flyin'? Ixnay, pard—not me. Those babies are after somethin' and I rise and say that whatever it is it doesn't belong to anyone o' them. It's a free-for-all, and I aim to get me in some tellin' body blows before those wisenheimers celebrate another birthday."

Gales had similar inclinations, but he was by nature more tactful. He folded the messages thoughtfully.

"We'll see what K.O. says," he said.

"It's just postponin', sweetheart, what we're gonna do anyhow. What I am gonna do, anyhow. I guess you better run home to your wife, anyhow."

"Now, no wisecracks, half-pint—"

HE STOPPED. There had been a knock on the door. Gales rose and crossed the room, opened the door, found a scrawny white man there blinking behind horn-rimmed spectacles.

"Mr. Gales? Well, sir, my name is Horning. I'm a combination reporter and news photographer from Hongkong. Lot of news around about your bit of adventure. Mind if I come in?"

"If it's a picture you want," McGill said, "come right in."

Horning laughed in a high, piping voice and came in with his sun-helmet in his hand. Gales waved him to a seat.

Horning looked around with nearsighted eyes. "News has been slow until this. I came up here to see you men on the off-chance that we could remedy that. Would it be asking too much of you if I could get the entire story, from beginning to end?"

"Well, we haven't reached the end," Gales said, smiling.

Horning smiled back.

"Well, I mean— Now"—he took out a note-book—"just where is this mysterious inlet?"

McGill expanded. "Well, it's about—"

"Just a minute," broke in Gales, quietly.

McGill gulped and looked up at his partner.

Gales was eying Horning mildly but steadily. "I'm afraid, Mr. Horning," he said, "that we have nothing to give to the newspapers. At least, not yet."

Horning looked hurt. "I'm sorry, sir, to intrude, of course. I meant no harm. If you wish it I can hold back all news till I receive other word from you. But I certainly would appreciate a lead, so that—"

"I'm sorry, Mr. Horning," said Gales, shaking his head.

Horning stood up, ruffled, slightly indignant. "I assure you you are not taking the proper attitude. I represent the Oriental Allied News Service and my word is as good as gold."

"I'm sorry, but no news," said Gales.

Horning colored. "Very well!" he snapped.

"But," said Gales, "if you want you can fly with us—if it so happens that we are going to fly."

Horning was taken aback. He laughed. "Well, I say!"

"We can let you know later."

"Well—well, of course, that will be splendid. I'll keep in touch with you."

When Horning had gone, McGill exploded, "Are you in your right mind? First you insult the guy and then—"

"Damper down, Mike," Gales drawled, lighting a cigarette. "That guy's no more a reporter than I am. He's another link in this confounded mystery."

"Yeah? Then why the devil are you takin' him along?"

"Because, little one, we can keep an eye on him. If I kicked him out of here we might walk down the street and get treated to a couple of bullets. If we take him along—well, he knows a lot of things we don't know. And there are a few things he doesn't know. He thinks we know them. One, for instance, is the location of that inlet."

"How come all this mind-readin'?"

"No mind-reading. I just happen to know Horning—and that guy is not Horning."

CHAPTER VII

PURSUIT

AT **ELEVEN** that morning a radio message characteristic of K.O. Pike came through by relays from Saigon.

> Use your head but don't blame me if you bust it. Sam Garrison is paying for the show. Am on my way to Singapore. Radio for help if you think it necessary but don't go dragging everybody into trouble. Stay sober.

"That last attempt at a wisecrack," Gales said, "is probably meant for you, Michael."

Down at the Airways wharf they found Horning in a high state of excitement. Gales was resolved to carry on the pretense that he and McGill believed the man's name was really Horning. Gales knew the genuine Horning well. More times than one had he carried Jerry Horning home from a Saigon sidewalk café in the days before he traveled the high trails with McGill. Oddly enough, the man looked something like Horning. He even carried an expensive camera.

Gales drew McGill aside. "Now get this, Mike. Make no cracks about this guy. Treat him like a pal. He's a queer one. He doesn't look like a killer to me, but you never can tell. Let me do the talking."

The first thing Gales did was tell Horning that he wouldn't be allowed to carry firearms on his person. Horning showed surprise.

"But the country is wild, Mr. Gales."

His surprise looked real.

"The air is our country, Mr. Horning. If we need your aid I'll give you your gun back. But it's an—er—company rule. I'll have to put it in the locker—under lock and key."

"Well—well, all right."

They bought two rifles and a lot of ammunition, and extra cartridges for the sub-machine gun. These they charged to the Agency. Garrison Airways had been good enough to fill the tanks and look over the motor. Garrison had radioed his Kuching staff to lend all aid possible to the partners. The old boy was hotter than a hornet because he felt Brunt and Willis had played a dastardly trick on him as well as on Gales and McGill.

Sampson said in a whisper to Gales, "That's a strange bird you're taking along."

"Shucks. Newspaper man."

"Oh, yeah?"

Gales changed the subject. He and McGill checked up the motor for their own benefit and McGill climbed in behind the controls.

"Don't forget," Samson said. "First sign of trouble radio us and if we haven't a plane here we'll relay your message to Singapore. Good luck, boys!"

Gales shook hands with him and climbed into the plane. Horning was sitting in the seat directly behind McGill. He looked innocent and genuinely excited. He was, indeed, a queer customer.

TWO BLASTS on a siren cleared the water. McGill got the motor hot and began to give it the gun. The prop screwed into the air and the Vought rocked a bit and then lunged forward.

Once under way, the plane gathered speed quickly and was soon streaking upward, her floats trailing beads of water.

The partners were optimistic. They had tanks full of fuel, plenty of ammunition, and a fairly definite objective. The purpose of this flight, according to Gales, was to ascertain what that blue circle on the Baron's map signified.

McGill of course had a hankering to return to the inlet and wreck the place. But Gales had talked him out of that, though he admitted it would be a good idea to wing over the inlet and see if the vessel and the plane were still there, much as he reasoned they would not be.

They did not follow the river, but went northerly over the roof of the jungle to save time and conserve fuel. McGill flew at three thousand feet and a flat one hundred miles an hour. Gales passed the time tuning up the radio set and Horning remained in his seat, blinking behind his big horn-rimmed spectacles. From time to time Gales looked around at him. The air trail was rough as a rutty woods road until the Vought reached the seacoast. Then they had a light beam wind and good visibility.

Gales was the first to spot the familiar spit of land. He pointed, and McGill, who had every good reason to remember, nodded and cursed crisply to himself. Horning got up and looked out of the window, roused no doubt by the new interest the partners were taking in the coast.

The partners saw no vessel. McGill cruised over the spit of land and Gales used binoculars to study the inlet. It was deserted. The plane was gone. He discovered that the shacks were gone, too. He saw ruins—charred ashes—blasted trees.

"Somebody burned the whole shebang," he told McGill. "I wonder if the plane was burned, too. Those guys from the ship—"

"Is this the—the inlet?" broke in Horning nervously.

Gales looked up at him. "Yes."

"I should like to take a photo of it, please—if you don't mind. I could open a window."

Gales said, "Go ahead."

Horning jumped to his task. McGill circled slowly and Horning took several pictures.

Gales was puzzled. It began to occur to him that there really might be two men by the name of Horning.

"All right," Horning called out, smiling. "Thank you."

McGill muttered, "Cripes, Bill, what is this guy's racket?"

"Be patient, Mike. We'll find out some day. Now here's our course."

He clipped a chart on the dashboard and McGill leaned forward to study it.

"Right to the vicinity of that blue circle, Mike."

"Okey."

THE VOUGHT picked up speed and drew farther away from the coast. Horning sat up and took notice. He seemed on the point of getting up and asking a question, but relaxed and narrowed his eyes thoughtfully.

What did he know? Certainly he knew something, perhaps much more than either of the partners knew. Yet there were a few things he did not know.

The sea was wide and deserted. But an hour later Gales picked up a dot on the horizon. He put glasses to his eyes and steadied them. It was a ship. McGill saw it, too, and kept the Vought headed in a bee-line. The ship began to take on familiar lines. It was headed north, leaving a wide wake behind it, McGill knocked off a bit of altitude. "What does she look like, Bill?"

"Sure looks like the *Krag Castle* to me."

"Says me! And if you ask me, pard, she was the tub anchored outside the inlet last night. And the guys in that smallboat were from her, too. Let's look her over close."

He cut his gun and drifted down toward the *Krag Castle*. A couple of men on the bridge were holding binoculars to their eyes. One kept pointing. A third man ran down from the bridge and went forward quickly, disappearing.

Horning exclaimed, "That's the *Krag Castle!*"

Gales nodded.

Immediately Horning jumped for his camera.

McGill growled, "Maybe the poor guy is just cracked in the upper story, Bill. Either that, or you don't know Jerry Horning at all."

"It may be all a big stall, Mike. Let him play along."

McGill tooled the crate lower and lower, until every man and every detail of the rusty tramp was visible to the naked eye. Two natives in the bow threw back a tarpaulin.

McGill started. "By cripes, they've got a cannon!"

He slammed the stick to the right and kicked right rudder bar. Horning had just finished taking a picture. He fell back with the camera, landing in a heap. The gun on the vessel boomed. Gales ground his teeth. McGill, with the throttle well up, pulled the Vought into a zoom and hiked wildly for altitude. The cannon boomed again. The shell missed by a margin. McGill kept going upward until he figured they were out of range. Then he leveled off and looked downward. The vessel was a mere dot on the sea below.

"Now what do you think of that, Bill?"

"You sure were quick on the stick, Mike. And I gather that Horning is not one of *that* mob."

Horning came tottering forward. "That was close, wasn't it? Imagine the nerve of the beggars!"

"I guess you're sorry you didn't stay back in Kuching, eh?" Gales said.

"Sorry? By no means! This is priceless!"

McGill ventured, "Hey, Bill, how's to go down and rake that packet with the sub-machine gun?"

"No." Gales shook his head. "A third time they might hit us. Besides, we want to find, if you don't happen to know it, what that blue circle indicates."

"Pardon my glove, master mind!"

The red-head lined out on his course again and in a few minutes the *Krag Castle* was lost to sight.

Now—Gales mused—either the flying-boat had been sunk at the inlet or was somewhere ahead. It seemed logical to think that Brunt and Willis were in a league with the master of the *Krag Castle*. But what had arisen at sea to make Brunt and Willis send out a call for a plane? A logical answer might be that they had a contact man on land somewhere.

Who?

Horning?

If so, then, why had Horning taken a picture of the vessel? Perhaps just to cover up.

Or maybe....

THE CHARTED course led the Vought farther away from land, until the Borneo coast became a blur that soon vanished in the distance. Nothing now but the wide sea and the empty dome of the sky. Gales began figuring closely on the chart, reasoning that the blue circle covered a diameter of ten miles.

The motor roared its endless song. The wind strengthened, on the bow now, and began to hoot and clap and strum in the wires. The ship rocked and the throttle had to be shoved up to maintain a good speed.

Horning never lost interest. His eyes kept blinking and he never took them from the horizon. Gales used his binoculars often. He expected at any minute to pick up the flying-boat, even though the possibility existed that it might have been sunk at the inlet.

Finally he said, "We're entering that circle now, Mike."

McGill cut his gun and went down to a thousand feet. They covered a dozen miles and then turned around.

"Start circling Mike," Gales said. "Go wide and then make 'em smaller and smaller. If this circle is just a hoax, we've been on a goose chase."

Round and round the Vought went, with Gales using his glasses all the time, rocking with the motion of the cruising ship. Suddenly he pointed. McGill squinted and heeled the crate over. Horning came forward to peer between them. Out of the sea rose a pinnacle of rock that grew in size with the passing minutes. White foam broke, and then Gales noticed wisps of smoke rising from the crest of the pinnacle.

"Could that be it, Bill?" McGill asked.

"Darned if I know, Mike. It's just a volcanic island or rock. About quarter of a mile wide at the base. Not a bit of growth on it. Doesn't seem possible—"

For some reason he looked up at Horning. Into Horning's eyes had come an eager light. He did not blink. His eyes seemed uncommonly steady.

Gales turned to McGill. "We're on the windward side. Maybe there's a lagoon to leeward. We might take a look, Mike."

"I think—"

Suddenly a plane appeared over the rocky mass. Its appearance was as mysterious as it was startling. It was an open cockpit job, two-place.

McGill pointed. "Now answer me that, Willie boy!"

"By George!" exclaimed Horning.

He ran aft for his camera.

"This camera fiend is just about gettin' on my nerves," McGill growled.

"Never mind him!" Gales clipped. "Watch that plane!"

He jumped up and swung aft, brushed Horning out of the way, got the sub-machine gun out of the locker. He came forward shoving a fresh cartridge drum into place. He opened windows on both sides.

The two-seater was drab-gray in color, a biplane with a long cowling. Suddenly she zoomed.

"Machine gun armed," Gales muttered. "This means trouble!"

"Well," the red-head said, "I never expected afternoon tea."

CHAPTER VIII

THE CLASH

McGILL YANKED back on the stick and hiked for altitude, too. Horning took a picture of the black pinnacle and then laid the camera aside. He seemed very excited, biting his lip, rubbing his hands together. And that eagerness was steady in his eyes now, apparent in every twitching of his features.

The gray biplane heeled over and seemed to hang poised for a brief moment. Then it dropped plummet-like, lying over on one side, giving the appearance of sliding sidewise toward the climbing Vought.

McGill, with full power on, heeled way over and swung beneath the falling biplane. Instantly the gray plane steadied its wings and whipped over. A Lewis gun spat jets of smoke from the rear cockpit. Lead hammered into the roof of the cabin job. Horning cursed—for the first time.

Gales shoved the Thompson gun out of the starboard window in the bow and put a line of marks on the biplane's flank as the latter swooped down past them. Again the biplane's gunner cut loose, and lead snarled in the cabin. Horning ducked, crouched on the floor, his lips pressed tightly together.

McGill leveled off sharply, whipping the plane's tail upward. He looked down. The biplane was flattening out below and hitting the air trail for another hard climb. McGill rolled toward it.

Horning ran aft to the locker. Gales saw him and started. Horning grabbed a rifle and leaped to one of the windows, throwing a cartridge into the breach. He braced himself in the open window, watching the gray plane.

The Lewis gun opened fire and its lead rapped into the underside of the Vought. Gales stuck his Thompson gun downward and kept his finger pressed to the trigger. Horning fired from the window aft. The biplane came wading up through the hail of lead its gunner raking the Vought mercilessly.

The planes passed each other in a blaze of gunfire. Then they shot away, and Gales clipped a fresh drum to his gun. Horning ran to the locker for more cartridges. Did he know who manned that deadly gray biplane? Gales swung aft.

"Listen, Horning. On the up and up, how do you figure in this?"

Horning blinked. "I? Well, sir, it looks to me as if I'm getting a big news scoop. My shooting may help. Look out!"

The gray plane was coming again, head on for the Vought's flank. Gales swung to one of the windows and raised his Thompson gun. He drove a line of lead at the biplane's shimmering prop. The biplane heeled over and the gunner opened fire, his lead whistling past Gales and Horning.

Suddenly Horning reeled backward. He banged into one of the seats and crumpled to the aisle. Gales leaped to bend over him. Glass shattered and rained down on him. He rolled Horning over. Horning was trying to speak. His chest was a bloody smear, his eyes bulged. Suddenly they remained fixed, glassy.

And so Horning died—with his secret.

GALES SCRAMBLED to his feet and hung on to a seat while McGill made a screaming turn. Gales saw the pontoons of the biplane sweep past the windows. That was close. He ran forward.

"Horning's dead!" he yelled.

"And so will we if that crate comes any closer!"

It was ironic indeed that Horning, who obviously knew something about the mystery, should die. His body rolled from side to side with the swaying of the plane.

Gales went to the window opposite McGill and watched the biplane turn around.

"I think he's reloading, Mike. Go after him."

McGill gunned the motor and swept around in a tight turn. The gray plane stuck its nose upward and climbed. McGill climbed to head it off. Then the gray plane stopped climbing and went into a sudden dive. It dived straight for the Vought's nose. Gales held his fire for a breathless half minute, then cut loose, driving his lead into the biplane's nose. The enemy's lead rained on through the floor, ripping seats apart.

Then a tongue of flame raced from the biplane's cowling and at almost the same time there was a terrific explosion that blinded Gales and McGill. Vaguely Gales saw a man pinwheel from the rear cockpit as the biplane rolled over. McGill heeled away from the burning plane.

Gales looked out. The biplane tumbled toward the sea in a mass of flames. It struck and sent up a cloud of steam. Gales put down his gun and rubbed a hand across his face. McGill cut the throttle and began to circle downward swiftly. He leveled off a couple of hundred feet above the sea and Gales leaned out. Bits of wreckage were visible, but they were disappearing rapidly. There was no sign of either of the men. McGill circled many times, to make certain, then shoved forward on the throttle and climbed upward, heading for the rocky pinnacle.

On the leeward side they saw a long lagoon guarded by a wall of ragged rocks. The only entrance to this body of water was a small cleft, so small that it would admit possibly a ship's dingy, but nothing larger. The lagoon water was smooth and afforded what appeared to be an excellent place to drop the plane.

"I'll go down," McGill said.

He cut his gun and drifted over the sea wall. He skimmed over the surface of the rock-bound lagoon. He sensed when his pontoons struck. But suddenly there was a rending sound. The Vought slewed around violently, reeled sidewise, and water snarled. The left wing sliced into the water, the plane spun and Gales was hurled against the side. Fabric and metal were ripped away. Water slammed white-foamed in through the windows.

The nose buried down. The tail, whipping all the way around, crashed into a rocky ledge and doubled.

Gales heaved McGill out of the seat. "The windows, Mike!"

But McGill was half-way through when he stopped. "She won't sink any more, Bill."

One crumpled wing pointed toward the sky. The other was doubled up under the water. The partners were in water to their waists and for a long moment each hung in a window getting his breath. "Now this is sweet," McGill said.

"This is the sweetest, lousiest story ever told!"

"This wagon will never fly again, Mike."

"And I doubt if we will. What happened, anyway?"

Gales climbed out of the window and up around the side of the plane. He squatted there and looked at the right pontoon jutting out of water, mangled beyond repair, like the rest of the plane. He climbed down to inspect it. Then he muttered and returned to the window.

"Simple, Mike. They shot holes into our undercarriage and it couldn't stand the strain when the pontoons hit the water."

THEY WADED ashore—or rather, they waded to the shelf of rock and hauled themselves up. There was no shore—nothing but jagged rocks and lava formations. Looking up, they could see the wisps of smoke rising from the pinnacle.

McGill observed, "I don't like this place. Suppose that volcano gets active? B-r-r-r!"

Disgruntled, he followed Gales along the rim of the lagoon. They came to a large depression and found a lean-to made of a tarpaulin. They found a primus stove and some provisions and a tin box in which some clothes were stored.

"Those two guys camped here, Mike."

"I ask you, why should anybody want to camp here? Dammit, Bill, there's nothin' here—nothin'. Only rocks. Look at that rock."

"There must be something else."

"What? If it was an island I'd say buried treasure. But nobody could bury anything here."

"You're right in that. Still—" Gales shrugged.

No, nothing could have been buried. But Gales said, "Maybe there's a ship buried in the lagoon."

"All right. Now look. Look how clear the water is. You can see bottom. There ain't no depth. Ask me, pard, and I'll say that we're at the wrong place."

"Oh, nonsense, Mike. This is the place all right. Somebody is going to come here. The *Krag Castle*, for instance. And I tell you what we're going to do. That Vought is done for, Mike. The engine's smashed and so is everything else. We'll burn her."

"Why?"

"To get her out of sight. Then we can hide in one of those crags up above."

But first they hauled out the body of Horning and searched his clothing. They found some money, but no identification. Then they fished out the Thompson gun, the other guns and all the ammunition.

Gales broke open the fuel tank and threw a match to the gasoline. In a minute the plane was a roaring inferno. It burned to a crisp, disintegrated. The motor fell to the bottom of the lagoon. Bit by bit every last piece of the Vought disappeared beneath the surface. Then the partners weighted Horning and dropped him into the water.

Gales murmured, "I wish I knew the secret he died with."

"And I wonder what his real name was, Bill."

They carried their guns and ammunition up the craggy face of the pinnacle. Half-way up they found a crevice that could not be seen from below, and here they stored their belongings. Then they went down to the camp on the ledge by the water and cooked a meal over the primus stove. They saw no fish—not even a sea bird. The pinnacle was grim and forsaken, and the only sound was the dull booming of the sea on the windward rocks.

The meal finished, they took blankets and climbed to the hide-out. Shadows were creeping over the sea. There was no sign of a ship, no sign of a plane.

CHAPTER IX

THE EAGLES WAIT

THERE WAS a windy dawn. The partners stirred from beneath the blankets and rose, rubbed their eyes. Visibility was not clear yet. They climbed down the crags to the ledge by the water and prepared breakfast—hot coffee, black, and biscuits, hard.

"I sure hate desert island stuff," McGill grouched. "When I think o' the swell times in Saigon, struttin' myself with the dames, and then look around here. There's a dame in Saigon— But then I forget, old horse, you're a married man, though if I seen as little of you as your poor wife does, I'd chuck you, if I was her."

"You're certainly in a fine mood today, lame brain."

"Ah-r-r, I feel like a burr in my own sock! Look at the good plane of ours gone! And what have we got for it? And what will K.O. say when he finds out? If nobody comes here, we starve. If somebody does come, it will be somebody we've never met formally—as your wife would say—"

"Never mind about my wife."

"Well, anyhow, no matter what happens we'll be just a memory to certain people."

Gales shrugged and walked off, swung among the crags, looked into fissures. McGill would get over that grouch, Gales knew. The red-head was usually hard to get on with around breakfast-time, anyhow.

The sky brightened. Gales sat down on a crag and smoked one of the cigarettes that had dried out during the night. The sun crashed into the east, spreading its color over the long reaches of the sea. Gales shaded his eyes with his hands. He started, peered intently.

Then he shouted, "Hey, Mike!"

He peered over the crag and saw McGill crawl into view below. He motioned for his partner to come up. McGill climbed rapidly and soon swung onto the crag. Gales pointed.

McGill rubbed his jaw. "Yeah, I see."

It was a ship crawling like a bug over the horizon.

"Let's go up to our hide-out, Mike," Gales said.

They climbed on upward until they reached the ledge. They sat down and waited.

AN HOUR later the *Krag Castle* hove to on the leeward side of the pinnacle. The partners lay on their stomachs watching. They heard the anchor chain roar, saw the anchor crash into the water. A white-capped man leaned in the starboard wing of the navigating bridge, looking over the sea-wall into the deserted lagoon.

After a while a small boat was lowered. Natives pulled at the oars and the small boat won through the narrow entrance. A man stood up and pointed. The white-capped man at the tiller said something and the natives began pulling. The boat slid up to the ledge where Gales and McGill had found the camp. From their hide-out the partners had a fair view of the ledge below.

The man who pointed now climbed out of the boat, removed his topee and mopped his forehead.

Gales gripped McGill's arm. "Brunt, Mike!"

"Well, doggone!"

"This is a break, kid," Gales said.

McGill said:

"Yeah—for Brunt."

Gales felt the blood pounding through his veins. He forgot to consider the danger attached to their predicament. In his mind now was the realization that they were spectators at the tail end of a mystery. It was certain that Brunt and Willis had been in a league with the *Krag Castle* from the beginning. Through trickery and murder, Brunt had finally reached what appeared to be his goal. And what would he find here among these barren crags?

He stood well back, gesticulating, speaking rapidly. The man in the peaked cap stood beside him, nodding, running his eyes back and forth across the lower crags. Out on the vessel, the man in the white-topped cap still leaned on the bridge. The natives kept throwing apprehensive glances at the coils of smoke that rose from the volcanic crest of the pinnacle.

Finally the smallboat returned to the ship and lay alongside. The natives swung up the rope ladder and began carrying bundles down into the small boat. The boat made a trip to the ledge, unloaded and then returned to the ship. This time a derrick lifted a big crate from the hold and lowered it carefully into the small boat.

"I wonder what that is," McGill said.

"We'll see later." Gales pointed. "They're rigging a derrick on that ledge down there, too."

They could see Brunt crawling among the lower crags industriously, while Willis remained on the ledge smoking. The small boat reached the ledge and it took the men half an hour to unload. Then they knocked the crate apart.

"Some kind of an engine, Mike," Gales said. "Bet it's a drill of some kind. They've got cables, too."

The men rested below. Then Brunt joined the man in the peaked cap and they stood looking up toward the crest of the pinnacle. Presently they started climbing. Occasionally Brunt stopped to speak and point from one crag to another. And then....

"Hell," McGill growled, "they're comin' *this* way."

GALES REACHED for the sub-machine gun. McGill gripped a pistol. Brunt and his companion kept climbing, their shoes scraping on the lava rock. Gales and McGill edged farther back into the recession. Presently Brunt appeared on the ledge, stopping to mop his face. His companion was the mate who had commanded the smallboat from which Gales and McGill first took Brunt and Willis.

The two partners remained motionless, tense. They did not care to clash with the men now. There were too many below to follow up. Gales hoped fervently that Brunt and his companion would pass on.

But suddenly Brunt turned and looked directly at them. He looked like a man struck dumb.

"Steady!" Gales clipped.

The mate whirled, took a look at Brunt, then followed the direction of Brunt's gaze.

"By cripes!" the mate snarled. "I'm seein' things!"

"Oh, no, you ain't, you punk," McGill said.

"Keep your hands up!" Gales commanded. "Mike, take their guns."

McGill got up and disarmed the men. They did not care to argue in the face of the deadly Thompson gun Gales held.

"Now," Gales said, "lie down flat."

"Look here," Brunt blustered. "You can't accomplish anything by doing this—"

"Get down, Brunt!" Gales barked. "You leave that to us."

Brunt and the mate lay down. McGill tore off their shirts, twisted the shirts into ropes and tied the men hand and foot. Then he hauled them back into the depression.

About an hour later Willis on the ledge below, began to show signs of anxiety. He called Brunt's name and kept peering up toward the pinnacle. Another white man had joined him and both began calling. Willis indicated with his hand the direction that Brunt and the mate had taken. After a while they called a couple of natives and started up the crags, separating. Every so often Willis stopped to call Brunt's name.

He climbed to the ledge in front of the partners' hide-out and was on his knees when he saw the muzzle of the Thompson gun. He swallowed once and remained motionless.

"Get him, Mike," Gales said. "Remember, Willis, one peep and you're done for."

McGill disarmed Willis, bound him and dragged him back into the depression. Then they heard a man calling Willis' name.

"Willis! Hey Willis, where are you? Willis!"

Suddenly a Lascar dropped to the ledge from above.

"Hands up, you fella!" Gales snapped.

The Lascar's eyes bulged and he reeled backward, losing his balance. He careened off the ledge, still screaming, and Gales rushed after him. For a brief moment Gales was in the open. Out of the corner of his eye he saw a white man standing on a crag fifty yards away.

The white man swore and swung up his gun. It boomed. Lead chipped lava rock near Gales' foot. Gales swung the Thompson gun around. The white man ducked as the gun rattled violently. Below, the Lascar was stumbling downward, screaming wildly.

"They'll come and get you now!" Brunt snarled.

"Will they?" Gales flung at him. "Don't you believe it!"

The ship's whistles roared. A man was waving his hands frantically from the bridge. Again and again he pulled the whistle rope, and the man who had shot at Gales could be seen from time to time on his race down the crags, followed by the two Lascars that had started out with him. They joined three more Lascars on the ledge by the water and piled into the smallboat.

The whistle kept roaring.

Brunt snarled, "That whistle—means trouble! Dammit, Gales, untie us!"

"Don't be a fool," Gales said.

The whistle stopped. Gales and McGill listened intently. Presently they heard a faint droning sound. They scanned the seascape, saw nothing. But they knew that sound. It was the sound of a plane in flight.

Gales muttered, "She's coming up on the other side of this pinnacle, Mike!"

The mate roared, "It's that flyin' boat! Gawd, cut us loose! I'm the only guy can handle that gun on board!"

"Yeah, and what happens to us?" McGill said.

Brunt cried, "Throw in with us!"

"Nothing doing," Gales told him. "You're a bunch of cheap killers. Throw in with *you?*"

"Ain't *that* a laugh!" McGill said quietly.

CHAPTER X

TREASURE

THEY SAW the big flying-boat go storming by overhead. The small boat was just swinging alongside the *Krag Castle.* The flying-boat dived mightily over the lagoon and roared over the vessel. Instantly the foredeck of the *Krag Castle* heaved in the grip of a terrific burst of flame. Guns spat from the flying-boat's windows, and the big crate lifted her nose upward and banked.

Some natives dived overside from the vessel. The skipper and a few others raced for the rope ladder, scrambled down it and piled into the small boat. The small boat began pulling for the lagoon. The flying-boat came back toward the *Krag Castle,* dropped another bomb that wiped away the superstructure. Flames spread over the vessel and the plane droned over the lagoon and started in a wide, lazy circle.

"What are those explosions?" roared Brunt.

"Your ship's in flames," Gales said.

Brunt groaned and heaved back and forth, jerking at his bonds. The mate swore.

The boatload of men reached the landing ledge and scrambled upon it as the plane came droning toward the lagoon. The two white men and the natives raced for the crags, clawing their way upward, seeking refuge from the plane.

The plane kept a level course, banked over the landing ledge. An object plummeted. Instantly the whole pinnacle seemed to rock and sway. Gales and McGill saw the burst of flame, saw rocks hurled far into the air, knew that among the rocks were the men who had sought refuge. Some of the rocks fell down in front of the partners' hide-out. Smoke rolled over the lagoon.

Tranquilly the big plane circled aloft, while the *Krag Castle* became a roaring furnace. The smoke over the lagoon and the lower crags cleared, and not a living man was to be seen there. Great wounds had been made in the lava.

Five minutes later the flying-boat nodded her nose downward and came floating down over the farther sea-wall. Her great hull split the water and the big wings rocked. Her motors beat unevenly, then died down, and the props swished around slowly. She drifted toward the landing ledge and men appeared, some holding guns, others mooring lines.

When the big crate was made fast the men began to crowd on shore. Gales counted ten of them, and then there was another—the Baron, who appeared last, immaculate in tropic whites. He strolled back and forth running his eyes over the destruction which the third bomb had done among the crags.

Eleven men....

Three of his men crawled about with drawn guns, peering cautiously. Others examined the engine that Brunt and his men had brought from the vessel. They laughed, and the rocks echoed their laughter.

SUDDENLY ONE of the three men called from among the crags. Gales heard his voice but could not see him. The others looked up and then started forward, all disappearing behind a bulge of rock.

Gales and McGill heard cries of excitement, but could not make out any words.

Brunt gasped, "What are they doing now?"

"They're out of sight," Gales said. "They've found something."

"They couldn't have!" Brunt muttered.

Gales and McGill made no reply. They continued to watch the point at which they had seen the men disappear. Presently four men appeared, carrying what looked like a big chest. Their labors indicated that the chest was heavy.

"Well, Brunt," McGill said, "they've got somethin'. They're carryin' a big chest."

"My God!" Brunt exclaimed.

The mate snarled, "I thought you said it was buried—"

"It was! It was! I remember! I saw it buried—before my very eyes. Ask Willis. Wasn't it all buried, Willis?"

"Yes," said Willis from the shadows.

The men carried the chest to the ledge and then went into the plane. They reappeared carrying picks and crowbars and returned to the crags, disappearing. Then the partners heard the ring of picks on stone. But they stared at the chest that had been brought out. Two men were hacking at it with hatchets.

Gales leaned back. "Well, Brunt, your game is up. They've got a chest down there and evidently they've seen another and are digging to get at it. So it was treasure all along, eh, Brunt?"

There was a moment of silence. Then Brunt said, "You've got eyes to see with, I guess. You see what's going on."

"How do you like the prospect before us, Brunt?" Gales mused. "Here we're on a crag in the middle of the ocean, off the trade routes. Even if you could get your hands on the treasure, it wouldn't do you any good. You couldn't get away. A hunk of rock went right through the bottom of the small boat and the *Krag Castle* just went down by the head. You had it coming to you, Brunt."

Brunt snarled, "How about you, eh?"

Gales said nothing.

The mate snarled, "Listen here, Brunt. I don't care to starve here. These two guys can fly a plane. Let's all pitch in and mop up those guys. If we get killed, that'll be too bad. But we might not get killed."

Brunt breathed thickly in the shadows. Then he said, "Gales—Gales, how about it? A five-way split if we make it, or a split according to as many of us win through. There—there's two hundred thousand down there in raw gold!"

Gales said, "Brunt, you tricked us. You would have killed us at that inlet if you'd got the chance. But you left us for the other gang to finish—and they damned near did. McGill and I fight our own battles, Brunt. We'll fight this one."

"But you can't—only two of you!" cried Brunt.

McGill said, "Boy, you just don't know us."

Gales looked down in time to see the Baron and two men hurrying toward the crags behind which the rest were hidden. They heard shouts of joy.

Gales drew close to McGill. "That ledge down there is clear for the time being, Mike. We've got to get closer. Take all the guns here."

McGILL MOVED quickly, gathering up the guns they had taken from their prisoners. In each back pocket the partners stuck a pistol, which meant two apiece. Added to these, McGill carried a rifle, and Gales carried another rifle across his back. In his hands he carried the Thompson gun.

"You leavin' us!" cried the mate.

Gales spun, snapped, "Talk loud like that again and I'll empty this gun in all of you!"

Quickly the partners slipped from the lofty ledge and began sliding down between other ledges. Gales dared not take a chance with the three they had left behind. He and McGill were determined to fight alone. Their grudge against Brunt was equal to their grudge against the Baron. They asked no quarter now, intended to give none.

They reached the water's edge unperceived and hurried along on the rock surface. They could hear the sound of the Baron's men more distinctly now but could not see them. They attained the landing ledge and saw the chest that had been brought down. It was still locked—a stout metal chest badly corroded.

Gales motioned to the plane. Tense, every nerve drawn tightly, the partners swung onto the plane, handicapped by the weight of the firearms. But they made the door and crawled in. There was hardly any motion. They prowled aft through several compartments, came finally to a dark compartment in the stern where odds and ends were stored. Here they sat down, breathing heavily, close to each other, each listening intently.

Gales whispered, "I think I've figured one thing out, Mike. That treasure was buried all right. Brunt brought a drill here and no doubt dynamite. That bomb the Baron dropped accidentally hit the rock where the treasure was buried and blew the rock apart."

"But how was it buried in the first place?"

"This is a volcanic peak. The treasure was probably landed here and temporarily hidden in one of the crevices. The volcano erupted and the lava flowed down and buried the loot. Brunt mentioned gold. There's been gold stolen from somewhere. The Baron and his men got a break in a big way. It might have taken days to drill that rock."

They sat on, huddled in the darkness. They heard voices draw nearer and assumed that the men had come back to the landing ledge again. They could have remained in their hide-out in all safety from the Baron's men, but they did not care to die of hunger and thirst. Fighting death was better.

And they still had hopes, no matter how slim.

ABOUT AN hour later they heard men inside the plane. They could hear footfalls, commands, shouting and sudden breaks of laughter. The partners retreated farther into the dark compartment, McGill holding a pistol in either hand, Gales gripping the submachine gun.

Once they heard a man right outside the compartment door. They tensed, ready to fight it out. But receding footfalls made them breathe easier.

They chuckled nervously, shook hands with each other, and continued to wait. Gales looked at his strap-watch. It was two in the afternoon. The sounds of activity died down a bit, but they could still hear footfalls somewhere forward.

Then there came a sound that made their blood spurt. The burst of a motor, and a vibration pulsing throughout the plane. Then another motor; finally a third. The three motors warmed up slowly, and the big flying-boat rocked gently. The sound diminished after a few minutes, but the motors were still turning over slowly.

Intermittent commands reached the partners' ears. Presently they could feel the plane moving. They heard the splashing of water. Then the plane seemed stationary again. A minute later the motors barked loudly, swung into a deafening roar that throbbed in every fiber of the plane.

Then the rush of wind, the snarl of water, the sense of swift, headlong movement. The partners felt the stern rise and fall, heard the greater roar of the water, the thunder of the motors. Then one of the sounds stopped—the sound of the water. The tail swayed, the rush of the wind was more noticeable, the roar of the motors steadier.

They were off—on the wing! The partners shook hands again. This was what they had hoped for. Now they could hardly believe that it was true. The first flush of excitement over, they settled down against the bulkhead. After five minutes they went into a significant huddle and spoke in quick, tense whispers.

Then Gales stood up and lit a match, holding it above his head. He pointed to the closed hatch above them. The match went out.

"Mike," Gales said, "we'll have to leave the machine gun and the rifles behind."

"Okey, Bill."

But they retained the pistols—two apiece. Gales unlatched the hatch and pushed it up against the wind. He swung up and shoved his head out, looked forward, then muscled his way out and squatted on top. He motioned to McGill. McGill appeared and Gales helped him out. Then they closed the hatch and remained for a few minutes clinging to the surface. Their jaws were set. Dangerous business lay ahead of them.

GALES STARTED first, flat on his stomach. He began wriggling forward in the face of the wind, offering as little resistance to the wind as possible. McGill crawled behind him. The ship kept to an even keel at a moderate speed. The partners made slow progress, pausing frequently to get their wind, then advancing slowly but doggedly. They reached the trailing edge of the high wing and paused again. The sea was two thousand feet or so below. They went on grimly, slowly, and reached the wing's leading edge.

They looked at each other, grinned, and the grin gave each of them fresh courage. They pressed on, Gales still in the lead, hugging the top of the plane with every inch of his body. They could see just the top of the pilot's head in the open cockpit in the nose. If that pilot happened to rise and look around they would be lost.

Gales paused to draw out one of his guns. McGill did likewise. Then McGill crawled up beside his partner and they crept on side by side. Three feet ahead of them was the pilot's head.

The pilot looked absently up at the sky. Out of the corner of his eye he must have seen Gales, for his head twisted around, a shocked look leaped to his eyes. Gales was leveling the gun at him, twisting his lips.

McGill leaped and landed in the cockpit. The pilot swung toward McGill. Gales stretched out and clouted the pilot on the head. The pilot wilted. His hand fell from the stick. Instantly McGill hauled him out of the seat. Gales dropped right into the seat and grabbed the controls. The attack had gone off so smoothly that the big ship hadn't altered the slightest in her flight.

McGill had the pilot on the floor. He motioned to Gales. Gales took off his necktie and passed it to McGill and McGill hastily tied the pilot's hands behind his back. Then the red-head hefted both his guns and looked down a short flight of steps in a small radio compartment. It was empty.

Gales peered at the chart before him, looked at the sun, ran his eyes over the dials. He shoved up the throttle, heard the motors roar louder and felt the big ship push through space at a greater speed. A hundred and fifteen miles an hour.

McGill went down into the radio compartment. The next door was closed, but there was a small glass port in it. McGill crept to this and peered into the next compartment. He saw ten men in there. He saw two large chests and one small one, all broken open. The men were in high spirits, a bottle was being passed around. Bars of gold were on the desk. The Baron was making notations on a sheet of paper while two of the men lifted more bars from the chests. One of the men was singing and swinging a drink back and forth.

Then suddenly the big plane banked. McGill knew: Gales was changing the course. Some of the men in the compartment reeled. Some of the gold bars fell to the floor. The Baron cursed.

McGill booted open the door and stepped in with a gun held level at either hip. The door swung shut behind him and shut out in a great degree the sound of the motors.

"As you are, you birds!" the red-head barked savagely.

THE MAN who had been singing and swinging a drink made a pass for his gun. He got it half-way, even while McGill shook his head. Then McGill fired. His right-hand gun hurled lead at the man and the man fell back against the desk, crumpled to the floor.

"Watch it, the rest of you!" McGill barked. "One fancy move and you get the same treatment!"

The Baron put a hand to his head. His features drew tightly together.

"Just little old me," said McGill. "And my partner, the celebrated Bill Gales, at the controls."

"You—you!" he cried hoarsely.

"We been ridin' a cloud."

The men could not speak. They were like men petrified. They stared at McGill in wild astonishment. They looked from the two unwavering guns to the two unwavering eyes.

McGill said, "Get this. If any of you birds thinks you can clear a gun, start right now. I'm waitin'. Or take a lesson by what happened to your chum there."

"Where are we goin?" snapped the Baron.

"My partner is figurin' that out, Baron. Just leave it to him. I'm stayin' right here—and so are you birds."

The Baron made a hopeless gesture. "Do you mind if I sit down?"

"Yes, I mind. You stand up with the rest."

The Baron looked around at his men with squinted eyes. "There is one man," he said. "We are nine. If we make a break he can't kill more than two of us."

The men's eyes shifted.

McGill crouched. "Start in," he snapped. "You start, Baron." One of his guns trained on the Baron's chest. The Baron swallowed and looked away from his men.

The big plane roared on over the sea, its throttle up to the last notch. Gales was restless at the controls. He kept throwing anxious glances backward. How was his partner making out? Gales had heard the first shot, had tensed and waited for a rush of men against his back. But they had not come. That meant McGill had fired.

The man on the floor beside him stirred. Gales drew his gun and leveled it, shaking his head. The man recoiled and lay horror-stricken. Gales kept the gun in one hand, controlled the roaring ship with the other.

McGill kept the nine men at bay. None had taken up the Baron's suggestion—not even the Baron. McGill's guns remained steady in his hands, his eyes never drooped. Challenge burned in them. This small red-head became a deadly menace in the eyes of the nine men, and tension sapped them until they became limp in body and mind.

One slumped to the floor. McGill's guns steadied, a harsh command ripped from his lips. But no man attempted to draw. They must have hoped against hope that something would happen—a failing motor, a clogged gas-line—

But the ship roared on over the sea, each motor working perfectly. Shadows came. McGill made one of the men switch on the lights. Darkness fell and Gales steered by compass and consulted the chart more frequently.

Another of the nine men crumpled—and another. The strain was too great for them. They lay on the floor mumbling, begging for mercy. While McGill carried on, the strain showing in his face. With a broken cry the Baron reached for his gun. McGill was like a rock. His lip curled, snapping out a warning. The Baron, his nerves ragged, fired into the floor. McGill's gun belched and the Baron fell across the desk on the bars of gold.

McGill said nothing. Only his eyes bit fiercely into the other men. But they made no attempt to pick up where the Baron had left off. They swayed on their feet, their eyes drooped, their shoulders sagged.

And the plane thundered on in the darkness.

CHAPTER XI

THE LAST HANGAR

SAM GARRISON tramped up and down the wharf office at Kuching, puffing furiously on a rank Sumatra cheroot. He had arrived that afternoon from Singapore at sundown. Samson tried to keep pace with him.

"Okey, Samson," the air chief rapped out. "We'll start in the morning. I got Gales and McGill into this. I'll get 'em out of it."

"Not a word from them," Samson said. "Nothing. I think they're done for, chief."

"Those guys couldn't croak, Samson. They don't know how. They're just stranded somewhere— What's that?"

Samson ran to a window and looked out in the darkness. He saw a man running and flung to the door, opened it.

"Plane, boss!"

"Turn on the floodlights, Miller!"

Garrison bowled Samson aside and ran down the wharf. Samson followed him and they stood on the pierhead and squinted up into the dark sky. The roar of powerful motors drew nearer. Then Samson pointed.

"There she comes, chief."

They saw lights in the sky.

The floodlights were switched on and the water sparkled.

The big flying-boat droned out of the darkness, dropped to the river and churned up white foaming water. The motors hooted, the crate rocked, then came plowing toward the wharf. A spotlight swept around and then steadied on the nose. A hand waved from the cockpit.

Garrison leaped in the air. "It's Bill Gales!" He waved both hands. "Hi, Bill, you old galoot!"

The plane slushed toward the wharf and the motors stopped. Men came on the run down the wharf.

Gales stood up in the cockpit, said, "Have armed men ready!"

McGill sagged against the bulkhead in the compartment, his eyes red-rimmed, his face muscles taut, his guns steady. On the floor was sprawled every man except the Baron, who sat in a chair, his eyes barely open.

Then McGill started as men rushed into the compartment. Armed men. Sam Garrison was there, puffing his cheroot, swinging his gun, snapping, "Where's them guys?"

McGill lowered his guns. He turned and saw Gales, haggard as himself, worn and weary from the hours of tension.

"How's every little thing, partner?" Gales muttered.

"Old pal, old pal!" McGill croaked, and reached out a hand toward him.

THE BARON lay on a cot, smoking. A doctor sat beside him. Gales and McGill and Sam Garrison stood looking at the Baron. The Baron smiled.

"Well, my time is up," he said. "I never thought it would be—so suddenly, at any rate. Plans of mice and men, eh? Well, that's that. The gold is there. All of it. It was shipped in the *Eastern Prince* a year ago, Singapore to Shanghai. I was a passenger. Jake Brunt was the ship's master, a man named Willis was the radio operator. They scuttled the ship off that rocky pinnacle—"

"The *Eastern Prince!*" exclaimed Sam Garrison. "I remember! Go on, Baron."

"I was a passenger, I said. Looking for fortune in a big way. I began to be suspicious when I found the ship way off her normal course. I heard them one night—in the skipper's cabin—planning: four of them, Brunt, the master; Willis, the operator; and the second mate and the second engineer. I approached them and made them a proposition. They had to take me in.

"The trick was turned at night. We chose four Lascars to help, intending to kill them, of course, when they were no longer needed. When the ship started to go down the five of us were in strategic positions on board. We shot down the other three passengers, the first and third mates, the chief engineer.

"We had a big dinghy and we loaded the gold in it. We got away and made for that rocky island, arrived safely. We planned to hide the gold there till a later date. We had food and planned to stay there a while. We hid the chests behind one of the crags. The volcano erupted. Lava swept down. The second mate and the second engineer were caught high up. Willis and Brunt and I piled into the dinghy and shot the four Lascars at sea, threw them overside. We removed the vessel's name from the dinghy. We landed on the Borneo coast and burned the dinghy to destroy all evidence.

"Willis and Brunt then tried to kill me. I escaped. I reached Singapore and worked up to Shanghai, collected some old army friends and we got enough together to buy that plane from a wealthy Chinaman for a mere song. It all took time. I sent two men in a small plane to stand guard at the island."

"And we finished them," McGill said.

"I SENT Gossman to that inlet with fuel," the Baron went on in his husky voice. "I had an idea Brunt and Willis were spying on us. Then one of my men reported that Brunt and Willis had left Singapore suddenly, but he didn't know with whom or how. We took off in our plane from Batavia. Brunt's man, who was spying on us, must have wirelessed the *Krag Castle*. How that man found out about the inlet, I don't know, but he must have seen our maps. I see now, however, how Brunt and Willis got you, Gales, and your partner, into the plot. They wanted to get to the inlet first, to destroy our base, and to find out more about our plans. Toward which end they killed Gossman. Up until a short time ago I was convinced that you two men were in with them.

"You know about the ship. We took off in the morning and were surprised to find it outside the inlet. We swung to bomb it but they surprised us with that gun. They crippled us and we fled up the coast, stopped for repairs, and then continued. As you know, we cleaned out the ship at the treasure island and accidentally blew up the rock beneath which the treasure was buried.

"We had had word before that the *Eastern Prince's* underwriters had a secret agent working on the case. That was our greatest worry. He was posing as an innocent newspaper man—"

"Horning!" broke in McGill.

The Baron began coughing and heaving on the cot. The doctor went to him. Garrison motioned to the partners and the three left the room.

Garrison said, "Well, boys, there'll be a big reward for you. We'll ship that gold to Singapore on my next westbound plane."

"We'll have to borrow one of your cabin jobs, Sam," Gales said.

"Shucks, you go ride in the passenger plane."

"It's not that, Sam. I mean those three guys we left at the island—Brunt, Willis and the mate."

Garrison poked Gales in the ribs. "You would be soft-hearted, wouldn't you?"

McGill winked at Gales.

Gales grinned, and retorted:

"Soft-hearted my eye! There's a price on their heads—and maybe you don't think we need it! They're unarmed and they'll come to us like babies."

"Well, anyhow," Garrison said, "come around to the hotel and have a drink and one of my cheroots."

McGill said, "Well, after all, Sam—just the drink. Cigars are too strong for my constitution."